THE PERILOUS *Journey* BEGINS

RICH RITTER

THE NEW VOICE OF THE AMERICAN WEST

THE PERILOUS *Journey* BEGINS

A MAGNIFICENT EPIC OF
SEVEN TRAGICALLY ENTANGLED LIVES

NOR THINGS TO COME:
A TRILOGY OF THE AMERICAN WEST

RICH RITTER
THE NEW VOICE OF THE AMERICAN WEST

PO Box 221974 Anchorage, Alaska 99522-1974
books@publicationconsultants.com—www.publicationconsultants.com

ISBN 978-1-59433-552-5
eBook ISBN 978-1-59433-553-2
Library of Congress Catalog Card Number: 2015948968

—First Edition—

Manufactured in the United States of America.

For I am persuaded, that neither death, nor life, nor angels,
nor principalities, nor powers, nor things present,

Nor Things To Come

... shall be able to separate us from the love of God ...
Romans 8: 38-39

Table of Contents

List of Excerpts from Muireall Anne Ravenscroft's One-Volume History of the American West

Prologue

San Luis Obispo, California
July 20, 1907

Azure eyes searching the distant sun-dappled hills above the polished rim of a porcelain cup, Muireall Anne Ravenscroft sipped green tea. She set the cup on the wide arm of her Adirondack chair and glanced sideways at John Ravenscroft, her beloved husband of eight years. He balanced over two-thousand pages of meticulously-typed manuscript on his legs while reading the last page of the prologue. When he had finished, he inserted the twenty-seven page introduction behind the table of contents and adjusted his reading glasses down his nose. A breath of cool air swirled across the veranda; John quickly laid his hands on top of the impressive pile to prevent the pages from scattering. Muireall waited for the gust to subside before tapping her foot and coughing in rhythmic counterpoint, a personal affectation John had come to know well.

"What did you think of the prologue?"

John lifted the top page from the colossal tome and pretended to read it. "The introduction is a lengthy work all by itself, isn't it? And I must say, I don't care at all for this title: *A Concise History of the American West*? Positively dry and unimaginative. Can't you do better? This immense manuscript is also crushing my legs. I'm not sure '*Concise*' is the right word. What do you think of this title: *A Leg-Crushing Account of the Old West?"*

Muireall fidgeted against the steep back of the Adirondack chair and scratched her fingernails into the arms. "You can't even get past the title without criticizing it? What's wrong with it? It describes the work perfectly."

"I did get past the title before criticizing it. You asked me to read the first draft and to critique it. Well, in my opinion the title is boring, especially given the promise of the introduction." A raven landed on the guttered eave of the veranda, squawking twice before scampering noisily across the copper roof, hurdling over each seam in a diagonal sprint to the ridgeline.

"You liked the introduction?"

"I did—I liked it very much—but I have some suggestions there as well. But first, I think you should do something about this title."

"Do you have a specific idea for an alternate title... other than the silly one you just suggested?"

"Not really. Just something less dull. The introduction is anything but dull. Besides, you're the writer. Use your imagination to come up with an imaginative title." John transferred the manuscript to a side table, pushed himself up from his matching chair, and strolled to the crafted wood handrail enclosing the veranda. "What a glorious, glorious day. I love these summer days when the sun warms the mountains and the cool wind blows in from the ocean. I love the smell of it." He pressed his hands down on top of the rail, stretched his back, and breathed in the fragrant afternoon air.

Muireall scrunched her brows mischievously. "Then what do you think of *A Glorious, Glorious History of the American West*. Is this more to your liking?"

John exhaled exuberantly. "Now you're the one making fun of me. But I do like it better, if only slightly. I might consider dropping the second *'Glorious'* though."

"Then I shall change the title to *A Glorious History of the American West*. I do like it better. But you said you had other suggestions for the introduction. Will you share them now, or has our discussion of the title exhausted your vigor?"

"You should know me well enough by now to appreciate that my vigor is seldom diminished by a spirited debate, especially on a subject this important."

"I know. Then present your first suggestion. I promise not to react like I did with the title."

John returned to his chair, nudged the reading glasses up to the bridge of his nose, and lifted the introductory pages from the top of the manuscript. He thumbed through the pages aimlessly, paused near the middle, read a few lines, then said, "I think you should revise the first sentence."

Muireall tapped her foot loudly against the wood decking of the veranda, but did not cough this time. She thought of rolling her eyes, but willed herself to avoid this irritating mannerism. "You just *pretended* to look somewhere in the middle of the introduction to avoid another argument. You were planning to criticize the first sentence all along."

John covered his mouth to conceal a smirk. "Absolutely not true. I really do have a suggestion for the middle, but I thought I should get the first sentence over with so we can move on to a more productive discussion."

"You're a cad, but I still cannot help but love you."

This time John did not conceal the smirk. "I know. No matter how much you try, you just can't live without me. I understand. I truly do. But you still should revise the first sentence. If you don't, I fear some readers may yawn and put the book down without reaching the second."

"I will remain calm and receptive to your suggestion. What is wrong with the first sentence—surely not the same problem as the title?"

John considered the best way to answer this question. He decided a frontal assault might work best. "The first sentence is dull. You should begin the introduction with something—"

This time Muireall could not will her eyes into submission and they rolled wildly. "Don't tell me. Something… more imaginative?"

"Yes! Something more imaginative. Just the word I was looking for. How did you guess it? You must be a mind reader."

Muireall regained control of her wayward eyes and settled comfortably into the chair. She raised her cup and sipped green tea. "It's the only possible explanation: I can read your mind."

"I'm afraid I've succumbed to my dishonest nature. I actually love the first sentence, but could not resist the temptation to tease you. I do enjoy it when you squirm about with such intense seriousness. It gives me great pleasure."

"You *are* a cad."

"Yes I am. But do not let any of my personal shortcomings distract you from the important task at hand. I promise to give you my honest comments for the introduction, and then shall spend the remainder of this lovely afternoon plunging through the first chapter. And I also promise I will not make fun of you again, even if I do enjoy it with all my heart."

"You really promise?"

John reached over and caressed Muireall's hand. "Actually, no. I'm just preparing you for some really good teasing later."

Muireall withdrew her hand in mock disgust. "I must find a better word than 'cad' to describe you. Somehow 'cad' is just too lenient."

John smiled as Muireall's hand retreated from his loving grasp. "I'm sure you'll think of something very imaginative. You are, after all, the most gifted writer I know."

Chapter One

Dunnet Head Lighthouse,
the Highlands of Scotland
April 1860

Gordania Sinclair twisted vigorously against the cool ground near a patch of heather until fresh grass slithered between her toes, bathing her feet in clean dew sparkled by the slanting light of a fresh morning. After gyrating comically for nearly a minute, she bent down to examine the green blades that now appeared to grow from the tops of her feet. She scrunched her face to focus her observation. Although a young lady of thirteen, she had nonetheless failed to lose any of her tomboyish fascination with the smallest details of nature, including—to her mother's unfailing horror—insects and frogs. Especially frogs. Once she kept a frog in a box beneath her bed—until her mother discovered it and forced her to return it to the wild land where it belonged. This unfortunate incident had not deterred her. She still sought the tiny amphibians when away from the house, and often concealed one or two of the creatures in a secret pocket she had sewed into her favorite play dress (while feigning interest in sewing to please her mother). But no longer a child, and growing in wisdom and maturity with each passing minute, she also released the frogs and insects—and whatever else she had collected—before returning home.

Duncan Sinclair prompted his daughter to make haste in a tone both stern and good-natured. "Please keep up Gordania. I intend to return to the lighthouse before noon to check the electric arc, and at the pace you are presently keeping there is no chance we will complete our journey by dinner."

Gordania looked back to fully assess the progress they had made since the conclusion of breakfast. Against a distant glaze of rain-grayed clouds she could still distinguish the top of the lighthouse above a smoothly-sloping hill: the black-painted dome, triangle-faceted glass above the orangey-yellow base, corbelled balcony, trellised railing, and a smidge of the gently tapered white cylinder below. When she squinted, she could also discern the top of one of the slit windows, trimmed in the same orangey-yellow as the base, just below the balcony. They had probably travelled only a thousand feet in ten minutes—a leisurely stroll at best. Ignoring the tender blades of grass growing between her toes, she ripped her feet from the ground and accelerated into a gallop. She arrived at her father's side before he could speak again. Forgetting the reason for her sprint across the heathered slopes, she burst out, "Are you going to let me shoot today, father? You said I could shoot soon. You said it last week when I asked. Is today soon enough?"

Duncan lifted his 12-gauge side-by-side percussion shotgun to his shoulder and reached down for his beloved daughter's dirt-smudged hand. Gordania rubbed her hand clean on the folds of her dress then raised it to his waiting grasp. She probed his expression for a positive reaction to her question. A grateful mariner had purchased the gun from John Dickson & Son in Edinburgh in 1857, and had presented it to the lighthouse keeper of Dunnet Head as a gift of honest appreciation. Duncan could not have afforded the finely-crafted gun on his meager lighthouse keeper's salary. "I suppose it is soon enough today. You have, after all, demonstrated a measure of patience beyond your age. But I only have seven rounds left, and we must return home with a bird for dinner. Therefore... I think you should fire the shotgun twice, because the first shot will surprise you, and the second will not."

Gordania released her father's hand and clapped with excitement. "Can I load it too? I want to learn how to load the gun before I shoot it."

"What has God given me? Only two daughters and no sons, but a daughter who wants to handle a man's shotgun just like any son. I must be especially blessed."

Gordania did not understand the comment. "Can we shoot now?"

“Not yet, my special blessing. We are still within sight of the top of the lighthouse, and your mother, should she climb up to the balcony and use the telescope, would not appreciate seeing her oldest daughter participate in this particular activity. I think we must walk a half-hour or more, until neither lighthouse nor mother are within view.”

Gordania brightened. “Then father, let us please hurry, for you must return to the lighthouse by noon.” She rushed away from Duncan, glancing back several times to confirm the briskness of his pace, her final glance to the top of the lighthouse searching for the glint of the telescope lens.

The sun arced higher above the eastern rim of the peninsula and warmed patches of the rolling hills through breeze-scattered clouds. When they had hiked exactly thirty minutes to the second (Duncan confirmed this with his English pocket watch), he announced, “Gordania, come back. We have gone far enough and it is time for me to fulfill my promise. And, if we are lucky enough, a red grouse or ptarmigan will arrive in time for the shooting lesson and we shall kill two birds with one stone.” Duncan reached into the ragged canvas bag strapped over his shoulder and removed two cartridges and percussion caps. When Gordania arrived, he instructed her to hold out her hand. “Here are percussion caps and cartridges for your shooting lesson. Take the shotgun in your other hand. Mind the weight of it.”

Gordania accepted the shotgun with her left hand, pulling it quickly against her chest. “It is heavy, father, but not too heavy for me.”

Duncan smiled. “Maybe you are indeed my son in disguise. Now, since you have no shoes, brace the butt of the shotgun on the toe of my boot and pull the rod from beneath the barrels.” Gordania dropped the cartridges and caps into her frog pocket and extracted the rod. “Good. Place one cartridge in each barrel and ram them all the way in with the rod.” When she began pushing the rod into the first barrel to set the cartridge, Duncan helped guide it.

“Father, I can do it without help.” Gordania completed the task and then shoved the second cartridge into place.

“Good, my delicate Gordania. Now take the shotgun in both hands, pull the hammers back until they click in place, and press a percussion cap onto each side. Mind the triggers so you do not pinch a finger.” Gordania struggled a bit with the caps, but completed the work successfully under

Duncan's amused and patient supervision. "Well done my little tomboy. Take care to aim the gun away from me. Shooting your father would prove more difficult to explain than a mere shotgun lesson. Now we are ready to shoot. Should we kill a rock, or wait for a plump grouse to wander by?"

Gordania's patience had ended. "We should shoot a rock, because who knows when a grouse will show up, and you must return to the lighthouse by noon."

"An excellent point." Duncan pointed toward a grassy outcrop of weathered boulders. "Set your feet like this. Press the stock firmly against your right shoulder. Lean forward a bit. Very good. See the small bead at the front of the barrels? Do not aim with it, but use it to point to the rocks. Now... hold the stock against your shoulder... set your finger gently on the first trigger... good... now squeeze your little hand... lean forward... squeeze... squeeze... squeeze...."

The finely-engraved John Dickson & Son side-by-side percussion cap shotgun recoiled violently against Gordania's petite shoulder as pellets spewed from the barrel in an explosive roar. The blast threw Gordania back against her father. Duncan, anticipating this very result, caught his precious daughter with one hand and the shotgun with the other. He quickly stood her up. "Now you know what it feels like. Do you still want to take the second shot?"

A fresh tear rolled down Gordania's cheek as she rubbed her bruised shoulder. She sniffed before answering, "You said I could have two shots." She reached out for the shotgun and Duncan let her take it.

"Yes I did, and you will. You know what to do. Let's aim at the patch of heather to the right. Do you see it?" Gordania prepared for the promised second shot, and to Duncan's amusement she set the butt against her left shoulder and placed her left hand on the triggers. "A splendid idea to try the other side." Gordania sniffed again and squeezed the second trigger: this time she did not falter. The blast chewed up the ground a few feet in front of the heather patch. "A bit low, but still a splendid shot."

Gordania trembled after she lowered the shotgun from her throbbing left shoulder. "I will do better when you let me shoot again."

"I have no doubt you will. But now we truly must make haste to find a succulent bird and kill it for our dinner. And with only five cartridges left, I must take care not to miss." Duncan reloaded the shotgun and slung it over his shoulder. "We should head back to the lighthouse and hunt along the way. Would you like a bird hunting lesson as well?"

Gordania nodded. "Yes father. I would."

"Is the pain in your shoulders tolerable?"

"Yes, tolerable."

"You will probably feel the soreness more tomorrow morning, but it will toughen you for the next shooting lesson. But let's not worry about it now. We have work to do if we hope to enjoy a grouse dinner tonight—if we are lucky enough to find one." Duncan turned in the direction of the lighthouse and began walking with the measured strides of a hunter.

Gordania ran to her father's side and then slowed to match his pace. "I know we will be lucky today, father."

A few minutes before the sun reached its noonday zenith, and after several hours of good hunting, Gordania and Duncan walked along a gravel roadway toward the stone wall that enclosed the Dunnet Head Lighthouse and grounds. Gordania carried a large grouse by the neck over her shoulder and played with two frogs in her secret pocket. Her shoulders still ached, but she didn't care. The roadway soon reached an opening in the wall flanked by whitewashed stone pillars, each topped with pyramids of stone stained by years of salt spray. The wall to the right turned at the pillar and continued along the side of the road in a sweeping arc terminating easterly of the lighthouse at a small gable-roofed building near the 300-foot sandstone cliffs of Dunnet Head. The wall to the left shot off in a perpendicular angle to the road and traced a gentle curve until it reached a small stone structure westerly of the lighthouse. Gordania released the frogs in a grassy puddle, and then touched every third stone on the top of the wall as she ran ahead of her father.

Whitewhiskered Erskine Mackay slathered another brushfull of whitewash down the jamb of the only window at the front of the gable-roofed building near the cliffs. The assistant lighthouse keeper spotted Gordania's approach along the curved wall in his peripheral vision. He addressed her without looking away from his work. "I see, Miss Gordania, that we are counting stones again in the usual pattern. And I see as well, although I mustn't turn my head to look more closely, some sort of feathered creature carried over your shoulder."

Gordania counted the last stone and touched the bucket of whitewash with her toe. "Father shot a fat red grouse for dinner, and he only used one percussion cap and cartridge. The second barrel is still loaded."

Erskine lowered the dripping brush and admired the bird. "Why yes, it is a fat one, and should make a wholesome dinner for all. But tell me little Gordania, how you know so much about the shotgun? I do not recall when sporting guns became of interest to little girls."

Gordania scrunched her face. "I'm not little, Mr. Mackay. I'm thirteen, and father said I'm a young lady now."

Erskine plunged the brush into the bucket and swirled it around to saturate the stiff bristles. "My deepest pardon, young miss. I can see you are surely a young lady. My remarks about the shotgun were poorly chosen."

"Father showed me how to shoot it. I got to load it and everything. But he said not to tell mother because it would make her unhappy. I shot both barrels at a rock and a patch of heather. I almost got the heather."

Concealing his amusement, Erskine lifted the brush to the wall and continued his work. "I see. But do not worry. Your secret is safe with me. I shall take it to my grave. You have my solemn word."

Just before Duncan arrived Gordania said, "Thank you Mr. Mackay."

Duncan balanced the butt of the shotgun on his toe. "Thanks for what?"

Erskine answered before Gordania could say anything. "Why, I was expressing my admiration of the lovely bird you bagged this morning, and Gordania was thanking me for my observation. She also told me you got it on the first shot. Quite a feat, if you ask me." Erskine winked at Gordania when he had finished his little deception.

"Yes, we had a bit of luck today. And we shall all enjoy the day's luck at dinner tonight. Now Gordania, take the bird to your mother. She will wish to admire it as well."

"Yes father. I know it will please her to see it." Gordania skiphopped past Erskine and the whitewashed building and ran to the stone wall between the courtyard northwesterly of the lighthouse and the plunging cliffs above treacherous Pentland Firth. She continued touching every third stone as she raced along the wall, counting rhythmically in cadence with each footfall. She found her mother pinning a bed sheet to the sturdy clothesline Duncan and Erskine had erected last summer. Rose Anne Sinclair, Gordania's younger sister by six years, rolled around in the freshly cut grass beneath the windflapping clothes. Gordania held up the plump red grouse as high as she could reach. "Look what father shot with the shotgun. It only took one shot and he's still got one shot left."

Fyona Sinclair struggled against the freshening afternoon breeze as she pinned the last corner. She bent down to observe the bird more closely. "My, and isn't this a fine bird. And who do you suppose will pluck it and cook it for dinner?"

Gordania forced the grouse up a little higher until she could no longer tolerate the ache in her shoulder. "Do you think it will make a good dinner? Father said you would admire it."

"I do admire it. And would you and Rose Anne care to help me pluck it?"

Gordania glanced over at Rose Anne, now attempting to stand on her head while leaning against the clothesline post. "I would like to help pluck it, but I thought I would play for a while since I've had a long day of hunting."

"A long day of hunting? I see. Yes you may play for a while, but first we will have a bit of lunch, and then you must take Rose Anne with you when you play. Your sister is very fond of you, and I believe she would enjoy your company."

Without expressing any special pleasure in the task, Gordania agreed obliquely. "She will have to keep up if she wants to play with me. I plan to run fast today."

Fyona touched Gordania's tangled hair. "Of course. But you might slow your pace a bit. Do you want me to brush your hair before lunch?"

Gordania shrugged. "Not today. I like my hair the way it is."

Swallowing the last of her bread and milk, Gordania pushed away from the heavy wood table and jumped from her chair. She darted to the front door and tugged at the massive wrought iron lever until the door swung open and afternoon light flooded the room.

Fyona clapped. "Gordania Sinclair! Do not forget to take Rose Anne with you. Remember our conversation before lunch."

Gordania skittered to a comical pose just as her dirt-smudged toes bumped against the stone threshold beneath the doorway. She turned slowly, very slowly, until she could barely distinguish her mother's form on the opposite side of the table. "I told you I plan to run fast."

"Nonetheless, you will sit patiently, without fidgeting, until Rose Anne finishes her lunch, and then you shall take her with you."

Erskine Mackay coughed and tapped his pipe on the table. "And while you are gallivanting around the highlands of Dunnet Head this afternoon, you might keep a lookout for Andrew Sutherland's missing Border Collie. I ran into him a few days ago, and he told me the dog had been acting strangely before disappearing altogether."

Unusual for Duncan, he betrayed a modicum of anxiety. "Acting strangely? And then disappearing altogether? Very odd, Erskine. Very odd. Maybe Gordania and Rose Anne should play near the lighthouse today."

Erskine sucked the pipe into his whisker-rimmed mouth and spoke between puffs of bluish smoke. "Don't think there's ... anything to worry about, Duncan. The Border Collie is ... naturally strange in my view. I've actually seen one spend ... an entire morning herding the ocean waves. And with a couple of sheep watching the whole thing from the hillside."

"I see your point, Erskine, but I still think—"

Fyona broke in. "Gordania knows how to handle herself around dogs. I don't think there's a reason to worry. She just needs to keep a lookout like Erskine suggests."

Rose Anne had drained her glass of milk when Erskine first mentioned the troublesome Border Collie. She had stood by the table during the entire dog conversation, her hands folded neatly behind her back. "I'm ready to play now. May I leave?"

Gordania jumped across the stone threshold. "Yes. Let's go Rose. We have a Border Collie to find, and not much time to find it."

Fyona pressed her hand against her chest. "Oh dear. Maybe we shouldn't have discussed the dog at all." She reached across the table and began collecting plates and cups. "You may go play Rose Anne, but do not lose sight of your sister. The two of you must stay together."

Gordania and Rose Anne fled the house and the endless slow-eating-tea-sipping-pipe-smoking-dog-conversation of the adults. They ran along the curved stone wall at such great speed that Gordania did not have time to touch every third stone. They ran through the first pair of stone pillars and then the second. They ran out into the grassy wilds of Dunnet Head far beyond the protective stone walls of the lighthouse grounds. They ran and ran and ran until they could run no more. Gordania collapsed into the soft grass near an outcrop of jagged boulders. Rose Anne arrived a minute later and crumpled next to her older sister with a melodramatic swoon. Together, as Gordania had promised her mother, they gazed up to the gauzy clouds and sprinkled blue skies above Pentland Firth. They listened to sea birds squawk far beyond the rugged cliffs. They felt the salty breeze flowing in from the crashing ocean waves puff against their cheeks. They sniffed the fragrance of nearby heather and grasses.

"I know what we should do." Gordania sat up and searched the meadows to the west. "We should look for frogs. I had two nice ones this morning, but I let them go when we came home from hunting. I need to find some more."

Rose Anne, eager to please her older sister, agreed with enthusiasm. "Yeah. We should look for frogs."

Their energy restored by the brief respite in the comforting grass, the girls ran up the gentle slope of a nearby hill. When they had both arrived at the top they shielded their eyes from the subdued brightness of the afternoon sky and searched for likely frog ground. Gordania spotted a small loch about 500 feet from the base of the hill. "There's a good spot to look for frogs, especially this time of year." The girls bounded down the hill toward the loch, nearly stumbling into each other twice. When they arrived at the edge of the water, Gordania fell to her knees and muddied the front of her dress. Rose Anne did the same and both girls crawled around in expanding circles. Gordania dug around in a thick clump of wet grass and pulled out a small frog. "I've got one. And it's a nice size too. He'll fit perfectly in my secret frog pocket."

Rose Anne stood, mud dripping from the hem of her dress, and skipped over to admire the frog. "He's a nice one. I hope I find a nice frog. But I don't have any place to keep it like you do. I wish I had a frog pocket."

Gordania held the frog close to study its thumbs. "Maybe I'll sew you a frog pocket too. Mother likes it when I sew. But first we should look for some crickets. They like crickets. They like grasshoppers too, but I think they like crickets more."

Rose Anne tilted her head to observe the frog better. "I can look for crickets. I've found them before."

Gordania slid the frog into her secret pocket. "Good. Then let's get started, because I have to help mother pluck the grouse before dinner and we don't have much time. She said you could help pluck the grouse too."

The girls ambled beside the southern boundary of the loch, their heads down, searching for crickets and grasshoppers. They had explored for several minutes, and had found three crickets and a grasshopper, when the rumbling growl of Andrew Sutherland's wayward Border Collie surprised them. Rose Anne froze, but Gordania spoke to the collie in a soothing voice. "Hello collie. I hear you're lost and looking for your home. Maybe we can take you there. We know where Mr. Sutherland lives."

The dog inched forward and woofed ominously.

Gordania grabbed a handful of Rose Anne's dress. Rose Anne nearly tripped on Gordania's feet. "Nice doggie. You just stay there. We're going to leave you alone now."

The collie lurched forward several steps and snarled.

Gordania pulled Rose Anne behind. "Rose Anne, I think you should run home now. I'll follow you in a minute, but I want you to run and not turn around. Do you understand?" Rose Anne nodded; tears began flowing down her pinkish cheeks. "Alright then. Run! Run now!" Rose Anne tripped and stumbled to the ground. Gordania quickly yanked her back to her feet and pushed her hard in the direction of the lighthouse.

Incited by the sudden movement, the furious collie charged them both. Gordania turned and the angry dog bit deeply into her stomach and ripped away a ragged patch of dress and skin just above the frog pocket. Gordania grabbed the dog around its neck to allow Rose Anne time to escape. The dog twisted in her grasp and bit into her neck. Gordania held the animal tightly and the dog tore another chunk of flesh away. Blood poured from the wound in her neck. Blood oozed from the gash in her stomach. Gordania waited until Rose Anne had vanished over the top of the hill, and then kicked the dog as hard as she could. The dog growled one last time before scampering away.

Gordania rested several minutes before standing. She felt woozy when she straightened up. Blood drenched the front of her torn dress and dripped down her legs. She reached into her secret frog pocket and pulled the frog out. The limp creature had survived a direct attack by the dog, but had then drowned in Gordania's blood. Gordania dropped the dead frog and a few blood-soaked crickets into a puddle and began walking in a wavering path back to the lighthouse. She wondered if her mother had begun plucking the plump red grouse when the first rain drops of an approaching squall dampened the distant hills.

Chapter Two

Shiloh, Tennessee
April 6, 1862

Manfred Herrmann slouched against the crinkled bark of an ancient hickory tree at the verge of a dense grove not far from the western shore of the Tennessee River and nudged the luminous petals of a fire pink with a black-powder-smudged finger. He twisted the fragile green stem between thumb and finger to spin the jagged tips of the petals against his palm, and briefly enjoyed the gentle touch of the scarlet flower. He pressed the fluorescent petals against his scraggly brown moustache and breathed in the nectar's sweet aroma, then exhaled the fragrant air with a satisfying whoosh.

"Silene Virginica."

Manfred stroked one of the pedals just as Sergeant-Major Gallagher stopped in front of him. "Beg pardon?"

"I said, Corporal Herrmann, Silene Virginica. The scientific name of the flower you're impaling on the unkempt bristles of your moustache. Also known, to the less educated of the Seventh Iowa, as the fire pink."

Manfred broke the long end of the stem off and threaded the flower through a button hole. "Saloon Veronica. I forgot…you collected plants before the war."

"It's Silene Virginica, not saloon veronica, and please refer to me as a botanist, not a plant collector."

"A *bottomless*. Of course Sergeant-Major. Please accept my apology. I will use the correct title from now on."

The sergeant-major stiffened. "Corporal Herrmann, your morning botany lesson has concluded, and I don't want to put you at any further risk of a general court-martial. Now round up your squad for parade and inspection. Colonel James M. Tuttle requires assurance that the brigade under his command can still march after the sloppy maneuvering he witnessed from Pittsburg Landing to our present bivouac."

Corporal Herrmann bent the stem of the fire pink to hold it in place. "Yes sir, but it's not yet six in the morning."

Sergeant-Major Gallagher grinned. "It is not our place to question the wisdom of the colonel. Now form your men up for the parade, and look sharp about it."

With the haranguing of lieutenants and sergeants, the ten companies of the Seventh Iowa Infantry Regiment—over 500 strong—poured from the bivouac of neatly arranged white canvas tents and formed loosely into four long files. A captain nodded, and Sergeant Gallagher bellowed: "By file, right, dress!" and each file stepped forward in succession and shuffled into smart alignment. With this maneuver completed and all eyes snapped forward, Sergeant-Major Gallagher continued: "Shoulder, arms!" and the men of the 7th Iowa heaved over 500 Springfield rifles and muskets into the air and snapped them against shoulders toughened by long hours of drill. When the strangely muted echo of hundreds of steel barrels chafing against wool jackets had faded, Sergeant-Major Gallagher intoned: "Company, right, face!" and the men of the 7th Iowa pivoted on heel and toe and snapped their feet together. With the company now facing the approved direction, Sergeant-Major Gallagher barked: "Mark time, march!" and the men of the 7th Iowa commenced marching in place, rhythmically stamping booted feet against the soggy ground. After waiting exactly six steps to allow the cadence of footfalls to synchronize, Sergeant-Major Gallagher prompted: "Forward, march!" and the men of the 7th Iowa stepped off. The ten companies of the 7th Iowa fell into line behind the men of the 14th and 12th Infantry Regiments, and the men of the 2nd Iowa Infantry Regiment fell into line behind them, completing the long blue column of the Union Army's First Brigade under the command of Colonel James M. Tuttle, Second Division under the command of Brigadier General W. H. L. Wallace.

Manfred peeked down at his flower several times to admire the still vibrant red petals. He thought of pulling the flower up from the button hole to enjoy the soothing fragrance again, but worried he might fall out of step and invoke the wrath of the sergeant-major. He adjusted his spacing from the man marching in front, and then checked his alignment in the rank. After taking another dozen strides, he noticed several men sitting on horses about a hundred yards ahead. He stretched his neck and raised his chin and squinted.

The soldier marching to his right spat a slimy gob of tobacco before declaring, "That there's General W. H. L. Wallace, leader of this here division we're a part of."

Manfred lowered his chin. "You don't say. I think I was about to figure it out for myself. My vision just gets a little blurry when we march."

Not losing a step, the soldier spat again and grinned. "Maybe you need some of them fancy spectacles if you can't see who's leading the division."

Manfred now reached within two-hundred feet from the seated horsemen, and still could not see the faces clearly or distinguish the emblems of rank on the uniforms. "I don't need any spectacles. I can see just fine."

"Couldn't see General W. H. L. Wallace sitting high up off the ground on a horse. Don't suppose you can see him now."

"I'm about to see him."

"Don't look like you is about to see anything. Like I said, you ought to get some of them fancy spectacles."

Manfred fumed, "See here, farm boy, I don't need any fancy—" A cascading volley of musket-fire rumbled in the distance behind and to the left of the marching brigade and echoed through the dense hickory and oak trees, interrupting the delivery of Manfred's angry retort. Manfred gazed up at the serene clouds. A second volley reverberated through the dense woods.

Surprised by the sudden and unexpected noise, the tobacco-chewing farm boy swallowed some of the brown goo. "Must be Union troops taking some early morning target practice."

Still angry, Manfred snarled, "And now you're an expert on the daily activities of the whole Union Army?"

At least three, maybe four trumpets shrilled to the southwest, and then a third volley chattered. Manfred listened for a fourth volley, but after a brief silence—no more than 10 seconds—scattered and chaotic rifle and musket fire erupted across the western horizon and rattled through the thickets of trees. The sound grew ominously louder with each footfall of the marching troops now passing on parade in front of the mounted officers.

Sergeant-Major Gallagher boomed, "Companies . . . halt!" and the men of the 7th Iowa came to an rolling standstill. Sergeants up and down the line echoed the same command to the other regiments of the First Brigade. Manfred now stood close enough to the group of men sitting on horses to recognize General W. H. L. Wallace. With some pleasure, he also identified Colonel Tuttle. He watched the general and the colonel and the other men surrounding them as they took turns standing up in their stirrups and pointing into the trees separating the regiment from the approaching commotion.

A sweat-lathered horse ridden by an agitated corporal burst from the trees and kicked up ragged chunks of muddy ground as it galloped along the western side of the long files of the 7th Iowa. When he arrived directly across from General W. H. L. Wallace and his entourage, the corporal pulled the horse up and yanked the snorting animal to the right and drove it between two of the ranks of the 7th Iowa, shoving shouting men to either side and nearly trampling their feet. The corporal trotted up to General W. H. L. Wallace, saluted, opened a black pouch slung over his back, pulled out a folded sheet of paper, and shoved it into the general's hand. The general opened the paper and read whatever message someone had scrawled on the page, folded it up again, and crumpled it in his hand. General W. H. L. Wallace leaned sideways in his saddle and spoke into the ear of Colonel Tuttle. Colonel Tuttle pulled his mount out of the line of officers and rode over to the bugler standing to his right. He bent down in his saddle and spoke into the top of the bugler's cap. The bugler saluted, spit twice, wetted his lips, raised the polished instrument to his mouth, and sounded the allegro eighth and sixteenth note command for "quick time." The four regiments of the First Brigade tramped ahead in a rolling surge.

Manfred struggled to match step with the men around him. He nearly stumbled to the muddy ground when the man behind him kicked the back of his boot. He glanced to his side and the farm boy grinned tobacco-stained teeth back at him. When he had finally settled into a comfortable pace, the bugler sounded the allegro sixteenth and dotted-sixteenth note melody to signal "double quick time," and the 14th, 12th, 7th, and 2nd Iowa Infantry Regiments accelerated in turn. Manfred nearly fell again when the regiment climbed over a bushy hillock and splashed across the slimy stones of a shallow steam. The four long files separated when the men swarmed around a copse of tangled oaks, then broke apart completely as the regiment stumbled across a deeper stream. Manfred's boots filled with icy water and water splashed against his crotch. When the men had reached the swampy ground beyond the stream, the four files of the 7th Iowa reformed behind the 12th Iowa before following a long, sweeping arc to the left. Manfred trotted along; muddy water squished from holes in the leather soles of his boots and his Springfield rifle slapped against his shoulder. The long column of the First Brigade emerged from the swampy ground and curved across the Hamburg-Savannah Road where it roughly paralleled the southerly-flowing Tennessee River. The column continued to veer until it pointed southwest and then south and then southeast. As the long files of men completed a final sweep and began to straighten, they quick-stepped into the scattered paths of wounded soldiers retreating east from the remnants of their shattered regiment. Hundreds of discouraged men trudged through the advancing Iowa regiments—alone, in pairs, in small clusters, limping, bent over, assisted by other men, on makeshift crutches, dragging rifles, empty handed, torn and blood soaked. The bugler screeched the presto sixteenth note call to signal halt. Sergeants and lieutenants darted along the lines screaming commands to form a line of battle two ranks deep. The four regiments of the First Brigade quickly reformed into a pair of ragged lines facing southwesterly. Muskets and rifles crackled beyond the forest of oaks and hickories, much closer than before—and the men waited.

Manfred spoke to the farm boy, miraculously still standing to his right. "That was a hell of a run. I didn't think I was going to make it across the second stream. Nearly fell in the deep water."

The farm boy grinned and spat a lump of chewed tobacco spit in front of Manfred's muddy boots. "I didn't think you was going to make it neither, seeing how you can't see much of what's going on right in front of your own nose."

Manfred's anger had diminished while crossing the swamps north of the second stream, and he took no offense. "Did you get a look at those stragglers? They'd been shot up pretty—"

The bugler sounded the lilting eighth and quarter notes in two-four meter to signal the command to "fix bayonets," and four regiments of bayonets rattled metallically as men yanked them from leather scabbards and rammed them into place. The bugler sounded presto quarter and eighth notes in six-eight time to call the Iowa men to move "forward," and the two-rank-deep line of battle, nearly a thousand yards long, marched over the uneven ground and advanced raggedly through the oak and hickory trees and tangled underbrush. A minie ball zinged overhead, and then another, and then two or three in quick succession, and as the shadows of the forest slowly gave way to the overcast light of an open field, Manfred Herrmann and the tobacco-chewing farm boy and the men of the 7th Iowa Infantry Regiment reached the shoulder of a sunken road just beyond the boundary of the trees. The field swept away from the road and revealed a battleground shrouded in bloody carnage and swirling smoke. The 12th and 14th Regiments formed the line of battle just inside the tree line along the sunken road to the left, and the two ranks of the 2nd Iowa formed to the right. The bugler trumpeted the command to halt, and the men settled into position. Before Manfred's pounding heart had begun to slow, two long gray lines of Confederate infantry issued from the blanket of smoke less than 200 yards away and marched directly toward the 12th and 14th Regiments—the new left flank of the First Brigade.

Ethan Plantagenet, a first lieutenant with the 8th Texas Cavalry, casually bent his knee over the smoothly-curved leather horn of his black saddle. He squinted through chaotic swirls of gloomy smoke to better observe the four infantry regiments of Brigadier General T. C. Hinden's First Brigade advance in long lines across an open field toward groves of oak and hickory just beyond a sunken road. Artillery boomed far away to the right. After first surprising and then overrunning the Union encampment in the dappled early morning light, the Army of the Mississippi now continued its relentless advance to the Tennessee River without meeting any organized resistance from the retreating Union troops. The chaotic Federal retreat promised the possibility of a complete rout. He tugged his grandfather's watch from an inside pocket and flipped open the finely-engraved cover with a white-leather-gloved thumb. He admired the miniature photograph of his late wife before checking the time. Not yet nine. At this pace of advance, forward Confederate units should reach the Tennessee by mid-afternoon. He cherished the idea of dinner on the peaceful banks of the river. Lieutenant Plantagenet lowered his foot to the stirrup and galloped back to his regiment.

Sergeant-Major Gallagher strolled purposefully along the front of the first rank of the 7th Iowa, stopping several times to contemplate the advancing Confederate infantry. He repeated the same commands at each new platoon. "Hold your ground. Do not yield. Hold your ground. Do not yield. Hold your. . . ." When he reached Manfred's platoon, he stopped again, but not to observe the approaching infantry—which had suddenly halted and was now preparing to fire on the 12th and 14th Iowa. "Corporal Herrmann. Do you still have your fire pink?"

Manfred watched the first rank of Rebel infantry take aim. "Yes, Sergeant-Major. I still have it." He glanced down at the flower and a wave of smoke exploded along the Rebel line. Seconds later, the men of the 12th Iowa (to his left) answered with a deafening crackle of rifle fire. Dozens of Rebel soldiers crumpled to the ground.

Sergeant-Major Gallagher did not flinch. "Do you perchance remember the scientific name I taught you this morning?"

Manfred thought back on his early morning conversation. He watched the second rank of Rebel infantry lower muskets and take aim. "Yes I do, Sergeant-Major. It is Silene Virginica." A second wave of billowing smoke ejected from the line, and again the 12th Iowa responded in kind. Dozens more Rebel soldiers collapsed in scattered mounds across the front of the diminishing line.

Sergeant-Major Gallagher stepped behind the ranks of the 7th Iowa and then faced the battlefield. "Very good Corporal Herrmann. But now we have work to do." A trumpet shrilled and the Confederates, bayonets flashing, surged into a running charge. The sound of a thousand stamping feet and whooping voices washed across the field and crashed against the trees.

Sergeant-Major Gallagher coughed to clear his throat, then boomed, "Fire by rank...company...left oblique." The two ranks of the 7th Iowa pressed over 500 Springfield rifles and muskets against their shoulders and swung to the left. Sergeant-Major Gallagher calmly observed the charging enemy troops as they approached the lethal field of fire he now prepared for them. "Front rank...aim...." He paused until a sufficient number of Confederates had entered the killing zone. "Fire! Load!" Hundreds of minie balls spewed across the open field to tear the flesh and break the bones of the advancing men. A Confederate officer waved his saber wildly in the air and screamed at his men to form a new line. A hundred men or more formed a ragged line facing the 7th Iowa and frantically poured black powder into hungry muskets and rammed lead balls into place. Sergeant-Major Gallagher continued without emotion. "Rear rank...aim...." This time he did not pause. "Fire! Load!"

After firing with the second rank, Manfred frantically plucked a fresh paper cartridge from the black-leather box slung over his shoulder. He used his teeth to tear off the end of the cartridge with the minie ball. He poured black powder from the cartridge into the barrel of his Springfield Rifle, then extracted the ball from his mouth with calloused thumb and finger and pressed it into the waiting barrel. He spit the paper cartridge remnant to the ground and rammed the ball and powder into place. He flipped open the lid of a small leather box attached to his belt and removed a percussion cap. His hand trembled and the cap fell to the ground. Without hesitation, he pinched out another, cocked the hammer one click, pressed the cap into place, and fully cocked the hammer. As he waited for the next command he peeked over his shoulder; the tobacco-chewing farm boy grinned at him again. Before Manfred could look away the farm boy's head fulminated, showering blood and teeth and a chunk of nose across Manfred's uniform. The farm boy, the side of his face shredded by a Rebel minie ball, tried to remind Manfred about the fancy spectacles but only gurgled incoherently before staggering backwards and stumbling over a rotten log.

Sergeant-Major Gallagher continued, "First rank ... aim ... Fire! Load!"

More Confederate soldiers fell to the ground, adding to the grim human litter now choking the open field. The Confederate officer waved his saber at the 7th Iowa and a bugle shrilled again. Hundreds of gray men pulled away from the assault of the 12th and 14th Iowa Regiments and charged toward Manfred's position.

Sergeant-Major Gallagher did not break his melodic cadence. When the charging Rebels reached within 50 yards of the 7th Iowa, he bellowed, "Second rank ...." The Rebels reached within 40 yards. "Aim ...." The Rebels reached within 30 yards. Sergeant-Major Gallagher waited, and a sweaty spasm convulsed across Manfred's back and rolled up his neck when he pressed his finger against the trigger. The rebels reached within 20 yards, and Manfred identified the delicate face of a young boy. "Fire!" The attacking Rebels vanished in a blanket of smoke, but quickly broke through the murky shroud and dove into the first rank of the 7th Iowa Infantry Regiment. The man in front of Manfred hissed when a Rebel bayonet stabbed through his gut and burst from his back. When the man slid off the blade and fell to the ground, he revealed the young boy Manfred had seen before the obscuring smoke had swallowed him up. The young boy aimed his bloody bayonet and lunged, but Manfred knocked the boy's musket to the side before swinging his rifle butt around to slam the boy to the ground. When the boy tried to stand Manfred kicked him to the ground again and pressed the sharp tip of his bayonet against the boy's chest, just below the throat. Manfred allowed a moment to appreciate the boy's dirt-smudged face, tangled brown hair, and age—fifteen, maybe sixteen at the most—and while tears bathed the boy's dirty cheeks, Manfred thrust the bayonet in. Then, as his hands trembled and the men of the 7th Iowa drove back the Rebel assault, Manfred watched the young boy choke on his own blood and the light fade from his brown eyes.

Excerpt from

A Glorious History of the American West

by Muireall Anne Ravenscroft

Shiloh: Prelude to the Decline of the Confederacy

The Battle of Shiloh, the first significant incursion of the Union Army into the Confederate West, is little understood and often misrepresented in the written histories of the American Civil War. Other engagements, such as Gettysburg or Chancellorsville, are often cited as more important, but my research has led me to this conclusion: Shiloh, also referred to as The Battle of Pittsburg Landing, was truly the decisive turning point of the Civil War. One need only refer to General Ulysses S. Grant's own memoir in which he declares that the battle was "...more persistently misunderstood, than any other engagement between National and Confederate troops during the entire rebellion...." to appreciate the fundamental underpinning of my assertion. Further, what appeared early in the day of April 6, 1862 as a potential rout -- after a dramatic early-morning surprise attack by Rebel infantry on the bivouacked Federals -- quickly transposed into a stunning Confederate loss by the conclusion of hostilities on April 7th, a loss from which the South, in my opinion, never recovered.

A significant aspect of Shiloh is the level of carnage achieved by green troops, a level not previously experienced in the war. The typical Confederate soldier marching from Corinth, Mississippi to the battleground of Shiloh had little or no combat experience and was poorly armed (some carried pikes instead of rifles), while roughly half of opposing Federal troops had not experienced actual combat. And yet, this pivotal and epic battle -- which pitted approximately 65,000 men of the Union Armies of the Tennessee (General Ulysses

S. Grant) and of the Ohio (Major General Don Carlos Buell) against the nearly 45,000 men of the recently-formed Confederate Army of the Mississippi (General Albert Sidney Johnston and General P. G. T. Beauregard) -- resulted in casualties of nearly 24,000 men killed, missing, or wounded in a scant two days of persistently brutal conflict.

In fairness to the combatants, much of the fog of war (a phrase I have borrowed from Clausewitz) that plagued the battle (and likely contributed to the level of bloodshed) can be attributed to the difficult terrain of southwest Tennessee. The undulating, heavily-wooded land to the west of the Tennessee River rises at points to bluffs more than 150 feet above the river plane and dives into countless deep ravines. The numerous tributaries of the three primary streams bounding the area -- Lick Creek to the south; Owl and Snake Creeks to the north -- crisscross the battleground. Swamps spread in scattered patches across the landscape, and were so characteristic of the terrain as to become a primary focus of Confederate strategy: to cut the Federals off from retreat to the Tennessee River and drive them northwest into the swamps of Owl Creek. Lastly, heavy rains days before the conflict rendered the few available roads, poor enough in decent weather, nearly impassable, especially by a large army attempting to surprise the enemy through quick deployment. In fact, General Johnston had originally intended to attack on April 4th, but was delayed until the 6th because of the condition of the Western Corinth Road. It was, according to Colonel Wills De Hass (commander of the 77th Ohio Infantry during the battle of Shiloh), "...the worst possible battleground."

Even given these many impediments to success, the Confederates still might have achieved victory were it not for an implausible event. At mid-afternoon of the first day (around 2:30 pm), while leading the advance on the Union left flank, General Albert Sidney Johnston, the Army of the Mississippi's most experienced and effective combat leader, was struck in the leg by a stray minie ball. An artery severed and his boot filling with blood, he collapsed within minutes and died. Without Johnston's inspired and focused leadership, the Confederate troops were diverted from his primary strategic objective -- the capture of Pittsburg Landing -- and instead intensified the offensive on the "Hornet's Nest," a hastily formed defensive line established along a sunken road near a peach orchard and the only Union position that had not yielded to the Rebel onslaught. This misguided tactic, which required numerous frontal assaults before achieving a breakthrough, produced heavy casualties on both sides and allowed General Grant seven precious hours to establish a new defensive line extending west from Pittsburg Landing on the Tennessee River then north up the Hamburg-Savannah River Road toward Owl Creek. Late in the afternoon of the first day, a final charge on this second line by two Confederate brigades was repulsed, and as the bloody day drew to a close it became clear that the late General Johnston's grand strategy of driving the Union Army away from the Tennessee River and capturing Pittsburg Landing had fallen short.

John Ravenscroft brushed sand off the top of the manuscript, now piled messily next to the folding chair, and dropped an oval rock on top to protect it from errant sea breezes. He removed his reading glasses and scanned the churning waves of Avila Beach. The afternoon light sparkled on the waves flowing over the smooth sands and crashing against the black-barnacled piles of Harford Pier. Far beyond the end of the pier, at least five miles or more, lofty cumulus clouds drifted on the prevailing winds northwesterly toward Morro Bay. John rubbed his eyes, fatigued by the ocean glare, and when he opened them Muireall padded through the sand into his vision. She wore the fashion of the day. The black, knee-length, puffed-sleeve wool dress hung down to conceal the ribbons decorating the bottom of her black bloomers. Rivulets of seawater ran off the hem of the dress and rolled across the long black stockings adorning her athletic legs before splashing on the black laced-up bathing slippers protecting her feet. A fancy cap, also black and trimmed with a twisty swirl of white piping, offered the only feminine touch. John attempted to imagine the sensual curve of Muireall's waist, but the bathing suit prevented it.

Muireall pulled the fancy cap off and reached for a towel to dry her dark, shoulder-length hair. "Make any progress?"

John rubbed his eyes again. "Yes I did. I just began reading the section on Shiloh."

"And?"

"I liked it, but. . . ."

"But what?"

"You use a lot of parenthetical phrases."

Muireall tossed the damp towel over the canvas back of her folding chair and plopped onto the canvas seat. "I like parenthetical phrases."

"I noticed. And you use commas, dashes, and even parentheses to punctuate them."

"Do you see a problem?"

"Not really. On the other hand, I'm truly impressed by the amount of information you are capable of packing into a single sentence. But when you string two or three of those packed sentences together. . . ."

"Is this a bad thing?"

"I suppose not, but it does make your writing a bit . . . turgid . . . at times."

"Turgid? At times?"

"You know what I mean. Thick. At times."

Muireall fluffed her hair to dry it in the slanting sun. "Do you think I should rewrite the section on Shiloh?"

"I don't know. Maybe you should consider inserting a short, pithy sentence from time to time. It might reduce the turgidity."

Muireall stretched her arms and legs and burrowed her toes into the warm sand. "Alright. Probably good feedback. I'll rewrite the section as you suggest." Muireall began to rise from the chair.

John reached over and pressed her arm down. "But not now and not tonight. How would you like to eat dinner here before we drive home? We could dress and drop by the Marre Hotel for seafood and a glass of wine. We could make a romantic evening of it."

Muireall smiled. "You don't think I should address the excessive use of parenthetical phrases tonight? Since you've pointed it out, I feel a tremendous urge to resolve the issue as soon as possible."

John released her arm with a tender caress. "The parenthetical phrases can wait until tomorrow." After enjoying one last view of the sparkling sea, John asked, "By the way—what's a minie ball?"

Chapter Three

Nanjing, China
July 1864

Tseng Longwei—born of peasant farmers in 1819 in the mountainous region of Guangxi in southern China; educated in math, science, English, and the ways of Jesus by Baptist missionaries as a youth; hardened in the coal mines of Guangxi as a young man; swept away by the peasant revolt of Hong Xiuquan against the corrupt Manchu Dynasty in 1850; wounded by sword and arrow during the victorious advance of the Taiping Heavenly Army into the Yangtze Valley through the years 1851 to 1853; elevated to the rank of colonel and granted command of a full regiment during the disastrous and bloody Taiping march on Shanghai in 1861—walked. Tseng Longwei, his mind filled with worry, his stomach twitching from hunger, his joints stiff from too little rest, walked along the wide path atop the ancient and lofty stone walls near the east gate of the city of Nanjing. He slowed his pace at intervals to inspect the remnants of his shattered regiment, depleted to fewer than 300 men by fanatical defense of Nanjing and the privations of a two-month siege. He peered through a slotted opening in the stone battlement to gauge the more than 80,000 troops of the Imperial Army now besieging the city and threatening the very existence of the rebellion. And he tarried near the battlement above the east gate and rested his hand on the hilt of his sword to consider the meaning of the untimely death of Hong Xiuquan—spiritual and moral leader of the Taiping Rebellion—and the presently uncertain future of the Taiping Rebellion and the Heavenly Kingdom of Peace.

Unsettling rumors shrouded Hong's death and flourished among his men. One said he had heard from a trustworthy source (someone close to one of the concubines) that the Heavenly King had deliberately poisoned himself to avoid the inevitable collapse of Nanjing and consequent shame from loss to the encroaching forces of the contemptible Manchu Dynasty. Another had heard from a general's assistant, who had overheard the whispers of Hong Xiuquan's own son in a darkened corridor, that Hong had died of a simple illness—nothing more, nothing less—although the specific symptoms of the allegedly simple illness were not described in any great detail. One of the more believable rumors proposed that the Heavenly King had suffered a horrible death from food poisoning after eating putrid wild vegetables collected from a foul swamp near the wall protecting the city, but no one could remember who had told this story nor had anyone actually witnessed the harvesting of the vegetables. One of Tseng's own captains—and only two of five remained in the regiment—declared on a daily basis that the Heavenly King had risen to Heaven to directly seek the protection of Nanjing from God himself, and that he would soon return with an army of angels, but only the most fanatical believed this outlandish claim.

Tseng Longwei had decided that insufficient information existed to sustain belief in any specific rumor, but he had not witnessed a public appearance by Heavenly King Hong Xiuquan for at least a month, and leadership of the Taiping Heavenly Kingdom and its capital, Nanjing, had appeared to transfer to Hong Tiangui Fu, Hong's eldest son, during this time. But only 16 years beyond the womb and unproven as a leader of any sort, Hong Tiangui Fu did not engender much confidence in Tseng Longwei's regiment of battle-hardened veterans. Tseng Longwei had significant doubts as well, and with the Emperor's Imperial Army surrounding the last stronghold of the Taiping Rebellion and choking off any possibility of escape or relief, a creeping splinter of cynicism encroached upon his thoughts and dampened optimism with increasing regularity.

Tseng Longwei found his senior captain—the one who had repeated, to anyone who would listen, the rumor of Hong's travels to Heaven to muster an army of angels—crouched against the stone parapet directly above the massive arch keystone of the east gate. The captain had nearly finished restringing his favorite Tarter bow, in his hands a more accurate and deadly weapon than the clumsy flintlock muskets preferred by some of the men in the regiment. Tseng Longwei addressed the captain with much respect: "Have you seen any movement, or do the men of the Imperial Army continue to sit in their tents and do nothing?"

The captain tugged at his new bow string to test its strength and grunted. "I have not observed anything to suggest alarm, but they do not sit in their tents and do nothing. Today they have become herders of cattle instead of warriors, and are moving many cows along the banks of the Yangtze River to the north. You can see the long trail of dust for yourself."

Tseng Longwei leaned against the rampart to view the Imperial warriors who had become herders of cows. He pressed his hand against one of the gigantic bricks of the serpentine wall and his fingers chafed along the Han characters embossed on the face of the brick. Instead of searching for cows, he studied the writing on the brick. "I have been told, by someone whose name I do not recall, that nearly every brick in this wall is identified with the location and name of its maker."

The captain snorted his disbelief. "Why would anyone go to such trouble for a brick?"

"I have been told, by the same person whose name still eludes me, that should the brick fail the maker could be found by the Emperor's civil servants and then tortured or put to death for incompetence." The dust cloud began veering away from the river and commenced a gentle southerly turn.

The captain continued his air of disbelief. "A steep penalty for the profit of a brick."

Tseng Longwei attempted a smile, but, when he surveyed the dust cloud, his lips refused to curl. "For one brick, yes. But for millions of bricks, possibly worth the risk."

"And what is the name of the unfortunate individual who may have profited greatly from the making of millions of bricks or may have been tortured or put to death by the Emperor's civil servants for the failure of a single brick?" The captain stood and pulled a fresh arrow from its quiver and tested the nock in the new bowstring, aiming defiantly in the direction of the herders of cattle.

Tseng Longwei bent closer to the giant brick and read the Hon characters: "The man who made the brick is one Yuan Zhuang of Shanghai, but he made the brick 500 years ago. I think he has probably outlived the risk of its failure."

Satisfied with the fit of the nock on the bowstring, the captain relaxed the Tartar bow and returned the arrow to the quiver. "This may be true, but the Emperor's civil servants could have put him to death in the most horrifying manner imaginable for the failure of another brick we do not know about."

"What you say is most plausible, or the Emperor's civil servants may have tortured Yuan Zhuang or put him to death for something unrelated to the manufacture of large bricks. There are many possibilities." Tseng Longwei removed a small telescope from a pouch he always carried slung over his back. He extended the brass tubes of the scope and examined the dust cloud through the tiny aperture of the eyepiece. He swung the telescope left and right across the lengthening cloud, lingering at intervals to study some aspect of the moving dust more thoughtfully. He focused on the rear of the dust cloud with great curiosity. Satisfied with his observations, he lowered the telescope and collapsed the tubes and slid it into the pouch. "The Imperial Army is driving the cows onward to uncover the many traps we have set in the fields before this gate. There are several wagons loaded with barrels traveling behind the cows. It is likely the barrels are filled with gunpowder."

The captain shrugged. "Do the Emperor's cow herders think a wall built from bricks made by the legendary Yuan Zhuang of Shanghai (who may or may not have been tortured or put to death in the most horrifying manner by the Emperor's civil servants for the failure of one brick), and which has stood for centuries can be breached by a herd of cows and few barrels of gunpowder?"

Tseng Longwei adjusted the brim of his bamboo hat until the shadow fell below his eyes. The cloud of dust had moved close enough to allow discernment of individual cows. "I fear the wagons carry more than a few barrels. I believe there may be hundreds." He again removed the telescope from its pouch and nervously clicked the tubes to full extension before bringing the aperture to his eye. "The cows at the front of the cloud are approaching the initial array of traps." A flash of early afternoon sun glinted off the polished scope's objective lens as he watched the first unfortunate cows break through the thin mat of earth and light supporting structure and tumble into the shallow pit of sharpened bamboo spikes. The following cows and herders and wagons loaded with barrels of gunpowder and Imperial Infantry quickly separated and flowed around the exposed trap. "They have found the first trap at the cost of five or six cows, and maybe a cow herder or two, but it is difficult to see through the dust." Tseng Longwei swung the front of the telescope across the line of dust and watched as cows tumbled into other traps. This pattern repeated until dozens of traps lay exposed. Tseng Longwei collapsed the telescope and set it on the stone parapet. "The Emperor's Imperial Army and its militia of cows have breached the defensive line of traps, and are now converging on this gate."

The captain offered the possibility of some optimism. "I assume at the loss of many soldiers and wagons loaded with barrels filled with gunpowder?"

Tseng Longwei did not look away from the advancing army. "I fear the traps have only killed a few innocent cows and peasants. The wagons and infantry have apparently passed through the field of traps unharmed. Ready the archers and musketeers to defend the gate."

The captain saluted. "I will give the order. We will not allow the Emperor's men to breach the gate."

Colonel Tseng Longwei spoke without sentiment or change of expression. "Although it pains my heart to say so, take particular aim on the innocent cows and peasants. It may be possible to slow the assault by creating a mound of dead animals. Then we can redirect our bows and muskets to the men who crawl over the mound. If we succeed in stopping the wagons, I believe we can survive this assault."

After the captain had departed to marshal the regiment, Tseng Longwei watched the cows and peasants and infantry and wagons loaded with barrels of gunpowder plod relentlessly toward the east gate. He stood erect and stoic as the archers and musketeers of his regiment, and those of two equally depleted regiments the captain had commandeered, lined the battlements above the gate and awaited the command to fire. He stood without flinching when the captain shouted orders up and down the line and hundreds of arrows and musket balls rained down on the unfortunate cows and peasants, creating the mound of corpses he had hoped for. He watched as the men of the Imperial Army broke through the mound and pushed ten wagons loaded with barrels toward the ancient east gate.

He glanced to his left and right without blinking as dozens of his men slumped against the stone parapet or crumpled to the stone path, victims of the Emperor's own arrows and muskets unleashed from below. He glanced up at the western sun and lost sight of the wagons when the peasants and Imperial Infantry pushed them against the gate.

The captain ran up to Tseng Longwei and spoke with great urgency. "It is my unfortunate duty, Colonel Tseng, to report to you that we have failed to stop the wagons. Do you think the gate will hold?"

Tseng Longwei drew his sword, anointed with the blood of more than 100 adversaries of the glorious Taiping Rebellion, from its leather scabbard and examined the chipped but still elegant blade. "Order the men to move off the wall and fall back, but do not allow them near the gate until after the explosion. We will defend the capital of the Heavenly Kingdom of Peace from the ground."

Tseng Longwei's shattered regiment, and the two equally-depleted regiments commandeered by his senior captain, raced down wide stone steps from the top of the east gate to the ground before deploying along the ancient stone wall to both sides of the gate. An explosion of nearly 40,000 pounds of gunpowder shook the ground and disrupted the tranquility of the warm afternoon. The concussive wave of the explosion ruptured one of Tseng Longwei's ear drums. Blood trickling from his damaged ear, he fell against the engraved bricks of the wall and sank to the ground. He watched in puzzled silence as hundreds of men of the Emperor's Imperial Army stormed through the cleaved gate—followed by several bewildered cows.

Tseng Longwei, his ears still buzzing wildly from the explosion at the east gate, buttoned the collar of his recently-procured Imperial Army uniform and watched the new moon float peacefully above the fallen city of Nanjing. He stretched his shoulders and shook each leg in turn to lengthen the fit of jacket and pantaloons, but to no avail. He glanced down at the man stretched out naked and motionless at his feet. He considered the idea of killing another Imperial soldier a few inches taller, but decided against it. Although the dark streets and alleys of the capital of the Heavenly Kingdom of Peace now swarmed with thousands of soldiers of the despised Manchu Dynasty, many who likely wore uniforms that might fit Tseng Longwei perfectly, the frenzy of killing also swarming the ancient streets rendered the search for longer sleeves needlessly dangerous. Tseng Longwei dressed the bleeding corpse in his uniform, and, although it pained him to do it, strapped his beloved sword around the dead man's waist. He did not much care for the weight and balance of his new sword, but did not imagine he would have a need to use it if he traversed the city, now littered with the mutilated bodies of his comrades, with the appropriate bravado of an officer of the Imperial Army.

During the gory retreat of his men from the east gate to the very walls of the Heavenly King's palace near the foot of Zhongshan Mountain, Tseng Longwei had fought courageously until the last man of his regiment, the senior captain who still waited for an army of angels, held off a horde of Imperial soldiers long enough to allow his escape down a narrow alley. Just after midnight, as the final defense of the Taiping Palace collapsed and the buildings of the palace were set ablaze, Tseng Longwei had found temporary refuge beneath a pile of executed Taiping men. But now disguised as one of the Emperor's officers, he strolled jauntily down the center of a large street to the west of the palace, hoping to find escape through one of the gates closer to the Yangtze River. He entered a large, open plaza southwest of the blazing palace grounds, and the sight of three Taiping women standing closely together invited his curiosity. He turned from his course and approached the women. A rectangular slab of wood with three neatly-aligned holes, the two sections of the slab secured together by heavy iron hinges, bars, and clasps, bound the unfortunate women together at the neck and weighed painfully down on their shoulders. The first two women wore the baggy sleeves, pants, and skirts of Taiping peasants. The third stood naked and shivered from exposure to the night air.

Tseng Longwei spoke cautiously to the naked woman, averting his eyes from her nakedness. "Who has taken your clothes, and for what purpose have they done so?"

The woman tried to step back from the Imperial officer who now spoke to her, but the heavy wood slab fixed her in place. "Your own men tore my clothes and violated me. When they had finished their work they did not have the decency to cover my nakedness."

Tseng Longwei did not deny her accusation. He walked away from the three women. He searched among the hundreds of bodies littering the plaza until he located a dead woman slumped over a stone lion near a well. He judged the corpse about the same height and shape, and then stripped her including cap and shoes. He returned to the three and began dressing the naked woman.

She spoke with utter surprise. "You are a soldier of the Imperial Army. Why are you dressing me?"

Without saying a word, Tseng Longwei pulled the pants and then the skirt up to the woman's slender waist and tied them off. He slit the front of the jacket open with his new sword and draped it around her shoulders. A platoon of Imperial soldiers stomped arrogantly across the plaza in neat ranks and files. The man leading the platoon glanced at Tseng Longwei briefly, but after noting his lofty rank resumed his march. Although Tseng Longwei had averted his eyes when he first spoke to the woman, he could not avoid noticing her loveliness when he dressed her naked body. "I do not have time to explain. Lift your foot so I can slip the shoe on. Now the other." Tseng Longwei's hand trembled when it touched the sole of her foot. He completed his work by setting the cap on the woman's head and twisting it into place. When he had finished, he abruptly turned to walk across the plaza.

The woman clasped the front of the jacket tightly in the shivering fingers of her calloused hand and waved with the other, the tips of her fingers scraping across the rough underside of the heavy wood planks. "Thank you. Your kindness will be rewarded in heaven." And then, impulsively, she said, "My name is Li Hua."

Tseng Longwei trudged away from the three bound woman without speaking. He did not imagine the new morning would find them alive. When he reached an intersection of three roads at the far end of the plaza, brightly illuminated by the flames of a burning structure, he veered westerly. He worked his way across the chaotic center of Nanjing and then turned onto a narrow street aligned northwest. Although the key to his escape remained the masquerade of the Imperial uniform complemented by an aggressive display of arrogance, he still preferred the less-travelled roads to minimize the chance of confrontation and subsequent discovery. After following alleyways, small roads, and major streets for half the night, he reached the ancient perimeter wall and one of the western gates, less than a kilometer from the Yangtze River. He noted a subtle glow in the eastern sky and judged that an hour or less remained before sunrise. He shifted his attention to the gate. A dozen men guarded the route of his chosen escape. Without slowing his pace or modifying the swing of his arms—except to pull on the sleeves of his jacket to temporarily increase the length—Tseng Longwei marched defiantly up to the soldier who appeared in charge. He planted his feet widely apart, rested fisted hands below the belt of his sword, mustered his confidence, and spoke with appropriate conceit:

"Move out of my way, underling. I have important business beyond the gate, and I am already late to my task."

The guard, a sergeant from Beijing, grimaced quizzically. "No one is allowed to pass through this gate tonight, not even someone with important business. I have specific orders from the captain."

Tseng Longwei did not know the rank of the officer he had killed, but feigned great indignation nonetheless. "Do you not recognize my rank!?"

"Yes, you are a major in the Ever Victorious Imperial Army."

A stroke of luck. Tseng Longwei had unknowingly slaughtered a senior officer serving with the elite Ever Victorious Army. "Yes. You are very observant. And what will happen when the general finds out that you, a lowly gatekeeper, have prevented one of his senior officers from passing through this gate to deliver a message critical to the final destruction of the despised Taiping Army? Do you imagine his pleasure will be multiplied by your incredible stupidity?"

"What is so important about the message?"

Tseng Longwei sputtered and stomped his foot. "Such incomprehensible insolence! It is no business of yours what the message contains or does not contain and whether it is important or not. I have no time for this lunacy. There is no more to argue. I shall return within the hour with an escort and have you put to death on the spot."

The sergeant fidgeted. He thought of asking his men for advice, but decided otherwise. "I will yield to your command. But only because you have assured me of the importance of your mission. You may pass through the gate to deliver the message."

Tseng Longwei shoved the sergeant aside. "When I return from my mission, I may still have you put to death for your insolence." He passed through the gate and marched beyond the ancient wall of engraved bricks and stone. Still maintaining the dashing stride that had brought him this far, he followed the path west and then north to the Yangtze River.

He walked along the river. When the morning sun broke over the eastern horizon and sparkled on the water, he encountered a fisherman and his family mending nets next to a small but well-maintained junk. After convincing the family that he did not belong to the Imperial Army—a task which required more effort than convincing the sergeant to allow him to walk through the western gate—he boarded the junk with the fisherman, his sun-leathered wife, and three sons. The fisherman and his wife raised the sail on the unstayed mast and pushed the vessel away from the shore. The junk drifted to the center of the river and, as a gust of wind billowed the sail to life, set a course downriver toward Shanghai.

Chapter Four

Fort Sedgwick, Colorado Territory
June 1867

Joshua Hotah patted the neck of his faithful appaloosa, then scratched the strong-willed animal along the base of her coarse mane. The horse tried to step away, but he pulled firmly on the leather reins and coaxed the animal back. The horse pondered Joshua's youthful face. He stroked the animal's white-and-brown-spotted nose with a delicate motion. The appaloosa exhaled a defiant snort, but she did not step away this time.

"I know you want to leave this place and ride across the open grass, but we must wait outside until the new captain finishes his long conversation with the war general." The appaloosa appeared to understand Joshua's soothing words, but shook her head in mock frustration anyway. Joshua stroked the nose more vigorously. "I know. I know. But you must learn patience in your new life. You cannot always ride when you want to and where you want to. Sometimes you must wait a long time inside the sharpened tree walls of the fort until the white man is done with whatever he is doing. The same is true for me."

Joshua Hotah had acquired the appaloosa from an aging Nez Perce warrior during the waning days of last autumn. At the time, Joshua had need of a new horse and the Nez Perce had need of a new rifle. Joshua traded a Sharps military carbine— converted to use the new .50-70 Government metallic cartridge—and thirty-seven rounds of ammunition for the spirited animal. Before the negotiations began, he concealed his Henry repeating rifle some distance away beneath a prickly yellowing bush to avoid any distractions. He preferred the range and accuracy of his Sharps, but had decided a repeater might provide more utility in his current occupation. The Nez Perce tried to barter the saddle and beaded bridle for more ammunition, but Joshua finally convinced him that he had given every last cartridge and might have to ride many days to find more. The Nez Perce chuckled at the conclusion of the transaction. Before pulling his horse around to gallop away, he declared: "I hope you are a very good rider, Joshua Hotah." Joshua answered back: "Do not worry about me old man," before he confidently mounted his new horse. The feisty appaloosa waited until Joshua relaxed, then instantly spun around and bucked him to the ground. Astonishingly, the animal did not run away, but instead contemplated his new "master" with a bemused look. Joshua brushed himself off and limped back to the defiant animal. His remarkable friendship with the appaloosa began at this moment.

Excerpt from

A Glorious History of the American West

by Mulreall Anne Ravenscroft

The Horse and the Indian: A New Way of Life

Although there is significant evidence that the ancestors of the modern horse thrived in both North and South America during prehistoric times, and that at some point these resilient animals migrated from North America to the eastern regions of Asia across an Arctic land bridge, horses nonetheless vanished inexplicably from the New World around 8,000 B.C. When the Spanish Conquistador Hernan Cortez first set foot on the Yucatan Peninsula in 1519, the horse was effectively reintroduced to the continent. The Mayans who inhabited the lands of the peninsula had never seen these magnificent animals before and, understandably, initially perceived the combination of horse and Spanish rider as a strange new ~~entity~~ beast. The Mayans, and later the Aztecs and Incas, learned to fear the mounted soldier during the bloody conquest of the peninsula, Mexico, and Central America.

King Charles V established the first Viceroyalty of New Spain in 1535 (a few years after the conquest of the Incas in 1532) to govern the new colonial territories in North and Central America. By the time Spanish rule of New Spain ended in 1821 this vast colonial empire extended south to Guatemala and north into the south-western United States including the modern-day states of California, Nevada, Utah, Colorado, Arizona, New Mexico, and Texas. The capital of New Spain was located in Mexico City. The second Viceroyalty of Peru was established in 1542 and originally controlled most of South America from its capital city of Lima. The third Viceroyalty of New Granada was established in 1717 and primarily governed areas now encompassing Panama, Columbia, Ecuador, and Venezuela. The fourth and final Viceroyalty of the Rio De La Plata was formed in 1776, the same year as American Independence, and roughly bounded the countries of Argentina, Bolivia, Paraguay, and Uruguay, with Buenos Aires as the capital.

After initial explorations north of Mexico by the Franciscan monk Marco Di Niza suggested the possibility of great riches, the Spanish Conquistador Francisco Vasquez de Coronado led a major expedition into what is now western New Mexico. His advance guard reached (and then captured by storm) the primary Zuni city (called a pueblo by the Spanish) in northwest New Mexico in July of 1540. Coronado sent exploration parties in every direction and discovered a rich and populous region with twelve pueblos and around 8,000 inhabitants. After a brief period of peace and cooperation, the Pueblo Indians reacted with hostility and resistance to the capricious behavior of the Spanish. This in turn led to horrific reprisals including the burning of 100 Indians at the stake and the slaughter of hundreds more. The subsequent years brought more expeditions, continued hostilities, the construction of numerous Catholic churches, and the baptizing of thousands of Pueblo Indians. By 1630 approximately 50 friars provided religious services to 60,000 Indians in over 90 pueblos, including a small but wild Apache contingent in the eastern plains.

The year 1680 marked a calamitous turning point for both the Spanish and Pueblo Indians. Inspired by the leadership of Pope, a chief from the pueblo of San Juan in northern New Mexico, the Pueblo Indians mounted a widespread and coordinated uprising and in the process killed over 400 Spaniards, including 21 missionaries, and temporarily drove the Spanish from their lands. The Pueblos also destroyed every mission including all records and furnishings. As the uprising raged on and the Spanish retreated in chaos, thousands of Spanish horses were released into the wild and migrated north. Because of their farming culture, the Pueblos had more interest in sheep than horses and did not act quickly enough to capture them in significant numbers, but the Comanche Indians to the east and the Utes to the north embraced the new animal. The Spanish horses continued to move north on both sides of the continental divide during the following decades and found the Shoshone by 1700, the Pawnee by 1720, the Nez Perce by 1730, the Crow and Blackfeet by 1740, the Cheyenne and Sioux by 1770, and had even travelled into northern California by 1775. Although the arrival of horses did not fundamentally change the hunter-gatherer lifestyle of the Indians, they did provide new and unimagined freedom over the vast distances of the west, thereby allowing the practice of a truly effective nomadic culture for the first time. And not only did the Indians conquer distance and time with the assistance of the magnificent horse, they also transformed themselves into superb riders and hunters of the great buffalo herds and legendary warriors, all within a handful of generations.

The appaloosa, a spotted horse possibly derived from the Spanish Andalusian breed, deserves special mention. The Nez Perce Indians of Washington, Oregon, and Idaho were possibly the only tribe to consciously and selectively breed horses for strength, speed, courage, intelligence, and the quality of the spotted markings. As such, the appaloosa was highly regarded and sought after by other tribes of the plains. These capable and strong-willed animals served the Nez Perce well until the very end when in 1877, under the leadership of Chief Joseph, the last free Nez Perce surrendered to the U.S. Cavalry after an implausible 1,400 mile fighting retreat through what many thought was impassable terrain. The appaloosa horses were taken from the proud Nez Perce and distributed amongst white settlers, and the purity of the breed was forever diminished.

John Ravenscroft slurped tomato soup from an oversized spoon as he read to the end of the paragraph about Chief Joseph and the appaloosa horses and the U.S. Cavalry. He licked the spoon clean and nestled it to the side of the saucer below the curved porcelain bowl then set the page down next to his wine glass. When he raised his eyes from the manuscript they instantly found Muireall's. "Not bad. Not bad at all. As a matter of fact, pretty interesting."

Muireall slurped a spoonful of tomato soup. "Thank you."

"Where'd you find this stuff? I've never heard about any of it."

"In magazines. In books I purchased at that cute little bookstore in San Francisco last year. In the California Polytechnic School library. At the San Luis Obispo Carnegie Library. Other sources I can't remember without checking the bibliography."

"Impressive. And if I understand this section correctly, the horse began in North America, crossed over some sort of land bridge into Asia before disappearing from the American continent for reasons we don't know, migrated west to Spain, boarded a ship with Cortez, crossed the

Atlantic Ocean to the Yucatan Peninsula, travelled to Mexico with the Conquistadors, then journeyed back to North America with Coronado after an absence of around 9,000 years when a Pueblo Indian named Pope sent the Spanish packing."

Muireall sighed. "Sounds about right, although you have condensed four pages and two days of hard work into an extemporaneous outburst of less than 100 words. I'm the one who should be impressed—with your gift of brevity."

Captain Ethan Plantagenet of the U.S. 2nd Cavalry stared blankly across the polished oak table, the only furniture in the room not covered with a thin film of dust, into the stoic face of General William Tecumseh Sherman. He generally found Sherman an honorable man, but occasionally struggled with the infamous "March to the Sea" of 1864. But then he reminded himself of his promise to set aside all such concerns in support of his rejuvenated career in the army, the only occupation that had ever provided him with true passion and commitment. He had tried shop keeping following the war, but after a drunken night of intense self-pity and a failed suicide he had sought out the military again the next morning. Distracted by these thoughts, and unsettled by the memory of the nearly-successful suicide, he did not choose his next words with care. "General... I think it ill advised to assign a Sioux half-breed to my company for what should be a straightforward mission. Frankly sir, I have not found any reason to trust them."

General Sherman maintained the clarity of his calmly indifferent expression. "You mean to say...you are not willing to trust them." Sherman lighted a cigar—recently imported from Saint Louis—and puffed a compact haze of smoke above the table. "Joshua Hotah is a superb Indian scout. His horsemanship is unsurpassed. He reads the trail with great skill. He is a better rifle marksman than any of the ragtag immigrants in your unit. He speaks both English and Sioux fluently, and a little Cheyenne and Nez Perce as well. He may speak other Indian dialects I am not aware of. I would not hesitate to trust him with my life in this savage wilderness."

Ethan shifted his weight and squeezed a pair of white cavalry gloves behind his back. "And which half do you suggest I trust, sir—the white or the red?"

Sherman released his stoic countenance with a brief smile. "I see your problem." He paused again to enjoy a long draw from the cigar. "An excellent cigar. Would you like one before you leave?"

Ethan shifted his weight again. "No sir. I don't smoke."

"A habit you should consider taking up. Nothing like a good cigar to break the tension of the moment." Sherman lowered the cigar to admire it. "And which half do *you* suggest I trust, Captain Plantagenet—the gray or the blue?"

Ethan felt the sting of this question. "I assure you sir, that you have my full and uncompromising loyalty. The war is over for me."

Sherman chewed on the cigar. "I know I do son, and I honestly have no doubt of it. But I assure you as well that you can trust Joshua Hotah with your life. Do we have an understanding?"

Ethan considered his next words more discreetly. He thought of pushing the argument a bit more, but then reconsidered. "Yes sir, we do."

"Good. Then listen carefully. Lieutenant Colonel Custer and over one-thousand men of the Seventh Cavalry departed Fort Hays nearly a month ago to quell some Indian uprisings near the Platte River. According to information I have just received, the regiment is encamped at the forks of the Republican River, about 90 miles southeast from here. I have a critical communiqué that must be delivered to Custer as soon as possible. I have placed the message in this envelope." Sherman slid the envelope, secured with his personal wax seal, across the polished table. "You alone are to carry the message. You alone are to personally deliver the envelope directly to Custer. Do not allow anyone to take the envelope from you and do not ask anyone to deliver the message on your behalf. Are these instructions clear?"

Ethan wrested the envelope from beneath Sherman's tobacco-stained fingers and then deposited it into a black leather pouch slung at his side. "Yes sir, your instructions are quite clear."

Sherman flicked a large cylinder of grayed ash from the end of the cigar. Ethan watched the ash float down and puff off the edge of the formerly pristine table. "Then you are to leave immediately. Take as many men from your company as you see fit, but I want you to leave the fort within two hours. Any questions?"

"No sir, none."

"Then on your way. And take a cigar with you." Sherman opened a leather box and presented it to Ethan. "You might change your mind."

Without a hint of indecision, Ethan selected one of the cigars. "Thank you, sir."

"And Captain…"

"Yes sir?"

"Don't forget to take Joshua Hotah with you."

"No sir." Ethan shoved the cigar into the pouch next to the letter, saluted smartly, pivoted cleanly, and strode briskly from the office. When he had passed though the heavy wood door and crossed the covered porch at the front of the building, he found Joshua Hotah standing beyond the margin of the roof's shadow and stroking an unusual spotted horse. He addressed him directly. "Are you the half-breed they call Joshua Hotah?"

Joshua looked up from his appaloosa, the oddly-feathered brim of his old army hat shading his face from the morning sun. "My name is Joshua Hotah."

Ethan clopped indifferently down the two porch steps and approached Joshua at a leisurely pace until he stood less than an arm's length away. Joshua's dark-blue regulation army jacket, wide-brimmed-black-felt Indian scout hat with golden crossed-arrows insignia and red and white acorn-tipped braid, and light-blue pants with a blue stripe down each side were in order, but the multi-colored-bead-adorned leather moccasins represented a notable lapse of military decorum. "General Sherman has assigned you to my company for a patrol to the forks of the Republican River." Ethan thought of the moccasins again. "I objected vigorously because I do not trust you or any other Indian scout. However, I have no choice but to bring you along because of the general's insistence. General Sherman informs me that you speak fluent English. Is this true?"

Joshua grinned. "Yes, I speak English. My father was a buffalo hunter who came from England in a ship."

Ethan noted the annoying hint of a British accent. "Then not only are you a half-breed, but neither half is American. Truly enlightening."

"My mother was Sioux."

"So I heard. As I said—"

The appaloosa shook its head violently and nearly yanked the leather reins from Joshua's hand. Joshua pulled the animal close and spoke soothingly in Nez Perce until the appaloosa had calmed. "I do not think my horse likes you much."

Ethan stepped back to avoid the skittish animal. "Then I believe, Joshua Hotah, that we have an understanding."

Joshua grinned a second time. "Yes, I believe we do…" and then the grin widened, "…old chap."

Ethan did not find this British vernacular amusing. He slapped his thigh with the white cavalry gloves. "Then we leave within two hours. Do not be late. I do not intend to begin the patrol by disobeying a direct order from General William Tecumseh Sherman, but if you do not arrive on time, I will leave without you."

Two days after departing Fort Sedgwick with 20 men and a half-breed Sioux scout, Captain Ethan Plantagenet pushed himself up on the stirrups of his cavalry saddle and scanned along the north and south forks of the meandering Republican River for evidence of Custer's Seventh Cavalry. As his vision swept across the horizon, his eyes paused at the strange image of Joshua Hotah—about 50 yards distant—on his hands and knees with his face pressed close to the ground only inches away from the spotted nose of the appaloosa. Although implausible, both man and horse appeared to find the same thing. When he squinted and refocused, it also appeared to Ethan that Joshua Hotah was conducting a discussion with the animal, and that the horse responded to each comment by moving its head. This observation did not improve Ethan's original impression of the scout. He spoke to his sergeant, an immigrant from Ireland and a veteran of the final year of the Civil War. "Wait here with the men while I have a little talk with our scout."

The sergeant spit. "Yes sir. A fine idea."

Joshua Hotah poked a stick into the remains of the abandoned campfire and stirred. A jet of sooty dust puffed up against the appaloosa's nose; the spotted horse shook her head and snorted. "You should not be so curious. Your only reward is a nose full of ash." Still on his knees, Joshua explored the ground for artifacts. He noticed a discarded tin can. He crawled over to the can and sniffed it. The appaloosa sniffed the can too. "Custer left this campsite a few days ago, probably more than a few days. And they did not clean up before they left. Maybe they have many soldiers and do not worry about leaving a trail behind." The appaloosa nudged Joshua's shoulder in apparent agreement. Joshua stood and walked southwest, without holding the reins of his horse. The appaloosa followed. He kneeled to the ground by a set of wagon wheel tracks running north and south. Before he had finished inspecting the tracks, Captain Ethan Plantagenet rode up and stopped in front of him, a few yards away. When Joshua raised his gaze from the wagon tracks to Ethan's face, he noticed the evening moon rising just above the peak of the captain's hat.

After waiting patiently for a report, Ethan leaned forward against the saddle horn. "What have you and your horse found? Anything worth noting?" Ethan observed the wagon wheel tracks in the fading daylight. He followed the tracks to the north, where they likely began, and then back to the south. "Looks like wagon tracks heading south. I assume Custer has gone in that direction."

Part of this observation impressed Joshua. "Yes, wagon wheels heading south. But I believe Custer has not gone with the wagon tracks. The path of the wagons does not have enough horse hooves. I believe Custer and the Seventh Cavalry must have followed a different path, possibly west."

Ethan glanced down at the tracks again, the moonlight now providing more illumination than the fading glow of the western skies. "Nonsense. I don't see how you can come to such a conclusion from the evidence right in front of us. I see wagon tracks and I see horse tracks, both heading south. I see absolutely nothing to suggest Custer and his main force went in a different direction. We camp for the night and follow the wagon tracks south at daybreak."

Joshua offered the possibility that Ethan had more correctly read the ground. "I am not certain what I say is true. I can agree with you on this. But we should scout a wider area to find Custer's path. If we follow these wagon tracks, we may not find him at all."

Ethan pressed his hand against the leather pouch containing the message from General Sherman (and the cigar). "We've had a hard two-day ride and the men are tired. I'm not going to waste more time scouting this endless country when the evidence of Custer's direction of travel is right in front of us. Tomorrow we follow these wagon tracks south. I am confident we will locate Custer before the end of the day."

Joshua thought about telling Ethan about the campfire, but decided against prolonging the argument. He would wait for an opportunity tomorrow to prove the wagon tracks did not follow Custer and the Seventh Cavalry. Maybe then he could talk Captain Plantagenet into a different path.

As the sun neared its zenith and the day continued to warm, Ethan halted the patrol. He rubbed the back of his neck, adding more sweat to a leather glove already soaked with sweat. He spoke to Joshua Hotah, now riding by his side. "Have you seen any evidence that Custer turned off this wagon trail? I certainly have not."

"I have not. But we have ridden so fast and stopped so little, it is hard to tell what I have seen and have not seen."

This obvious excuse did not convince Ethan. "Or maybe you are not as good a scout as General Sherman imagines."

Joshua did not take offense. "Maybe not, if this is what you wish to believe. But it is difficult to read the trail when we are riding very fast above it."

"It is really not necessary for you to read the trail at this point. These wagon tracks point to Custer, and we will follow them to the end."

The Irish Sergeant jabbed Ethan on the arm. "Sir, we've got company, and I don't think it's the Seventh Cavalry." The sergeant pointed.

Ethan followed the end of the sergeant's finger to a long column of riders stretched along the top of a low ridge running southwesterly to his right, about 300 yards away. Ethan began counting them, but stopped when he reached a hundred. He pulled a small telescope from a saddle pouch, extended the tubes, and squinted at the riders. He lowered the telescope and declared, "Indians." He handed the telescope to Joshua. "Ever use one of these before?"

Joshua did not answer the question. He took the telescope and held it up to his left eye. "Lakota ... and Cheyenne. They have been following us."

Ethan shifted in his saddle. He had bravely faced Union infantry, cavalry, and artillery in the war, but the sight of Indians on the plains of northwest Kansas frightened him in a way he did not think possible. "How many? What are their intentions?"

Joshua collapsed the telescoped and pressed it into Ethan's hand. "Over one-hundred, with maybe more behind the ridge. I do not know what they intend."

Ethan privately prayed that General Sherman knew more about Indian scouts than he did. "What do you suggest we do?"

Joshua answered, "I think we should ride east to Beaver Creek and look for cover. And we should not ride slowly."

Ethan did not argue. He gave the order to the Irish sergeant. "Sergeant, you heard our scout. We are heading east to Beaver Creek, and we are not riding slowly."

The sergeant answered stoically, "Yes sir. Sounds like a good plan to me."

The patrol veered off the wagon trail to the east, and at the command of the sergeant broke into a trot. Some of the men could not keep their eyes forward, and regularly checked the Lakota and Cheyenne riders behind them. Captain Ethan Plantagenet did not look. After fifteen minutes of silence had passed, he renewed his conversation with Joshua Hotah. "What are they doing now?"

Joshua twisted just enough to see the Indians at the rim of his vision. "They are still following us. They are getting closer. They are riding faster than we are."

Ethan looked back for the first time since the patrol had abandoned the wagon trail. "I see what you mean. What now?"

"I think it is time to run."

"Do you think we can outrun them?"

"No, we cannot outrun them. We should ride to someplace where we can defend ourselves. This is our only chance."

This answer alarmed Ethan. "I see." He turned to the sergeant. "Sergeant, it's time to make a run for it and to find a defensive position. But don't blow the damn bugle." He turned back to Joshua Hotah. "Joshua, you take the lead. We will follow you."

This time the sergeant smiled uneasily. "Yes sir." He gave the troopers the order to gallop and the patrol rushed forward with Joshua Hotah and the appaloosa in front. This maneuver ignited an instant response from the Lakota and Cheyenne riders, and for the first time the troopers could hear the exuberant cries of the nearest warriors.

Joshua led the patrol easterly, the churning legs of the galloping horses—sweat-lathered and weight-burdened with cavalrymen and leather and wood and iron—smashing violently through the flowing grasses and scattered wildflowers of the prairie. The rugged ground began a gentle rise toward an undulating ridge running northeast to southwest. Beyond the ridge, in a shallow valley, Beaver Creek and Sappa Creek and Prairie Dog Creek flowed southwesterly and offered the possibility of a defensive position. Ethan strained to see clearly through stinging splashes of sweat and cutting slaps of wind as he watched the nimble appaloosa and Joshua Hotah bound over the ridge. When he had reached the ridge himself, he swung his exhausted mount around to confirm the proximity of the Lakota and Cheyenne. To his eternal horror, he beheld the closest warriors overtake two troopers at the rear of his patrol and beat them to the ground with stone clubs. One of the fallen soldiers, a recent immigrant from Germany and only one month in the saddle, stood and began staggering in small looping circles. The man struggled to remove his pistol, but a Cheyenne spear pierced him cleanly through the breast and drove him down again. Ethan spun his panting horse around and commenced a ragged gallop down into the valley. Moments later he spotted Joshua and the appaloosa gesturing at him to follow them toward the swirling waters of Beaver Creek, now visible and seemingly within reach. When Ethan arrived at Joshua's side, they renewed the desperate run to Beaver Creek together. Nearby, another trooper—a young man from Massachusetts with two Lakota arrows plunged deeply into his back—finally released his flagging grip on the saddle horn and tumbled clumsily off his mount into yellow waves of prairie grass where the merciful ground instantly shattered two vertebrae at the base of his skull.

When Joshua and Ethan arrived at Beaver Creek, with the sergeant and 16 remaining troopers trailing in disarray, they pivoted abruptly and raced along the stream, splashing in marshy pools swollen beyond the meandering shore. Joshua suddenly pulled up next to Ethan and reached across the narrow space separating them and tugged at the blue wool of his arm. Ethan glanced over to Joshua, who pointed behind them before slanting away from the creek and slowing to a walk. Ethan and the remaining troopers did the same.

Ethan, his horse shivering with exhaustion, spoke to Joshua without moving closer. "Where did they go? They were right behind us."

Joshua scrutinized the ridge to the left, now some distance from Beaver Creek, and then scanned along the creek to the northeast. "I believe they are walking the same path we do, but on the other side of the hill."

"Why are they doing this? They could have easily killed all of us."

"They are taunting us. We should find protection quickly, because they will soon attack again. Some of the warriors may be moving in front of us now. We should cross Beaver Creek and move away from the hill."

Joshua and the appaloosa trotted across the creek. Ethan and the sergeant followed without offering any commands, and the ragged line of troopers followed without speaking. Joshua turned at a gully littered with boulders and flanked with thorny bushes. Ethan and the sergeant pulled up next to him.

Joshua dismounted, removed his feathered cavalry hat, and coaxed his long black hair back over his shoulders. He swung around in a complete circle and studied the terrain, then appraised the position of the sun before walking to Ethan's side. "It is not the best place, but the day will end soon and we do not have time to look for another. You are the soldier. Do you like this place?"

The leather of Ethan's saddle chirped when he twisted back and forth to review the defensive possibilities of the rocky gully. "I agree it is not the best. I would prefer the high ground, but this is less exposed. I think we should make our stand here. Sergeant Doyle, do you have anything to add?"

The sergeant stiffened. "Yes, sir. Can you find another 50 troopers before dark? It would be a service, sir."

Captain Ethan Plantagenet dismounted. "Sergeant, tie the horses up near those large boulders and spread the men out along both sides of the gully. Mr. Joshua Hotah, I want you at my side tonight. Right or wrong, we make our stand here. And may God help us."

The gloomy face of a new moon and the deafening howl of prairie wind offered little hope to the 19 men spread thinly along the jagged sides of the shallow gully. The sun plunged below the western horizon and bluish skies faded to murky blue then to inky blue then to terrifying blackness. During this darkest of nights, Lakota and Cheyenne warriors drew lots and then one-by-one waded noiselessly across Beaver Creek and crept silently over the grassy soil to the far ends of the gully where individual soldiers lay blind in the shadows of darkest midnight and deaf in the swirling rush of wind. And then one-by-one, the soldiers perished when a stony club crushed a man's head or a sharpened blade slashed across his throat or a length of leather cut off the air from his gasping lungs. The silent killing proceeded down the lines of men throughout the dreadful night, and by dawn, when the rising sun finally dissolved the hideous shadows of night and the cool freshness of the morning diminished the relentless wind to a tender breeze, only Captain Ethan Plantagenet of the U.S. 2nd Cavalry and the half-breed named Joshua Hotah remained alive.

Joshua slithered back to Ethan's side and rolled over to his back. He raised his shoulder off a sharp rock and reported in a low voice, "It is as we feared. Everyone is dead. Only the two of us have survived this long night."

Exhausted by lack of sleep but forced awake by apprehension, Ethan asked weakly, "The sergeant is dead too?"

"Yes. But I think he may have fought a little, because his throat is not slit and there is much blood on the ground. He may have stabbed his attacker before he died." Then Joshua added, "Five of the soldiers are missing their balls."

"The Indians took their ammunition?"

"Yes, they took their guns and ammunition too."

Ethan pulled his Colt 1860 Army cap-and-ball revolver from its black-leather holster and rested it across his stomach. He had used the pistol throughout the Civil War, and found the familiarity of the polished steel barrel and hand-smoothed wood grips oddly comforting. "Not a pretty thought. Maybe we should try to make a run for it. We still have the horses. We could take two and scatter the rest to divert the Indians."

Joshua considered this idea briefly. "A possibility, but I do not think our chances are good. We are probably surrounded and would have to ride through the Lakota and Cheyenne. The appaloosa might make it, but your horse probably would not."

Ethan smiled darkly. "Any chance they will just let us go?"

"I would call it wishful thinking. But if we did run for it, maybe they would kill us in the saddle. Then we would not be captured and tortured to death. Maybe the men who died quickly during the night are the lucky ones today."

Two gaunt ravens fluttered overhead and landed raucously in a scrawny cottonwood about thirty feet away. The ravens leered down at Ethan and Joshua, twisting their glossy heads right and left to improve the view. The raven to the left, the larger of the two, began issuing a strange chortling sound reminiscent of a contented cat while the other continued his thoughtful examination of the narrow ravine and the two men stretched out on the ground below.

Ethan removed his cavalry hat and pretended to adjust the sweat-soaked-dust-caked brim while watching the two ravens and listening to the odd sound. "Ravens have arrived to witness our demise. Do you think they know something we don't?"

Joshua chuckled. "Ravens always know something we don't. It is a bad sign. I have not had good luck with ravens around."

Ethan carefully positioned the crumpled hat on his head. "I know what you mean. I felt pretty good about our situation myself until those two birds arrived. Now I'm really—" The raven to the right, the smaller of the two, exploded in a wing-flapping-squawking show of alarm. The other raven quickly joined in the display.

Joshua peeked above the rocks. A lone Sioux rider approached, a lance in one hand and a rifle in the other. The rider stopped about 30 strides from the shallow ravine and waited.

Ethan rolled and cocked the hammer of his Colt in the same smooth motion and prepared to take a shot. "I think I can hit him. I killed men at Shiloh from a greater distance while riding a horse. I ought to be able to shoot an Indian sitting still."

Joshua reached over and pressed Ethan's arm down. "Do not shoot."

"Why? We might as well take a few of them with us."

"He is my half-brother. I believe he has come to talk to us. Do not shoot."

"Your half-brother?"

"Yes, our mother is the same."

Ethan lowered the revolver until the barrel rested on a tuft of buffalo grass. "Astonishing. What's his name? What do you think he wants?"

"Running Bear, and I think we should find out. Do not bring any guns."

This alarmed Ethan. "I do not think it wise to walk out in the open without our weapons."

"If you bring a gun, you will die. Our only chance is to walk out with empty hands. Put down your revolver and stand up."

Ethan waited until his hand had flinched a few times, then sucked in a deep breath and exhaled and set the Colt gently on the ground and stood. Joshua stood in unison then rested his Henry repeating rifle against a rock with a melodramatic flourish. They advanced side-by-side to talk to Running Bear. When they had reached a small mound covered with wildflowers about two strides in front of the horse, they stopped. Joshua waited for his half-brother to begin the conversation.

After an unpleasant delay, Running Bear frowned and said, "Txay huh wan chee youn kay shnee." *(I did not see you for a long time)*

Joshua raised his chin to see his half-brother's face better. "Cante waste nape ciyuzapo." (*I greet you from my heart*)

Running Bear waited again. *"You would have died last night if I had not convinced the others to spare your life."*

"I thank you for sparing our lives, my brother, but what have you to tell us now?"

"Because we share the same mother, you may leave, but the soldier must stay."

"The soldier is my friend. I will not leave him here so you can cut off his balls like you did to the others. You must let both of us leave, or kill us both together."

This surprised Running Bear. He drove the lance into the ground in anger. Ethan touched Joshua's arm. "What did you just say to him?"

Joshua snarled at Ethan without taking his eyes off his half-brother. "It is none of your business what I say or do not say to my brother."

Running Bear chuckled. *"Your friend is very stupid. Does he know what danger he is in?"*

Joshua smirked, *"Yes, the white man is stupid in many ways, but very clever in other ways you do not appreciate. You would do well not to underestimate him."*

Running Bear nodded slightly. *"I do not have the heart to kill you today, even if you deserve it for helping the soldiers invade our lands and kill our buffalo."*

"Then you must let us both go. I will not leave without my friend."

Running Bear glanced back at the Lakota and Cheyenne warriors waiting hidden behind the crest of the hill. *"You are very presumptuous, but I must honor our mother. You may go with your friend, but the horses must stay."*

"It is a long walk. You should allow us to take one horse."

"The horses are the price you must pay to live. Now leave before it is too late."

"Thank you my brother. Until we meet again."

Running Bear's countenance dimmed. *"I must tell you, child of my mother, the next time we meet I will kill you. You are given only this one chance."*

Joshua Hotah nodded. *"I understand. Then I shall pray we do not meet again."* He pulled Ethan's arm. "Start walking away from here. Do not look back. Do not say a word. Walk quickly, but not too fast."

"I need to fetch my Colt."

"No, you must leave everything here. We cannot take the chance."

"No horses?"

"This is the agreement, but I think we will see the appaloosa again—after she throws her new rider to the ground and follows after us."

Joshua Hotah and Captain Ethan Plantagenet hiked south until they reached Sappa Creek then southwesterly. The appaloosa joined them, as Joshua had predicted, about two miles before they rediscovered the wagon wheel tracks that had originally led them to disaster. They took turns riding the horse. They talked about many things. They smoked General Sherman's cigar. And eventually the wheel tracks led them to Fort Wallace, about 40 miles from the massacre in the gully. They arrived at the fort hungry and dehydrated, but alive. Joshua waited outside an impressive stone building while Ethan gave an abbreviated report to the fort commander. They ate and drank separately, and then each slept for nearly two days—again separately.

Ethan discovered Joshua early in the morning a day later, preparing to leave with the appaloosa. He greeted him with renewed vigor. "Good morning Joshua. Where are you going?"

Joshua slipped a new Henry repeating rifle, donated by a sergeant at the fort armory, into a leather saddle sheath. He answered without turning his head. “Your sergeant has replaced my lost rifle, and for this I am grateful.” Then he turned. “I am no longer a scout. Today I head west, then maybe north.”

Ethan felt a tinge of melancholy. “What will you do? You’re a damn good scout, if anyone would care to listen to you. You should reconsider.”

“Thank you for saying it, but I have decided to look for my father and mother. I lost them some years ago, and it is time to find them again.”

“Is there anything I can do for you?”

“No. This is something only I can do, but thank you.”

Ethan held out his hand. “Then goodbye, my friend.”

Joshua grasped Ethan’s hand and they squeezed without shaking. “Yes, goodbye my friend.”

Joshua Hotah mounted the appaloosa, kicked the feisty animal in the loins, and trotted through the open gate. He rode about a mile before circling west. With the sun warming his back and cumulus clouds rising in the distance, he began the search for his parents.

Chapter Five

Sitka, Alaska
October 18, 1867

Roshan Kuznetsov, stinking of skinned sea otter and three months of unwashed tromping through the rainforests and waterways of Baranov Island, loitered unreasonably close to the polished double-B-flat tuba. The distorted reflection of his bearded, unwashed face just beneath the flared bell of the tuba amused him, and reminded him that he had once again returned safely from the wilderness of bear and spruce to the booming metropolis of New Archangel. When he tired of playing with his reflection, he switched his attention to the man holding the heavy instrument. He found the dark blue uniform, the odd hat with no flaps for the ears, the golden-fringed epaulets, and polished knee-high black boots quite amusing. Roshan swung behind the man to investigate the neatly-trimmed back of his head, and then continued around to his other side where another man stood at attention brandishing a shiny trombone.

After obeying the earlier command to stand at attention, the tubaist could no longer remain still or silent. He broke ranks to confront Roshan. "Do you mind stepping away, sir? I have to play in a few minutes, and I need the time to catch my breath."

This surprised Roshan. "I speak of sometime English. Do you speak the Russian?"

This exasperated the tubaist. "I certainly do not. Now please step away."

Roshan persisted because he had not yet completed his inspection. "You must sorry me, but I still have much to find of your tuba. I must share with you I want to play the tuba when boy, but my parents did have not the wealth to afford of a large thing. There is also problem of finding a tuba for to buy, but is not of the story."

"Very sad, and I'm very sorry your parents could not afford a tuba, but could you please just move away? Your stench is truly suffocating. I fear I won't be able to breathe when we begin playing."

"My stench? What is stench? This is new word I have not to hear."

The trombonist broke ranks as well, and held his nose while addressing Roshan. "It means you stink. And frankly, my friend, I've never smelled such a stink, not even on the farm back in Missouri."

Roshan grinned. "Yes, I know what is stink. You cannot take the breathing because stink is too good for you. But I do not know the stink—I mean 'stench' because I should practice the new English word you have told of me—because I do not smell it any more after many months in the forest looking for the otter pelts."

The tubaist attempted to regain the conversation. "Yes, I think we have all agreed you stink, so please move away as quickly as possible. I'm beginning to feel light headed for lack of fresh air."

Roshan nodded agreeably. "Yes, I would please to move, but first you must answer a question of confusion to me."

The trombonist held his entire hand over his nose. "Yes, yes, but please ask your question quickly. I do not think I will last much longer."

"Good. Then the question I ask," Roshan paused to gesture expansively with his arm, "is what is it doing this day in New Archangel, and why do a tuba and a trombone in blue pants and many other instruments I do not understand the names stand in front of the Baranov Castle three months before now stand on this place I am now from the trees?"

The tubaist had hoped for an easy question, but it took him several seconds to sort out the jumble of words. "You haven't heard? How is this possible?"

Roshan dropped his arm and frowned. "There is something to hear of the possible?"

The trombonist answered on behalf of the tubaist. "This town and all of Alaska belong to the United States of America now. The Russians sold the territory last April, and today is the day we take down the Russian flag and raise the stars and stripes."

Roshan sputtered, "The stripes of stars?"

The tubaist corrected, "The stars and stripes. The American flag!"

Roshan took off his ushanka[*] and kneaded the soft otter fur between his fingers. "How possible is this? What of my trade of the otter furs if the American stripes are in the air because the Russian flag is not?"

The trombonist began gasping for fresh air. "Listen here. We answered your question, now you're supposed to step away. That was the deal."

Roshan took a step back, but the stink persisted. "That is a deal? But I do not this belief it is true. How can Russia sell the all of Alaska? It is too much to understand in a short day."

The tubaist continued, "Your confusion is not our problem my stinky fellow, now move away like you promised."

Roshan dropped his chin and walked away, but not because the tubaist and trombonist had told him to. He walked away in disbelief because Russia had sold Alaska. He muttered in Russian, "This is not possible. How could this be? Trapping sea otter has been my life for more than 20 years. What will I do when the Americans are in charge? Will they allow me to continue my work? Will they allow me to stay in New Archangel at all? What if they ask me to leave? What then? What will I do? What will I do?"

Roshan ambled sadly away from Castle Hill, mumbling incessantly of his loss. The sounds of the U.S. Army band playing the Star Spangled Banner echoed off the wood buildings to either side. He glanced back, and the stars and stripes of the American flag fluttered into his view above Baranov's Castle. Roshan watched briefly before resuming his mumbling walk.

Roshan Kuznetsov, still stinking of skinned sea otter and three months of unwashed tromping through the rainforests and waterways of Baranov Island, marched angrily up the weathered wood steps and across the weathered wood porch into the gable-roofed-wood-sided headquarters of the Russian-American Company to demand answers of Prince Dmitri Petrovich Maksutov, the current and—if the accusations of the tubaist and trombonist were true—last chief manager of the company and last

[*] The *ushanka* is a Russian fur hat with ear flaps that can be tied over the top of the hat or under the chin to protect the ears and lower jaw from the cold.

governor of Alaska. A rear admiral in the Russian Imperial Navy, and a hero of the Battle of Sinope in the Crimean War, Prince Maksutov had proved reasonable in past encounters. Roshan prayed that the regrettable events of the last few months had not made him less affable as he passed by the ornate desk with the Prince's flamboyantly-attired assistant sitting in an equally-flamboyant cushioned chair just behind. The assistant stood immediately and chased Roshan into Maksutov's office, but failed to stop the determined trapper of otter.

The assistant spoke from behind Roshan. "My deepest apologies sir, but I could not stop this smelly man from entering your office unannounced. He has no appointment."

Maksutov, balding with luxurious moustache and sideburns framing a naked chin, looked up from a box partially packed with books and papers. "Let Roshan Kuznetsov in. He never has an appointment when he comes here."

Roshan snatched his ushanka and swept it away in a wide arc as he bowed at the waist; a puff of stench wafted across the Prince's desk. "Thank you my grace. It is always a pleasure to meet you in your luxurious office."

Maksutov pressed his hands down on the cluttered desk separating him from Roshan. "Roshan, stop. We both know you want something and take no pleasure in coming here. And, as usual, you smell of dead otter and other smells I can only guess at. Please come to the point before I am suffocated by your presence."

Roshan restored the stinky ushanka to his unwashed head. "Then I shall move directly to my complaint. I was just told by two very reliable individuals that Russia has sold all of Alaska to the Americans. At first I thought this impossible. Who would be so foolish as to commit an act of such unthinkable stupidity? But then I realized both individuals who stood in front of me were in fact Americans, and what they were telling me could be true. I then said to myself, there is only one way to find out what is the truth: to speak directly to Prince Dmitri Petrovich Maksutov, chief manager of the Russian-American Company and Governor of Alaska. There you have it. This is a summary of my complaint."

Maksutov gestured toward a large samovar, well maintained but surprisingly unadorned (considering the lofty credentials of its owner), on a table near a tall double-hung window. "Although I hate to suggest a reason for you to reside in my office longer than necessary, would you care for some tea?"

Roshan glanced around until he found a large baroque chair painted in gold. He dragged the chair into position in front of Maksutov's desk and plopped into the crimson-red cushions. "Yes, I will drink tea while I listen to your answer."

Maksutov positioned a cup beneath the samovar's polished spout and opened the valve to pour some hot tea. "Sugar?"

Roshan scooted forward. "You have sugar? I have not tasted sugar for two months. Yes, I will have two spoonfuls of sugar."

Maksutov balanced the cup on a dainty saucer, handed the tea to Roshan, and sat behind the desk. He picked up some papers then set them down again before speaking. "As I think you know, Roshan, the fur trade is not as good as it used to be. It is costing Mother Russia far more than it is worth to maintain Sitka. It has simply become a very expensive proposition, one which we can no longer afford."

Roshan gulped some of the overly-sweet tea. "Yes, the otters are not as numerous as they once were, but they will return again soon. I am sure of it."

"The otters are no longer numerous because of men like you, Roshan."

"It is my passion to trap the otters. I cannot help it if I am good at it."

Maksutov leaned back in his chair and clasped his hands. "Wishful thinking my friend, but there is another problem you should consider."

Roshan slurped the last of the tea and set the saucer and cup on top of a pile of documents at the front of Maksutov's desk. "Are there not problems enough already?"

"The Tsar has larger concerns than either one of us can truly understand or appreciate."

"Tsar Alexander has concerns of Alaska?"

"Yes. He worries the British may simply take Alaska from Russia without any compensation whatsoever. At least the Americans are willing to pay a lot of money for the privilege to own it. Then they can suffer the cost of maintaining it."

Roshan slumped in the chair and then sprung to a rigid sitting position. "But if the Americans own Alaska, what of the fur trade?"

Maksutov sighed. “I do not think the Americans have as much interest in otter pelts as we Russians do. But I have heard they are quite interested in gold. Maybe you should consider a change of profession.”

“A change of profession?”

“Yes, it is a thought. I heard there is gold in California. Or you could return to Russia and continue doing whatever it was you were doing before you left.”

Roshan’s arms fell to the sides of the chair. “I was not doing anything before I left Russia because there was nothing for me to do. I could not even find a tuba to play. This is why I travelled to Alaska in the first place.”

“You came to Alaska because you could not play the tuba?”

“No, I came to Alaska because I could not find anything to do in Russia. I just mention the problem with the tuba as one example of the many reasons I left Russia.”

Maksutov pressed his fingers together. “There is an American naval ship sailing for San Francisco early in the morning. I believe it is called the USS Ossipee. If you wish, I could arrange passage for you. Captain Emmons is a personal friend of mine. I will compensate you this afternoon for the pelts you have delivered. This should provide you with more than enough money to begin a new life in California.”

“But where is this California?”

“It is to the south, my friend. And it is very large, possibly larger than Alaska. I doubt you will have any trouble finding it.”

Roshan stood and bowed. “Thank you Prince Dmitri Petrovich Maksutov. I appreciate the advice. But I must take some time to think on it. Such a momentous decision cannot be made in the blink of an eye.”

Maksutov stood as well. “Do not think on it too much, or you will miss the ship and your one chance for easy transport to California. You must let me know of your plans within the hour to allow sufficient time to make proper arrangements with the captain.”

Roshan bowed his head and reached across the desk and shook the hand of the last Governor of Alaska, then stomped out of the office. When Roshan had exited the building, the flamboyant assistant entered the office and immediately held his nose. He spoke to Maksutov between gasping breaths. “Would you like me to open a window?”

"No, do not open a window. Open them all. And when you have finished, take this chair outside and burn it. I don't think even the Americans will want it in its current condition."

The flamboyant assistant cringed. "Do you expect me to touch it?"

Maksutov gazed through the window. "Yes, I expect you to touch it. Now get to work. We still have much packing to finish before we forever leave this unforgiving land."

Roshan Kuznetsov, his back hunched over from the carefully-selected accouterments of his profession he thought might prove useful in the goldfields of California—or which he could not bring himself to part with because of an overwhelming sense of nostalgia—blundered through the muddy, narrow, meandering, log-and-timber-building-rimmed streets of Sitka at 5:27 in the morning on October 19th in the year 1867, a persistent southeasterly blowing dreary mist into his already saturated beard. He paused at an intersection of muddy streets to enjoy one last view of the Russian Orthodox Cathedral of Saint Michael the Archangel, rising magnificently from the mud in horizontal-wood-siding splendor at the end of the lane. He considered the idea of walking into the cathedral to pray for a safe and prosperous trip, but feared the priest might discover him and force him to attend confession. After deciding God did not require an extravagant building with a metal-clad dome and spire to justify a simple prayer, he crossed himself and prayed where he stood:

"My dearest Lord...especially in difficult times, of which we both agree there have been a few...you know I have sinned...yes, many times... alright, many, many times—more than I can possibly recount from memory standing in the rain and wind at this moment. But even so, I also know you are a forgiving Lord, and that it would please you if I were to experience a safe trip to California—a place I'm sure you know where it is even if I have not heard of it—and then to find only a little wealth after I get there so you would not have to spend as much of your precious time worrying about me." Roshan adjusted the heavy load weighing down his shoulders before continuing. "And another thing Lord, something I have never shared with you, or anyone else, until this very moment when I am about to depart on a ship to only you know where, but I truly beg your forgiveness for killing so many—"

"So many what?"

Roshan turned and the swerving load of accouterments nearly knocked into the man standing behind him. "Father Dmitri. I did not know you stood right behind me or I would have taken more care when I turned around."

"Do not worry about it Roshan. So many what?"

"So many what? Oh, yes. So many what, you ask? Why, I was merely talking to myself about something which matters very little now because there are many reasons to not worry about thinking of it ever again."

"I see. It sounded like you were praying. Maybe we should walk over to the cathedral and I can hear your confession."

"I would like nothing better than to confess my sins to you this very morning, Father, but unfortunately I am late for the ship that will take me to California, so I must beg your forgiveness and hurry on my way."

"I see. Then I will pray for a safe trip."

"Thank you, Father."

"But as to the wealth, we must both leave it in God's hands."

Roshan jumped to raise the load higher on his shoulders. "Why, thank you Father. I did not know you stood next to me for so long."

"I heard your entire prayer. And Roshan ..."

"Yes, Father Dmitri."

"True wealth is not always what you think."

"Yes, Father Dmitri."

"Now on your way, or you will miss the ship and your new adventure in California. And one last thing Roshan."

"Yes, Father?"

"Take a bath when you find the time. You smell like a rotting beaver."

"Yes, Father Dmitri. I will."

After shaking hands with Father Dmitri, Roshan continued his march to the boat yards where he hoped to find the ship named...the ship named...named...well...he could not remember the name of the ship.

But, he reasoned as he tromped along, how hard could it be to find a large American ship? When he arrived at the end of a wharf jutting favorably above the incoming tide, he discovered three large ships anchored in the bay. He could not even guess which one had the name he could not remember. Then he realized an important detail: if he had remembered the name of the ship, he had no way to get out to it anyway. He dumped the load from his back into three separate piles, one for each ship, sat on the largest, and waited. He did not wait long. At precisely 6:00 am, a small boat with seven sailors in blue uniforms and peculiar hats—six oarsmen and one boatswain with an elegantly manicured moustache standing near the bow—arrived below the wharf. Roshan stood, stretched his back, sauntered to the edge of the dock, and peered down on the man with the moustache. The man peered up at Roshan and curved his hands around the moustache to form a small megaphone and yelled:

"Are you Rushing Koozesstough?"

"No, I am Roshan Kuznetsov. I belief you have heard for the wrong man who is not standing in the here."

The boatswain removed a crumpled piece of paper from his pocket, unfolded it, and yelled, "Are you Roshing Kooznetasoov?"

"No, you are still speaking of a person I have no idea."

The boatswain produced a pair of reading glasses, shoved them on his nose, and read the words on the piece of paper again. "Are your Rooshan Kooznetsove?"

This articulation of Roshan's name proved close enough. "Yes, I am Roshan Kuznetsov. Why do you ask?"

The boatswain folded the paper and stuffed it into the same pocket. "I have orders to lighter you to the USS Ossipee."

This delighted Roshan. "You know which ship is the one you just said the name of which I cannot remember?"

"What did you say?"

"You know of the ship?"

The boatswain pointed at a sleek, wood-hulled, three-masted, steam-powered, sloop of war floating serenely in the deeper waters of the bay. "The USS Ossipee is the one in the middle."

Roshan decided further conversation was not necessary. "Do not worry of more answer than you have said. I bring my things down to beach and we can move in small ship to the one with the name I cannot remember even when Prince Dmitri Petrovich Maksutov told me of it in his office just before today and you told me of it again in the morning."

The boatswain sent two men to help Roshan transfer his gear into the boat. To everyone's surprise, they loaded the gear with extraordinary haste. When Roshan had settled into the boat, stinking even more of skinned sea otter and three months of unwashed tromping through the rainforests and waterways of Baranov Island than he had in Maksutov's office because another full day had passed, the boatswain (a seasoned man of great experience) sucked in an enormous breath of Roshan's stink and nearly gagged his breakfast over the gunwale. He ordered the six sailors under his command to shove off immediately and then to row as if their lives depended on it. This created a strong breeze which provided temporary relief. After the boat moored alongside the USS Ossipee, the boatswain and the six sailors escorted Roshan and his gear up the narrow ships ladder with astonishing efficiency.

The boatswain quickly issued an order to two of the oarsmen. "Please escort Mr. Rooshin Koosetoss and his gear below decks and find him quarters with the U.S. Army Band."

When Roshan and his gear and the two oarsmen arrived below decks, the tubaist and the trombonist were playing cards and drinking coffee. The tubaist stiffened and sniffed the air. "Three please. Do you smell something? It smells like the same stink we smelled at the flag ceremony. How is it possible?"

The trombonist dealt three cards from the deck. "Good Lord! It *is* the same stink. I'll never forget that smell as long as I live."

Roshan rushed to the sides of the tubaist and trombonist and slapped his arms around their shoulders, sending a shower of playing cards into the air and spilling cups of coffee across the table. "It is my new friends of America! We see ourselves once again, and I must speak to you I have not forgotten the new English word you told of me at the changing flags to America. The word you are wishing to tell is 'stench.' I have *stench* you do not forget because you live as long as you forget. But I see better news for you than the stink of my stench. Today, I travel with you on the big ship all the way to California, even when I do not know where California have been and I cannot remember the name of ship. We have much time to find many new English words to speak with when my English is the best you can believe."

The trombonist held his nose, then exclaimed to the tubaist, "Oh lucky day."

Chapter Six

Budapest, Hungary
May 1869

Csongor Toth delighted in the serenity of a spring afternoon as he strolled contentedly along the Széchenyi lánchíd* above the sun-sparkled Danube River on his way to the Royal Hungarian University School of Law. He lingered near the center of the span to admire the smooth catenary of the massive iron chains supporting the horizontal structure of the bridge between two massive stone piers and beyond where the chains vanished mysteriously into stone-clad riverbanks. His gaze followed the flat curve of one of the chains until it reached the stone face of the eastern pier, an impressive structure rising with classical elegance more than 150 feet above the surface of the cleanly-flowing water. He studied individual links in the chain (prodigious iron plates more than six feet in length) and the enormous iron rivets connecting the iron links to countless iron verticals attached to the iron roadbed beneath his feet and sustaining it from collapse. He wandered to the very edge of the narrow roadbed to evaluate the foundations of the stone river piers. When he leaned over the ornately-understated iron railing, the bow of a river barge glided into his view. A young woman of no more than twenty assisted a grizzled and sinewy man, likely her father, with various lines looped across the deck

---

* The Széchenyi lánchíd or "Széchenyi Chain Bridge," a stone pier and iron chain suspension bridge named after Count István Széchenyi and completed in 1849, was the first permanent bridge constructed across the Danube River in Budapest.

of the barge. Although Csongor's intensely-logical mind briefly resisted the distraction, his attention shifted fully to her unbuttoned bodice, and while he admired the sweat-glistened curve of the young woman's bosom all thoughts of bridge engineering receded. When the barge had cruised beyond the bridge and he could no longer see the young woman clearly, Csongor backed away from the iron railing and continued his walk in the pleasant warmth of the afternoon sun.

After passing respectfully beneath the imposing pair of stone lions defending the end of the bridge with silent ferocity from atop equally-imposing stone pedestals, he drifted southerly and worked his way through a multitude of pedestrians down to the Belgrád rakpart.[*] He quickened his pace and darted around a mother and father pushing a newborn in a sky-blue baby carriage. When he passed the family he remembered that he had once considered engineering as a profession. His supple mind had always excelled at mathematics, and with fluency in three languages (his own as well as English and German) he had imagined the possibilities of designing engineering masterpieces in all of the great cities of Europe. During this period of youthful infatuation with both the science and art of engineering, Csongor had dreamed of graceful bridges spanning the widest channels of the Thames in London, stunning railway trestles clinging to precipitous snow-dusted cliffs in the lofty peaks of the French Alps, and dazzling towers of the most inconceivably-delicate structures shooting boldly into the skies above Budapest itself. But in the end, when his maturing mind had finally accepted that it craved not the analytical rigor of math and engineering but rather the messy uncertainty of debate and philosophy, he chose the law.

Csongor's eyes shifted right across the Danube and swept up the sharply-rising slopes of the Gellért Hegy[†] to the sprawling stone walls and parapets of the now obsolete Citadella.[‡] He recalled a lesson from a compulsory history class in which a senile professor, hunched over with age and tapping his cane on the polished marble floor behind the podium at the end of each sentence to emphasize the punctuation, droned on

---

[*] Belgrade Embankment.

[†] Hill.

[‡] Citadel.

for an entire hour about the Hapsburg Dynasty and the construction of the Citadella in 1854 to guard the city from the rebellious masses and the transfer of the Citadella to the city after the Compromise of 1867 between Austria and Hungary and the symbolic destruction of portions of the fortified walls in two places and other useless facts he did not care to remember on such a pleasant afternoon.

When the odd reverie of the stooped professor and tapping cane had dimmed, Csongor's eyes snapped from the Citadella to the path directly in front of his rushing feet, but then began jumping around as interesting distractions fell into his field of view. The boundary of his moving shadow, projected off to his left by the low afternoon sun and softened by cirrus clouds floating miles away, vibrated chaotically over the uneven joints of bricks inlaid along the walking surface next to the river. He instinctively swerved a few steps to the left to avoid a woman's umbrella, and the head of his shadow scattered across a line of chairs set near a continuous stone curb hugging a much wider walkway running in front of a long arc of monumental buildings facing the Danube. The head of the shadow leaped from the ground when it collided with an ancient tree growing from the brick walk, and leaped again when it plowed into a cast iron light post, then fluttered across more chairs before crashing into another tree and another light post and more chairs and another tree. Csongor dashed back to the right until the fingers of his outstretched hand slapped the fluted iron stanchions of the iron railing that prevented him from plunging headlong into the swirling waters of the river. He began counting the stanchions—an obsessive habit he had failed to cure himself of—without slowing his pace: one, two, three, four... twenty-seven, twenty-eight... one-hundred-and two, and three, and four... two-hundred... and seventeen, and eighteen, and nineteen... a man lounging in one the chairs shook his fist at something, but this time Csongor did not see it... three-hundred, and one, and two, and... a child screamed after falling and cutting her knee on the sharp corner of the stone curb, but he did not notice her either... and thirty-five, and thirty-six, and thirty... rapid footsteps pounded behind him, growing louder and louder, but he did not hear them... forty-two, and forty-three, and—

A sweaty hand clutched Csongor's shoulder from behind. Csongor whirled around, a fist concealed behind his back. The sweaty hand spoke before Csongor could strike. “Csongor, I’ve been searching for you. You were supposed to meet me at four. When you didn’t show, I guessed I might find you here.”

Csongor relaxed the belligerent fist. “I apologize, my treasured roommate Kelemen. The serenity of the afternoon and the golden warmth of the sun encouraged me to forget our appointment. I trust you will forgive me.”

Kelemen frowned. “Of course I will forgive you, Csongor. Don’t I always forgive you? Have I ever not forgiven you?”

The corners of Csongor’s delicate mouth lifted imperceptibly. “You are right. I cannot think of a single time you have not forgiven me. A remarkable achievement.”

“I could not say if it is remarkable or not, but that is not the point. Would you like a pilsner? The afternoon is very hot, and I would like some refreshment before we talk.”

“A grand idea. I would never refuse a beer purchased by someone else. It always tastes better when I do not have to pay for it.”

The two continued south on the Belgrád rakpart until they arrived at a small restaurant with spotless picture windows, colorful flowers springing from earthen planters, and tables and chairs meticulously arranged on the brick pavement outside in the waning light of the fading day. They sat at one of the small, square, white-table-cloth-covered tables at the side of the street and each ordered a beer from the mustached but slightly-balding waiter. The street noise amplified when people departed places of work and scurried along the rakpart to return home for the night. A young couple emerged from the river of people flowing in front of the restaurant and occupied an adjacent table to enjoy a few glasses of red wine before continuing homeward. When the beers arrived, Kelemen immediately lifted the tall glass to his lips and downed half of the pleasantly-bitter lager.

Csongor sipped twice from his glass then set the drink next to the small candle located precisely in the center of the table. “You must be thirsty. I have never seen you drink this much beer at one time.”

Kelemen fidgeted, and then lifted his glass again. “I do not think it is the thirst. I think it is because I am nervous.” He poured the remaining beer down his throat with a single unbroken motion and slammed the empty glass on the table.

Csongor lifted his glass and sipped again. "Nervous? Nervous about what?"

Kelemen raised his left hand above the table and displayed a splinted little finger. "This is why I am nervous."

Csongor shrugged. "You are nervous of your little finger?"

Kelemen elevated his chin to conceal the utter disgust of his visage. "No, of course I am not nervous about my little finger. I am nervous about the man who broke it two nights ago."

Csongor smirked, more noticeably than before. "Is there much pain?"

This time Kelemen did nothing to conceal his disgust. "Of course there is much pain. It hurts like holy hell. Why do you think I am drinking this beer? I am trying to dull the pain. I will likely drink a few more beers before we leave this table tonight. If I'm lucky I will collapse into a coma and there will be no pain whatsoever."

Csongor's smile faded. "And what is the name of the unruly brute who broke your little finger? And, I might add, to what purpose?"

Kelemen concealed the splinted little finger beneath the white tablecloth and waved with his good hand at the slightly-balding waiter. The waiter hurried to the table. "Another beer please. No, I've changed my mind. Do you have a good supply of pálinka?* I might drink very much tonight." The waiter nodded. "Then bring me a large glass of pálinka. I don't care which one. Csongor… another beer?"

"No thank you. Unlike you, I have no desire to stumble into the Danube and drown before I return to the flat."

Kelemen spoke to the waiter. "Fine. Just the pálinka then, a very large one."

Csongor touched the rim of his glass, but did not drink. "Is it wise to mix beer and pálinka in the same minute? I have never known you to drink this much."

"You would drink too if you faced the dilemma now confronting me."

"Ah, yes. The broken finger. This *is* a dilemma."

Kelemen slapped the damaged hand on his leg and winced from the shot of pain. "Damn it, the finger is not the point. The police officer,

---

* Hungarian fruit brandy, similar to cognac.

Mészáros—the one who patrols evenings near the School of Law—he is the point."

"How is officer Mészáros, who I have met only once, the point?"

The waiter arrived with the large glass of pálinka. Kelemen gulped half of it before proceeding with his explanation. "Really Csongor. You are tedious at times. Officer Mészáros is the one who broke my little finger two nights ago."

The conversation suddenly intrigued Csongor. "And the purpose?"

"Have you not heard of his reputation? To begin with, he despises lawyers. Secondly, he despises students of the law even more. Thirdly, he imagines we students of law are all very wealthy. And fourthly, he has demanded some of us to pay for his personal protection to keep us safe from harm when we travel to and from the school at night."

"How much does he want?"

"100 forints[*] a week."

"This is an amount you can easily afford. Why don't you just pay officer Mészáros and be done with it?"

Kelemen squirmed in his chair then swigged another gulp of pálinka. "Whether or not I can afford the amount is as much the point as is my little finger. I told Mészáros I would not pay him a single krajczár[†] for his so-called protection."

"And what did he say?"

"He did not say anything. He broke my little finger. Then he said something. He told me to deliver 200 forints to him in front of the School of Law tomorrow at midnight or he would break more fingers."

"I thought the cost of his protection was 100 forints?"

"He charged me extra for the trouble of breaking my finger."

Csongor lifted his beer and poured a healthy swig across his tongue. "Sounds fair."

Kelemen's face reddened as he sputtered his reply. "It is not fair at all! Nothing about this is fair. I refuse to pay anything to this so-called

---

[*] A forint was the primary currency in the Austro-Hungarian Empire between 1868 and 1892.

[†] 100 krajczár equals one forint.

policeman who is extorting money from innocent law students. I refuse. I will never pay him."

"How many broken fingers can you afford?"

Kelemen calmed himself before finishing the last of the pálinka. He waved at the waiter: "Waiter, another pálinka—in a larger glass this time," then addressed Csongor. "This is why I am talking to you and buying you beer so you do not have to pay for it yourself."

"You imagine there is some way I can help you with this problem?"

"Of course I imagine you can help me with this problem. You have helped me in the past with other problems. You have a special gift with people. You are the most skilled and ruthless debater in the school. And, more importantly, you are absolutely fearless. I want you to talk to the policemen and convince him to leave me alone."

Csongor reflected before speaking. "It would cheer me greatly to talk to officer Mészáros and convince him to find someone other than you to protect. However, because of the inherent risk I would not accept this assignment without proper compensation."

"You would not?"

"No, I would not."

Kelemen's eyes narrowed. "What manner of compensation are you thinking of."

Csongor stroked his chin. "I was thinking of… 100 forints a week, but only until the end of the semester."

Kelemen slammed his injured hand on the table then groaned at the pain. "Csongor…"

"Yes my beloved roommate?"

"You are an ass."

Csongor simpered uncharacteristically. "Yes, I know. Then it is agreed. To be fair, I will provide said legal services on a contingency basis. If I successfully convince the good officer to relinquish his claim to provide you with protective services, then you will pay me. If I fail to convince him, then you can either pay him or let him break more of your fingers."

"You are still an ass."

"Do not worry about tomorrow night. I will meet officer Mészáros at midnight in front of the School of Law on your behalf. You can stay in the flat and rest your little finger."

The next day, fourteen minutes until midnight. Kelemen sat at his Bösendorfer baby grand piano* (a gift from his mother three years ago on his twenty-first birthday) in the spacious flat he had shared with Csongor for three semesters. The splinted little finger on his left hand throbbed with each beat of his anxious heart. Another glass of pálinka, his fourth of the evening, waited patiently next to the finely-carved wood music rack angled above the polished white and black keys. He thought of playing a few notes, but then remembered the broken finger. He tapped his left thumb on middle C, and plunked down the scale C...B...A...G..., but the splinted finger bounced annoyingly on the white keys, and then wedged painfully between two of the black keys. He swore, reached for the pálinka, and before the glass touched his....

Police officer Mészáros endured the passing minutes beneath the glow of a street lamp on Szerb Utca† near the Royal Hungarian University School of Law. Light rain sprinkled down and glistened the street. Nearly midnight, and his 200 forints had not yet arrived. *Not to worry. Still a few minutes to go. And if the forints do not arrive, I will break another finger. Maybe a thumb or a wrist. Who knows?* He paced beyond the dispersed rim of the light, then pivoted back into the light. He leaned indifferently against the damp lamp post, then bent his knee and rested the heel of his boot on the cast iron base. He yawned. He rubbed the back of his neck. Footsteps. He stood erectly and peered into the shadows beyond the rim of light. Splashing. Louder. Footsteps. Louder. Csongor Toth, his overcoat buttoned to his neck, stepped into the light.

Surprised, Mészáros snorted, "Who the hell are you?"

Csongor introduced himself with an elegant bow. "I, my good sir, am Csongor Toth."

"Where is the spineless law student Kelemen? He is the one I want. He owes me money. A lot of money." The rain intensified.

---

* Manufactured in Vienna in 1860.

† Serbian Street.

Csongor advanced closer to Mészáros to assess his build and height. "Kelemen will not be coming to see you tonight. He has sent me to meet with you on his behalf."

Mészáros yawned without covering his mouth. "On his behalf? Then I assume he sent you to pay his debt."

Csongor shrugged. "In a manner."

Mészáros expanded his chest aggressively. "In a manner? What the hell do you mean?"

Csongor did not back away. "I am here to make an offer."

"An offer? I'm not interested in any offer. Just pay me the 200 forints or I will break more of his fingers. Maybe I will break his thumb or his wrist. I have not decided yet."

Csongor leaned forward to purposefully collapse the space separating him from Mészáros. "I offer you a single lump sum payment of 2,000 forints, but only on the stipulation that you never bother Kelemen again."

Mészáros's eyes widened. "2,000 forints?"

Csongor winked nonchalantly. "Yes, 2,000 forints, but only on the stipulation. . . ."

Kelemen drained the last swallow of pálinka and set the empty glass on the piano bench. He considered refilling the glass, but decided the pain in his little finger had dulled sufficiently to diminish the need. He also felt a bit lightheaded, and leaving the stability of the piano bench could offer the risk of falling and hurting his other hand—or possibly breaking his neck. The delicate gears in a French bell-strike clock centered on the stone mantel above the hearth whirred and the bell rang twelve times. Kelemen pulled a watch from his pocket and flipped open the engraved cover. Four minutes after midnight. He noted to himself that he should adjust the mantel clock forward by four minutes. He decided to practice major scales with his right hand, beginning with C major. He placed his thumb on middle C and raced smoothly up the white keys to the highest C of the instrument and then back down again. He moved his thumb up one half-step to C-sharp, and raced up and down again, playing mostly black keys. He glanced across the room to a large window, and observed the rain for the first time. He moved his thumb up another half-step to D, and executed the thumb under at G cleanly and then added C-sharp as the hand travelled up and down the keyboard again. He set his index finger on E-flat to play the. . . .

Officer Mészáros suggested a compromise. "Maybe I should offer you my protection too. Then I can collect 200 forints every week and I will have 2,000 in only ten weeks."

Csongor's sober expression hardened. "I would advise against adding me under the wing of your dubious protection. I strongly recommend acceptance of my offer. I truly believe this is in your best interests."

"Another law student lecturing me on my best interests. I have dealt with the likes of you before. Maybe I should break your finger too, and then you will understand." Mészáros chuckled.

"I can see you are a determined negotiator. I am willing to increase the amount to 3,000 forints, but this is my last offer."

"That is a lot of money, and begins to interest me." He stroked his chin. "Here is my offer to you. I will accept the 3,000 forints, but will expect the law student Kelemen and you to begin paying me 100 forints each week beginning the first day of September. You will have my protection for the entire summer, and then you will begin the weekly payments for continued service."

Csongor listened attentively. "We will not be here during the summer."

Mészáros snorted, "It is not my problem."

Csongor reflected briefly. "I will accept your offer." He reached inside his raincoat and produced an envelope. "The money is in this...."

Playing major scales with one hand did not relax Kelemen as much as he had expected, but he decided to forge ahead to the last scale anyway: then he could tell Csongor he had accomplished something useful this night other than drinking too much. He placed his index finger on A-flat to play an A-flat major scale. Only four flats. Not too hard. When he had finished, he moved his thumb up one half-step to A to play A major, the final scale that would reach the highest note on his piano.* His hand accelerated up the keyboard, and when he reached the last A at the last white key at the very end of the keyboard, a note he rarely played, and his little finger deftly pressed the key—Kelemen recoiled. *What a thin, inadequate sound!* He pressed the white key again, and again the same. He tapped it repeatedly to loosen the action and still could not produce the fullness of sound he expected. This is odd, he thought to himself. He shoved the piano bench back and stood.

* Kelemen's Bösendorfer baby grand piano has seven octaves beginning and ending with the note A. The highest note on a modern 88-key piano is the note C.

He raised the lid to its highest position and set the prop. He eyes bounced along the strings, and when they reached the highest note, he discovered that one of the three strings was missing. *What is this?* He tried to remember if he had ever played the highest key before and decided he had. Who would have taken a string from his Bösendorfer baby grand piano? And why? He slumped down on the piano bench and....

After finding a good spot directly under the light, Mészáros shoved his finger under the envelope's sealed flap and ripped it open. He pulled a tight stack of forints through the jagged tear, licked his thumb, and began counting. It did not take him long to count the large denominations. He began stuffing the money back into the envelope. "I must say I'm surprised. Like you promised, there are 3,000 forints here. But how did you know we would agree to this exact—"

Holding two wooden dowels connected with a thin wire, Csongor Toth advanced swiftly until he stood directly behind Officer Mészáros. Csongor looped the deadly ligature over the officer's head and pulled it taut against his throat. Mészáros clutched the 3,000 forints in his hand until his shuddering grip relaxed and the money fluttered erratically across his jerking leg into a shallow puddle of dark rain spreading away from the toes of his meticulously polished boots.

Kelemen, still wearing pants and socks from the night before, sat at the side of his bed and rubbed his throbbing head with his throbbing left hand. He stood and stretched. When he bent backwards and arched his spine he noted a touch of unpleasant nausea at the back of his tongue. The rain had stopped and sunlight glowed on the window sill beneath the blinds. He thought of making a cup of tea, and waddled unevenly across the bedroom to the door that led to the main living area of the flat. He opened the door and the brightness of the room throbbed inside his head. It took him a moment to notice Csongor Toth relaxing on the settee.

"Csongor. Why are you up so early? I didn't hear you come in last night."

Admittedly a little tired, Csongor politely covered his mouth and yawned. "It is after lunch, my lazy roommate. I thought you had died with your pants on."

"After lunch? No wonder I feel terrible. I think I shall make some tea. Would you like a cup?"

"Delighted."

Kelemen massaged his jowls. "But before I make tea, I have to share something quite odd with you."

"You assume I want you to share something odd?"

"Last night, just after midnight actually, when I was practicing major scales with only my right hand because the splint on my left hand kept sticking between the black keys, I noticed for the first time something wrong with the high A."

Csongor feigned surprise. "Something wrong with the high what?"

"The high A."

"And what was wrong with the high A?"

"It took some work to figure out, but I finally opened the lid and discovered one of the strings is missing."

"Missing?"

"Yes, completely gone."

Csongor shrugged indifferently. "You are sure it did not just break?"

"No. I would have seen part of the wire. Here, let me show you what it sounds like." Kelemen walked to the piano and tapped the key. The note sounded perfectly. He struck it again, and again the note rang out full and true. "This is not possible."

"Maybe you are playing the wrong note. And you should have the piano tuned. The A sounds a touch flat to my ear." Csongor yawned again.

This angered Kelemen. "I am not playing the wrong note. I swear to you the note did not sound properly last night."

"I noticed the empty bottle when I arrived this morning. Maybe you were too drunk and just imagined the problem."

This possibility concerned Kelemen. "I could not have been so drunk to have misheard the note and to have seen a missing string when it was not missing."

Csongor sniffed. "Not that anything you just said makes any sense, but all manner of things are possible when you drink too much. But enough of this: I have something more important than an unruly note on the piano to discuss with you."

"Something more important?" Kelemen shook his head then winced at the throbbing and sat down on the piano bench.

Csongor stood and kicked a small suitcase with his foot. "I have decided to take a holiday. I leave on the train in less than two hours."

Kelemen swung around on the bench and slouched. "A holiday? But the semester ends in a few weeks. Can't you wait till then?"

Csongor lifted the suitcase. "It does not matter to me. I tire of classroom law and stuffy professors who put us to sleep and should have died years ago."

"Where will you go? When will you return?"

"I do not yet have the answers to those questions, but maybe I will go anywhere I please, and maybe I will never return."

"Will you write to me?"

"Likely not. But I do have one last bit of business with you."

"Business?"

"Yes." Csongor plucked a sealed envelope from his pocket and presented it to Kelemen. "Listen carefully my treasured roommate. You are to keep this envelope in a safe place, a place only you can find. Never open the envelope. When three years have passed, burn the envelope and its contents then scatter the ashes."

"Never open it?"

"Yes, but there is one, and only one, exception."

Kelemen grew more worried with each spoken word. "And what is this one exception?"

Without sentiment, Csongor responded smoothly, "If the police come to arrest you because of your involvement with the policeman Mészáros, then you may give them the envelope."

"Csongor, I do not understand what you are talking about."

Csongor lifted the suitcase with ease and carried it to the front door of the flat. He hesitated when his hand felt the chill of the cylindrical knob. "It is good you do not understand. Adieu my comrade. I wish you a successful career in the law." And with a casual flick of his hand to signify a wave, he opened the door and walked out.

Chapter Seven

Salt Lake City, Utah Territory
May 1871

Priscilla Kimball—brown pigtails bouncing in the Saturday morning sun, white cotton dress swirling wrinkled across graceful legs, slender arms swinging in exuberant tempo—skipped urgently along the dusty edge of East Temple Street. Now three months beyond the milestone of her fourteenth birthday and full of youthful vigor, she weaved skillfully between muscled working men unloading wood-staved-iron-ringed barrels from an ox-drawn wagon and danced by the eleven neatly-dressed children of a strolling family. At one point she pranced athletically around a gnarled hitching post to avoid a group of quarrelling men and then sprinted behind a row of three sturdy farm horses. As she passed the last horse and angled back toward one of the brick buildings lining the street, she ran her delicate fingers along the animal's flank and felt the coolness of fresh sweat. Without breaking the pace of her cadenced skipping, she sniffed the pungent sweat before wiping her hand in the billowing folds of the white dress. The horse, reacting to the unexpected caress, shook its head and whinnied. Priscilla glanced back at the calling sound before losing sight of her path and blundering headlong into the arms of James Kimball, her older sibling by five years.

James caught Priscilla in his sinewy arms, hardened by years of obedient work and bronzed by the sun to the boundary of his rolled-up sleeves. "Priscilla. Where are you off to? You were supposed to meet father and mother at the general store an hour ago. Now I find you here in the street skipping along as if nothing mattered in the world."

Priscilla loved James above all her brothers and sisters, but also knew of his relentless loyalty to mother and father. She had not forgotten the appointment. She had merely chosen to ignore it for a while. "I was on my way to the store now. This is why I was skipping. I did not want to be tardy beyond what father and mother could tolerate."

James released his grip. He loved Priscilla above all his brothers and sisters, but also knew of her cleverness with words. "Then I suppose, since you are on the way to the store right now, it would not matter if I accompanied you to your intended destination."

Priscilla smiled mischievously, a smile James had witnessed many times before. "You may accompany me, my brother, but I fear your presence at my side may slow me down. I was moving quite fast before you stopped me, and now I am not moving at all."

James removed his wide-brimmed hat and shook a spray of sweat across the ground. "I do not believe speed is the issue at this point. I think your safe arrival at the general store is the reason I should walk with you. I would not want a horse to distract you again and make you even later."

Priscilla grasped James's left hand and tugged. "Then let us get moving my beloved brother. I do not want you to make me any later than I already am."

James placed the wide-brimmed hat on his head and stepped off briskly to keep pace. "There are times, my little sister, when you are a lot of trouble. It makes me wonder why I care for you so much."

Priscilla immediately shot back, "No more trouble than you yourself, big brother."

Priscilla and James resumed the serpentine path through erratic crowds of people congregated beneath canvas awnings and haphazard piles of loose farm implements and materials and cascading boxes of freshly picked apples and rolling wagons and more sweat-glistened farm horses and another family with children and a second throng of bickering finger-pointing farmers and an unpleasant mongrel of a dog tied up to one of the hitching posts and nipping at anyone who got close enough to nip at until they arrived at the key-stoned brick entry and display window arches of the two-story general store. They stopped before entering to gaze up at the wrought iron letters pegged into the joints of the brick fascia above the entry:

KIMBALL AND SMITH EMPORIUM
& GENERAL STORE
ESTABLISHED SALT LAKE CITY 1862

James squeezed Priscilla's little hand. "It should not take that long to read the name of the store, little sister, especially when you have read it many times before. You must go in and speak with father and mother. You can delay no longer."

Priscilla released her brother's hand. "Thank you, big brother. Will you accompany me into the store? I would appreciate your company."

James balked at the idea. "I would like to, little sister, but I must return to work before both of us are in trouble. I only came here to find you and deliver you to father and mother at the general store. I must return to my job and leave you alone to your task."

Priscilla felt her resolve flag a bit. "I ... I understand James ..." then tried to conceal it, "... then on your way, and thank you for delivering me safely to my destination. I may never have arrived without your help."

James nodded once and shoved both hands into pants pockets. "I'm sorry—"

Priscilla held up a little hand with the palm facing her brother's lips in the manner she had learned by observing her mother. "No need to say anything more. Just go. I do understand."

James turned slowly and walked away. Priscilla watched his sweat-stained back vanish around a corner before climbing up the stone steps to the wide landing and opening the massive doorway at the main entry and skipping blithely into the Kimball & Smith Emporium and General Store.

A man of gentle temperament and enormous patience, Thaddeus Haglund waited. A man of straightforward integrity, Thaddeus Haglund did not judge the reason for waiting. A man of great personal wealth obtained through vision and honest hard work, Thaddeus Haglund now possessed the financial resources to achieve the purpose of waiting. A man of profound religious beliefs and now only a few months from the age of thirty, Thaddeus Haglund had decided to take a second wife.

Priscilla's mother twisted her hands together as if scrubbing with unseen soap and paced behind the wood chair now occupied by respected Salt Lake City banker and entrepreneur Thaddeus Haglund. "I really do not understand what has delayed my daughter, Mr. Haglund. I am certain she knew of the location and time of our meeting. I reminded her this morning during breakfast."

Thaddeus Haglund rested his plumpish hands on the top of a simple wood cane with a tastefully decorated brass handle. "Do not worry, Mrs. Kimball. Your daughter is young and cannot be expected to demonstrate the maturity of an experienced woman such as yourself. I shall simply wait until she arrives. I know she will arrive before too long."

Priscilla's father maintained a stoic expression and offered no discernible indication of the agitation twisting his stomach. "Nonetheless, Mr. Haglund, it is not right for her to be late. I expected better of her. I shall certainly have words with her later."

Thaddeus Haglund hunched over his walking cane and peered intently at the main entry door to the emporium and general store. His countenance brightened when the door swung open, but quickly dimmed when a bearded wrangler stumbled in. "I do not think that will be necessary, Mr. Kimball. It would not be my desire to intentionally create any ill will between me and your daughter over such a tiny lapse of responsibility. In my opinion, we should ignore the clock, wait patiently, and strive to conduct a pleasant meeting when she does arrive. I do not imagine we shall wait much longer."

One of the local wives approached Priscilla's mother with a nearly empty bolt of sky blue fabric with tiny white dots. "Good morning Mrs. Kimball. How much for this fabric?"

Mrs. Kimball, still washing her hands with imaginary soap and water, glanced at the fabric. "That is a remnant, Mrs. Smith. As such, I would be willing to sell it to you for—"

The entry door swung open again, and Priscilla skipped into the general store. The bearded wrangler, who had not managed to get beyond a row of boots displayed just to the right of the entry, closed the door behind her. She did not stop skipping until she arrived at a spot approximately one skip in front of Thaddeus Haglund's wood and brass cane. She waited for her father to begin the conversation, but when he remained silent she said, "Sorry I'm late, but I lost track of the time when I stopped to admire a horse. I do love horses."

Thaddeus leaned back in his chair and smiled. "Perfectly understandable, my dear. However, I do not believe admiration of horses is a proper avocation for my future wife."

Priscilla clasped her dainty hands behind her back and pressed her toes together. "And who might that be?"

Priscilla's father finally joined the conversation. "Priscilla, this is Mr. Thaddeus Haglund. You have met him at church several times during the last few months. Your mother and I have been talking to Mr. Haglund at great length concerning your future, and we are pleased to say he has graciously agreed to take you as his wife."

Priscilla frowned. "But Mr. Haglund already has a wife, and she has a wart on her cheek."

Priscilla's mother took her turn. "Yes, we know dear. Mr. Haglund has decided it is time for him to take a second wife. Father and I could not be more pleased that he has chosen you for this sacred duty. Mr. Haglund is highly respected in the community, a businessman of great means, and a pillar of the church. He will offer you the blessing of a good life."

Priscilla protested, "But I hardly know Mr. Haglund."

Priscilla's father replied, "You will know Mr. Haglund through holy marriage, Priscilla. This is a wonderful opportunity for you and all of our family. But there is no reason to belabor a decision already made. We have scheduled the wedding for one month from today, and there is much to do in preparation."

Thaddeus Haglund stood, and for the first time Priscilla observed that he was not a man of much physical prowess. "Yes, one month from now suits me fine, Mr. and Mrs. Kimball. It will allow sufficient time to prepare my household for Priscilla's arrival. After, of course, our trip to the state of New York, which I promise will be memorable."

Priscilla's mother exclaimed joyfully, "And it will allow me sufficient time to sew a wedding dress for Priscilla. I will select the fabric today and begin the work tonight."

Priscilla nearly asked a foolish question about New York, but held her tongue because the question served no purpose other than to create needless turmoil in the family.

A glorious morning of blue skies and gentle breezes had graced the marriage of Priscilla Kimball to Thaddeus Haglund. The groom had presented himself surprisingly dapper in a tailored pinstripe suit accentuating an illusion of broader shoulders and slenderer waist. The bride wore a wedding gown of purest white (her mother had fussed over it every night during the preceding month). Several of the attendees commented that the gown's understated elegance gave Priscilla the appearance of a woman nearing the age of twenty. Because of Thaddeus Haglund's standing as an important businessman in Salt Lake City, many of the community's leading families attended the ceremony. And now that the nuptials had successfully concluded and the couple had become forevermore Mr. and Mrs. Thaddeus Haglund, many of the same families attended the outdoor reception to celebrate the blessed day.

The couple stood side-by-side, near a table covered in white table cloths and piled with food and drink and flowers, to greet the long queue of well-wishers. A string quartet performed Mozart somewhere by a thicket of sycamore trees, the lilting string notes mixing pleasantly with the sound of quavering leaves. After shaking hundreds of hands and hugging dozens of friends, a small break in the line allowed the opportunity for Thaddeus to utter the first informal words to his new bride. "I trust you have enjoyed the day, Priscilla?"

Priscilla rubbed her nose on the gown's embroidered sleeve. "I believe I have, Mr. Haglund, but I really have no previous experience to compare it to."

Thaddeus reached over and squeezed her little hand. "Quite understandable, my dear. You do not have the advantage of a previous marriage like I do. Completely understandable." He released Priscilla's hand to shake another and then hugged a distant relative who had recently borrowed money from the bank. "I have been thinking about our conversation at the general store, particularly what I said to you about horses."

Priscilla adjusted her veil and hugged Thaddeus's distant relative. She did not remember the discussion of horses at the general store. "Did we talk about horses? I do not remember."

"Yes we did, and I now regret what I said to you."

Priscilla still could not remember any talk of horses. "And what did you say to me that you now regret, Mr. Haglund?"

"I told you I did not think the admiration of horses was proper for my future wife. Do you remember now?"

Sunlight flashed across Priscilla's face and she squinted. "I apologize, Mr. Haglund, but I still do not remember the conversation of horses." A local rancher wearing recently washed clothes smelling only slightly of manure, and who almost never travelled to town unless absolutely necessary to purchase supplies, stopped in front of Priscilla and stretched out his arms to offer a heartfelt embrace. Priscilla bent slightly to accept the hug.

Thaddeus bowed to shake the next hand. "Well, I have thought much about my remarks, and now that we are married I have experienced a change of heart in regard to your love of horses."

"And what change of heart are you speaking of, Mr. Haglund?"

"I have decided to honor you with a special wedding gift, something I believe you will like very much. I would like to show it to you when this seemingly endless line of people has ended, and I see, with the exception of a few latecomers, the end is finally near."

Priscilla held a petite bouquet of flowers bound with a white ribbon up to her nose and sniffed the subtle fragrance. The pungent smell of impending rain tainted the nectar's perfume. She noted the grayish cumulus clouds gathering from the southwest. "I have bought you no gift, Mr. Haglund. Was I supposed to?"

"No, no, my dear. Do not worry about it. My gift is merely a demonstration of the deep love I hope to nurture with you in the coming years, and a sign of repentance for my thoughtless words when we met at the emporium."

The end of the line finally arrived in the person of forty-seven-year-old Wilhelmina Scott, a local seamstress who had, scandalously, never married. She spoke to Thaddeus before addressing Priscilla. "Congratulations, Mr. Haglund. I wish you well in the coming years. And you, my little princess, are a lovely bride. I wish you prosperity and happiness in your new life. And please do not hesitate to come by the store if you should need any sewing, or even if you just wish to share a cup of tea."

Priscilla nodded and responded politely, if a little impatiently, "Thank you Miss Scott. I may certainly take you up on the offer of a cup of tea." And then spoke quickly to Thaddeus. "May we go see the gift now? The line is finished."

Thaddeus chuckled. "Certainly, my 'little princess.' I think it's a wonderful idea to take a small break from the scores of people who have attended the reception to wish us well." He clasped her tiny hand. "This way to see the gift. It is only a few minutes' walk from here." A muffled rumble of thunder echoed off the mountains to the east, and the morning breeze freshened as he led her around the lavish reception table and past the string quartet near the rustling sycamore trees.

Priscilla squeezed Thaddeus's hand. "Why didn't you just bring the gift to the reception? You could have given it to me there."

Thaddeus chuckled again. "You will see."

Thaddeus and Priscilla crossed a broad sun-scorched lawn and then a patch of raw earth speckled with chuckholes until they arrived at the rear of a heavy-timbered-red-painted barn where one of the local blacksmiths worked. Thaddeus quickened his pace and pulled Priscilla around the corner to a small corral built against the side of the barn. A beautiful chestnut-colored horse raised its distinctive head and whinnied. Thaddeus lifted Priscilla up until she stood on the lower fence rail to allow her to see the horse clearly. "This is my wedding gift to you, Priscilla. It is an Arabian horse purchased from a respected stable in New York and shipped by train to Salt Lake City just this week. This is an intelligent animal of even temperament, and it possesses both great speed and endurance. The Arabian horse was originally bred by the nomadic peoples of Arabia for the desert; he should feel quite at home here in Salt Lake City." Thaddeus waited for a response, but Priscilla did not say a word. He tried to prompt a response. "I hope you like it."

Priscilla tilted her head enough to reveal the rivulet of a fresh tear on her tender cheek. "What's its name?"

Thaddeus pressed his shoulder against one of the corral posts. "It has no name that I am aware of. The naming of this magnificent animal is up to you, my dear."

Priscilla scrunched her face in thought. She had actually considered several horse names in the past, but had never imagined she would actually possess her own horse. "I will name him Ezekiel, after the prophet of the Old Testament."

This surprised Thaddeus. "An awfully serious name. Do you not wish to name him something of a lighter attribute?"

Priscilla persisted. "No. Ezekiel fits him, and this shall be his name. Can I ride him?"

This also surprised Thaddeus. "But Priscilla, you are wearing a wedding dress. I don't think now is the time."

"Then I would like to at least sit on Ezekiel before we return to the reception. Do you have a saddle and halter?"

Thaddeus could see that his new bride had no intention of relenting. "Yes, I have a saddle. I will talk to the blacksmith, and he will prepare… Ezekiel…to allow you to sit on him." Thaddeus disappeared into the barn. He returned a few minutes later with the blacksmith who carried an English riding saddle and matching bridle. The blacksmith brushed Ezekiel's back then saddled and bridled the animal. When he had finished the task, he nodded to Thaddeus and sauntered back to the barn. Thaddeus opened the narrow corral gate and gestured with an open hand. "Your mount awaits, my lady."

Priscilla skipped into the corral, the hem of the white dress catching on the bottom of the splintered gate post, and hopped to Ezekiel's side. "Help me up, please."

"Do you want me to hold your flowers?"

"No. I want to keep the flowers. They smell nice."

Thaddeus grasped Priscilla around her youthful waist and lifted her up until her foot reached the metal stirrup. She flung her leg over the black saddle and the folds of the wedding dress cascaded across Ezekiel's muscular shoulders and rump. Priscilla raised the flowers to her nose and sniffed. Thaddeus waited briefly before speaking. "Are you ready to dismount? It looks like a storm might be coming in. I'm sure Ezekiel would like to retire to the shelter of the barn."

Priscilla lowered the flowers. "I would like to sit a little longer. You may return to the reception if you are worried about rain. I will join you in a few moments."

"But... I'm not sure it is a good idea to leave you here sitting on... Ezekiel."

"Just awhile longer. Do not worry, Mr. Haglund. I will join you shortly."

Thaddeus lifted the reins up to Priscilla's eager hand. "I suppose it wouldn't hurt for you to enjoy your gift a few minutes more. Do you like it?"

"Yes, I love your gift. I will never forget this special day."

"Alright my dear. I shall meet you at the reception shortly. I just felt a sprinkle of rain on my hand. The ladies may require some assistance moving the food indoors. You won't be long then?"

"No, Mr. Haglund. I won't be long." Priscilla smiled broadly.

"Good. I shall see you in a few minutes. Be careful not to soil your wedding dress. Your mother worked very hard sewing it for your special day."

"I won't."

Reluctantly, Thaddeus Haglund walked out of the corral, leaving his young bride sitting atop the Arabian horse recently named Ezekiel. He did not care for the name. He had expected something different, but there was no way to reverse the decision now.

Priscilla watched Thaddeus stroll around the corner of the barn. The distant sky flashed with jagged lightning above the sycamore trees and light rain moistened the sleeves of her wedding dress. She waited five minutes before coaxing Ezekiel over to the gate. She lifted the loop of rope that secured it and rode out of the corral. When she had reached the street in front of the barn, she pulled Ezekiel left and nudged him into a trotting gait. At the boundary of Salt Lake City, with the thunderstorm spreading quickly across the town and her little hand still clutching the flowers, she kicked Ezekiel into a full gallop and headed north.

Chapter Eight

East China Sea
October 1867

Approaching the smooth arc of the Ryukyu Islands south of Japan and the eastern extent of the East China Sea, the Pacific Mail Steamship Company steamer "China" plowed easterly through the heavy seas and patchy rains of autumn. A side-wheeler capable of achieving 10-knots in favorable seas, the ship lumbered along at less than eight as the steeply-angled bow shuddered through swarming waves. Driven on by hissing gusts of scalding steam, the massive side wheels advanced defiantly and the paddle blades slapped the surging foam in a tediously incessant rhythm. The ship dove into a rogue wave higher than the bow and rolled aggressively to port.* Icy-green water stormed over the plunging gunwale† and washed along the decks before spitting out of scuppers to return to the sea. The steamer then rolled wildly to starboard‡ before finally righting itself in time for the onslaught of the next phalanx of angry waves.

Outfitted in rain-slicked-yellow sou'wester coat and wide-brimmed sou'wester hat, a beleaguered first mate (and former harpooner from Nantucket) named Obadiah Hancock held fast to the taught rigging near

---

* Left-hand side of the ship.

† The upper edge of the side of a ship or boat. Pronounced "gunnel" with the accent on the first syllable. If you pronounce it as spelled, people will immediately know you are a landlubber.

‡ Right-hand side of the ship.

the base of the main-mast aft[*] of the black-smoke-belching stack. When he had regained his bearings, he trudged forward along the pitching deck toward a lone man clinging tenaciously to the port-side railing just beyond the forward life boats and paddle wheels amidships.[†] An unexpected gust stung his face with briny spray and tossed him against the freshly-painted wood hull of one of the life boats, almost taking his breath away. The timber yards[‡] groaned ominously above as they twisted against the swirling wind. He clung to the lifeboat's bow davit[§] with both hands and waited for a period of calm; when the ship had swung to near vertical and remained steady for a few seconds he jogged fearlessly along the slippery wood deck until he arrived at the side of the man who now leaned precariously over the railing, dry heaving into the churning darkness below. As his calloused hands slid across the top rail and felt the roughness of it, he noted that the time had arrived for a vigorous scraping and a fresh coat of paint. He would mention this to the captain under more auspicious circumstances.

Grasping the railing vigorously with one hand, Obadiah Hancock cupped his free hand to the side of a close-cropped beard and yelled at the man attempting to vomit into the East China Sea. "Ahoy there! The captain says no one allowed on deck during the storm. Ye have to go below at once."

The seasick man, his head covered in a makeshift canvas hood, pushed himself upright and swiveled enough to glimpse Obadiah at the periphery of his wind-blurred vision. "If I return below, I will surely heave my guts out for all to see after smelling the stench of seasickness again. I would rather die in this storm than go below for another foul breath."

This presented a serious dilemma to Obadiah. The steamer powered laterally into another big wave and began to roll to starboard. "Hang on. We're going to roll again." They both clung desperately to the top rail when

---

[*] Toward the stern or rear of the ship.

[†] Midway between the bow and the stern.

[‡] A yard is a spar on a mast from which sails are set. The yardarms are the outermost tips of the yards. The PMSSC China had three masts, two of them square-rigged, to supplement the primary steam power.

[§] A davit is a small crane that projects over the side of ship and is used to launch life boats.

the deck slanted away beneath their feet. After the deck had stabilized to a tenuously horizontal alignment again, Obadiah repeated his plea. "But you must return below. If you do not, the captain will surely send more men, and they will force you below whether you like it or not."

The man tasted another squirt of bile at the back of his tongue and dry heaved again. When he had finished, he defied Obadiah's threat. "If I see more men coming to force me below, I will jump over this railing and take my chances in the sea."

Obadiah offered a compromise. "Then come below with me to my cabin, and I will give ye some molasses and ginger to settle the stomach. You can rest there until your stomach has improved and then return to the steerage* deck where the captain wants you."

A fresh swirl of wind obscured the lone man's hearing. He dry heaved again before asking, "You will give me mole glasses and finger?"

Obadiah spotted another monstrous wave swelling toward the steamer's bow. "No. I will give you molasses and ginger. Ginger!"

The lone man released his grip on the railing, and the bow of the steamer began its vertical ascent up the face of the wave. "Then I will go with you."

As he watched the new wave rise above the bow, Obadiah grabbed a handful of rain-soaked fabric above the lone man's shoulder and yanked him away from the railing. "We must make haste." He pulled the lone man across the rising deck to a central hatch just forward of the smoke stack. Obadiah lifted the hatch with practiced skill and shoved the lone man awkwardly into the opening. The wave crashed over the bow and spilled across the deck just as Obadiah slammed the hatch shut. The two men rested on the steps below the fragile protection of the hatch and listened to the raging squall above.

Obadiah slapped his sou'wester hat on his knee and seawater sprayed against the wall. "It's not safe for any man to be out in this storm. What's your name, friend?"

The lone man folded the makeshift canvas hood neatly on his lap. His black hair and long ponytail glistened in the dim light below the hatch. "My name is Tseng Longwei."

---

* The section of a passenger ship providing the cheapest accommodations.

After seeing the man's almond eyes and olive skin, Obadiah blurted with impulsive astonishment, "You're a Chinaman. I did not guess your origin from the way you speak English."

Tseng Longwei answered slowly and indifferently, "I learned to speak English from Christian missionaries at a very young age. I believe they were from America, but I do not remember if this is true."

Obadiah Hancock swore amusingly. "Well I'll be damned. A Chinaman who speaks English like an American from Massachusetts." Obadiah unbuttoned his coat. "We'll catch our death sitting here in these wet clothes. Follow me to my cabin and I'll give you the molasses and ginger I promised. And when we have settled, you can tell me about China. This was my first trip to that strange land, and I did not make it into Shanghai more than a hundred yards beyond the end of the dock." Obadiah pushed himself up and descended the steps.

Tseng Longwei stood, a little unsteadily as the ship slid along the face of another wave, and the nausea swelled in his stomach. He followed Obadiah Hancock to the bottom of the steps where they turned right and then left down a narrow passageway dimly illuminated at lengthy intervals by flickering brass oil lanterns. The lanterns swayed on elegantly-curved brass wall brackets in sympathy with the rolling steamer. The motion of the lanterns and the flickering light of the kerosene wicks did not diminish the misery of Longwei's unsettled stomach. Obadiah pulled a large brass key ring from somewhere inside his jacket when they arrived at his cabin and shoved a key into the door lock and twisted it with a heavy click to open the door. When they had squeezed into the cabin, comfortable for one but cramped for two, Obadiah lighted a small gimbaled oil lamp and invited Longwei to sit and rest on the only chair. He dove to his hands and knees and fished around beneath the bunk for the molasses and ginger. He pulled a modest leather-bound trunk from beneath the bunk, opened the lid, reached in with both hands, and then displayed two glass jars—one with blackstrap molasses and one with ground ginger powder. He set the jars on a small side table at the end of the bunk before retrieving a tarnished metal cup and spoon from the only shelf in the cabin.

Obadiah spoke into the cup while he prepared the allegedly therapeutic concoction. "This will fix ye right up. It is not often I've been sick, but the few times I've felt it coming on the molasses and ginger has fixed me right up." After swirling the mixture around vigorously, Obadiah handed the cup to Tseng Longwei.

Longwei examined the black liquid suspiciously. He held the cup up to his nose to sniff the sweetness of the molasses and ginger and then set the cup on his knee. "I fear this remedy will make me sicker, if this is even possible."

Obadiah sat on the bunk and slapped his knee. "Just drink it down. I promise ye will feel better within minutes. And if not, what's the harm?"

Longwei raised the cup again. "I will try your medicine, but do not blame me if it ends up on the floor of your cabin." He pushed the rim of the cup against his lips, tilted his head back, and swallowed the molasses and ginger down in three quick gulps. "I do not feel better."

Obadiah frowned. "You must wait a bit. Ye cannot expect it to work before it arrives in your stomach." The steamer lurched to starboard. "Another big wave, but I believe the storm is settling down."

Longwei handed the cup to Obadiah. "It does not feel like the storm is settling down. It feels just the same, if not worst."

Obadiah laughed. "It is because ye are seasick, my friend. And, I would guess, because you have never been to sea before. But we should try to pass the time more pleasantly while the medicine does its work. Tell me about Shanghai. Tell me about China. Where did you live? What things have you seen?"

Longwei covered his mouth and burped. "There is very little to tell. I have lived and worked in Shanghai for three years. Before then I lived in many places and saw many things." Rising up another swell, the steamer's massive wood keel issued a sustained, rattling creak, then creaked even more violently when the ship crested and surfed down the other side into a long, dark depression between waves.

Obadiah pressed for more information. "What work did ye do in Shanghai?"

Longwei slumped back in the chair and contemplated his last occupation. "I pulled a rickshaw along the waterfront in Shanghai. Many foreigners live in Shanghai now. British. French. Germans. Danish. Even Americans like yourself. I pulled all of them in my rickshaw."

Obadiah scanned Longwei's face for evidence of improvement in the wavering light of the gimbaled oil lamp, now tilting to starboard. "Are ye feeling any better yet? I think the molasses and ginger should begin working any time now."

Longwei took in a deep breath and exhaled slowly. "I am not sure. I think I feel maybe a little better, but when the room moves I feel sick again."

"At least ye have not puked in my cabin. There is some improvement."

"Yes, what you say is true."

"Then tell me more about Shanghai. What is the reason many foreigners live there?"

Longwei wiped sweat from the back of his neck and sighed. "I cannot honestly say why they were there. The Americans and English lived in different settlements on the Huangpu River. I worked there often because there were many people who wanted to ride in my rickshaw. There were also men from other places. France. Germany. Denmark and Australia. One afternoon I gave a ride to an English and an American at the same time. I did not speak to them, so they did not know I could understand their words. They complained about the weather because it had rained. They talked of the cost of silk and cotton and fertilizer. The American asked a question about opium and the English gave a strange answer which I did not understand. They spoke of the many hardships of living far from home in such a strange land where almost no one spoke English. They insulted the Chinese Emperor two times, which I did not object to. The American paid me twice as much as the English when we arrived at the end of the ride. They both wore strange hats and shiny shoes. This is all I remember."

Obadiah drummed his fingers on his knee, then offered a mundane question. "Does it rain often in Shanghai?"

Longwei chuckled. "Does it rain in Shanghai? Yes, it rains very much, maybe one-hundred days a year. There are sometimes typhoons in the summer, but spring and autumn are often pleasant…unless it rains. The thermometer is often very hot in July and August."

Obadiah remembered the comment about opium. "Is there much opium in Shanghai?"

Longwei lamented, "Yes. The opium trade is a great evil. It is slowly devouring the people of Shanghai and of China."

Obadiah perked up. "Where does the opium come from?"

Longwei's countenance hardened. "The British bring it into the city, on fast clipper ships. They bring the opium in, and take the silk and tea out. There are many opium dens in Shanghai, and many who smoke opium, and those who smoke the opium are never the same."

"What did the English gentlemen say to the American about opium that ye did not understand?"

The ship plowed through another wave and the steam engines rumbled the floor beneath Longwei's feet. "He talked of the great cost of shipping opium from India. He said it was the only thing China would buy in trade for tea and silk. But I do not think he believed this answer."

"Ever go to one of these opium dens?"

Longwei thought of a particular evening. "Yes, but I did not stay long, and I did not go inside. A wealthy Chinese, an Imperial official, asked me to take him to the Blue Lotus opium den on Fuzhou Lu.* When we arrived I could hear music coming from inside. There were many banners and lanterns hanging on the front of the building, and I could see men hanging over a balcony above the street. Prostitutes worked outside of the entry to the Blue Lotus, and many people dressed in fine clothes. I left quickly after receiving payment. I did not like the place and had no interest to stay."

Obadiah frowned his disappointment. "Then ye didn't go inside and take a look?"

"No. I did not like the look of the place. But the beautiful hair of one of the woman did catch my attention. I am ashamed to confess to you that she tempted me for a moment. Thankfully, I did not fall prey to her."

"Did she have large bosoms?"

"I did not notice."

"Ye saw her hair, but missed her bosoms?"

Longwei remained stoic. "I only saw her hair, which was enough to tempt me."

Obadiah straightened up and grinned. "So ye had a strong desire to f—"

Longwei slammed his feet against the floor and jerked in his chair. "Never say that word in my presence! Never!"

---

* Foochow Road.

Longwei's angry tone astonished Obadiah. He asked wickedly, "Never say what word?"

"The word you were about to say."

"You mean, the word—

"Stop! Yes, that is the word you are not to say."

"Why not? I find it a right handy word when things go wrong on the ship, which happens more than a few times every single day."

"Because the Christian missionaries who taught me to speak and read English told me I would burn for eternity in the everlasting fires of Hell if I ever used the word."

"But it was I who was about to speak the word, not ye."

"What you say may be true, but it also worries me to hear the word."

"Then did ye not even think of touching her—"

"Do not speak that word either!"

Grinning, Obadiah quizzed, "What word?"

"The word you were about to say."

"Hair? Hair is a bad word too?"

Surprised and relieved, Longwei relaxed. "No, you may say hair. I thought you were about to say—"

"Ass?"

"No!"

"Cunt?"

Longwei sighed helplessly. "Breast, I thought you were about to say breast. Please. I beg you not to speak any more bad words. I fear for the safety of my soul if you do."

"Then, my friend, I will do my best to use only good words. And after being sorely tempted by the temptress—even though we know nothing about her except her hair—did ye still not think of going inside the opium den? Had you no curiosity to learn more about the place?"

"No. My shame prevented me."

"Your shame prevented you? How unfortunate. I would have liked to have heard about an opium den."

"Then you should visit the Blue Lotus when you return to Shanghai. But I do not think it wise to smoke opium or sleep with prostitutes. If you do, you may spend the rest of your life in opium dens smoking and sleeping and you will never return to the sea you love."

Obadiah grinned. "Wise council my friend," and after clicking his tongue, asked, "and how are you feeling now? You seem improved since we first met on the main deck."

Longwei straightened in the wood chair and evaluated the condition of his stomach. "Because the talk of the Blue Lotus so disturbed me I did not notice the sickness is nearly gone. I do not have any desire to 'puke' as you have said."

"Good news!"

"Yes."

"Then before you leave my cabin and return to the steerage deck where you belong, I would appreciate it if ye would tell me one last thing."

"Yes. Before I return to steerage deck where there are too many Chinamen sitting in every corner and huddled around bowls of rice and hot metal pots of tea I can answer it. What is your last question? I will hope to know the answer."

"Why are you on this ship, and what is your business in San Francisco?"

"You have asked two questions."

"True enough. Will ye only answer one of them?"

"No, I will answer both because of your kindness with ginger and molasses. I have chosen to cross the sea to San Francisco to work for…" Longwei reached into a small satchel strapped to his side and removed a folded paper. He opened the paper with difficulty because the storm had dampened the creases and then held it close to the gimbaled oil lamp. "… to work for the Central Pacific Railroad."

This surprised Obadiah. "And where did you find this paper about a railroad in another land?"

"I tore it off the wall next to the doors of the Blue Lotus opium den, after receiving payment from the Imperial official."

Feigning concern for Longwei's eternal soul, Obadiah declared, "You tore it off the wall? Isn't that akin to stealing?"

"No. Not when I do not believe anyone going to the Blue Lotus to smoke opium and sleep with prostitutes would have any interest in working on a railroad in San Francisco. I did not want to forget what the paper said."

Obadiah slapped his thigh and laughed. "Well that surely explains all."

Longwei squinted. "I believe it does."

"Then you gave up a steady job pulling rich gentlemen in a rickshaw for the uncertainty of work in a new country?"

"I do not mind the rickshaw, but for me it was not safe in Shanghai. It is better to be sitting on this ship in the great ocean puking and drinking molasses and ginger than waiting for danger to arrive at my feet in Shanghai."

Obadiah perked up a second time. "Danger? What danger did ye fear in Shanghai?"

Longwei folded his hands in front of his chest and rocked. "I cannot say what danger. There may be some on the ship who would not understand. It is best to say nothing to you, because the danger could come to both of our feet now that we have sat together in your cabin."

"No one saw us enter."

"You cannot be sure of it. And now, because I am feeling better, I should return to my rightful place on the deck with too many Chinese."

"Steerage Deck."

"Yes, that's the word. Steerage."

"You do not care to talk more of prostitutes and opium dens and Shanghai?"

"No."

"Then ye best be on your way. It pleases me the molasses and ginger have calmed your stomach. And it pleases me we had a chance to talk about China and Shanghai."

"Yes, it pleased me too. Thank you for your kindness."

Obadiah Hancock opened the cabin door. He leaned into the passageway and peeked both directions. "The way is clear if you leave now. Turn right then left at the second ladder. It will lead you down to the steerage deck. Goodbye my friend."

Tseng Longwei stood and noticed that the ship had settled into an easy roll. The storm must have diminished during the conversation. He nodded to Obadiah without speaking, dashed through the cabin door, and vanished beyond the dim light of the passageway.

Tseng Longwei shouldered his way between two fellow Chinese immigrants to secure a narrow slot at the railing near the spot he first met Obadiah Hancock. He pushed up on his toes, wedged his stomach against the top rail, and lunged perilously beyond the gunwale. He looked down the slanting side of the ship into the oil-slicked water lapping against the wooden hull and flowing around blackened wood pilings only a few feet away. The steamer China pressed the oily water against the pilings and then nudged the floating pier at the Pacific Mail Steamship Company docks in San Francisco, California.* The slimy hull squealed when it rubbed along the row of barnacled piles. On the heavy timber dock below sinewy men with rolled-up sleeves and heavy boots skillfully handled snaking lines and tied off the bow and stern of the steamer to heavy iron cleats, polished smooth by thousands of lines from other ships. Tseng Longwei lifted his head and breathed in a deep breath of the new land; the aroma of briny sea mixed with smokestack exhaust filled his lungs. He coughed twice, then blew a gob of blackened snot from each nostril over the railing. With his breathing restored, he commenced a careful study of the buildings and facilities beyond the dock.

A single-story-wood-sided-gable-metal-roofed structure stretched neatly down the center of the dock beginning at a group of flat-roofed warehouses and pitched-roofed sheds clustered near China's stern and extending to the end of the pier a hundred feet beyond China's bow. Men appeared and disappeared through dozens of closely-spaced white-trimmed doors puncturing the building in a repeating pattern. Two men, one tall and brawny and one short and gaunt, shouted profanities and pointed accusatory fingers at a broken barrel with a dark fluid oozing from jagged cracks. The black smokestack of another steamer thrust ten feet or more above the ridgeline of the gable-metal-roofed structure. Two smaller steamers, smokestacks disgorging billows of black smoke that joined above the ships before blending with a skim of low fog to form a blue-gray mist, waited for loading or unloading of people and goods and equipment on either side of a short pier 50 feet or more from the Steamship China's starboard. The spar-bristled masts of other ships poked above the roofs of other buildings along the waterfront inland from the China. More ships, both steam and sailing, floated offshore in the fog-shrouded bay and awaited patiently for a place at one of the docks.

---

* California became a state in 1850.

Shouting deckhands and the clanging of a gangway bouncing against the splintered dock interrupted Longwei's thoughtful observation of the Pacific Mail Steamship Company shore facilities. The men at his sides shoved away from the railing and pushed into a surge of people eager to leave the ship. Longwei, in no hurry to disembark when the steamer did not roll in the stormy waves of the sea, held his position at the railing. He resumed his observation of the land, and attempted to discern the outline of the city of San Francisco through the diaphanous plumes of fog.

A muscular calloused hand squeezed his shoulder. "Are ye not going ashore with the rest? Do you like molasses and ginger so much that ye wish to taste it again on the return voyage to China?"

Longwei turned around to admire the sea-weathered face of Obadiah Hancock. "Have you arrived in time to teach me more bad words before I leave the ship?"

"I believe ye have heard nearly all during our many conversations. But I do not believe you will try to remember any of them."

"There are more bad words of which you did not speak to me?"

"A few there are. But they are generally spoken only by sailors like me. I'm supposing ye will have little use for them ashore."

"I can thank God for that."

"You're damned right you can."

Tseng Longwei glanced toward the gangway: the crowds of Chinese and other passengers had diminished. "Although I have enjoyed our conversations, it is time for me to go."

"Surely it is. No more rickshaws for you. Now it's the railroad, and only God knows where he'll take you from here. Farewell my friend." Obadiah shoved his hand out.

Longwei and Obadiah shook hands for the first time. "Yes, farewell my friend. Keep safe in the storm. And do not forget the ginger and molasses. And try not to say too many bad words. There is still a chance God will redeem you."

Obadiah Hancock grinned. "I'll do my damn best."

After their hands released, Longwei lifted a small canvas sack by his side, walked across the deck to the top of the gangway, bounded down the narrow plank to the dock below, and pivoted toward China's stern and the city of San Francisco. He walked along the busy dock until he had reached the cluster of flat-roofed warehouses and pitched-roofed sheds close to China's stern. He followed a group of passengers through a winding alleyway between the buildings and turned left at a ragged dirt road on the other side. He followed the road past a mound of gravel and turned again at a long fence pointing back to the water. Someone had painted the side with large white letters, and Longwei read the words as he drifted along the fence. C. C. HASTINGS & CO. LICK HOUSE CHEAPEST CLOTHING....

A barrel-chested man wearing a white shirt and black felt derby bellowed from atop a flatbed wagon and gestured an invitation. Two more wagons waited nearby. "Men from China. Come with me to work for the Central Pacific Railroad. We will feed you and pay you. Work for the railroad. Free food and housing." A second man held up a poster with a picture of a train. Dozens of Chinese fresh off the Steamship China ran to the wagons.

Tseng Longwei did not hasten his pace. When he arrived at the wagon he spoke calmly to the derby man. "If I board this wagon, you will take me to the railroad?"

The derby man peered down at Longwei. "A Chinaman who speaks good English? Quite a novelty, if you ask me. Yes. I will take you to the railroad. But you must get on before there is no space and you are left behind."

Longwei tossed his canvas sack onto the wagon and climbed aboard. As the derby man had predicted, the wagon quickly filled with Chinese. When the wagon pulled away, Longwei muttered to himself, "This is truly unfortunate. It appears there was no reason to steal the railroad paper from the wall of the Blue Lotus."

Chapter Nine

Seattle, Washington Territory
May 1868

Excerpt from
A Glorious History of the American West
by Muireall Anne Ravenscroft
The Birth of Seattle

Any discussion of the importance of the Pacific Northwest in American history must begin with Seattle. A young city when compared to the urban centers of the eastern states, much of the rolling terrain of today's Seattle consisted of luxuriant green forests shrouded in rain and mist at a time when eastern cities were firmly established. Although the ancestors of the contemporary tribes of Puget Sound likely migrated from the north some 12,000 years ago, the first Europeans did not discover the area until 1792 when Captain George Vancouver explored the inland waterways of the Straits of Juan de Fuca and Georgia.* This fact alone places the Puget

* The Strait of Juan de Fuca is bounded on the north by Vancouver Island and on the south by the Olympic Peninsula. The Strait of Georgia extends up the northeastern seaboard of Vancouver Island.

Sound, and the Pacific Northwest in general, among the last American lands explored by the Europeans.

The Duwamish tribe lived on the site of present-day Seattle, and much like the Suquamish, Nisqually, Muckleshoot, Snoqualmie, and other major tribes of Puget Sound, was intrinsically tied to the rivers, lakes, and the sea. This is in stark contrast to the Plains Indians (Blackfoot, Crow, Cheyenne, Sioux, and Arapaho, to name a few), who lived east of the Rocky Mountains from eastern Montana down through central Texas and thrived primarily as nomadic hunter-gatherers. The names of several Puget Sound Tribes are telling on this point. The name Duwamish means "The People of the Inside," which refers to Elliot Bay, the Duwamish River, and the other rivers, lakes, and waterways that connected the tribe's ancestral homeland. The name Suquamish translates as "People of the Clear Salt Water," which invokes vivid imagery of the pristine waters off the Kitsap Peninsula and Bainbridge Island. These and other Puget Sound Indian tribes harvested salmon, cod, and shellfish from the water and deer and elk from the land, then stored this bounty in quantities sufficient for the long months of winter. They built ornately-carved canoes for transportation. They developed intricate trading networks connecting permanent settlements on the rugged coastlines and along meandering river valleys. They housed extended family groups in architecturally significant cedar log structures with ventilated fire pits. And they developed elaborate social structures with powerful chiefs, complex systems of religious clans, and economies that used goods to measure wealth. Sadly, these vibrant cultures of the Pacific Northwest commenced a precipitous and irreversible decline beginning with the arrival of the Americans.

Early European interest in Puget Sound centered on the abundance of beavers and otters thriving in the numerous rivers and waterways of the region. The Hudson's Bay Company, originally incorporated by British royal charter in 1670 and one of the world's oldest companies, controlled the entire fur trade of the Pacific Northwest from Fort Vancouver on the northern bank of the Columbia River, just north of present-day Portland, Oregon. Established in 1824, this massive center of commerce and trade encouraged American migration into the Pacific Northwest and eventually served as one of the final stops for many of the pioneers traversing the legendary Oregon Trail. The Hudson's Bay Company originally sought to restrict American settlement to the lands south of the Columbia River, but with roughly 53,000 Americans arriving in the area between 1843 and 1860 many pioneers pushed northward into lands controlled by the Hudson's Bay Company. Understandably, boundary disputes between the United States and Great Britain intensified during this period of determined western migration, and in 1846 Great Britain lost all control of the region when the Americans and British agreed to establish the border between the United States and Canada along the 49th parallel.

The history of Seattle begins with two brothers from New York: Arthur and David Denny. In 1851 they led a wagon train of intrepid pioneers along the 2,000 mile Oregon Trail with the objective of settling in the Willamette Valley, the ultimate destination of most travelers of the Oregon Trail in those days. Along the way they heard colorful stories of vast and fertile lands near the waterways of the Puget Sound, and when they arrived at Portland they made the momentous decision to continue north. The pioneers of the Denny party eventually staked claims on Alki Point, the location of present-day West Seattle, but only a few months later relocated to a more agreeable site on the other side of Elliot Bay, the site of Pioneer Square and downtown

Seattle. They named the new settlement "Seattle" after the Duwamish Chief Sealth.

These early pioneers found the mud flats to the south excellent for oysters but unsuitable for civic development. Consequently, they set to work clearing the rolling hills to the north, and eventually built schools, churches, and other civic structures. Entrepreneur Henry Yesler arrived in Seattle in 1852, and built the first steam-powered sawmill on the Elliot Bay waterfront at the foot of Mill Street (now named Yesler Way) a year later. The original name of Mill Street was supposedly inspired by the numerous logs that were "skidded" down the steep hill by horses and mules from the constantly-eroding tree line of the area's old growth fir forests (likely older than a thousand years). The sawmill provided many jobs for the early settlers, as well as the Duwamish Indians, and soon became the town's principal economic driver. Much of the sawmill's product, first logs but later milled lumber, was shipped to the booming city of San Francisco in California, but the mill also provided lumber to new towns and communities throughout Puget Sound. In fact, the city of Seattle would come to rely on the lumber industry for economic growth and prosperity for decades to come, and while other....

John Ravenscroft tugged the feather pillows under his head and nudged Muireall's shoulder without releasing the page of manuscript from his hand. "Muireall. I have a question about this bit you wrote on Seattle."

Muireall lifted her chin without opening her eyes. "What? You have a question about what?"

"Seattle."

Muireall stretched one arm above the simple wood headboard, glanced at the clock on the side table, and talked through an involuntary yawn. "It's seven o'clock. What are you doing reading the manuscript this early in the morning?" She yawned again.

John repositioned his reading glasses. "I couldn't sleep anymore and, believe it or not, I actually enjoy reading your manuscript. I'm constantly learning new things I never knew existed."

"How nice... but it's still seven in the morning."

"It's Saturday. Why do you care what time it is?"

"I know it's Saturday. I just like to sleep in a little on Saturday."

"You can sleep in after you answer my question about Seattle."

"OK. I give up. What's the question?"

"Why does any discussion of the Pacific Northwest in American history have to begin with Seattle? What about Portland? Couldn't one make an argument that Portland is just as important to the development of the Pacific Northwest?"

Muireall plopped her head against the pillow. "I like Seattle."

John squinted at Muireall quizzically. "You don't like Portland?"

"Portland's alright, but I like Seattle better."

John removed the reading glasses and set the page and the glasses on his stomach. "And this is the intellectual justification for your historical assertion?"

Muireall wedged her hand beneath her head. She yawned before saying, "Only partly."

John waited for a continuation but none occurred. "Only partly?" Muireall said nothing. "Are you going to tell me the rest of the intellectual justification?"

Muireall rubbed her toes along John's calf. "No, I'm not."

"No? You're not going to tell me? Why?"

Muireall smiled playfully and her eyes narrowed to tantalizingly-mischievous slits. "Because... now that I'm wide awake at seven o'clock on a Saturday morning, I had something else in mind."

...tautly-stretched ribbons of golden-flashed end-of-morning sunlight
shooting through rough-edged weathered roof holes
and dusty window glass sparkling hazy clouds of swirling sawdust
exuding freshly pungent smells of newly-cut wood
and hot friction-vaporized tree sap.

Gusting plumes of billowing hot-scalding steam,
moist and tingling on the nose hairs, all mixed together
with ear-ringing-quick-whirring pulleys and iron levers
clanking brightly against iron, a counterpoint to
allegro-churning boiler-driven pistons
vigorously singing percussive melodies.

Sight-blurring blades of all sorts and sizes
cutting clean and straight through tight-grained ancient timber
screaming defiantly with greased shafts spinning hard against....

Roshan Kuznetsov plunged a sap-stained index finger into each ear and shut his eyes tightly while the recently-sharpened teeth of the enormous circular saw sliced a clean quarter-inch kerf* down the length of a thousand-year-old log. When the spinning blade had reached the end of the log, Roshan and a fellow sawyer named Erland Bech seized the bark-crusted slab† at each end and carried it to the base of a large pile of slabs. With numerous grunts they swung the slab back then forward again and tossed it about three feet up the side of the expanding pile. The unruly slab teetered momentarily, then rotated and slid to the ground. Roshan jumped away just before the slab nearly crushed his toes.

Erland wiped the sweat from the top of his head with a sticky sap-smudged hand. "I told you we should've stacked the slabs better to begin with. Now our lives are in danger with each new cut. I do not think we will make it to the end of the day."

Roshan examined his toes and then the slab that had nearly cut them off. "Yes, yes. You always say we should have done the stack better even when I do not forget when you never said the better in the first place."

Erland shook his head as they shuffled back to the tirelessly moving carriage‡ to retrieve the next slab. "It is now clear to me, Roshan. I have

---

* The groove made by a saw.

† A slab is the outside piece cut from a log when squaring it for lumber. Slabs were often cut into firewood to fuel the sawmill boiler.

‡ The carriage is the horizontal device on which a log moves back and forth through the saw blade to produce slabs and lumber. The log is turned on the carriage before making each new cut.

worked with you at this sawmill far too long. It frightens me to think of it, but I actually know what you just said even though what you just said makes no sense at all."

Roshan grabbed his end of the next slab when it fell away from the log. "No, you have it the backwards. You stay with me not long enough to make sense and then we will see what the difference the sense makes."

Erland altered his grip and they carried the slab to the pile. "My point exactly, Roshan. I know what you mean, but anyone listening to this conversation from the outside would have no idea what you just said."

Roshan's face transformed to a knowing expression. "Yes. But they could not listen outside because we are not in the outside. If you take the care to look around the back of me you can see not the outside of the Yesler Sawmill on the Mill Street where the horse and mule pulls the forest to your feet and the place I work for the many months now because they gave me job if you look hard enough to see when I should be in San Francisco looking for the gold but now I look for no gold and have no reason."

Erland frowned and they tossed the slab onto the pile. This time it did not slide to the ground and nearly crush Roshan's toes. "And this is another thing that's been bothering me, if you must ask. You have told me you trapped otter for a living in New Archangel way up north in Alaska, and you said the Prince of New Archangel, although the title makes no sense to me, somehow convinced the United States Navy into shipping you to San Francisco so you could look for gold, and yet here you are, working as a sawyer in a sawmill in Seattle. You have never explained why you are not in San Francisco." He slapped his hands together to knock off some of the sawdust.

Roshan was not sure he could adequately explain the reason he had ended up in Seattle—a town of only 2,000 people and endless mudflats and steady rain and with no possibility of finding gold or silver at all as far as he could tell—instead of San Francisco. But he tried to explain the events of that day to the best of his recollection. "It is the longer of stories, and not of the easy to remember the reason, but I will give you the best I know to remember."

A steam whistle shrilled, signaling a short break for lunch. "Good. You can tell me the story while we eat. I'd like to hear it, because I'd like to stop worrying about it."

After retrieving their lunches, Roshan and Erland sat on a convenient slab not too distant from the carriage. The whirring pulleys and billowing steam and thumping boiler pistons did not cease during lunch. Roshan opened a small package and discovered a hearty chunk of rye bread. An apple fell out and rolled on the ground by his feet, but he did not notice. "Yes, Prince Dmitri Petrovich Maksutov of Russia, and a hero it is true of the famous war I cannot remember the name, sent me to the American ship called Ossipee, a name I do not know why it means to anyone, to go to San Francisco for the gold."

Erland bit into a slice of cheddar cheese. "I do not care about the name of the ship. Go on about why you are here in Seattle instead of San Francisco."

"Yes, I can tell you of it. It begins the trombone and the tuba played the poker, a game I am sure you heard, and they teach me to play the game until I have almost little of the no money. Still then, I do not worry about it because of the gold I will find the soon in California, a place I do not know the name but San Francisco is at the same."

"Musical instruments took all of your money?"

"No, you have it the wrong. Not musical instruments took the money—the trombone and the tuba played the poker until I have money left of little."

Erland picked up the errant apple, rubbed it vigorously on his shirt to remove the sawdust, and handed it to Roshan. "You lost your apple. Never mind about the musical instruments. I don't think it probably matters anyway. You still haven't explained why you got off the ship in Seattle. That's the part I'm interested in."

"Yes, I will come to Seattle in short. I play the poker, a very game of fun if you have the time and a deck made of many cards and the Ace of Shovels, and the ship stops in the water and does not move where I can see the Yesler Sawmill at the bottom of the road Mill Street we have spoken of before the begin and we sit at this time eating apple and cheese. I stand next to the trombone and the tuba on top of the large Ossipee and my both lips see the Yesler Sawmill of name I did not understand at the time and I point the arm," Roshan gestured with the apple to demonstrate, "to the Yesler Sawmill where we eat and I talk to the trombone and tuba and say, 'Is this the place San Francisco in the California where I go to find the gold?' and the tuba talks to me, 'Yes, Roshan, this is San Francisco, and the place where to go to get on the land and find the gold you are looking.' And then the trombone talks again and speaks, 'Yes, this is the San Francisco where you go if you must lift your bags and go.' If you can think of it, it makes me happy to find San Francisco and begin my look for the gold. I lift my bags and walk down the ship and here I am in the today."

"It sounds like the musical instruments lied to you. They told you to get off the ship in Seattle when they knew full well you wanted to go to San Francisco."

"I do not think they tried to tell lie. I think they thought wrong of Seattle and told me the wrong time to lift the bags. I think they feel the bad for it when Ossipee arrives in San Francisco and they find the mistake."

"If you say so, but I still think they lied to you."

"I do not believe the tuba and the trombone would tell Roshan the lie when they took the much time to show me poker and the cards of deck."

"But now you're stuck in Seattle, and instead of trapping otters or prospecting for gold you're cutting logs for a living. Such a shame, and truly a sad story."

"Yes, you speak the truth I have not found San Francisco and the gold, but the tuba and the trombone did give me to speak English with more words I did not know."

"The tuba and trombone taught you new English words? Like what?"

"Many important words of the English. I say them for you in the now when you know the tuba and the trombone felt the bad when Ossipee found San Francisco and they found a mistake. *Poker face. Full house. Royal flush. Two of a kind. I see you and raise you five. These cards are jinxed. Gentlemen, read 'em and weep. Who is idiotsonofabitch who dealt this shitty hand?* And many other new English words I do not have the time to think of now."

"You picked up quite a vocabulary from the tuba and trombone. I'm glad you at least improved your English on the trip to Seattle."

"Yes, I think of it too. But I have not much the chance to speak the words since beginning in my time in Seattle. Maybe it is because there is no the poker to play."

The steam whistle shrilled again, signaling the end of lunch. Erland Bech stood and stretched. "But it's still a sad story."

Roshan stood and flung the apple core over the top of the pile of slabs. "What is sad, because is not the gold in Seattle?"

"No, it's sad you're stuck in Seattle. And it's sad you'll never make it to San Francisco to follow your dream of prospecting for gold and becoming rich."

"Yes, I see how you tell it. It is much sad. But it is not of the too much bad in the Seattle. The many rain does not make me little happy and helps me think of the trapping otter in rivers of New Archangel, and I smile to think of it. So it is not much bad."

"I guess you could look at it that way, if it cheers you up."

With little forewarning, fifty-seven-year-old Henry Yesler—carpenter, millwright, sea captain, builder, entrepreneur, real estate agent, future mayor of Seattle, and founder of the Yesler Sawmill—appeared through the light-dappled haze of suspended sawdust. He spoke with the forceful confidence of a successful businessman. "You two. What are your plans during the next month?"

Surprised by the sudden arrival of Henry Yesler, Erland spoke first. "Plans? We have no plans. We never have any plans. Roshan, do you have any plans?" Roshan thought of San Francisco and shook his head. Erland continued, "No sir, Mr. Yesler. We have no plans at all. We just work for you here at the mill, day in and day out, rain or shine, shine or rain."

Henry Yesler shoved a hand into the side pocket of his tailored suit jacket. "Good. Very good. Then let me tell you why I'm here and what I've got in mind. I have a special shipment of select vertical grain lumber and beams, the finest wood you ever saw, set to sail tomorrow at the crack of dawn. It's being loaded on the ship as we speak. I am in need of two reliable men to accompany the lumber to the destination and to make sure it arrives safely and intact. It'll take a good month to get there and back. Maybe longer. I know it's short notice, but I need to find two volunteers this afternoon, so I'm in a bit of a hurry."

Erland and Roshan gaped at each other. Roshan was about to speak, but Erland pressed his hand against his chest and calmly spoke for the both of them. "We don't know, Mr. Yesler. I'd have to say... we like it in Seattle. Babysitting a bunch of special lumber on a ship full of scoundrels sounds like a lot of trouble to me. Can you tell us where the lumber's going to?"

Henry Yesler pulled his hand from the jacket pocket, thoughtfully stroked his neatly-combed beard, then hooked his thumbs behind the tailored jacket lapels. "I certainly can. Some big expensive hotel under construction in San Francisco. Interested?"

Chapter Ten

Liverpool, England
July 1869

A high-necked cotton dress concealing the scars on her neck, Gordania Sinclair nestled the delicate glass between thumb and finger and peered down into the slanting surface of red wine while she sipped. Her emerald eyes slowly rose to the mustached face of the dapper gentleman sitting across the table as she placed the glass on the flawlessly-white linen tablecloth a few inches from the rim of the china dinner plate. She self-consciously joined her hands and lowered them beneath the table to conceal a tattered sleeve she had repaired with needle and thread an hour before dinner. The hissing steam engines of the SS Tarifa rumbled deeply beneath her feet and rattled a sterling silver butter knife resting on a bread plate.

The dapper gentleman—fascinated by Gordania's rustic beauty, emerald eyes, and the tattered sleeve of her plain cotton house dress—waited graciously after she had set the wine glass down before restarting the conversation. "I see. And did you actually miss the train?"

Gordania spoke with the evocative brogue of northern Scotland. "No. Even though it was my first trip to Glasgow, and I had never visited such a large station before, I found the correct platform just after the train began to move and ran alongside before jumping aboard. I only carried one small bag; it did not cause me any difficulty."

The dapper gentleman attempted to visualize the event. "You ran alongside the train in a dress? Carrying a bag?"

Gordania demurred. "I know it was not proper, but in truth I have run in a dress my entire life. I hope you do not think less of me for it."

The dapper gentlemen smiled, but not sufficiently to portray obvious amusement. "No, I do not think less of you at all. I find it both amusing and charming at the same time. I can clearly picture you in my imagination, running like a swift-footed gazelle down the platform in a cotton dress and leaping aboard a moving train. Simply delightful."

Gordania blushed. "I'm not certain a gazelle is the appropriate likeness. I would think a large farm animal would be a more believable choice."

"You do not allow yourself sufficient credit, Miss Sinclair. But then what? Did you encounter other adventures on your journey from Glasgow to Liverpool?"

"Not to speak of, although I did experience something quite extraordinary when I boarded the first train at Golspie Station."

"The first train of your trip to Liverpool?"

"No, the first train in my life. My father had driven me from Dunnet Head Lighthouse to Golspie Station, a distance of some 80 miles, in the family wagon. We did not speak much on the trip, and when we did, we did not talk of serious matters. It sprinkled a bit on the way, but otherwise we enjoyed reasonably good weather. After we arrived at the train station, a quaint little stone building with tiny dormers and two large chimneys, my father presented me with a small package wrapped in brown paper tied with a string. He asked me to open it right there. I carefully opened the package to save the paper and found a leather-bound diary, a small bottle of ink, and my father's cherished fountain pen. I told him I had no intention of taking his pen, but he insisted and said he wanted me to keep a written record of my journey to America and to write letters home to my mother and sister. I promised I would do it. Then he hugged me harder and longer than I ever remember as a child. When he let go, I noticed a tear on his cheek. I had never seen him cry before. It was quite extraordinary."

The dapper gentleman struggled to appreciate the emotion. "Your father must love you very much. Did he not agree you should leave?"

Gordania sipped her wine again. Now some distance from the Princess Dock, the SS Tarifa steered northwesterly toward the centerline of the River Mersey on a course that would take the iron-hulled steamer into Liverpool Bay and then westerly to the Irish Sea. Squawking seabirds soared above the stern. A heavy-laden, black-smudged freighter steamed by the Tarifa to port heading for the cranes and railways of the Herculaneum Dock, two miles up the river, to unload a shipment of coal. "No, quite the opposite I'm afraid. My father was the one who actually thought I should go to America. Mother did not approve at first, but later agreed. I saved what little money I could over the next two years, mostly by working as a nanny, but in the end it was not nearly enough. Then my parents surprised me during a Sunday dinner at the lighthouse and gave me the remaining money I needed to pay for the train and sea voyage. With luck I will actually have a little bit remaining when I arrive in Boston; sufficient, I pray, to last until I find work and a place to live."

"You have made no prior arrangements in Boston?"

"No. How could I? I do not know anyone in America."

"Then why do you go, when you have family in Scotland and no friends in America?"

"My father has made clear the reason: to make a better life for myself. He did not believe there was sufficient opportunity in Scotland, especially for a woman. He believed, and still believes, there will be opportunities in America that simply do not exist in Scotland, and he has always wished the best for me."

"Certainly. And the trip from ... what did you call it?"

"Golspie."

"Yes, Golspie. Of course. Charming name for a town, especially in Scotland. And the trip from Golspie to Glasgow? Uneventful?"

"Yes. I enjoyed it very much, especially when we stopped at one of the railway stations along the way and I had time to watch the different people who boarded the train. When the train arrived at Inverness, I had never seen such a large city before.* I thought of getting off to explore, but worried I might miss the train when it left the station."

"You did not yet know of your skill in running after and jumping aboard moving trains?"

"I did not. But then we arrived in Glasgow, and when the train travelled through the city, I realized how small Inverness was. Growing up in

* The population of Inverness, Scotland in 1869 was approximately 14,000 people. The Inverness railway station opened in 1855.

a lighthouse on Dunnet Head does not adequately prepare one for the realities of the larger world."

While Gordania described her observations of Inverness and Glasgow, the dapper gentlemen produced a silver cigarette case (engraved with his initials), opened it with a click, extracted a slender cigarette with a gracefully subtle flourish, lighted it, and puffed a thin swirl of smoke. The SS Tarifa sailed beyond the mouth of the River Mersey and the steamer rolled a little to starboard when it encountered the rougher waters of Liverpool Bay. The ship slowly accelerated until it reached a speed of 10 knots. "My dear, a life in a lighthouse in Scotland is not less worthy than a life in a big city such as Glasgow. I believe you have seriously underrated the advantages of your upbringing."

"What you say may be true, but my lack of experience has made me naive. As you know, when I changed trains in Glasgow I lost my way and nearly missed the train to Liverpool. If I had arrived at the platform even a minute later, I would not have had the opportunity to run to catch it."

"In a cotton dress."

"Yes, but as I told you—"

"You have often run in a dress. True, but you did arrive at the platform in time, which speaks well of your intellectual persistence. And you did catch the train by running and then leaping aboard a moving platform with a suitcase in hand—a feat I doubt any city girl could achieve, even if her very life depended on it—which speaks well of your athletic prowess. I do not think you will remain naive for long. And you are already less so than when you hugged your weeping father on the platform of the train station in ... in ... what did you call it again?"

Gordania smiled. "Golspie."

"Yes, that's it—a name which is so foreign to me that I will probably never remember to say it correctly in a complete sentence without your help."

"Thank you for your kind words, but I suspect your praise is unjustified."

"That is for me to decide, my dear Miss Sinclair. And what of your experiences after Glasgow? Did you run after any more trains on your way to Liverpool?"

"I did not have the opportunity, because I took special care to avoid the same unfortunate circumstances. But when I arrived in—"

The head waiter, nearly as dapper in stiff collar and bow tie as the dapper gentleman, suddenly appeared by the table. "Will you and the lady be having desert, sir?"

The dapper gentleman spoke without releasing his gaze from Gordania's emerald eyes. "I think not tonight, but do you have a good cognac?"*

The head waiter bowed, slightly. "Yes sir. We have a very nice Courvoisier."

The dapper gentleman thoughtfully puffed his cigarette. "And the age?"

The head waiter stiffened proudly. "Extra old, sir. I believe at least 10 years."

"Excellent. Please bring two glasses of Courvoisier."

Gordania waited until the head waiter had scurried away to fetch the cognac. "I have never tasted cognac before. I hate for you to spend the money when I do not know if I will like it."

"Do not worry, Miss Sinclair. If you do not like it, I will gladly finish the rest. And you were saying before the waiter interrupted us? Something about arriving?" The dapper gentlemen crushed his partially-smoked cigarette into a porcelain ash tray.

"Oh yes. I was about to say... when I arrived in Wigan† I had to change trains again. Since I had to wait almost half a day for my departure to Liverpool, and because I did not want to sit in the train station, I found the courage to explore the city streets a bit."

"Miss Sinclair, I doubt that you possess a deficit of courage." The head waiter arrived with two tulip-shaped wineglasses of cognac balanced deftly on a polished serving tray. He skillfully placed the glasses in front of Gordania and the dapper gentleman then pivoted with military precision

---

* Cognac, named after the town of Cognac in France, is a variety of brandy. Legend has it that several barrels of Courvoisier were hidden aboard the ship that transported Napoleon Bonaparte to his final exile on the island of Saint Helena in 1815.

† Wigan is approximately 20 miles east of Liverpool, and was one of the first towns in Great Britain to be served by a railway. The population of Wigan expanded dramatically during the Industrial Revolution, reaching nearly 32,000 by the middle of the 19th century. Wigan was dominated by coal mines and cotton mills beginning in the late 18th century.

and marched away. "And now the cognac of Napoleon has arrived to prove your courage. Please take a sip, as you promised."

Gordania stared at the glass of amber liquid before offering a light-hearted protest. "But I have already had two glasses of wine. I don't think I should drink any more less I become faint."

"You did not finish your second glass of wine. It is still sitting in front of you only half-empty as proof. And you promised to take at least one sip. I do not think a single sip, if it is all you can manage, will make you woozy. But before you drink, you must raise the glass to your nose and smell the fragrance of the cognac. Then you may take a small sip."

Gordania lifted the tulip-shaped glass to her nose as instructed and sniffed the fragrance of the cognac. "It smells like jam."

The dapper gentleman smiled knowingly. "Yes. I assume it smells of very expensive jam. Now take a sip."

Gordania tilted the glass until a small taste poured over her tongue. After swallowing, she exclaimed, "It is wonderful. I may decide to finish the entire glass by myself and you shall have none of it."

The dapper gentleman lifted his glass of Courvoisier with a sweeping gesture and sniffed, "That, my dear, is the proverbial idea," then swirled the cognac and sniffed again. When he appeared satisfied, he drank. "And now that you have sniffed and sipped, you may enjoy the remaining cognac at your leisure. Now, may we return to Wigan? I have heard of it, but have not had the opportunity to visit this city of cotton mills and coal mines because I travelled to Liverpool from London via Manchester."

Gordania enjoyed one more taste and then set the tulip-shaped glass down next to the half-finished glass of wine. "The platform of the Wigan Central Railway Station was very crowded with passengers and baggage, and it took me several minutes to find my way through the crowd. When I finally reached the front doors and stepped into the street, I was confronted by the strangest skies I have ever seen, and the most unusual odor of smoke I have ever smelled."

The dapper gentlemen chuckled slyly. "You will get used to the smell of smoke on this very ship, especially if you are not mindful of the direction of the wind."

Gordania shrugged in her chair. "I cannot imagine the smoke produced by the Tarifa will match the smoke of Wigan."

"Then to put your theory to the test, we must take some walks together on the leeward deck of our steamship and you can compare the two." The Steamship Tarifa churned deeper into Liverpool Bay. When the vessel had achieved sufficient distance from the mouth of the River Mersey, it tacked sharply to a course that would lead westerly to the Irish Sea and then southerly between England and Ireland into the Celtic Sea—a blob of an ocean body touching Ireland, England, and a trace of France near the town of Brest. "The ship is turning again. We are truly on our way to America now. But on with your tale of Wigan. You were about to describe your exploration of this industrial town of gray skies and pungent smoke."

Gordania continued without agreeing to walk with the dapper gentleman. "Yes. I travelled only a bit further down the street, but because I found the skies so depressing and the air so foul I quickly retreated to the railway station."

"The gray of the skies and the smell of the air compelled you to return to a crowded railway station? How odd!"

"You would understand if you had ever breathed the sweet air of Dunnet Head or witnessed the pristine skies above Pentland Firth after a storm."

The dapper gentleman briefly closed his eyes to consider these images. "Yes, I suppose I would. And if I am fortunate, maybe I shall breathe your sweet air and view your pristine skies before I pass from this earthly life."

Gordania rested her forearms on the table. "I fear you are heading in the wrong direction if you wish to experience the air and skies of northern Scotland." But, remembering the tattered sleeve, quickly dropped her hands to her lap.

The dapper gentleman feigned no awareness of the sleeve. "As are you, my dear. And what of your travels from Wigan to Liverpool?"

Gordania relaxed back in the chair and unconsciously covered the tattered sleeve with her hand. "No special adventures to speak of. When the train finally arrived at the Liverpool Exchange Railway Station,* I disembarked

* The Liverpool Exchange Railway Station opened in 1850 and was originally known by two names because two different companies shared the line in Liverpool. The Lancashire and Yorkshire Railway called it the "Exchange Station." The East Lancashire Railway called it the "Tithebarn Street Station." The two companies amalgamated in 1859 and the station was named the Liverpool Exchange.

without difficulty, made my way down the crowded platform without incident, and easily located the front doors. I was very impressed by this station because all of the platforms were covered with a high roof with rows of glass to let in the light. I walked down the steps to Tithebarn Street, and turned right to find my way to the docks. I had talked to the porter and he had given me directions so that I would not get lost and end up in the wrong part of town."

The dapper gentleman nodded. "Quite prudent of you."

Gordania nodded. "The streets were very crowded in front of the station with people arriving and leaving from all directions. After I had walked along Tithebarn a minute or two, I looked back at the station. I was in such a hurry that I had not noticed the beautiful stonework and arches, the stone railing at the top, and the graceful chimneys. But the stone was very dark, and the sky above the Liverpool Exchange very gray."

The dapper gentleman opened the engraved silver case and fingered another cigarette. "And the smell of the air? Did it remind you of Wigan?"

Recalling the scent, Gordania breathed deeply. "It smelled of the sea, but not the crisp scent of Dunnet Head." She paused to enjoy a sip of cognac. "I continued my walk toward the docks, but I must have misunderstood the directions given by the porter, because I turned onto a narrow street, walked some distance, and turned again into a narrow alley. I could hear the sound of ships above the dark buildings, but had entered a sort of maze and could not find my way. This is when the two men approached me."

"And then what did you do?"

"I tried to leave the alley, but a third man appeared and blocked my way. I tried to run by him, but he grabbed me by the hair and pulled me to the ground. The other men began groping through my bag while the man who had pulled my hair held me down with his knee across my stomach. When they could not find any money or other valuables, they became angry and began screaming foul words at me."

"You had no money in your bag?"

"Fortunately, at the advice of my father, I had hidden the money in my bloomers. But I think this only caused a delay in the robbery. I believe they were about to look further on my person... just when you arrived."

"When I heard commotion inside the alley and saw you on the ground with three brutes about to take unfair advantage of your helplessness,

I decided to intervene." The dapper gentlemen puffed his cigarette and exhaled a luxuriant whorl.

"Yes, and I'm deeply thankful you did. When you first approached and asked if you could be of assistance, my heart sank. But when you produced a rapier from your walking stick and stabbed the biggest man through the shoulder... I have never seen a sword disguised as a cane before... and slashed one of the other men across the cheek—"

"A useful device at certain times. It was my deepest pleasure to assist you, Miss Sinclair. And now that we are safely on our way to America, have you fully recovered from this unfortunate ordeal?"

"I believe I have." Gordania removed the leather-bound diary and fountain pen from a tattered purse, opened the diary and uncapped the pen. "Before I forget to ask, could you please spell your name? I want to record it accurately in my diary, and to write of my ordeal when I return to my bed in steerage."

"Delighted, my dear. My name is spelled C... S... O... N... G... O... R... T... O... T... H." Without apology, he clarified, "The C is silent."

Gordania scratched Csongor's full name at the top of a blank page. "Thank you Mr. Toth. And now I must compensate you for my share of this lovely meal."

Csongor tapped his knuckles on the table in mock irritation. "You shall do no such thing, Miss Sinclair. The delight of your company has compensated me for the cost of the meal many times over. It is I who should compensate you."

Gordania presented a serious countenance. "Then, although I do not agree with your argument, we shall call it even."

"Your suggestion is more than fair."

"And Mr. Toth..."

"Yes?"

"I do have one more question for you before I retire for the night, if you do not mind."

"Please ask your question."

"When did you decide to travel to America? I know my reasons, but you are clearly a wealthy man who appears to have no need for adventures in a new land."

"Simple, my Scottish lass. I decided to board the Steamship Tarifa and sail to the New World after I met you."

Csongor Toth and Gordania Sinclair did walk the decks many times during the long transatlantic voyage: to compare the smoke of Wigan to the smoke of the Steamship Tarifa and to talk of America and Dunnet Head and Budapest and many other things.* And Csongor invited Gordania to dinner, much to Gordania's objection because she was never allowed to pay, nearly every day. When the Tarifa arrived in Boston in late July of 1869, the two spoke only briefly on the dock alongside the ship as a gentle rain fell from the gray-streaked clouds above. Csongor wished Gordania success in the New World, tapped his sword cane on the ground, and marched away without nary a handshake. Suddenly abandoned, Gordania stood on the rain-glistened boards next to the black iron hull of the Tarifa and stared into the gray buildings across from the dock for a long time before lifting the small bag with her meager possessions and stepping off into her new life.

---

* The trip likely required 15 days.

CHAPTER ELEVEN

Clayton County, Iowa
June 1870

Manfred Herrmann, now in the final day of the final week of the final month of his final year at Wartburg Theological Seminary, gazed dreamily through one of the clear glass windows that beckoned the slanting light of the Iowa prairie to flood the sanctuary. He squirmed in one of the simple handmade pews near the center of the sanctuary of St. Sebald Church as he listened to Professor Strathmore drone on endlessly of the ethical complexities of comparing the ideal of God to the reality of the world. His eyes snapped to a specific point on one of the whitewashed plaster walls between two windows and then blurred to momentary unconsciousness. Professor Strathmore transitioned to a discussion of the relevant ideas and philosophies of Johann Konrad Wilhelm Loehe;* Manfred's mind instantly flared to full awareness. Manfred admired Loehe's courage to denounce sin without fear, to speak plainly like the prophets of old, and to live the pious life. But at the same time he felt agonizingly troubled by his own shortcomings of courage, which hindered the same path.

Professor Strathmore droned, "And I believe, to clearly understand Loehe's fundamental beliefs and their relevance to our lives and mission in the church, one must consider the five dimensions of his Ecclesial

---

* The roots of the Wartburg Theological Seminary originate with the missionary vision of Johann Konrad Wilhelm Loehe, a Lutheran pastor who served in Neuendettelsau, Bavaria from 1837 to the end of his life in 1872.

Theology. Only then can one truly appreciate the depth of his thought and the power of his ideas. For example, if we begin by..."

Manfred thought to himself: *Now this is interesting and finally worth listening to. It certainly took long enough for Professor Strathmore to get to the point.* He scratched his shoulders against the hardwood back of the pew, raised his chin slightly, and closed his eyes—a habit indicating a state of intense focus more often than the beginning of an afternoon nap.

Professor Strathmore stepped around the large dry-goods box that functioned as the church's alter. "... when the dimensions are thought of separately or taken as a whole. Firstly, his ecclesial theology is *pietistic*. For Loehe, the consistently pious life leads to a profound sense of the living God's activities in our day-to-day existence. This same intense focus on pietism is what has motivated Loehe to become a devoted supporter of mission work here in America and throughout the world, including..."

His eyes still closed and his chin rising a little higher, Manfred's focus sharpened momentarily on the words "... consistently pious life..." then quickly drifted to thoughts of his plentiful failures to achieve the pious life. Dark images of Shiloh began tearing at the murky fringes of his consciousness, but he held them out by forcing his attention back to Professor Strathmore's monotonous voice.

Professor Strathmore noticed Manfred leaning back in the hardwood pew with raised chin and closed eyes. He began walking in Manfred's direction. "And if we consider the second dimension, that his ecclesial theology is *confessional*, we begin to achieve true insight into the reason Johann Konrad Wilhelm Loehe has strongly defended the Lutheran confessional identity and his subsequent resistance to unionism of the Protestant churches in Germany and..."

Manfred's attention ebbed and, unexpectedly, a particular memory of that terrible day, grotesquely distorted by the passage of eight years, flooded into the darkness and filled his conscious mind with chaotic light:

Manfred Herrmann looms over the prostate body of a young boy, serenely pale from loss of blood. Caustic black smoke swirls around the scene, stinging his eyes and searing his skin. The steady din of rifle and cannon fire shatters the air and pounds inside his ears. The orchard tree boughs drooping above tremble in the heat, then explode in flame and shower his back with glowing timber shards. Manfred brushes a burning chunk of wood off his shoulder and quickly returns to the task at hand. He lunges forward, and, as waves of intoxicating ecstasy convulse through his body, drives the deadly bayonet into the pale boy's slender neck. Surprisingly, the boy does not flinch. Manfred stomps hard on the boy's swollen belly with a muddy boot and the stomach explodes in a shower of rot and maggots. The maggots swarm up Manfred's leg and slowly devour the flesh below his knee. Manfred studies the exposed bone and tattered ligaments with dreamlike curiosity as the maggots swarm inexorably above his knee. He grips the rifle securely with both hands and when he pulls the bayonet, now oozing with lumpy smears of coagulated blood, from the lifeless body the boy's delicate lips open and a monstrous sucking noise rattles from deep inside the cruelly punctured throat. Then, unexpectedly, the pale boy lifts his head from a pool of voracious maggots and looks up at Manfred. When Manfred probes the vacant, lifeless eyes, the pale boy asks the same question he has already asked a thousand times: "Manfred Herrmann, why have you killed me again? I am already dead."

After a leisurely stroll from the alter down the center aisle of the sanctuary, Professor Strathmore arrived at Manfred's pew. "And then we come to the third dimension, one I find very interesting, that Loehe's ecclesial theology is *liturgical*. What this means, is ..." he placed his fist on the back of the pew, "... but why don't we allow Mr. Herrmann the opportunity to explain Loehe's third dimension since he appears to be deep in thought on the subject. Mr. Herrmann, would you care to join the discussion and offer your opinion?"

Manfred opened his eyes and the horrific image of the pale boy retreated to the veiled depths of his unsettled mind where it thrived in ominous secrecy. He knew the ghastly dream would return at a time of its own choosing, but he had other worries at the moment. Manfred shifted toward Professor Strathmore and casually crossed his legs. "What do you care to know about Loehe's third dimension?"

The question briefly disrupted Professor Strathmore's clumsy attempt to catch Manfred sleeping in his class. "That ... is not the point, Mr. Herrmann."

"Then what is the point?"

"The point is, I do not tolerate students sleeping in my class. Especially students who should be capable of demonstrating more discipline."

Manfred rested is arm on the back of the pew. "I agree. But then my question remains as originally stated. What do you care to know of Loehe's third dimension?"

Professor Strathmore sputtered, "Alright then. Since you were listening to the lecture so intently, why don't you take a few minutes to summarize the lesson thus far?"

Manfred stood, clasped his hands in front of his chest just below his chin, and closed his eyes in prayer. When he had finished, he opened his eyes, folded his hands behind his back, and commenced his summary. "The ecclesial theology of Johann Konrad Wilhelm Loehe, born in the year 1808 and now serving as the village pastor of Neuendettelsau in Bavaria, can be organized into distinct dimensions or aspects, of which the following five are the most significant: pietism, confessionalism, liturgical renewal, *diakonia,* and mission. One might ask, what does this mean to us as Christians? Let me offer the following outline of each of the five dimensions before I delve into a more detailed explanation. Firstly, Loehe's ecclesial theology is *pietistic.* Which is to say, his pursuit of the pious life has underpinned his relentless interest in mission work, and has given him—as you so eloquently noted, Professor Strathmore—a profound sense of the living God's activities in our day-to-day existence. Secondly, Loehe's ecclesial theology is *confessional.* He has always promoted the Lutheran confessional identity, and has therefore resisted pressures in Germany to reunify the Lutheran and Reformed. Thirdly, Loehe's ecclesial theology is *liturgical.* In fact, Loehe's scholarly study of the liturgical traditions of the early church have became the basis for the liturgical order used here in America, as well as in some parts of Germany. Fourthly, Loehe's ecclesial theology is *diaconal.* Because of this dimension, he has taken a lead role in founding a deaconess order in Germany. This vital work can be further attributed to—"

Professor Strathmore interrupted. "Manfred . . . enough."

Manfred dropped his hands to his sides. "But I am not finished yet. In fact, I have much more to say about Wilhelm Loehe."

"I know you have much more to say on the subject, probably more than any of us cares to hear, but by advancing beyond today's lesson you have failed to convince me you were not sleeping in my class."

Manfred scrunched his face in disbelief. "I assure you…I was not sleeping. I had merely closed my eyes to allow me to listen more intensely to your lecture of Loehe's courage to denounce sin without fear, to speak plainly like the prophets of old, and to live the consistently pious life."

Professor Strathmore smiled. "Regrettably, I believe you. See me in my office after class. I have something important to discuss with you."

Manfred Herrmann sat uncomfortably—just as he preferred—in the armless-hard-backed Quaker chair across from the simple unadorned table Professor Strathmore used for an office desk. Professor Strathmore peeked through narrow reading glasses as he organized several files of loose papers. He began the discussion without looking up. "I picked up the chair you are sitting on during a missionary trip to Pennsylvania. What do you think of it?"

Manfred ran his hands along the smooth edges of the hardwood seat. "Very simple and useful. I like it."

Professor Strathmore removed his glasses. "Yes, I imagine the simplicity of the design does appeal to you. Manfred, I worry about you at times."

Manfred appeared surprised by this remark and quickly crossed his arms in front of his chest. "You worry about me? Why?"

"Yes, I do. I worry about your intensity. I have never met anyone who is so intensely devoted to the Lutheran Church. Frankly, it scares me at times."

Manfred relaxed. "I thought you brought me here to chastise me for sleeping in your class."

Professor Strathmore tapped the table. "No, of course not. I knew you were not sleeping today. I merely had a bit of fun with you. Evidently, you did not appreciate the joke."

"Evidently, I did not. You played your role perfectly when—"

"Manfred…"

"Yes, Professor?"

"You never get the joke. This is why I worry about you. It's fine to be devoted to your faith, but one can be devoted to the point of missing the point."

This comment did not sit well with Manfred. "Miss the point? And what, then, is the point?"

Professor Strathmore sighed. "The point is... it is not a requirement for you to always be in a state of suffering. Yes, there is a time and place to suffer, but God wants you to enjoy life too."

Manfred thought of the pale boy hidden away in the gloom of his darkest thoughts, waiting, waiting, waiting, always waiting.... "It is difficult for me—to find much joy in life. I do not see life as an experience to be enjoyed, but rather as an opportunity to atone for my sins, to constantly pursue the pious life, and to—"

"Manfred, calm yourself."

"Calm myself?"

"Yes, calm yourself. We are all sinners. You are not the only one who sins."

"Yes, I appreciate this. But there are sins, and then there are sins. I believe, without a shred of uncertainly, that some sins will lead us to everlasting suffering and regret until the very day we perish from this earthly life."

Professor Strathmore grunted. "Very poetic, but also utter nonsense."

"Nonsense? Why?"

Professor Strathmore shrugged. "Let me give you some examples. Have you ever worshipped something above God? Money, for example. A very common sin."

Manfred tilted his head and considered the question. "Yes I have."

"Was it money?"

"I'd rather not say."

"Never mind then. I have committed this sin too—as recently as last week—and it was money. I find this a particular weakness. That's why I suggested it. But let's move on to another example. Have you ever used the name of the Lord in vain? I stepped on a nail last year and drove the darn thing clear through my foot. I misused the name of the Lord repeatedly over a period of several minutes. Fortunately, there was no one close enough to hear it."

Manfred slouched in the Quaker chair. "Yes, I have sworn too."

"Good. Then we are even on this account as well. Have you ever failed to remember the Sabbath? You know, to keep it holy?"

Manfred slouched a little more in the hard-backed chair until his heels rose off the floor. "I must confess to you: I have."

"Do not worry about confessing to me. Confession is for the Catholics. You can confess directly to the Lord. I skipped church and went fishing once." Professor Strathmore pressed his hands together as if in prayer. "Actually twice, maybe three times. I cannot remember for sure. But the point is, we have both committed this sin. Have you spoken ill of your mother or father, or sassed them when you were young, or anything of the sort?"

Manfred scrunched his face. "Of course I have. Who hasn't?"

"My point exactly. How about adultery? I assume you haven't committed actual adultery, per se, but have you ever thought about committing it? Thinking about it is just as bad, you know."

Manfred straightened up in the armless chair and pressed his knees together. "I have thought about it, many times. I just thought about it a second ago when you asked the question. I couldn't help it."

"There you go. I have thought about it too, so we have again sinned equally. Well then, have you ever stolen anything? Maybe as a child you took something from the general—"

Manfred interrupted, "You skipped one."

"I skipped one?"

"Yes. You skipped the fifth commandment: Thou shall not murder."

Professor Strathmore rocked in his chair. "Of course I skipped it. I didn't imagine it was relevant to our discussion."

"It is completely relevant."

"Why, have you thought about murdering someone?"

"Only in a dream. Actually, more of a nightmare."

"Then why is this relevant?"

"I have actually murdered."

Professor Strathmore frowned his surprise. "You murdered someone? Who did you murder?"

Manfred looked down at a spot just in front of his toes. "I murdered fourteen men, maybe more, all in the same day."

Professor Strathmore's frown turned suspicious. "In the same day? How could you possibly know how many you killed?"

Manfred did not look up. "Because I counted the ones I killed with my bayonet. I may have killed others when we fired into the advancing soldiers, but I could not see them."

"You counted them? Why?"

"Because after I killed the first one, a young boy who I still see in my nightmares, it became a sort of game to me."

"A game?"

"Yes, a game." Manfred appeared to drift away for a moment. "This is why I spoke of everlasting regret. You see, I am convinced that I would enjoy the game today just as much as I did on the battlefields of Shiloh eight years ago. I am not free from the sin. I have only learned to control it."

Professor Strathmore pushed away from the table and twined his fingers together against his mouth. "Manfred, I have decided on some important mission work for you, and I hope you will accept it."

Manfred lifted his chin. "Mission work? I would be honored, but I'm confident you can find someone more worthy in the seminary. There are many fine candidates."

Professor Strathmore lowered his hands without untangling his fingers. "I have thought about it for a long time, and today's discussion convinces me even more that sending you is the right choice."

"I will do whatever you ask."

"Good, then I will send you to Silver City."

"Silver City? I've never heard of it."

"Yes, Silver City. You'll find it in the Idaho Territory,* somewhere in the south near the Oregon border. We'll find someone who can draw you a map before you leave."

"A map would be comforting."

"I'm sending you to start a Lutheran mission church in Silver City. The Catholics are already there, and I doubt there are any Lutherans. Think you're up to it?"

"Do you?"

After breathing deeply, Professor Strathmore answered, "Yes, I do," then he clarified, "I really do." And then he grinned. "But first, I'm sending you to Chicago."

"Chicago? Why Chicago? It's in the wrong direction."

---

* President Abraham Lincoln signed the act that established the Idaho Territory in 1863. The new territory was created from portions of the Washington and Dakota Territories, and Lewiston became the first capital. The modern boundaries were set in 1868, and Idaho was admitted as a state in 1890.

Professor Strathmore pointed an index finger at Manfred. "To spend a few days in a civilized city before you head west. There are also many good German Lutherans in Chicago. I will arrange for you to meet a few of them while you're there. You should find it educational. It may even improve your sense of humor. Pack your things. You leave tomorrow."

"Tomorrow?"

"Yes, tomorrow. I shall pray for a memorable trip."

Chapter Twelve

Boston, Massachusetts
July 1870

A three o'clock appointment with a prospective client now imminent, and his interest in the afternoon's work flagging because of the stuffy dampness of the air, Csongor Toth swiveled in his chair, stood, took two steps, and raised the lower section of the only operable window in his office. Although small in area and consisting of one room and a tiny storage closet, the office did command exceptional views of the city from its position just beneath the stone-corniced roof of the Revere Bank building. He leaned precariously over the hand-hewn granite window sill until he could view the intersection of Franklin and Devonshire Streets five stories below. A small wagon pulled by a single horse had stopped in front of the main entry doors, but from his angle and distance he could not determine the purpose of the oddly-shaped materials and equipment strewn across the wagon bed. The horse kicked at the ground and a small wisp of dirt puffed into the air. When he turned his head and gazed along the street he could more clearly hear the squawking gulls and smell the ocean salt of Boston Harbor to the east. An unpleasant rush of warm, humid air drifted across his face, and he decided to close the window and return to the relative coolness of his office. A mantle clock chimed three times, signaling the arrival of the client for which he had only partially prepared. *Not to worry,* he thought to himself. Although he had not organized for the meeting in his usual manner, he had prepared sufficiently to carry on any likely conversation with acceptable verve and confidence, qualities which occasionally penetrated his otherwise impenetrable personality. Seconds after the third chime of the clock, a confident fist knocked at the frosted glass of the office door. The brass hinges squealed for lack of oil. A finely-dressed businessman strode assertively into the small office, his polished shoes tapping percussively on the marble floor.

Csongor pushed away from the window and pranced around the desk until he had closed the distance with his prospective client. He held out his hand and greeted the man with a faintly British accent tempered with a subtle hint of Hungarian. "Mr. Brewster I presume. It is my pleasure to finally meet you in person."

Not fond of lawyers, but appreciating their occasional necessity, Meredith Brewster grasped Csongor Toth's outstretched hand with both suspicion and vigor. "Mr. Toth. Sorry I'm late. I had important business to conclude at the mercantile and could not have arrived any sooner."

Csongor did not belie his excitement over a potentially lucrative contract. "Not to worry, Mr. Brewster. In any event, by my accounting you are only late by a few seconds."

Meredith Brewster grunted. "Yes, but late nonetheless. In my line of work, punctuality is the primary virtue of a successful businessman."

Csongor motioned Meredith Brewster to a leather seat with curved armrests. "Just so. Then shall we waste no more time and get to the point of our meeting?"

"I agree." Meredith Brewster removed his felt bowler and perfectly fitting leather gloves before sitting in the chair.

"Then what business brings us together on this fine Tuesday afternoon?"

"I will discuss it in due time, Mr. Toth. But first, I want you to understand something: I am not fond of lawyers, and I am not fond at all of the law, especially when it gets in the way of my business. I find lawyers, even in the best of circumstances, a necessary evil. In fact, I have fired the last two for incompetence and other professional indiscretions. I am telling this to you because I want no misunderstandings between us from the very beginning. I have only approached you because a business associate has spoken highly of your work, and, unfortunately, I have need of legal services at the moment. If this were not the case, I would not bother to speak to you."

Csongor listened to Mr. Brewster's remarks with intense fascination. He pressed his fingers together just below his chin. "All well and good, Mr. Brewster. Your philosophy of lawyers and the law does not concern me in the slightest. Shall we move on to the point of our meeting?"

Meredith smiled coolly. "Not quite yet, Mr. Toth. You may have received a good recommendation from my business associate, but I still want to hear of your background for myself. I must also have full confidence that whatever I say will remain between the two of us and go no further."

Csongor flexed his fingers, but otherwise did not move in the chair. "Might I assume that one or more of your previous lawyers has violated this latter precept?"

Meredith frowned. "Precept?"

Csongor leaned forward a little. "Did one of your lawyers share confidential information with someone else?"

Meredith coughed against the back of his hand. "Yes. In fact, both of my previous attorneys failed on this account." He also leaned forward in his chair. "Can I assume you will not fail me on this ... precept?"

Csongor relaxed. "You have nothing to worry about, Mr. Brewster. Nothing you say to me will go beyond this room. Nothing."

Meredith Brewster relaxed. "Good. Then before we discuss the reason I have come to your office, I would appreciate some knowledge of your background. I have not yet decided if you are the right man for the job."

Csongor lowered his hands and comfortably intertwined his fingers. "Certainly. I would ask the same if I were in your position. There is not much to tell, really. My parents are Hungarian. I was educated at the Royal Hungarian University School of Law in Budapest. When I left Budapest I ranked first in my class. I speak three languages fluently, including my parents' tongue and German. You can judge for yourself my fluency in English. I have also achieved modest proficiency in French, but I rarely have the opportunity to practice these days. I am independently wealthy and have no need of this occupation other than to provide a dash of light entertainment. I therefore cannot be influenced in any way by the offer of money. I am not afraid of confrontation, either intellectual or physical. And most importantly, I am absolutely ruthless when it comes to protecting the interests of my clients. Do you need to know more?"

Meredith nodded approvingly. "No, Mr. Toth. I've heard enough. I believe you are the right man for the job. Shall we begin?"

"Please."

"I have need of a new will. Because of certain events in my life, my current will is unacceptable."

"Simple enough, but any lawyer can prepare a will for you. Why do you seek my particular services for such a straightforward task?"

"You may not think so after I explain what I want."

"Then please proceed, and we shall see."

Surprisingly, Meredith abruptly stood and began pacing. The size of the office prevented him from wandering too far from the front of Csongor's desk. "My current will leaves everything to my wife. I wish to make a change. Due to certain events of the last few years, Eva is unstable and cannot be trusted with such wealth. I therefore wish to leave control of my entire estate to my only son, Jonathan. Do you see any problems with my idea?"

Csongor deliberated while Meredith paced the length of the desk twice. "Given the existence of the current will, and this sudden change in perspective, your wife could contest the new will. How old is your son?"

Meredith returned to the chair just as abruptly as he had left it. "Jonathan is twenty-two. "

"Is he of sound mind and body? And, more importantly, will he be more trustworthy than your wife with such … wealth?"

Meredith gazed through the window behind Csongor's desk. "He is a vindictive little cuss, if you want the honest truth, and lazy when it comes to hard work, but otherwise very capable, and under the circumstances I want him to control the estate, not Eva. I have lost all confidence in her ability to make any decisions, let alone good ones."

"Then I would have no problem writing a new will for you, one which should achieve your purpose and also survive any legal challenges by your wife. It would be wise then to establish her instability in fact. Perhaps you should invite me to your home, where I may personally witness said instability. This would also enhance my credibility at a later date should I be asked to attest to the fact that I have met your wife and that she is unfit to manage your estate."

"Good. This is the kind of advice I needed. My business partner told the truth when he said you were ruthless."

Csongor did not take offense. "Then it appears I did not need to waste your time informing you of the fact."

"Can you come to the house Friday morning, say around ten?"

"Certainly. And you live on Linden Place in Brookline?"

"Yes. How did you know where I live?"

Csongor stood and quietly wheeled the banker's chair back. "It appears, Mr. Brewster, that you are not the only one who prepared for this meeting."

The small town of Brookline.* Hills billowing like deep ocean waves, verdant green, speckled with tranquil groves of ancient trees. To the southeast a pristine brook meandering, gurgling along mossy shores overhanging smooth rocks. Gracious streets lined with mature overhanging trees and trimmed with neatly cut and fitted stone curbs and brightly whitewashed wood-framed and stone-capped fences. Elegant homes of Greek revival and Colonial revival and Gothic revival and Victorian Gothic and Shingle style and mansard style and brick and stone and wood. Porches and verandas and porticos in front and to the sides and around back, cool in the fragrant afternoon breezes flowing between Greek Doric and Roman Tuscan columns. Churches of stone and glass and copper and wood and brick, Romanesque and Gothic spires shooting into blue skies and visible from the hazy outlying hills. A village park, a primary school, a library, a high school, a bank, a town hall, a general store, a cemetery. To the west the Brookline Station with sun-gleamed polished tracks twisting serpentine through the town before veering smoothly east and west. And the Lindens area of Brookline, a planned community in the very center of the town, pastoral, idyllic, vaguely aristocratic, for those of sufficient means who wished to escape the increasingly overcrowded environs of Boston, but close enough to offer the possibility of a pleasurable carriage ride home after a long day of toil in the city.

---

* Brookline is located approximately four miles westerly of downtown Boston. The Lindens area was the earliest planned development of Brookline, with construction of the first homes beginning in 1843.

In the clammy heat of a summer morning, Gordania Sinclair felt unpleasant rivulets of sweat stream down her athletic legs as she rushed beneath the spreading trees along Linden Place in pursuit of two small girls. When she sighted her employer's home—a whitewashed Greek Revival structure with comfortably-shaded porches and rows of fluted columns along each side—she noticed an elegant black carriage with black horse and white-gloved-black-suited driver waiting patiently in the street. The girls slowed their pace and headed toward the horse, ostensibly to touch its tail and pet its belly, but Gordania deftly ushered them away from the menacing animal and then past the carriage without greeting the driver. She maneuvered the girls into a narrow but charmingly-landscaped lane separating the adjacent property and leading to the main entry at the southeastern side of the elegant home. A Mourning Dove—concealed by the speckled sunlight and leafy branches of an English elm (planted years ago in the front yard by the previous owner)—issued a melancholy *cooOOoo-woo-woo-woooo* before flutter-whistling into the air and streaking overhead. Gordania watched the nimble bird vanish beyond the guttered roof eave of the second story. She gently tugged the sleeve of the younger girl and directed her up three wood steps across the line of a sharply-edged shadow cast by the sun approaching its noon azimuth.

The older girl, nearly ten and named Bethany by her father, pointed to the sky. "Was that a baby owl, Miss Sinclair?"

Gordania reposed in the shade of the porch. "I only saw it briefly, but from the sound of it I believe it was a Mourning Dove."

The younger girl, nearly seven and named Bathsheba by her father, jumped and clapped her hands. "Is that the bird's name because it flies early in the morning?"

Gordania smiled. "No, my precious dear. The bird's name is spelled M-O-U-R-N-I-N-G as in a great sadness, not as in the part of the day before noon. I would assume the name comes from the bird's mournful song."

Bethany defended her earlier assertion. "It sounded like a baby owl to me, Miss Sinclair."

Gordania replied with the now familiar lilt of Dunnet Head. "Yes, it did have the sound of an owl about it, but I don't think you'll be hearing any owls at this time of the day, especially baby ones." She kneeled down and caressed each girl's arm. "But let's not dawdle on the porch. Your father and mother will be wondering where we've gone to. We should hurry inside the house to let them know we have arrived safely."

Bathsheba jumped and clapped again. "Yes, and there will be lunch."

Gordania rotated the polished brass lever on the heavy wood door (inlaid with colorful stained glass) and opened it wide. "Yes, there will be lunch. And then maybe a nap too, before our afternoon adventure."

Bethany toddled backwards into the marble-floored entry foyer. "A trip to the river to look for tadpoles?"

Bathsheba turned and backed into the house in step with her older sister. "Please, Miss Sinclair. We love to look for tadpoles. Can we go to the river after our nap? Can we?"

Gordania followed the rearward-marching girls into the house. "We shall see. But first I must speak with your father to see if *he* has any afternoon plans for the two of you. Then we shall think about organizing an expedition to hunt for tadpoles." She shepherded the girls, still marching backwards, into the kitchen where Miss Johnson, a former slave from Virginia but now a cook and housekeeper of the Brewster family, had nearly finished preparing a wholesome lunch.

Miss Johnson, busily cutting an apple into neat slices, ceased her work when she heard the girls stumble backwards into the kitchen. "Why, Bethany and Bathsheba, you have come back from your morning walk with nanny, and just in time for lunch, too."

Gordania waved. "Thank you Miss Johnson. I will take the girls upstairs for a nap after they have finished lunch."

"There's lunch for you too, Miss Sinclair." Miss Johnson set her hands on her full hips and glared sternly at Bethany and Bathsheba. "Have you two washed your hands? From the look of your dirty little faces, I would guess not."

Bethany and Bathsheba answered in near unison. "No Miss Johnson." Then Bethany explained, "We've been playing tag and looking for squirrels in the park down by the corner with Miss Sinclair."

Miss Johnson calmed her face. "What you do with Miss Sinclair is none of my business. Now off with you. And do not return to this kitchen until you have washed."

After the girls ran by, Gordania folded her hands at the front of her plain white dress. "Thank you for the offer of lunch, Miss Johnson, but I must first speak to Mr. Brewster about his plans for the afternoon. He may wish to take the girls out himself after their nap."

Miss Johnson chuckled. "You can ask him, but he's been talking to some fancy-dressed lawyer in the parlor for most of the morning. I'm thinking he has other plans this afternoon."

Gordania curled her slender upper lip. "What you suggest may be true, Miss Johnson, but I still have the obligation to ask him of his plans."

Miss Johnson grinned. "You can ask him, but I'd bet money his answer will be the same as it always is."

Gordania nodded and said, "Thank you for the advice, Miss Johnson, but I must ask, nonetheless."

Miss Johnson waved a sharp paring knife in the air and offered some final words of encouragement before Gordania opened the door to the foyer. "Good luck, Miss Sinclair."

Gordania discovered Mrs. Eva Corrine Brewster standing at the base of the stairs when she walked across the foyer to the parlor doors. She bowed her head. "Good afternoon Mrs. Brewster. I was just about to ask Mr. Brewster of his plans for the afternoon. I thought he might want to take the girls out after their nap."

Eva spoke with a hint of cynicism in her voice. "Yes, of course Miss Sinclair. But please knock before you enter the parlor. He may not want to be interrupted from his obviously important meeting with his new attorney. This is the second time he has visited our home in the last week, and unfortunately my husband has not shared with me the purpose of his business."

Gordania nodded again. "Thank you Mrs. Brewster. I shall take your advice." She tapped three times on one of the acid-etched glass panes inlaid into the carved frame of the right door leaf.

A few seconds passed, and then Meredith Brewster's baritone voice boomed from the room. "Yes, yes. Come in. Come in."

Gordania breathed deeply, opened the door, and stepped into the parlor. "Mr. Brewster, I am truly sorry for interrupting you, but I must speak with you about your afternoon plans, and if you care to take the girls out after their nap."

Meredith Brewster smiled broadly when Gordania entered the room instead of his tedious wife of twenty-three years. "No reason to apologize, Miss Sinclair. Please come in. I'd like you to meet someone."

Gordania advanced into the room until she could see the top of a man's head above the back of an upholstered Victorian chair. The man stood and slowly revolved.

"Gordania, this is Mr. Csongor Toth, my new attorney. He has kindly brought some important documents for my signature. Mr. Toth, this is our lovely and talented governess, Gordania Sinclair."

Gordania froze. Csongor bowed as if nothing was amiss. "Miss Sinclair. I am delighted to meet you. Mr. Brewster has already spoken of the excellent work you do with his youngest children."

Uncharacteristically, Gordania stammered her surprise. "W... Why... M... Mr. Toth. I merely take pride in doing a job well."

Delighted to have shocked and confused Gordania, Csongor smiled—an affectation which did not feel normal. "Yes, Miss Sinclair. I imagine you do." He produced a business card and placed it in Gordania's hand. "If you should ever need legal services, Miss Sinclair, here is my card. You can find my office in the Revere Bank building at the corner of Franklin and Devonshire in downtown Boston. I'm on the top floor."

Gordania held the white business card up and reviewed the perfectly centered printing:

Csongor Toth, Esquire
Revere Bank Building
Boston, Massachusetts

"Why, thank you Mr. Toth, but I doubt I shall ever require legal services, especially when one considers—"

Meredith Brewster interrupted, "Enough, Mr. Toth. You cannot have her. Now, Miss Sinclair, as to the afternoon... I have important business in town and will be gone until late tonight. I plan to dine with a company associate and then return on the nine o'clock train. If you don't mind, Miss Sinclair, would you please tell my wife of my plans? I shall be leaving straightaway and it is unlikely I will have the chance to speak with her."

Gordania bent her knees slightly and bowed her head. "Yes, Mr. Brewster. I shall tell her of your plans for the evening."

"Thank you. Now, Mr. Toth and I have a few more items of business to discuss. If you don't mind, Miss Sinclair...."

Gordania did not react immediately, but instead appeared surprised and confused again. "Yes, Mr. Brewster. Of course. I shall go enjoy lunch in the kitchen and then take the girls upstairs for their afternoon nap."

Csongor bowed decisively. "Good bye, Miss Sinclair. It was a pleasure meeting you."

"Goodbye, Mr. Toth." Gordania glided out of the parlor and closed the French door with a faint click. She did not find Eva Corrine Brewster in the foyer, and she did not find her in the kitchen when she joined the girls and Miss Johnson for lunch. After Gordania had taken Bethany and Bathsheba upstairs for their afternoon nap, she stopped at the door to the master bedroom. She raised her hand to knock, but hesitated when she heard Eva sobbing.

Chapter Thirteen

Fort Laramie, Wyoming Territory
Late March 1871

Riding the feisty appaloosa west on the Oregon Trail, Joshua Hotah fidgeted in the wind-scoured saddle he had purchased in Lincoln, Nebraska, and considered his four years of wandering since leaving Fort Wallace. Sensing a subtle tension on the reins, the appaloosa slowed, and then feeling a slight tug to the right, she swung around to the east. Consumed by a fleeting remembrance of the unexpected handshake and authentic claims of friendship from Captain Ethan Plantagenet, the better part of a minute passed before Joshua noticed that the late afternoon sun now warmed his back instead of his face. His dreamy thoughts evaporated, and he reached down and stroked the appaloosa's short mane. "You are a fine horse—the finest I have ever known—but you should not believe everything I tell you. What if I had fallen asleep in the saddle? We might have gone the wrong direction many miles before finding out. And then we could be lost, too." Joshua pulled on the reins. The appaloosa twirled smoothly and continued west. "But I should not forget the time when I slept so soundly I fell from the saddle. It is to your credit that you waited for me and did not run away."

A rifle shot echoed beyond a grassy hillock some distance to the north. Joshua pulled the reins and the appaloosa stopped. After a short wait, a second shot crackled the tranquil air. Joshua listened until the echoes had faded into the flowing prairie grasses. "I know the sound of the rifle. I have heard it before. We should ride to the sound and meet the one who owns it." The appaloosa glanced back at Joshua and snorted. "Yes, then we are in agreement." Joshua nudged the appaloosa and she galloped off the trail to the north. The appaloosa raced a thousand feet up the southern slope of the grassy hillock and plunged over the smooth crest. Another thousand feet to the north, a magnificent herd of buffalo stretched east and west far beyond the boundary of Joshua's vision. A third shot reverberated, and Joshua's head snapped to the visage of a lone man sitting south of the milling herd, about 400 feet away. Joshua slowed the appaloosa to an easy walking gait. He bent down and whispered into the animal's peaked ear, "Do not be afraid, my spirited companion. It is only a buffalo hunter. I'm sure he has no interest in horses such as you."

Joshua and the appaloosa trotted up to the buffalo hunter until they stood ten feet behind him. The appaloosa whinnied stridently, spooking the nearest cluster of buffalos. The frightened buffalos began scattering in different directions. Panic soon rolled through the herd, and the agitated animals stampeded. The buffalo hunter hurriedly loaded another round in an effort to take one more animal, but the agitated herd erupted into a full run and veered to the northeast away from his position. The man released his finger from the double-set trigger of the Sharps. He lowered the buffalo rifle and scooted around on his butt to see who had ruined his afternoon of hunting. Then he scooted up to his knees and stood, the rifle dangling in his right hand.

"Who the hell are you, and what on God's green earth are you doing out here?"

Joshua studied the stocky man who now confronted him. He perused the wide-brimmed-round-topped-gray-felt hat with a chunk of buffalo hide and a feather tied to the rear of the brim with a knotted length of leather. He eyed the man's flowing brown beard, which someone had apparently trimmed with a dull knife. He examined the man's dark-red shirt with a ragged tear near the collar. He inspected the man's leather chaps with uneven rows of leather fringe clumped together in three places with dried mud. He scrutinized the man's leather boots, covered in buffalo dung. "My name is Joshua Hotah. I am searching for my parents."

The buffalo hunter noted Joshua's gentle features, bronze complexion, and dusty black hair tied into a ponytail at the back. He also noticed the moccasins and the dark blue uniform shirt of the U.S. Cavalry with the gold buttons missing. "What the hell are you? Some kind of half-breed Indian scout, or something?"

Joshua answered flatly, "My mother is Lakota Sioux. My father is English, and a buffalo hunter like you. I was a U.S. Cavalry scout for two years. I am finished now."

The buffalo hunter grunted. "English, huh. And an Indian squaw for a mother. And somehow they got together out here on the damn prairie and made you? Hard to believe."

"What do you mean?"

The buffalo hunter ignored Joshua and nestled his rifle down on a leather scabbard. He fingered a booger from his nose and flicked it in the general direction of the disappearing heard, then tromped up to Joshua until close enough to give the appaloosa a kiss. "Your damn horse needs to learn a few manners. I've been tracking that heard for three days, and when I finally get them in my sights I only bag three animals before they panicked. That's only one buffalo a day by my reckoning. Now I've got to chase after the damn varmints all over again."

Joshua refused to apologize for the appaloosa. "Speaking of manners, what is your name? I did not hear you mention of it."

"My name? Why sure. My name's John Runyan. And like you already observed, I'm a buffalo hunter by trade. But I don't plan to do this my entire life. I've got bigger plans once I make my fortune."

A little more relaxed, Joshua set his hands on the saddle horn and shifted in the saddle. "Bigger plans? Like what?"

John Runyan grinned, exposing teeth stained from nearly constant use of chewing tobacco. "Bigger plans! Like moving to California and finding a nice place on the ocean. I've been told by someone who's seen it that the Pacific Ocean is beautiful and you can't help but stare at it until your eyes are sore from the looking."

"The Pacific Ocean? I do not know of it."

John Runyan slapped his thigh. "It's easy to find, my boy. Just head due west and you can't help but run into it. It's big—bigger than you've ever seen."

Joshua Hotah leaned back. "I was heading west on my way to Fort Laramie before I heard the shot. I should like to see it someday."

John Runyan pulled at his beard. "Fort Laramie? Now that you mention it, I might head there myself."

"Then you know how far it is? I am low on cartridges for my Henry. A man in a wagon told me I could buy some at Fort Laramie."

"Not more than 10 miles, my boy. And you can buy them bullets and anything else you might be wanting at the Sutler's Store. We can get there before the sun sets if we hurry. Give me a hand skinning these measly three buffalo and loading the wagon and we can get there sooner. Thanks to your horse it's turning out to be a more relaxing day than I expected."

"You can butcher three buffalo in such a small time?"

John Runyan looked up at the cloud-speckled sky and cackled. "There's no market for the meat worth the effort. I can get over two dollars a hide from a seller at Fort Laramie, maybe three if the hides are clear."

"You leave the meat to rot on the ground?"

"You've got the idea, my boy. It's the only way to make any decent money in this trade. Three is nothing. Why, I've left over 200 carcasses rotting on the ground on a good day. Now let's get cracking. Time's a wasting."

"I thought you said you had to chase after the heard again?"

"I did. But when you mentioned Fort Laramie, I changed my mind. I've got a certain whore I want to check on before the night's over."

"You can find a whore at this Sutler's Store?"

John Runyan spoke with renewed excitement as he slid the buffalo rifle into the leather scabbard. "Probably can, although I've never tried at that particular mercantile. No, my boy. After we buy you some bullets at Sutler's Store, we're heading to the Three-Mile Hog Ranch.* And I've got a whore in mind for you too. I think she's just the one for a half-breed like yourself."

"A whore for me?"

"Yes, my boy. I can tell you are in desperate need of a whore by the sorry look of you."

---

* The Three-Mile Hog Ranch was established by local entrepreneurs Jules Ecoffey and Adolph Cuny in 1873 as a "social center" for the soldiers of Fort Laramie. I have fictionalized its establishment prior to 1871 for the purposes of this story. Initially a trading post and saloon, it soon became notorious for excessive drinking, gambling, and prostitution. The ranch is now listed on the National Register of Historic Places.

Joshua squirmed in the saddle and the appaloosa shivered. "I don't know. I've never slept with a woman before. What is her name?"

John Runyan gathered up two bandoleers of bullets, a dented canteen, and a frayed woolen blanket before speaking with a tinge of disgust in his voice. "You don't sleep with a whore, unless you're willing to pay a lot of money for absolutely nothing. Her name's Martha Canary, and she's just the one for the likes of you."

John Runyan tugged the brim of his hat down to shade his eyes from the sun. He clicked his tongue and snapped the leather reins to encourage the pair of horses pulling his wagon—now loaded with a paltry three buffalo hides and one forlorn buffalo tongue—to a brisker pace. Joshua Hotah heel-tapped the appaloosa and accelerated until he drew even with John Runyan. One of the wheels bounced over a sun-hardened wagon rut then got all tangled up in some prairie grass before jerking a big clod out of the ground.

Joshua Hotah yelled above the noise of the trudging horses and grinding wagon wheels. "How much more to Fort Laramie?"

John Runyan clicked his tongue again. "Just over the gentle rise up ahead. Nestled in a big loop of the Laramie River. Can't miss it... unless you're a damn fool."

Joshua cupped his hand around his ear. "Who is a damn fool?"

John Runyan shook the reins and grunted. "Never mind, ya damn fool."

The wagon shuddered up the trail to the top of the gentle rise, then momentarily slowed before pitching to the other side. The horses broke into an exuberant trot; the wagon rattled violently and John Runyan bounced comically on the wood seat. Without prompting, the nimble appaloosa jumped to a gallop and raced ahead of the wagon. Less than a mile away, the buildings and tents and roads of Fort Laramie spread from bank to bank of a looping bend in the Laramie River. In the center, a large parade ground rimmed with buildings and punctuated with two flagpoles. And in the distance, two long files of cavalry returning from patrol. The last flare of the sun settled below the smooth hills beyond the encampment and the sky turned pale red.

John Runyan, the Sharps buffalo rifle clamped in one hand and the forlorn buffalo tongue dangling from the other, threw open the heavy whitewashed-wood-door and stomped into Sutler's Store with practiced bravado. Joshua Hotah trailed closely behind, momentarily concealed by John Runyan's ample shadow. Two kerosene lamps suspended from the ceiling, one with a spherical frosted glass shade and one with a conical brass shade, flickered when the door slammed against the wall. Three soldiers drinking and playing cards at a small table in the narrow barroom ignored the commotion. A large buffalo head mounted on the wall at the far end of the barroom gawked into the somber distance. John Runyan glanced around the store, then strolled across the dusty wood-planked floor up to the long brown-stained wood counter stretched out in front of rows of wall-mounted shelves—festooned with cans, wash bowls and pitchers, china plates and cups, coffee pots, cast iron skillets, glass bottles filled with colorful liquids, brass buckets, empty glass jars, dark brown wood boxes with gold letters emblazoned on the sides, ceramic jugs, and all manner of unusual merchandise—and smacked the bloody tongue down next to a set of scales with brass weighing pans. He glared at the slender, bespectacled man standing behind the counter and shook the heavy buffalo rifle. "How much for this tongue? I've got three buffalo hides out in the wagon too. How much?"

The bespectacled man winced in horror at the monstrous tongue and the trade counter now splattered with glossy blobs of coagulated buffalo blood. "I just cleaned this counter, sir. No more than ten minutes ago. And now look at it."

John Runyan spat on the floor. "Damn nice counter. How much?"

The bespectacled man tilted his spectacles and sneered. "Give you two dollars each for the hides, and 25 cents for the tongue."

John Runyan recoiled at the offer. "25 cents? Why, I could get at least three dollars for this tongue at one of those restaurants where people dress up to eat."

The bespectacled man sneered a second time. "Then you should take it to one of those restaurants right now and sell it to them. I'll give you no more than 25 cents."

John Runyan pushed the tongue across the counter until it nearly touched the white sleeve of the bespectacled man. "Alright you good-for-nothing cheapskate of a scoundrel. I'll take the 25 cents, and the six dollars for the hides," then he nodded at Joshua, "and my friend here needs some rounds for his rifle. Got any?" Joshua peeked around John Runyan's shoulder.

The bespectacled man leaned to the right until he could see Joshua clearly in the light of one of the kerosene lamps. "We've got all kinds of ammunition here, but we don't sell to Indians."

John Runyan slammed his palms on the bloody counter and laughed. "He ain't no damn Indian. He's a damn half-breed. Can't ya tell by looking at him?"

"Don't matter what kind of breed he is. Still not going to sell him any ammunition."

John Runyan pulled at his beard. "Fine. Can you sell the ammunition to me?"

"I can sell it to you."

John Runyan barked at Joshua, "Get around here boy, and stand up here at this gentleman's fine counter, the one he just cleaned ten minutes ago." Joshua stepped up to the counter. "What kind of ammo you need, and how many rounds?"

Joshua scanned the shelves. "A hundred-and-twenty rounds. For my Henry."*

John Runyan shouted at the bespectacled man, "I need a hundred-and-twenty rounds for my Henry. You got 'em handy?"

The bespectacled man sneered a third time. "I don't like this. You're just going to give it to him. Same thing as selling it to him directly."

John Runyan slammed his fist on the counter and smeared some of the tongue blood. The card-playing soldiers ignored him again. "You have no idea what I'm going to do with it. Now, you going to sell me the damn ammunition or not?"

---

* The Henry repeating rifle used a .44 rimfire cartridge, had a capacity of 16 rounds, and was the precursor to the famous Winchester repeating rifle. The potential for rapid fire compensated for the maximum effective range of 200 yards.

The bespectacled man squirmed and rubbed the thinning hair on top of his head, but then relented. "It comes in boxes of fifty cartridges each. I'd have to break a box to sell you a hundred-and-twenty."

John Runyan spoke to Joshua without looking at him. "A hundred rounds enough?"

Joshua did not look at John Runyan either. "Yes, a hundred rounds will do."

John Runyan continued his pretense with the bespectacled man. "I'll take a hundred rounds so you don't have to go to all the damn trouble of breaking open a damn box."

The bespectacled man disappeared below the counter. When he reappeared, he dropped two boxes of .44 rimfire cartridges on the counter. "You owe two dollars and fifty cents."

John Runyan turned to Joshua. "You got two dollars and fifty cents?"

Joshua examined the boxes on the counter. "Pretty expensive, but I need the ammo."

John Runyan turned back to the bespectacled man. "Two dollars and fifty cents! That's highway robbery you worthless piece of crap. I can get a hundred rounds of this ammunition for less than two dollars in North Platte."

The bespectacled man sneered one last time. "Then I suggest you ride there to buy the ammunition. Shouldn't take you more than a week."

"Scoundrel!"

"Take it or leave it."

Joshua pushed two dollars and fifty cents across the counter. John Runyan snatched the money and shook it in an angry fist inches from the bespectacled man's nose. "Here's your damn money for this overpriced ammunition." He threw it down on the counter. He stacked the boxes then handed them to Joshua. "Let's get the hell out of this den of thieves, my boy. Time to head over to the Three-Mile Hog Ranch where they know how to treat a customer with hospitality." John Runyan stomped to the entry door, threw it open with a defiant slam, and stormed out. Joshua Hotah trailed closely behind, and nearly failed to avoid the slamming door. The card playing soldiers paid no attention.

True to his assertion of superior hospitality, three brightly-dressed ladies greeted John Runyan and Joshua Hotah when they burst through the front door of the one-story, U-shaped, lime-grout* building that housed the saloon at the Three-Mile Hog Ranch. And in stark counterpoint to the relatively sedate atmosphere of Sutler's Store, dozens of off-duty soldiers and men who likely were not soldiers and other prostitutes and a woman who did not much look like a whore filled the saloon with a muddled roar of incomprehensible conversation and laughter.

John Runyan swept his arm around the nearest woman and squeezed her against his side. "Daphne, my gal. Just the one I was looking for. Are you available? I just made a big haul with three buffalo hides and a tongue, and I'm celebrating."

Daphne, not unattractive but well into her thirties, pushed away from John Runyan. "Three hides? Why, it'll cost your entire take to spend the night with me."

John Runyan roared with laughter. "What can I get for a dollar? I have to save some for a little boozing and some cards."

"Is that all you think of me, John Runyan? One dollar? Why, I'm worth at least two."

Temporarily distracted, John Runyan did not hear Daphne's question. "Where the hell is Martha? I want her to meet a friend of mine." Joshua Hotah peeked out from behind John Runyan's ample form.

Daphne ogled Joshua Hotah. "You brought an Indian in here?"

John Runyan boomed, "How many times do I have to explain this? He's not a damn Indian. He's a damn half-breed. Now where's Martha? I want her to meet my half-breed friend here."

Daphne waved her hand. "She's standing over there, by the bar."

John Runyan's eyes flitted along the bar until they found Martha Canary. "Pretty as usual. C'mon Joshua. We've got some introducing to do." He grabbed a wad of Joshua's sleeve and pulled him across the crowded room bumping against the backs of chairs until they arrived at Martha's side. Without releasing Joshua's sleeve, John Runyan removed his feathered hat and bowed. "Martha Canary, I'd like you to meet Joshua Hotah, half-

---

* Lime-grout was used in the same manner as concrete.

breed and former scout with the damn U.S. Cavalry, but now he's looking for his parents and he don't work for them no more."

Martha Canary plucked a small cigar from her unpainted lips. She studied Joshua Hotah's black hair and bronze complexion, then scanned down to his moccasins. "Why's he looking for his parents?"

"How the hell do you expect me to know? We just met today. His damn horse spooked an entire herd of buffalos and left me nearly penniless. Why don't you ask him yourself?"

Martha Canary simpered, picked up a shot glass of whisky from the beer-glistened bar, and tossed the burning liquid back into her throat. She rattled the glass down and wiped her mouth. "Tell me, my dear... why are you looking for your parents?"

A quizzical expression flowed across Joshua's face. "I suppose... because... they are lost?"

Spewing spittle across the bar, John Runyan erupted into laughter and slapped Joshua hard on the back. "Now there's a hell of an answer, my boy. A hell of an answer."

Martha Canary sniggered, then reached up and brushed Joshua's hair. "Are you sure you're not the one who's lost?"

Joshua answered more forcibly this time. "I am not lost. I know where I am. I just do not know where I am going."

A young soldier with his shirt unbuttoned and sleeves rolled up jumped to his feet and threw a handful of cards down on a nearby table before screaming at the civilian sitting across the table from him, "Full house, jacks over eights. Beat that asshole!"

The commotion did not distract Martha Canary, and as she stared compassionately into Joshua's eyes and continued the conversation with soothing words, Joshua imagined an empty room with only the two of them standing alone at the bar. "Not exactly what I meant, my dear, but if it's how you see things, who am I to disagree with you. Who are your parents?"

Joshua relaxed a little. "They were lost when I was very young. But my mother is Lakota Sioux, and my father is a buffalo hunter from England."

Martha Canary stiffened. "A buffalo hunter from England with a Sioux wife?"

John Runyan shattered Joshua's reverie. "That's what he said, Martha. Ain't you listening?"

Martha Canary snapped at John Runyan. "Quiet, John. I'm trying to carry on a conversation with Joshua here, and I don't need any help from you to do it."

Joshua broke in. "Yes, a buffalo hunter from England with a Sioux wife."

Martha Canary touched Joshua's shoulder. "Joshua, I met them. I'd say less than two years ago, here at Fort Laramie."

Joshua sucked in a quick breath. "Do you know where they were going?"

Martha Canary tapped her head. "They did say where they were going, but I don't remember. Let me think. Think. Think . . . ."

John Runyan slurped a large mug of beer, which had suddenly appeared, then wiped his sleeve across his face. "C'mon, Martha, think."

She snapped at John Runyan again. "I *am* thinking John. Can't you see me tapping my head?"

"I can, but I don't know why tapping your head would help anyone think."

Martha Canary clutched the front of Joshua's blue cavalry shirt with both hands. "Oregon City. I remember now. English accent. Sioux wife. They were on their way to Oregon City. I'm sure of it."

Joshua pulled away. "Thank you, Miss Martha, but I have to leave now."

John Runyan slapped Joshua on the back again. "What are you talking about, my boy? You just got here, and the fun's about to start. I think Martha Canary likes you, and she looks to be available to boot!"

Joshua backed away. "Thank you, but I have to leave. Where is Oregon City?"

Martha Canary grinned. "Head west until you get to the end of the Oregon Trail. You can't miss it." She kissed her fingertips and touched Joshua's cheek.

John Runyan objected. "But it's night. You can't travel at night. You might run into some Indians or thieves."

"I have travelled many times at night. I do not mind it." John Runyan and Martha Canary did not offer another word as Joshua Hotah hurried out of the Three-Mile Hog Ranch saloon into the pellucid moonlight of a clearing sky.

Excerpt from

A Glorious History of the American West

by Muireall Anne Ravenscroft

The Buffalo Hunters

The buffalo hunters flourished in the American West during the years after the Civil War until around 1884. By this time the 50 million wild buffalo that had once roamed the Great Plains west of the Mississippi and east of the Rocky Mountains had disappeared forever and only a paltry remnant of no more than 2,000 animals remained.* Many complex and interconnected events aligned to create this horrific and unprecedented slaughter including a severe economic depression after the Civil War that drove men west to seek work as buffalo hunters and skinners; an increased demand for beef that prompted the expansion of cattle ranches into the Great Plains and created predictable conflicts with the nomadic Indians and migrating herds of buffalo; the establishment of numerous Army posts to protect the westward-migrating pioneers and the subsequent contracts to local hunters to provide buffalo meat for the soldiers; the growing demand in the east for buffalo coats for warmth and rugs for decoration; the use of buffalo hides for the manufacture of machine belts and the use of ground buffalo skulls and bones for fertilizer; completion of the First Transcontinental Railroad in 1869, which provided a viable and economic means of transporting large quantities of buffalo hides and bones; and, ultimately more ominous, a policy of the U.S. Army to intentionally eradicate the buffalo to remove the primary subsistence

* During my research I have discovered claims of anywhere from 25 to 60 million buffalo in existence prior to the Civil War, and as few as 300 remaining in 1884. I have therefore chosen the numbers 50 million and 2,000 as reasonable compromises.

food source of the Plains Indians thereby forcing ~~them~~ troublesome tribes onto reservations.[*]

The Plains Indians had hunted the buffalo for food, shelter (skin tipi covers), clothing, fuel (dried dung), weapons (shields and bow strings), tools, and other necessities for thousands of years before the arrival of the first Spanish explorers. This subsistence relationship between Indians and bison might have lasted indefinitely but for the introduction of the horse, the modern rifle, and an eastern market for buffalo hides. The horse and rifle allowed the Indians to kill the bison in greater quantities with far less effort. And with a new market for buffalo hides emerging in the 1820s, the decline of the seemingly countless buffalo that had roamed the Great Plains for millennia had commenced. The decline advanced steadily into the 1860s, and then dramatically increased in the years following the Civil War when the victorious North began rebuilding and industrializing its economy and the subsequent demand for beef, hides, and tallow escalated. Because Texas alone could not supply the new demand for beef, ranchers turned to the lands of the Great Plains for expansion of the cattle industry. Unfortunately, American notions of ranching, private land ownership, and fenced lands conflicted with the nomadic lifestyle of the Indians and the migrating herds of buffalo. This conflict produced growing pressure to eliminate the buf-

---

* Regarding this latter issue, consider the following statement of General Philip Sheridan, leader of the Army of the Shenandoah during the Civil War, to a group of Texans concerned about the slaughter: "Let them kill, skin, and sell until the buffalo is exterminated, as it is the only way to bring lasting peace and allow civilization to advance." Ironically, Sheridan's personal crusade in later life was the protection of Yellowstone, where a small herd of buffalo was preserved to help save the animal from extinction.

falo and to contain the Indians on reservations to establish clear boundaries of land ownership and control. Alliances were possibly formed between cattlemen, the railroads, and the U.S. Army to this end.

Other pressures contributed to the demise of the buffalo. As more Americans journeyed west, the necessity for additional military forts to provide protection from the increasingly hostile Indians escalated as well. With the sudden influx of soldiers, and the need to feed them, the U.S. Army issued contracts to local hunters for buffalo meat. There was also a demand for buffalo meat to feed railroad workers building the Transcontinental Railroad (until its completion in 1869). Later, in large part due to the development of an economic method for tanning hides into leather for luggage and similar items, and the willingness of buyers to pay up to three dollars per clear hide (without cuts or holes), the economic benefit of the meat diminished or vanished altogether and the unparalleled slaughter of the buffalo herds truly began.

The combination of a depressed economy brought on by the war and the opportunity for work lured thousands of adventurous men into the profession of buffalo hunting, several with familiar names like Wyatt Earp, Bat Masterson, Pat Garret, Wild Bill Hickok, and William F. Cody. Armed with long-range, high-powered rifles like the Sharps .50-90* or the Springfield .50-70, a single buffalo hunter could kill as many as 250 animals in a single day. Although physically demanding and requiring both patience and skill, the technique was relatively straightforward. After locating a herd, the buffalo hunter selected a position downwind from the animals with a good field of view. Next the hunter set

* The Sharps Rifle Manufacturing Company developed the .50-90 black powder cartridge in 1872 specifically for buffalo hunting.

his rifle on a pair of wooden cross sticks secured with rope or twine near the top to provide a stable shooting stand. After carefully observing the herd, the buffalo hunter picked out the lead bull and shot it first. When the bull collapsed to the ground, the other buffalo would usually stand around in a daze, ostensibly waiting for a new bull to assume leadership. During this time of confusion, the hunter would attempt to shoot as many buffalo as possible, often 50 or more, before the herd panicked and scattered. This required great precision and focus to consistently achieve the necessary one-shot kills. And although rifles like the Sharps .50-90 incorporated heavy octagonal barrels to minimize over-heating and improve long-range accuracy, the excessive rate of fire often required the buffalo hunter to douse the barrel with drinking water from a canteen to cool it down for the next shot. When the herd had scattered and the killing was finished, the skinners went to work. If no contract or market existed for the meat, they would take only the hides, leaving the carcasses and edible meat to rot on the ground. Sometimes they took the tongues, but only if there was sufficient demand for this particular delicacy. By the early 1880s, over 5,000 buffalo hunters and skinners worked the rapidly shrinking herds of the Great Plains.

The killing reached its peak during the years 1872, 1873, and 1874. Although there is no corroborating documentation to prove this, one experienced buffalo hunter used first-hand accounts and shipping records to reach an estimate of 4,500,000 animals destroyed during this three-year period alone. As more and more of the herds were decimated, tensions with the Indian tribes that depended on the buffalo for survival magnified and the number of Indian attacks increased. This in turn led to more aggressive reprisals by the U.S. Army, and ultimately to the adoption of a policy to exterminate the buffalo. The primary goal of this policy was to eradicate the animal that provided the fundamental basis for the nomadic lifestyle of the Plains Indians -- a lifestyle proving incompatible with American western migration -- and thereby force the Indians onto reservations to allow the possibility of better separation and control.

Historic images provide a glimpse in time of the inconceivable breadth of the carnage. A photograph taken circa 1870 shows an impressive mountain of buffalo skulls at least 30 feet to the peak and over 100 feet at the base waiting to be ground into fertilizer. Another, taken at the Rath & Wright's Buffalo Hide Yard in Dodge City, Kansas in 1870, presents the image of a mustached gentleman sitting comfortably on a long pile of 40,000 buffalo hides awaiting shipment to a tannery. A lithograph published in the December 14, 1867 edition of the Harper's Weekly illustrates dozens of passengers on the Kansas Pacific Railroad shooting buffalo from platforms and windows while the train slows to match the speed of the migrating herd. The accompanying article includes the following note: "When the 'hunt' is over the buffaloes which have been killed are secured, and the choice parts placed in the baggage-car, which is at once crowded by passengers, each of whom feels convinced and is ready to assert that his was the shot that brought down the game." The article goes on to explain how the women also....

John Ravenscroft waved the page of manuscript at Muireall just as she began removing an apple pie from a square-sided whicker picnic basket. A bumblebee arrived to inspect the pie, but after hovering noisily buzzed away towards a more promising cluster of California Lilacs warmed by the sun. "Wait a minute!"

Muireall arranged the pie next to a slab of cheese with a knife stuck in it. "Wait a minute? Why?"

John waved the page again. "No, no…not the apple pie…this article about the buffalo hunters. Wait a minute!"

Muireall dug her hand into the basket to remove a pair of sandwiches wrapped neatly in wax paper. "Alright. I can wait a minute. Then what?"

"No, that's not what I mean either. I mean I have some questions, not that I actually want you to wait a minute."

Muireall pried two small porcelain plates from the basket and began unwrapping the sandwiches. "I hope you like roast beef. I couldn't find any fresh buffalo meat at the market."

John lowered the page. "Very funny."

"I thought it was. What's the question?"

"Actually, I have two questions. Maybe three depending on the answers."

"And…?"

"First question. Are you serious when you write that 50 million buffalos were hunted until only 2,000 remained? Unbelievable!"

"I am serious. Believe it. If you read the footnote, you'd know the numbers could have spanned between 60 million and 300."

"I did read the footnote, but those numbers are even more impossible to believe. Second question. They shot buffalos from moving trains for sport? You have good documentation of this?"

"They did, and I do."

"But a 30-foot high mountain of buffalo skulls?"

"Yes, and that's three questions."

"I have one more question."

"You originally said two, or maybe three depending on the answers."

John did not allow Muireall's rebuff to derail his continuation. "Where did you find all of this technical information about the buffalo hunters, like the kinds of rifles they used and the caliber of the rounds and pouring water on the barrel to cool it down and the rest? I didn't think you knew anything about such things."

"I chanced upon a real buffalo hunter and interviewed him. We talked at great length over a year ago. It's in the bibliography."

"Amazing. Truly amazing. Where did you find a buffalo hunter?"

"He lives in a cute little cottage in Pismo Beach, but he's retired now."

"I should hope so, especially if he lives in Pismo Beach. What's his name?"

"John Runyan."

"Never heard of him."

"Not surprising."

"How'd the interview go?"

"He swore a lot, and at one point he made the outlandish claim that he was a personal friend of Calamity Jane.* He even suggested their relationship was more than platonic."

"No kidding?"

"No kidding. Ready to eat?"

---

* Martha Canary was better known as Calamity Jane.

Chapter Fourteen

The Oregon Trail, Idaho Territory
June 1871

Excerpt from

<u>A Glorious History of the American West</u>

by Muireall Anne Ravenscroft

Glenn's Ferry and Three Island Crossing

Arguably one of the more fascinating sites along the Oregon Trail, Glenn's Ferry was the entrepreneurial brainchild of Gustavus "Gus" Glenn. Constructed in 1869 (the same year as the completion of the Transcontinental Railroad), the ferry offered passage across the Snake River far safer than the traditional Three Island Crossing -- the location two miles downstream where pioneers had previously forded the river -- and at the same time reduced the length of travel to Fort Boise by nearly 20 miles.

The Three Island Crossing may have been the most difficult of all the river crossings on the Oregon Trail. Pioneers could certainly choose to follow a longer and more difficult route along the southern banks of the Snake River, but roughly half made the decision to ford the river at this point to gain access to a direct freight road to Fort Boise with more abundant water and better feed for the animals. Pioneers typically used at least two of the three islands to ford the narrowed river channels. Even then, the crossing often proved perilous and could result in loss of life, animals, provisions, and in some cases entire wagons. An excerpt from the 1845 pioneer diary of one Samuel Hancock reveals the inherent dangers: "We lost 2 of our men, Ayres and Stringer. Ayres got into trouble with his mules in crossing the stream. Stringer, who was about thirty, went to his relief, and both were drowned in sight of their women folks. The bodies were never recovered."

Gus Glenn originally built his ferry to expedite the handling of freight, but it soon became the primary method of transport across the Snake River for pioneers who had chosen to use the Oregon Trail instead of the train. The ferry boat could hold two wagons at a time; multiple trips were required with a large wagon train. The ferry provided service until 1878 when Indians sunk the boat during a Bannock War skirmish. Glenn's Ferry was never reconstructed, but became a stop for overland stage service in 1879 and then a major railroad center in 1883.

"This bit about Glenn's Ferry is quite interesting. I've read of the Oregon Trail, but I've never heard of Glenn's Ferry. Come to think of it, I've never heard of Three Island Crossing either."

Muireall scratched her spoiled calico cat behind the ears and sipped a cup of tea. "I'm thinking of deleting it. I've got another comprehensive section on the Oregon Trail, and this part strikes me as a little too narrow and fussy, especially considering the intended broad reach of the book. After all, this is a one-volume history, and I had originally titled it: *A Concise History of the American West,* before you suggested the change."

John Ravenscroft sipped his cup of tea as well. "You could make it a sidebar."

The cat stretched. "Too long for a sidebar."

"You could make it a footnote."

The cat sneezed. "Too long for a footnote."

"You could make it shorter."

The cat yawned. "It would take me longer to make it shorter than it did to write it in the first place. I'd rather delete it altogether."

"If you are going to delete interesting stuff like this, then maybe you should change the title back to the way you had it in the first place."

The cat trilled. "Maybe I will."

"Then maybe you should."

"Then maybe I will." The cat trilled.

A brisk westerly fluttering the tattered canvas cover stretched across rows of arched hickory bows, the iron-rimmed wheels of a lone prairie schooner[*] rattled sharply over the hardened mud swirls of a dry gulch, each bounce and rumble and vibration translating from the sturdy axels to the wagon bed through a pair of rusty springs beneath the splintered driver's seat directly to the battered rumps of Ferd Tucker and his wife, Joniah. Each of the four straining oxen[†] pulling the schooner grunted in turn when they reached the steep upward slope on the opposite side of the gulch, and then grunted even more when they hauled the heavily-loaded wagon up onto more level ground. The unpleasant bouncing diminished once the wagon had cleared the gulch, but only a little. A young boy and girl giggled in the back, although the noise of the rumbling wagon concealed the sound from their parents.

Once unquestionably attractive, and in earlier years often noted for the fairness of her skin and shine of her hair, more than half a decade

---

[*] More suitable to the demanding rigors of the Oregon Trail, the prairie schooner was a half-size version of the much heavier Conestoga wagon. The prairie schooner weighed approximately 1,300 pounds unloaded.

[†] Primarily because they could not live off the available prairie grasses, horses were quickly rejected for use on the Oregon Trail. Oxen were reliable, strong, gentle, and less expensive animals, and could eat almost anything; however, with a travel speed of two miles per hour they were slow and plodding. Mules were the next best choice: they could also survive on the prairie grasses and were significantly faster than oxen. Unfortunately, the cantankerous personality of the mule caused great suffering for many of the pioneers.

on a homestead had aged Joniah far beyond her otherwise tender age of twenty-eight. The homestead, a tiny dirt-floored structure measuring no more than 12 feet by 14 feet and a 160 acres of isolated, rocky, windswept, arid, godforsaken prairie land in eastern Kansas, had nearly broken her spirit. She had arrived at the homestead in June of 1865 a new bride full of anticipation. She had forsaken the homestead in April of 1871, leaving behind the graves of two infants and most of her youthful hope. After much coaxing by her husband she had agreed to pile the meager family possessions into a prairie schooner and join a wagon train leaving from Independence, Missouri—although she didn't understand at the time how this might improve the family's often desperate situation on the homestead. She pulled at the brim of her bonnet to shade her tired eyes from the western sun, and spoke to Ferd in little puffs of voice as she bounced uncomfortably against the hardwood seat. "It worries ... me when ... we have not ... caught up to the ... other wa ... gons yet. I do not want ... to spend the night ... alone, es ... specially with ... the children. I do wish we ... had found a way... to leave ... earlier."

Ferd Tucker, accustomed to speak in succinct phrases (which often fit neatly between the more aggressive bumps), gazed intently at the trail beyond the bobbing heads of the lead oxen pair and answered without sympathy. "Couldn't leave earlier. Had to fix the wheel. You know this. You were there."

Joniah crossed her arms in frustration and the brim of the bonnet fluttered up, revealing the sun-reddened creases of her forehead. "I know I was ... there. You don't have to ... lecture me about ... what happened this ... morning. All I'm saying ... is ... I wish we'd left ... earlier so we... weren't so far be ... hind the other ... wagons." She jerked the brim of the bonnet down again, nearly poking herself in the eye when the left front wheel slammed into a deep fissure.

Ferd Tucker pulled the reins to the right in an attempt to steer the plodding oxen around another hole. The massive beasts did not respond quickly enough and the wagon bounced into the jagged depression. "Not trying to lecture. Just stating the facts."

Joniah shivered when she thought of travelling alone in the noisy wagon after dark. She shivered again when she thought of camping alone in the dark. "Where will we catch ... up with them? Did you talk ... to the wagon ... master?"*

The wagon rolled over a particularly rocky section of the trail and Ferd could no longer answer Joniah's questions with short sentences. "Other side of the ... Snake River. Glenn's Ferry. He said the ... passage was already ... paid for. Should make it ... before dark I ... reckon."

Joniah yanked at the brim of her bonnet. "Should have taken ... the train ... I reckon."

Ferd Tucker had met Joniah at a church social in Saint Louis, Missouri in 1864. Their courtship had lasted only four months before he proposed marriage. Because Ferd possessed sufficient carpenter skills to allow the possibility of employment and was not unhandsome—and because there were so few decent men available to choose from at the time—she had hastily agreed. Joniah would have found their small residence near her parents' home in Saint Louis adequately satisfying, but Ferd had heard rumors of free land for the taking in Kansas and had persuaded Joniah to pack up and head west. They searched nearly three weeks before finding 160 acres of surveyed government land that appeared farmable, although Ferd had no particular farming experience at the time and did not confess to Joniah until later that he had guessed about the quality of the land. He had built the tiny home to the minimum dimensions required by the Homestead Act of 1862 in an effort to conserve resources, and then promised Joniah he would improve the size and quality of the home in due time. Unfortunately for both of them, the rigors of squeezing a meager existence from the marginal land prevented fulfillment of the promise—although he did add a small window in the summer of 1867, and a covered porch large enough for a rocking chair in 1869. Now they were heading west again, and Joniah had no particular reason to expect anything better than she had endured in eastern Kansas.

Curious as to why her older brother spent so much time viewing the monotonous prairie landscape through the same small tear in the

* A wagon train was led by a "wagon master," sometimes called a "captain." The wagon master signaled the beginning of the trip, woke the pioneers up every morning at dawn, and made all major travel decisions including when and where to take breaks and camp for the night.

canvas cover, Clarinda jabbed Seth with her elbow. "Why do you keep looking through that hole, anyway? You're always looking through the same hole."

Seth stretched the tear wide open with both hands to see through the hole with both eyes. "None of your business why I looks through this here hole."

Clarinda, Seth's younger sister by 14 months, protested immediately. "Must be a reason. Tell me why. Maybe I want to look through the hole too."

Seth scoffed, "Look through the big hole at the back of the wagon. You can see a lot better."

Clarinda poked Seth in the shoulder with her finger. "I don't want to look through the back of the wagon. I want to look through your hole because there must be something to see or you wouldn't be looking through it all the time."

Seth decided to taunt his sister, a tradition which had successfully survived the recent family transition from homestead to wagon train. "I'll tell you, but only if you leave me be. I like looking through this here hole because it's a magic hole. It lets you see things you can't see anywhere else." He pretended to see something that didn't exist. "I just saw a prairie dog! It just stuck its head up out of the ground."

Clarinda clapped her little hands. "Let me see! I want to see the prairie dog through the magic hole!"

Now that he had gained Clarinda's innocent attention, Seth elaborated his taunt. "Oh, look, there's another one. And another. And another. They're popping up all over the place!"

Clarinda begged, "Please let me look through the magic hole. I want to see the prairie dogs!"

Although his parents would never condone telling a lie, Seth knew they could not hear his words above the rumble of the iron-rimmed wagon wheels and decided to magnify the audacity of his fabrication. "Oh my, hundreds of the little varmints are just pouring out of the ground. Just pouring! I've never seen anything like it."

Clarinda squealed, "Please let me see. I want to see the prairie dogs!"

Seth grinned as he peered through the meaningless little hole at the monotonous prairie passing by at no more than two miles an hour. He suddenly screamed, “Now a bunch of hawks are diving out of the sky and snatching the prairie dogs up! They’re running all over the place but can’t get away. I’ve never seen this many birds in my whole life!”

Clarinda pleaded for a turn. “Please let me see through the magic hole. Please! I want to see the hawks too.”

Seth escalated his shocking vision again. “I can’t believe it! Now wild horses are coming over the hills and chasing the hawks away. And the prairie dogs are jumping on the backs of the wild horses and riding ‘em.” Then, unfortunately, he pushed the lie too far. “Oh my goodness, now a whole bunch of buffalos just showed up!”

Even Clarinda did not believe the part about prairie dogs riding on the backs of wild horses, and she especially did not believe a whole bunch of buffalos had suddenly arrived. She crossed her arms. “You little liar. I bet there never was a prairie dog in the first place. You just made the whole thing up. You’re a little liar, that’s what you are.”

Seth pressed his face against the canvas, but could not hide the smirk. “They’re all gone now. I guess I should of let you take a look through the magic hole when it still had some magic left. Now it’s too late.”

“Liar!”

“I’m telling you the truth. I saw a bunch of prairie dogs. Must have been hundreds. And the hawks swooping out of the sky. And the wild horses too. And the prairie dogs riding ‘em. Then the buffalos showed up. I saw everything through this magic hole.”

“Liar!”

The argument could have easily progressed to fisticuffs, but the wagon skidded to a dusty halt and the incessant rumble of the trail diminished to a peculiar silence—except for the wind. Ferd and Joniah Tucker both squinted at the small white dot that had unexpectedly appeared where the meandering trail joined the horizon.

Joniah spoke first. “What is it? Do you think it’s Indians?”

Ferd transferred the reins to his left hand and lifted the brim of his hat up with his free hand. “Not sure. Don’t think so. Getting pretty late in the day. Might be one of the scouts coming back to look for us. Don’t think it’s Indians.”

Joniah scooched forward. “Is it coming this way?”

Ferd sniffed. “Think so. Looks like it’s getting bigger.”

The dot vanished into a depression in the trail. When it reappeared it was larger and faster. Joniah squinted. "It's definitely a horse and rider. Doesn't look like one of the scouts. Maybe the wagon master has come to find us. Looks like it might be his horse."

Ferd squinted. "Don't think it's the wagon master. Horse is too big and rider's too small and dressed in white. Wagon master wears mostly black. Never seen him in white except once in his—"

Joniah sat back. "Maybe you should get the rifle out, just in case."

"Don't need the rifle for a lone rider."

"You sure it's not an Indian?"

Ferd snorted his loss of patience with Joniah's endless questions. "Stop your worrying. What's one small Indian going to do?"

Joniah glared. "Kill the whole family and eat the oxen?"

The rider and horse approached within a hundred yards then slowed to a walk. Ferd blinked three times. "Well I'll be. Looks like a little girl to me."

The rider and horse approached to within 75 yards. Joniah stood up in the wagon and shaded her eyes with her hand. "It *is* a little girl, and she's wearing a fancy white dress. I can see it."

The rider and horse approached to within 50 yards. Ferd tied the reins off and stood next to Joniah. "Just look at the size of the horse. That there's a large animal."

The rider and horse approached to within 25 yards. Joniah put her hands on her hips. "There's something you don't see every day. Her fancy white dress is a wedding dress, but it's all torn to shreds. And unless I'm not seeing right, there's a wedding bouquet stuck in the saddle—all shriveled up by the heat."

The rider and horse pulled up to Joniah's side of the wagon. The little girl—no older than 15, hair tangled into matted balls of filth, cheeks sun-blistered red, lips cracked and swollen from the wind, thorn-slashed legs visible through the shredded remnants of a once-beautiful wedding dress—spoke with a raspy sweetness. "Do you have any food you could spare? My horse needs some food too. He doesn't like much of the grass around here."

Ferd started to tell the little girl they didn't have any food to spare—especially for a horse—but Joniah interrupted. "Of course we can spare you some food. We might even have a little feed leftover we can give to your horse. It's a beautiful animal."

The little girl coughed into her hand. "Yes. I named him Ezekiel. He was a prophet from the Old Testament. But he's not been doing very good lately. I think he's hungry. And he's been limping. Since two days ago."

Seth and Clarinda poked their little heads out of the wagon beneath the roughened hem of a canvas flap. Seth spoke for the both of them. "Why did we stop? Who's she?"

Ferd pointed his finger at the children and admonished, "This is no concern of your'n. Get back in the wagon and don't make a sound." Seth and Clarinda quickly vanished behind the canvas flap and commenced giggling.

Joniah hopped down from the wagon and walked to Ezekiel's side. She bent down and examined the animal's legs. "Ezekiel's got a bad cut here on his knee." Then she discovered the little girl's bare leg through the tattered wedding dress. "Probably the same thorns you got cut on. Did you ride through a patch of buffalo berry?"

The little girl shrugged. "Don't know, ma'am. We were hiding from some men who I thought were after us. When we rode down though the bushes next to a stream we got all cut up. Ruined my dress too. Happened a few days ago."

Ferd perked up and his mouth hardened. "Some men was chasing you? How come?"

The little girl wriggled in her saddle and then quickly concocted a lie. "I don't know why, but I think they've been following me for days. Maybe they want to steal Ezekiel from me. There were three of them. I thought I might try to get to Fort Boise, but I didn't have any money for the ferry. The man who runs the ferry told me I shouldn't take the other route 'cus it's a lot longer and a lot more dangerous."

Joniah smiled and pressed her hands together. "Well then, you'll just have to come along with us. The wagon master already paid for us to take the ferry, and they won't know you weren't part of our family in the first place."

The little girl stroked the horse's neck. "What about Ezekiel?"

Ferd was about to say there's no way on God's green earth he's bringing her dang horse along, but Joniah spoke before he could open his mouth.

"We'll just tie Ezekiel to the back of the wagon. The man at the ferry won't know he doesn't belong to us. Why don't you come down, and we'll find you a clean dress and get you something to eat. I have a spare dress you can wear. It might be a little big for you, but we can roll up the sleeves and pin up the hem."

Ferd tried to complain indirectly. "But we don't even know her name or where she comes from. And there's three men chasing after her. I don't think this is—"

The little girl swung her leg over the saddle and jumped down to the ground. "My name is…" A pair of sage sparrows darted overhead, distracting the little girl and causing her to hesitate. "My name is… Mary… Smith, and I come from… Brigham City, just south of here."

Joniah accepted the statement without judgment. "Well then, Mary Smith from Brigham City, let's get you something to eat and into a clean dress."

"Thank you, ma'am. I appreciate it. And Ezekiel?"

"Yes, and some feed for Ezekiel too."

Ferd complained directly this time, and made little attempt to conceal his displeasure. "We got to make it to Glenn's Ferry before dark. We don't have time for no sewing and feeding a horse who don't even belong to us. You said you didn't want to travel or camp alone at night."

Joniah glared at her husband. "Of course we have time. It'll only take a few minutes. After we're finished we'll head straight to Glenn's Ferry. Now, where did I pack that dress?"

Chapter Fifteen

Promontory Mountain, Utah Territory
April 28, 1869

Burly Sam Logan. Born in Texas of impoverished Irish immigrants. Raised as a young boy in Los Angeles before California statehood. Displaced to Sacramento at fourteen to find work. Fluent in Irish, English, and Spanish (but not Chinese). Red hair flaming beneath a well-worn derby. Green-and-black-plaid flannel shirt fluttering across sinewy back muscles. Freshly promoted to crew foreman because of his relentless devotion to the Central Pacific Railroad. Burly Sam Logan marveled at the random clusters of scrubby green bushes and sporadic outcrops of wind-and-rain-weathered rocks and waves of sun-yellowed grasses flowing over the lumpy hills cascading away to the west. His gaze found the elegant railroad tracks and adjacent row of neatly-spaced telegraph poles completed just yesterday, and then followed both track and telegraph to a tiny vanishing point at the juncture of land and sky. He searched for a white man among the hundreds of Chinese laborers swarming along both sides of the railhead: he found two standing next to a water wagon. A whistle shrilled, and his attention jerked to the approaching engine and 16 flatcars loaded with materials sufficient for two miles of track. He confirmed the time on his pocket watch, deftly dropped the watch into a vest pocket, and bellowed encouragement to the six Chinamen under his direct supervision. "Eleven minutes to seven my lads, a beautiful morning of blue skies and white clouds with a bit of coolness in the air, and we have the honor of loading the first handcar."[*] Plumes of hissing mist foamed around the polished wheels of the soot-blackened steam engine when the material train braked at the staging area. Sam Logan removed his timepiece again and counted the seconds down. Hundreds of men clambered up both sides of the flatcars and threw down bundles of fish plates[†] and kegs of bolts and spikes. Some of the kegs ruptured on the ground and scattered spikes and ragged shards of wood and bolts and rusty iron hoops across the track bed. When the fish plates and kegs were cleared, men scrambled over the 30-foot-long rails and wrestled over 700 of the 560-pound iron bars to the ground in an astonishing eight minutes. When the work had ended and the frenzied roar of shouting men and exploding kegs and clanging iron rails had diminished, the locomotive wheels spun into reverse and the empty material train pulled away to make space for the next material train, already approaching.

"Get ready my lads. Only a minute now. A few seconds more. Seven o'clock on the dot. Let's get started." Sam Logan and his crew of six Chinamen jogged along the north side of the track until they reached the first pile of materials. Sam Logan and five Chinamen organized into pairs and seized three of the heavy rails. The sixth man lifted a keg of bolts over his shoulder then trudged behind the last rail. Sam Logan and his Chinamen hauled the materials forward to the first handcar then dashed back for more. When they had accumulated 16 iron rails and sufficient bundles of fish plates and kegs of bolts and spikes, Sam Logan tied the neatly-whipped end of a stiff hemp rope to an iron ring dangling at the front of the handcar and the entire crew of seven men leapt aboard. Two horses with riders, one behind the other, jerked the rope taught and the car lumbered east. The riders dug their heels into the flanks of the

---

[*] A railroad handcar is typically a small flatbed vehicle with a device located on one side consisting of an arm that pivots on a base like a children's seesaw. The arm must be alternately pushed down and pulled up to propel the car. Because of their small size and relatively light weight, handcars are easily placed on and removed from the tracks to allow passage of trains (and other handcars). However, because 30-foot rails were removed from both sides of the handcars used this day, and because the handcars were pulled by horses, it is likely that they did not incorporate any propulsion equipment.

[†] A fish plate, also called a splice or joint bar, is a metal bar bolted to the abutting ends of rails to rigidly connect them together in a track.

straining horses and the handcar accelerated toward the railhead, only 200 feet ahead.

The Chinaman standing next to Sam Logan looked back at the next handcar where another crew of six Chinamen and one Irishman began loading rails and kegs and bundles. He faced into the wind and addressed his new crew foreman with appropriate respect. "Not to doubt the wisdom of the great Central Pacific Railroad, but is it really possible to lay ten miles of track in a single day?"

Sam Logan watched the knot vibrate under the tension of two surging horses. "Your name is Tseng Longwei, is it not? You're the one who handled the nitroglycerine at the Summit Tunnel."

The Chinaman chose not to repeat his original question. "Yes, I am Tseng Longwei. And yes, I worked at the Summit Tunnel."

Sam Logan grinned just before a big-green-spiky-legged June bug buzzed into his derby and tumbled to the gravel bed between the tracks. "I remember now—the coolie who has no fear and speaks English like an American. Quite a novelty, if you ask me."

Tseng Longwei agreed indirectly. "Yes, I suppose you could call it a novelty in a way. But is it really possible to—"

Sam Logan finished Longwei's sentence. "—to lay ten miles of track in a single day? I have no idea if it is or is not, my lad. But those bastards on the Union Pacific said it can't be done by anyone, especially a bunch of coolies, so we're sure as hell going to try."

Tseng Longwei cringed, but repeated the untoward word anyway. "Yes, those bastards—as you call them—on the Union Pacific do not believe the Chinaman and the Irishman can work together to lay ten miles of track in a single day." The handcar slowed. "Today I think we prove them wrong."

Sam Logan leaned back and shouted his approval, nearly losing his balance and falling off the handcar when it braked short of the railhead. "That's the spirit, my lad. That's the spirit!"

Sam Logan and his crew of six Chinamen jumped off the handcar, and a gang of four men armed with picks and wire cutters stepped aboard. The men broke open the tops of the kegs with decisive strokes of the picks and cut the bundles of fish plates with rapid snips of the cutters before tossing the materials to both sides of the handcar. Other men rushed forward to fill rusty buckets with spikes, bolts, and fish plates, then plodded away to distribute their heavy loads beyond the railhead. When only the rails remained, a single horse pulled the handcar a few yards more until it bumped the wood-framed iron track gauge at the terminus of the tracks. A handpicked crew of eight Irish rail handlers, under the direct supervision of Track Foreman H. H. Minkler* and Gang Foreman George Coley, marched back (four to each side of the handcar) until they had properly aligned with the ends of the 30-foot-long rails. A pair of men clamped the front of each rail with iron tongs while men at the back slid the rails to either side of the handcar and set them on iron rollers. The tong men pulled the rails over the rollers until they advanced 30 feet past the track gauge and the men at the back dropped the rails into place. The track gauge was quickly dragged forward and the new tracks bolted and spiked into place by yet another track gang. Men pushed the handcar east another 30 feet and the handpicked Irish rail handlers repeated the process until they had extended the track 240 feet. Another handcar loaded with 16 rails, bundles of fish plates, kegs of bolts and spikes, one Irishman, and six Chinamen, approached seconds before the track gang hammered the last spike into place.

Sam Logan strolled alongside his advancing handcar—at a pace equivalent to a team of oxen pulling a prairie schooner across the Great Plains—and held his timepiece in front of his nose to better observe the ticking second hand and the handpicked Irish rail handlers at the same time. Exactly 67 seconds after his arrival at the railhead, the handlers wrenched the last pair of rails off the car and pulled them forward on the iron rollers. He waved his crew of six Chinamen into action with an expansive sweep of both arms and a shout. "Let's get this empty handcar out of the way men." Sam Logan and his crew of six Chinamen lifted the car up, muscled it off the newly-installed section of track, and carried it back 50 feet where they remounted it to the rails. Sam Logan roped another pair of horses to the front of the car and they were promptly off on their first return trip to the material dump to collect more rails, bundles of fish plates, and kegs of bolts and spikes.

---

* Horace Hamilton Minkler is credited with laying the last rail before the golden spike was driven at Promontory Summit, Utah on May 10, 1869.

Tseng Longwei resumed his earlier conversation with Sam Logan as the handcar gained speed. "What we just did required less than two minutes. At this speed of construction…" He completed a precise mental calculation: *Sixty minutes each hour times 120 feet per minute equals 6,000 feet plus 1,200 feet which equals 7,200 feet of track per hour.* "…the 10-miles of track will be done in less than 10 hours."

Sam Logan roared, "Not so fast, my lad. You have not accounted for the curves; we have more than a few of those to deal with before the day is done."

"Yes, the curves. I had not considered the curves. But I am not the one who knows of the curves. I only know what I see in front of my own face and feel below my own feet."

"Not to worry, my lad. I do not know where the curves are either. We are both in the same boat. I only know the curves will come, and they will take longer to lay than our first stretch of track." The handcar slowed as it neared the material dump. One Irishman and six Chinamen loaded another handcar just ahead. "But the curves are not our problem." The handcar rolled to a stop. "Our problem is to get this handcar off the tracks. Off we go, lads." Sam Logan and his six Chinamen leaped from the handcar, lifted it off the track, and pulled it to the side moments before the next car rumbled by on its way to the new railhead. They hauled the handcar back to the rails and dropped it down with a metallic thud. The pair of horses pulled the hemp rope taught and the handcar rolled into place between a mound of kegs and a stack of iron rails.

Burly Sam Logan and his crew of six Chinamen worked throughout the long morning: loading iron rails and bundles of fish plates and kegs of bolts and spikes at the material dump, riding the heavily-loaded-horse-pulled handcar to the new railhead where men installed the materials in minutes, riding the empty handcar back to the material dump, repeatedly removing the handcar from the tracks to allow other handcars moving east to pass without losing speed, each round trip longer than the one before by 240 feet. When work suspended for the noontime meal, only five hours since the effort had begun, the nearly 4,000 men and hundreds of horses involved in the heroic endeavor had accomplished six miles of track at a pace very close to Tseng Longwei's calculation. But they could not maintain the astonishing speed of the morning. When work continued after lunch, the rising slopes of Promontory Mountain and greater number of curves slowed the advance, and a full six hours were required to achieve the last four miles. Even so, when the work halted for good at seven in the evening, a miraculous length of 10 miles and 56 feet stretched west back to the day's starting point. To consummate the achievement, a steam locomotive raced the entire length of new track at a speed of 40 miles per hour, arriving safely at the new railhead before the weary men began preparing the evening meal.

Strangely alone among thousands of men gathered around hundreds of fires twinkling in the darkness along both sides of the railhead, Tseng Longwei stirred the hot coals of his campfire with a blackened stick. When he had completed this task, he drank tea from a dented metal cup. On this day of days, his calloused hands twitched from gripping too many heavy iron rails, his hardened shoulders throbbed from hauling too many kegs of bolts and spikes, and his strong back ached from lifting the handcar too many times. A lone coyote howled in the distance, but the sound did not awaken the eleven exhausted men scattered around him. He thought of sleeping himself, but the exhilaration of the day's achievement kept him awake. Tseng Longwei tossed the blackened stick into the fire and watched it smoke and burst into crackling flame. He stretched out his legs to move his feet closer to the warmth of the fire and a cramp erupted on the back of his leg just above the right knee. He dropped the cup of tea in pain and massaged the unruly muscle with the tips of his fingers. When the spasms had abated and he felt more comfortable, he noticed the familiar clicking sound of hooves against rocks. He listened to the sounds of the hooves grow louder, and when he explored the darkness and tilted his head a little he discerned a shadowy man on horseback. The man and horse appeared more distinctly in the glow of a nearby campfire, and then disappeared in the darkness outside the light of the fire. The man and horse appeared again and vanished into the gloom a final time, and then gradually reappeared in the flickering light of Tseng Longwei's fire until both horse and man stopped a few paces before trampling on a sleeping Chinaman only twenty feet away.

Tseng Longwei finally spoke when the man did not utter a word or dismount. "You there on the horse. Are you looking for someone?"

A leather saddle creaked when the man slouched over the horn. He answered Longwei's question with apparent joy. "I finally have the good luck to riding through the many of men who do not speak the English but are the sleep too and maybe it cannot be told if they speak the English or no, but who cares if it can be told or not of sleep because I have found who speaks the English and has no sleep in the now."

This incoherently bombastic outburst suggested the possibility of a dangerous lunatic; Tseng Longwei chose his next words with care. "Are you certain you are not lost? I do not think you have found the person you are looking for."

The dangerous lunatic laughed, dismounted, and shambled toward Tseng Longwei. "It is not my lost of your problem. There is no lost when I speak the English and the men who are not sleep in the dark speak words who are not the English. But you speak the English; I stay here tonight near the fire you have poured. If you do not know of a problem I cannot."

Tseng Longwei decided that he would rather talk to the dangerous lunatic than move, and attempted to interpret what he had just heard. "Are you asking me if you can stay next to my fire tonight?"

The dangerous lunatic squatted down very close to Tseng Longwei. "Yes, it is what I mean to say, not when there is a problem or not."

Tseng Longwei stretched his legs again and, luckily, the annoying cramp did not return. "Yes, you can stay. I do not care. I am too tired to care. And if you wish, there is still some tea in a pot near the fire. Please take some."

The lunatic smacked his lips and rubbed his hands together. "I would love the tea cup, even tea not in a samovar like it is proper to make tea. But after much the miles riding on the forever track through the tunnel it is good to drink tea when is not in a samovar." He stumbled back to the horse, groped around in a saddlebag, and returned with his own cup. He found the pot, poured hot tea into the cup, and sat to Longwei's side. "This is good to have the tea cup. I thank you for it and wish you the good."

Tseng Longwei inclined on a folded blanket propped against a large rock. "You are welcome. And do you wish to share your name and tell me where you are going?"

The lunatic slurped some tea. "This tea is truly of the hottest. Yes, I wish no problem to tell you of my name and the meaning to where I go. My name is Roshan Kuznetsov from Sitka of the north, and I walk on my horse of many miles above the road of tracks from Sacramento to the land of Silver City to find my wealth."

This statement intrigued Tseng Longwei. "Where is this land where you will find wealth?"

"The land of Silver City?"

"Yes, the land of Silver City. I have not heard of it. Why is it the land of wealth?"

Roshan Kuznetsov finished the hot tea in two blistering gulps. "The land of Silver City is in the land of Idaho very close to the land of Fort Boise. But I am told by the who to turn one day to the left side, and it is hard to find the day."

"And the wealth?"

"Oh, yes. It is the land of wealth because a man who also walked on his horse on the forever track told me I can pick up the biggest maggots of gold and the silver up from inside the river water when I arrive there in the months to come."

Tseng Longwei's interest increased, but also his skepticism. "You have been told of this gold and silver? How do you know it is true? There are always stories of gold and silver you can pick up with your hands without doing any work. I have heard these stories myself, but I have not yet found a reason to believe any of them."

Roshan grinned, but Longwei could not see the grin in the darkness. "The man who said of the biggest of maggots in Silver City is the man who walked on the horse and said of my turn to the left some day when I find the day."

Longwei kneaded the back of his leg. A Chinaman sleeping a few feet away coughed. "If I understand you, only one man told you all you know about Silver City? This is the extent of your knowledge?"

"No, he is the one man who walked on the horse. The story is arrived at other men who did not walk on the horse. But of this I do not think you are of concern. Are you glad to hear the gold and silver in the land of Silver City? I hear of pleasure in the voice of your words."

Tseng Longwei speculated on the consequences of his next words. "Yes, I am interested in what you say. My work on the Central Pacific Railroad will end soon, and I must find other work to keep myself occupied. It is possible I may decide to travel to this Silver City, even if I do not fully trust you to know what you are talking about."

Roshan Kuznetsov rolled onto his knees and stood. His back creaked. "Wait here, my newest of the friend. I must seek of something only my horse is know of." Roshan successfully traversed the clutter of sleeping men to his horse and back without stepping on anyone. He plopped into a seated position and scooted his rump across the dry prairie ground. "We must drink of the vodka to celebrate the beginning of our friendly before we turn to the left side on the right day to the land of Silver City where there will big maggots to be, as you said, you can pick up with your hands without doing any of work." Roshan poured vodka into each of two glasses he had also fetched from somewhere on his horse and handed one to Tseng Longwei. The campfire glinted in the swirling liquid of Roshan's glass when he raised it up.

Longwei accepted the glass with a query. "Are you proposing a partnership?"

Roshan chuckled. "No, I am proposing vodka to celebrate our friendship on our travel to the left turn on the right day, where we are wealthy to the both of us."

Longwei's tone suggested apprehension. "I see. And what is it each of us brings to our travel to the left turn on the right day?"

Roshan reached out in the darkness and clicked Longwei's glass. "It is of the simple. You bring the best English to tell people of what I say of the land of Silver City, and I bring the knowledge which we must turn to the left side when I find the right day."

Longwei swiftly considered his options before clicking Roshan's glass in return. "Yes, I will travel with you to Silver City as your business partner to seek great wealth."

Roshan announced, "Hah!" then tossed the vodka into his mouth. "It is of goodly news you say to travel with Roshan to the land of Silver City. I overjoyed myself with the thought. If you say it is yes, we walk on our horses in the fast of morning."

Longwei tasted his vodka. "I do say yes, but we cannot leave tomorrow. I have signed a contract with the Central Pacific Railroad, and I must first finish my work on the tracks. We can leave when I have fulfilled my obligation."

Roshan rested the empty glass on his knee. "We wait to the end of the railroad? How much days for the end? The gold is arriving in the water now."

"I don't know, but I will not leave until the railroad is finished."

Roshan Kuznetsov had grown fond of his new business partner, and decided the best course was to wait. "Good. I wait for the railroad to the end. Then we walk the same on our horses to the land of Silver City."

Tseng Longwei, unexpectedly elated with his new opportunity, finished his vodka in two rapid gulps and stretched out his hand. "Also good. Then we shake on it."

"Yes, we shake on it, and it is the deal."

The new business partners shook hands vigorously in the gloom shortly after midnight. A white-faced barn owl clinging to one of the few surviving branches near the perimeter of the encampment screeched its approval.

Early in the morning of May 10, 1869 (nearly two weeks after Roshan Kuznetsov and Tseng Longwei had arranged their unusual business partnership), the Union Pacific Number 119 locomotive travelled to within a hundred feet of the opposing Central Pacific Railroad locomotive—the word "JUPITER" emblazoned on the side of the tender*—and squealed metal-on-metal to a standstill. Dozens of railroad dignitaries, including Central Pacific Railroad President Leland Stanford and Union Pacific Railroad Vice-President T. C. Durant, stepped off the platforms of special cars trailing behind each locomotive and merged into the already-waiting-decidedly-peculiar crowd of Irish and Chinese laborers, Mormons, Army officers (a few with wives), frontiersmen, Mexicans, buffalo hunters, Indians, mule skinners, camp followers, and even a couple of eastern bankers. The dignitaries and their entourage marched through the multitude of over 500 onlookers until they arrived at the spot chosen for the final tie. The two superintendents of construction, Strowbridge of the Central Pacific and Reed of the Union Pacific, carried that final tie—fabricated of polished California laurel with a commemorative silver plate nailed to the center—to the appointed spot and waited. After a reverend

* The tender is the attached container holding both water and fuel, such as wood or coal, for the steam locomotive's fire box.

from Massachusetts offered a lengthy prayer of thanks, Tseng Longwei smoothed the ground with a square-ended shovel, the superintendents dropped the tie in place, and the last two iron rails were installed.

Tseng Longwei retreated into the crowd when Vice-President T. C. Durant strutted forward to drive a spike of gold, silver, and iron from Arizona and a spike of silver from Nevada. Two mule skinners and an Irishman shoved in front of Longwei and blocked his vision of the historic proceedings. Longwei heard the sharp metallic clang of hammer on spike and the cheers from the men around him but failed to see anything. He dropped to his knees and crawled between a U.S. Army Lieutenant and the wife's frilly dress just in time to witness a man hand a spike of California gold to President Leland Stanford. Longwei tried to stand, but the excited crowd shoved him backwards and he fell to the ground. Again he heard the clang of hammer on spike and the cheers but did not observe the momentous event. The crowd surged forward. Tseng Longwei turned and trudged away. When he arrived at the rear of the dispersing multitude, he felt two brisk taps on his shoulder.

Roshan crossed his arms impatiently. "Do you see of the spike of the last gold as you wished in spite of you?"

Tseng Longwei dropped his head and focused on the toes of Roshan's dusty boots. "I did not see it. My view was blocked by too many people."

Roshan harrumphed indifferently. "Then can we leave about time for the land of Silver City in the Land of Idaho when you are now the ready?"

Longwei considered the significance of the two opposing steam engines one last time. "Truly, it is time to go."

Excerpt from
<u>An Abridged History of the American West</u>
by Muireall Anne Ravenscroft
The First Transcontinental Railroad:
Technological Marvel of the 19th Century

Many historians, myself included, rank construction of the First Transcontinental Railroad as the very acme of American technological achievements in the 19th Century. Some might suggest the construction of the

Eerie Canal of 1825 for this honor, but when one considers the difficulty of the terrain, the speed of construction, and the methods employed, there should be little doubt of the railroad's place in history. But before an evaluation of the technology can be undertaken, it is important to understand the political, cultural, and historical context of the transcontinental railroad.

Planning for the Pacific Railroad (the initial name of the First Transcontinental Railroad) really began in 1838 when a convention was convened by John Plumbe: a civil engineer, photographer, publisher, and early advocate for an American transcontinental railroad. John Plumbe personally surveyed potential railway routes in 1829, and is credited with arguing that a transcontinental railroad "...would hasten the formation of dense settlements throughout the whole extent of the road, advance the sales of the public lands, afford increased facilities to the agricultural, commercial and mining interests of the country...and enable the government to transport troops and munitions of war." Plumbe promoted the idea of the railroad throughout his life by petitioning Congress and publishing articles in newspapers and other publications, but died in 1857 -- six years before construction of the First Transcontinental Railroad had commenced.

Various bills supporting the Pacific Railroad through land grants, subsidies, and in one case an outright allocation of $90,000,000 for construction, were submitted in Congress during the 1840s, but none passed because there was no consensus on the route. The disagreement broke uniformly between northern and southern congressmen, and was intrinsically tied to the intense debate of whether or not slavery should be allowed in the new western states. Ongoing discussions bogged down in Congress until January 1848, when the discovery of gold near Sutter's Mill (located less than 50 miles northeast of present-day Sacramento) and the subsequent exodus of over 75,000 people into California in 1849 suddenly elevated the importance of a transcontinental railroad. Representatives of the southern states continued to press for a southern route, which was called the "South & Pacific Railroad," and the Gadsden Purchase* of 1853 rendered this a distinct possibility.

Nonetheless, Congress could still not make a decision, and in 1853 ordered five different surveying teams into the wilderness to explore likely routes to California. The surveyors finished their work in the fall of 1854 and sent written reports to the former Senator from Mississippi and then Secretary of War Jefferson Davis. Not surprisingly, Secretary Davis reviewed the reports and concluded that a southern route running through the recently procured lands of the Gadsden Purchase would allow the most efficient and cost effective project. However, disagreements on the route continued to rage in Congress, and proposals to fund this southern route could not secure sufficient votes to pass. The future of the transcontinental railroad languished in Congress until 1861, when the imminent secession of southern states unexpectedly emptied the Senate and House chambers of all opposition to the northern route. Free of legislative resistance, the remaining northern Congressmen funded work on the transcontinental rail-

---

* Named after James Gadsden, the ambassador to Mexico, and purchased in a treaty signed by President Franklin Pierce on June 24, 1853, the Gadsden Purchase was the last major territorial acquisition in the contiguous United States. Congress ratified the treaty on April 25, 1854 to procure a land area the size of Scotland south of the Gila River and west of the Rio Grande. The primary purpose of the land purchase was to allow the possibility of the construction of a transcontinental railroad along a southern route.

road without delay, and, because Confederate artillery had just fired on Fort Sumter in Charleston Harbor, hastily determined that the northern route through Nebraska would best serve the military interests of the Union in the Civil War to come. After passage by the House of Representatives on May 6, 1862 and the Senate on June 20, 1862, President Abraham Lincoln signed "The Pacific Railroad Act" into law on July 1, 1862 to "... aid in the Construction of a Railroad and Telegraph Line from the Missouri River to the Pacific Ocean...." The act established a corporation by the name of "The Union Pacific Railroad Company," and also authorized the existing Central Pacific Railroad Company of California to "...construct a railroad and telegraph line from the Pacific coast...to the eastern boundaries of California, upon the same terms and conditions in all respects [as are provided for the Union Pacific Railroad]." Further, the act awarded land grants to each company along the proposed right-of-way, and subsidized the construction $16,000 per mile over easy grade, $32,000 per mile in the high plains, and $48,000 per mile in the mountains.

The Central Pacific Railroad began construction in Sacramento, California on January 8, 1863. The Union Pacific Railroad began construction in Omaha, Nebraska on December 2, 1863. Initially, the Central Pacific made good progress through the Sacramento Valley and the Union Pacific advanced rapidly across the easy terrain of the Great Plains. However, natural and cultural obstacles soon slowed construction from both directions. The Sierra Nevada Mountains and, more significantly, winter snow storms dramatically reduced the progress of the Central Pacific from the west. In the east, the Plains Indians -- who viewed construction of a railroad on their traditional lands as a violation of existing treaties with the United States -- harassed the railroad laborers and tore up whole sections of track.

The Union Pacific reacted to this threat by increasing security and hiring buffalo hunters to kill the roaming bison, which were both a physical threat to the railroad and the primary source of food for the Indians. These acts escalated the conflict and the Indians countered by killing laborers. The Union Pacific further strengthened security, but at the expense of rapid progress. Then, new and unexpected problems arose in the west.

At first the labor forces of both railroads consisted primarily of Caucasian workers, the majority of these Irish. Two events changed this on the Central Pacific route. First, work in the Sierra Nevada Mountains required the construction of numerous tunnels (fifteen in all and one, the Summit Tunnel, was over 1,600 feet in length through solid granite). Together with the harsh winter weather these tunnels presented an increasingly hostile environment for the laborers. Second, the discovery of silver in Nevada in 1865 significantly depleted the Central Pacific workforce as men sought less dangerous and more lucrative opportunities. To solve the labor shortage, Charles Crocker, one of the original leaders of the Central Pacific Railroad and responsible for labor, proposed the idea of hiring the Chinese to fill the shortage of white workers. This suggestion caused great consternation among the managers of the Central Pacific Railroad, who believed the Chinese were not sufficiently skilled or hardy for the work. Nonetheless, Crocker won the argument, in part by reminding his business partners of the Great Wall of China, and was ultimately allowed to hire 50 Chinese workers on a trial basis. The company eventually hired thousands. When the Chinese took over the more backbreaking duties of pick and shovel and wheelbarrow and the blasting of tunnels, the Irish, who were initially resentful on racial grounds, were unexpectedly elevated to more prestigious jobs such as foremen of the

Chinese crews, "expert track handler and iron layer," and the like. The company paid its Chinese laborers $1 per day, which did not include room and board, and its Irish workers $2 per day including room and board. Even with this unfortunate disparity of compensation, the Central Pacific Railroad has carried the "stigma" of having hired Chinese instead of white workers into the labor relations of the current century. It is therefore exceedingly ironic to....

Exhausted from a late night of sketching followed by a long day of more sketching and a very long meeting, John Ravenscroft stumbled into the entry, dropped a leather valise and a roll of drawings on the stone floor, and shuffled into the living room. He plopped into his chair next to the picture window with an exquisite view of the coastal mountains—if he had cared to enjoy the view. Sitting comfortably at her writing desk, Muireall quickly scribbled the words necessary to complete a rather convoluted sentence. "How did your meeting go with the new clients?"

John Ravenscroft sighed uncharacteristically. "Not as well as I had hoped."

"Really? Did they not like your design for their new house?"

John sighed again and scrunched down into the chair. "Generally, yes. But they want to completely rework the second floor... and the kitchen. They have provided me with the most woebegone sketches I have ever seen to demonstrate their intent. I thought I had explained to them that they should let me do the drawings, but—"

Muireall set her pen down. "Woebegone? Is this an architectural term?"

John scrunched a little more into the chair. "No. It's a polite way of saying utterly wretched and pitiful in appearance."

"Utterly wretched and pitiful?"

"Utterly."

"The woebegone sketches aside, was the meeting otherwise successful?"

"I suppose, if one considers the potentially lucrative fees. But I do not really care to talk about it at the moment. I would prefer for you distract me from the day. I see you are writing again. What is the project this time?"

Muireall snatched the pen from the desk and crossed off a word. “Nothing new. I’ve decided to revise the section on the First Transcontinental Railroad.”

“You have? But I liked that section.”

“I appreciate that you liked it, but nevertheless, I have decided—”

“This discussion does remind of something I meant to tell you the other day.”

“It does?”

John sat up in the chair and his expression relaxed. “Yes. I’ve been thinking about your book title again.”

“Again?”

“Yes, again.”

Muireall rolled the pen over the page and a shot of blue ink squirted across the right margin. “What now?”

John pressed his fingers together and lowered his chin. “After giving the matter much thought, I think you should change it back to: *A Concise History of the American West.* I’ve read it out loud a few times, and I’m not very fond of the word ‘abridged.’ Seems awfully stuffy.”

“Stuffy? I see. Anything else?”

“Yes, I did have one more thought. Maybe you should drop the word ‘American.’ I think everyone knows the ‘West’ is the ‘American West.’ If you made this change it would make the title even more—”

“Concise?”

“Precisely.”

Chapter Sixteen

Brookline, Massachusetts
May 1870

Not willing to part with even a small fraction of her meager savings to purchase a railway ticket, Gordania Sinclair hiked over five miles from the center of Boston to the reposeful hills of Brookline beneath the pristine skies of a glorious spring morning. The day had opened unfavorably with scattered showers of cold rain, but then quickly transitioned to billowing white clouds and a dazzlingly blue sky. And now overheated from the vigorous hike in the sun, and uncertain of her precise location, Gordania rested in the dappled shade of one of the massive trees lining the manicured street. She reached into a pocket at the front of her white dress and removed a folded piece of newsprint—carefully torn from a copy of the *Boston Herald* found discarded beneath a bench. She unfolded the paper and read the partially-smeared words:

> WANTED: Full-time governess to care for children. Must be willing to live at residence. Private room with board provided. One day off every two weeks. Must have prior experience. Salary negotiable. Apply to Mrs. Eva Corrine Brewster, Linden Place, Brookline.

Gordania read through the text a second time before carefully refolding the paper and slipping it into the same pocket. She appraised the whitewashed Greek Revival structure with comfortably-shaded porches and rows of fluted columns along each side now looming impressively beyond the neatly-maintained front yard. A dark-skinned gardener pruning an unruly shrubbery down the street had given Gordania directions to this house, and had also assured her, with an accent she did not recognize, that the Brewsters and their two little girls lived here. She breathed deeply to restore her strength then walked to the left. She turned into a narrow but charmingly-landscaped lane that separated the adjacent property and led to the main entry at the southeastern side of the elegant home. She walked up three wood steps, across a generously-shaded porch, and stopped at a heavy wood door inlaid with colorful stained glass and secured with a polished brass lever. She knocked on the varnished wood stile at the edge of the stained glass: three crisp taps, a quarter rest, and one final tap. A few seconds passed before she heard delicate footsteps inside. The door opened without a sound. Someone must have oiled the hinges recently. A slender woman with the blackest skin and blackest hair and blackest eyes and whitest apron Gordania had ever seen stuck her head through the opening.

"May I help you?"

He mouth dry from a long walk without a drink, Gordania coughed and licked her lips. "My name is Gordania Sinclair. I have come to apply for the position of governess ... the one advertised in the newspaper."

The slender woman eyed Gordania's expression and manner of dress. "I heard they was looking for a new one. The last one didn't last but three weeks. I hope you is better."

Surprised, Gordania clarified, "But I have not yet interviewed for the position."

The slender woman chuckled. "I can see by the look of you...you shouldn't have any trouble getting the job. Just make sure you tell them you is not afraid to discipline those wild girls when you have to, and you'll do just fine. Come on in. I'll fetch Mrs. Brewster for you. She's the one doing the nanny hiring around here. I'm just the cook and housekeeper."

Gordania stepped across the stone threshold onto the marble floor of a spacious entry foyer. "The position is for a governess, not a nanny. And may I inquire of your name? And where you are from?"

The slender woman chuckled again. "My, but ain't we the nosey one! And feisty, too. But sure you can, Miss Sinclair. I'm Emma Johnson from a plantation way down south in Virginia, but I came here a few years ago—after the war."

Gordania followed Emma to a pair of French doors near the base of a wide stairway. Emma opened one of the doors and waved Gordania in. "You just wait here in the parlor. I'll fetch Mrs. Brewster for you right away."

Before entering the parlor, Gordania queried, "The war?"

Emma stretched out her arm and touched Gordania's shoulder. "You don't know about the war? Where you been child?"

"I arrived less than a year ago, by ship from Liverpool. I have not heard of any wars."

"Liverpool? And where might that be?"

Gordania walked into the parlor. "Liverpool is in England."

"England?" Emma's chuckle swelled to an exuberant laugh. "Is you an Englishman, then?"

Gordania smiled—the first time since her arrival in Brookline. "Hardly. I'm from Scotland. Dunnet Head, to be precise. Liverpool was merely my point of departure."

Emma slapped her white apron with both hands. "Dunnet Head? Never heard of it either."

"Few people have. It is very far from here."

"Well then. I'll fetch Mrs. Brewster. I'm sure she'll want to hear all about where you is from all over again. You're just wasting your time telling me about it. Sit down and make yourself at home, Miss Sinclair."

"Thank you, Miss Johnson, but I prefer to stand until Mrs. Brewster arrives." After Emma had gone to find Mrs. Brewster, Gordania walked slowly in a small circle. Elegant chairs with patterned cushions and a settee arrayed all around an ornately-carved table with large picture books on top. Original oil paintings painstakingly aligned on flawlessly-smooth plaster walls. Floor-to-ceiling wood shelves, on both sides of the French doors leading to the entry foyer, filled with leather-bound books and carved sculptures of dogs and glazed ceramic vases and a twelve-and-one-quarter-inch-high bronze songbird by Alfred Dubucand* (although Gordania did not know this at the time) and a carefully arranged formation of lead revolutionary war soldiers

---

* 19th Century French sculptor, primarily of animal subjects.

marching away from a gimbaled oil lamp. Polished oak floor strewn with elaborately-woven throw rugs. Exterior glass doors leading to a covered porch and flagstone patio and green lawn and pruned trees and beautiful flowers and a stone bird feeder with moss growing on one side. A gleaming-black upright piano fitted into the corner with sheets of music organized across the—

"Miss Sinclair?"

Gordania spun around and discovered a woman standing just inside the French doors. Middle-aged but still attractive. A hint of sorrow in the eyes. Wholesome bosom and hips with an enticing remnant of hourglass. Fastidiously-shaped flaxen hair with a few telltale steaks of gray. Elegant dress decorated with pleats and silk bows and ivory buttons. Smooth hands obviously saved from manual labor. Expensive and overly-large broach glinting a ray of light from the garden. "Yes, I'm Gordania Sinclair."

Eva Corrine Brewster noted the various repairs on Gordania's high-necked white dress. Clearly intelligent. Beguiling green eyes. Good posture. Naturally pretty but not in an overly pretentious manner. Stunning auburn hair braided to a loose ponytail hanging below the waist—functional if not fashionable. Obviously in need of money. "I understand from Emma that you have inquired about the job of governess?"

Gordania curtsied slightly. "Yes, ma'am."

Eva gestured toward the settee. "Then please do sit, and we will discuss your qualifications."

"Then you have not yet filled the position?"

"No, but we have interviewed several good candidates already. Please sit."

Gordania nestled into the settee next to Eva Brewster. "I am prepared to discuss my qualifications as requested in the newspaper announcement."

Eva folded her hands. "Your accent. Are you British?"

Gordania folded her hands too. "Scottish, ma'am. I was born at Dunnet Head, in northern Scotland, in a lighthouse."

Eva's eyebrows lifted. "A lighthouse? My goodness. And what has brought you from the lighthouse at Dunnet Head to the shores of America?"

"Quite simply, ma'am, to find a better life. My father thought I should come to America, although my mother did not agree with the idea."

"Really. How interesting. And can you read and write? Although my husband does not believe it is necessary, I am looking for someone who can teach my daughters to read with understanding and to write with skill."

Gordania answered assertively, "Yes, ma'am. My mother and father taught me to read and write, as well as the basic rules of English grammar and spelling, and I have previously taught young children to read and write in Scotland."

"You enjoy reading, then?"

"Yes, ma'am. Very much."

"I see. And what have you read that might convince me of your proficiency?"

Gordania allowed a few moments to reflect because she thought a poor answer might cost her a chance at the position. "I have read *Paradise Lost* by Milton. I have read many of the Shakespeare plays; my favorite is *As You Like It.* I have actually never seen a Shakespeare play, but I would like to. I have read many of the poems and other works of Elizabeth Barrett Browning. I have read *Ivanhoe* by Sir Walter Scott, and also *The Talisman.* I love Charles Dickens, and also Emily Bronte, although she only wrote the one novel. Jane Austen is an exceptional author, but I have only read *Sense and Sensibility* and *Pride and Prejudice,* although I have read both twice. I should try one of her other novels someday. My father inspired me to read Robert Burns, but I do find his writing a bit heavy at times. When I was a very young girl, around twelve, I read several works by—"

Eva lifted her hand and presented the palm to Gordania. "Miss Sinclair, have you not read any American authors?"

This question surprised Gordania. "I read the books available at the lighthouse."

"The lighthouse?"

"Yes, ma'am. The lighthouse at Dunnet Head."

Eva lowered her hand. "Of course. The lighthouse in Scotland. But did you grow up there as well? Did you not have opportunity to read books at other places? A local library, perhaps?"

"No, ma'am. I did not travel far from Dunnet Head until my voyage to America, less than a year ago."

Her voice flat and businesslike to this point of the interview, Eva now spoke with improved compassion. "Oh, my dear. I did not mean to belittle the books you have read. I only asked an innocent question." She adroitly shifted the topic. "And when were you born?"

"February 24, 1847, ma'am. I'm twenty-three."

"A long time to live in a lighthouse."

"I did not mind it. I had the love of my family. I always had food to eat. I always had tasks to keep me busy. And I learned how to maintain the light—an uncommon skill for a girl."

Eva breathed deeply. "Yes. Family is certainly. . . ."

Gordania waited an uncomfortably long time for Eva to finish her incomplete sentence before ending the silence with her own question. "Do *you* spend much time teaching your daughters to read and write, Mrs. Brewster?" She regretted having asked the questions before the last word passed her lips.

Eva did not appear offended by the impertinent question. "I would love nothing more. Unfortunately, I have suffered periodic bouts of melancholy since the birth of Bethany, my oldest daughter. It is not possible to properly educate my daughters when there are times I cannot even arise from bed, sometimes for a week at a time. And I do not care for the roughness of the local school in Brookline. It is really no place for my daughters." Eva touched Gordania on the hand. "This is why we are hiring you to be their governess."

Gordania blinked. "Have you given me the job, then?"

Eva smiled. "Don't act so amazed, Miss Sinclair. Yes, I have given you the job. You will be the perfect governess for this household. Can you begin tomorrow?"

Several months had passed since Gordania's first day as the Brewster family governess, and an unexpected meeting with Csongor Toth in the parlor just before lunch had troubled her beyond what she thought possible. After escorting Bethany and Bathsheba upstairs for their afternoon nap, she stopped at the door to the master bedroom. She raised her hand to knock, but waited when she heard Eva sobbing. She held up the crisp white business card Csongor had given her and mouthed the first line: CSONGOR TOTH, ESQUIRE. Wedging the card beneath the fingers of her fist, she knocked on the door using her rhythmic habit: three crisp taps, a quarter rest, and a final tap. The sobbing diminished and then stopped altogether. Gordania moved her cheek close to the door until her lips nearly touched the smooth paint. "Mrs. Brewster, is everything alright?" Nothing. She tried again. "Mrs. Brewster, are you—"

Eva Corrine Brewster interrupted Gordania with a faintly quavering voice. "Yes, yes... Miss Sinclair. Everything is fine. I am merely feeling a little downhearted today. Please see to the children. I hope to improve after a little rest. I may join you all for dinner."

Gordania stuffed the now crumpled card into a pocket. "I will see to them, ma'am, as you wish. Do you want me to wake you for dinner?"

Eva sniffed and then coughed. "Please, no. Miss Johnson will fetch me for dinner when it is time. But thank you for the offer. I do appreciate it."

"Yes, ma'am. I shall leave you to rest, then. Please call me if you need anything."

"Thank you. I shall."

After this odd conversation with Mrs. Brewster, Gordania sat on the porch and read three chapters of *Moby-Dick* while Bethany and Bathsheba slept. When the girls awoke from their nap, they galloped down the stairs, skipped across the foyer, and raced into the kitchen in search of their governess. Emma Johnson chased them out of the kitchen with a large wooden spoon and sent them to the porch. When they found Gordania, they reminded her of the promised afternoon trip to the river to look for tadpoles. She acknowledged the promise in a halfhearted manner, but admonished that an hour of study was first required to justify the adventure. Bathsheba complained, but Gordania held fast and sternly ushered the girls to the library to read and study the finer points of the semi-colon. When they had completed the lessons, the girls ran out of the house and galloped down Linden Avenue toward the river with Gordania trailing some distance behind. The three had only captured seven tadpoles when ominous clouds dark with moisture began scudding in from the turbulent seas to the east. Gordania and the girls fled the river with haste. The first rain drops splattered against the roof just after they had arrived beneath the protection of the porch.

Eva did not come down to the dining room for dinner. Miss Johnson had spoken with her through the locked bedroom door twice, and explained to Gordania and the girls that Mrs. Brewster had lost her appetite and felt quite exhausted since the afternoon. Because Mr. Brewster had not yet returned from Boston, Emma, Gordania, Bethany, and Bathsheba enjoyed a fried chicken dinner by themselves. Gordania read to the girls after dinner while Emma cleaned up the dining room and kitchen, and after playing a spirited game of hide-and-seek for an hour or more Gordania tucked the girls into bed around nine. Emma retired for the night a half-hour later. Normally in bed by ten, Gordania decided to wait in the parlor for Mr. Brewster to return so that she could tell him of Eva's condition. She had completed three more chapters of *Moby-Dick* and had extinguished the kerosene lamp before retiring for the night when the front door slammed and Mr. Brewster staggered into the foyer. Gordania set the heavy book down on a small table next to the settee and listened. The storm still raged against the windows looking out into the garden, and distant rumbles of thunder reverberated off the trees. Something shattered against the hard marble floor, possibly the flower vase on the table next to the kitchen door. Gordania stood and called out, "Mr. Brewster, is that you?" More thrashing about and then an alarming bump against the wall just outside the French doors. "Mr. Brewster, is everything alright?" The French doors opened, but Gordania could not see in the darkness. "Mr. Brewster?" Lightning flashed a few miles east of the house and the illuminated foyer silhouetted Mr. Brewster's massive frame. "Mr. Brewster?"

Meredith Brewster, his overcoat soaked from the storm, his blood seething with alcohol, his breath rancid with the smell of whisky, spoke in angrily-slurred tones. "Where ish my wife. I want to make yuv…to her. I haven't…made yuv to her…for three, three years. Where ish she?"

Gordania clutched the fabric around her neck. "Mr. Brewster, you are drunk!"

"Where ish my wife?"

"She is not well today. Please leave her alone and go to bed, Mr. Brewster. And do it quietly, or you will wake the girls."

Meredith Brewster took two steps into the room and wavered. The anger in his voice intensified. "Who are you…to tell me if I can shee my wife, or not. If I cannot…make yuv to my wife, then you will have to do."

Gordania's voice tightened. "Mr. Brewster, you have been drinking and you are not in your right mind. You shall do no such thing. Now please go to bed, and I will do the same, and we will agree to forget everything." Gordania attempted to walk around the intoxicated man who blocked her way.

Meredith reached out and snatched Gordania's neatly-braided ponytail. "Yooer not going aneeewhere, my lille girl." He jerked Gordania backwards and shoved her hard against the bookshelves next to the French doors.

The back of Gordania's head slammed against a hardwood bookshelf and flashes of light exploded chaotically behind the fluttering lids of her partially-closed eyes. She nearly swooned from the sudden pain, but the sound of fabric ripping away from her scarred neck and the feel of a clammy hand on her naked breast renewed her stamina. She pushed against his chest with both hands but did not possess enough strength to deter him. "Stop this Mr. Brewster. You are not well!" The hem of her dress rose above her knees and a hand pulled her bloomers down. "Mr. Brewster. Please stop." A forearm pressed roughly across her throat and lifted her heels off the floor. Clawing fingers probed between her thighs. "Mr. Brewster, I cannot breathe!" Gordania's arms flailed against the leather-bound books, and her knuckles scraped along the outstretched wing of the bronze songbird she had admired many times before. As Meredith Brewster fumbled with the buttons on his trousers and pressed even harder against her throat, Gordania seized the songbird with her left hand, raised it high above her throbbing head, and screamed: "Mr. Brewster, if you do not stop this instant, I will . . . ."

The bodice of the white dress soaking wet and shredded beyond repair, rivulets of icy rain dripping from the matted hair of her tattered ponytail, and her pleasing derriere splattered with mud and shivering wildly against the cold granite step, Gordania Sinclair clutched the top of her dress in a forlorn attempt to conceal the hideous scar while she waited next to the main entry of the Revere Bank Building at the corner of Franklin and Devonshire Streets. She had fallen to the ground seven times in the raging storm and darkness, and now both knees throbbed with pain. She began rocking back and forth and massaging her swollen knees when an elegant black carriage with a black horse and white-gloved-black-suited driver—

she recognized the carriage instantly—clattered up to the entry. A dapper Csongor Toth disembarked, waved the driver on after opening a stylish umbrella, approached the entry doors with confident strides, and halted abruptly in front of Gordania three steps down. He casually retrieved a pocket watch from his vest and clicked open the cover. "My dear Miss Sinclair. Whatever has brought you to my doorstep at seven-twenty-seven in the morning on such a miserable day? I can't imagine, but I am confident you will tell me in good time." He observed the torn dress and matted hair. "And I see that you have primped for our rendezvous. How sweet of you to think of me in this way."

Gordania's natural courage evaporated when she forced herself up and put weight on her knees. "Csongor. Something terrible has happened, and I didn't know where else to go for help."

Csongor remained composed as he continued his evaluation of Gordania's frightfully disheveled appearance. "Oh come now, Miss Sinclair. Nothing could be as bad as you say. Please accompany me up to my office, and we shall talk about this alleged terrible thing." He held out his arm and Gordania rested a shivering hand on top.

"You don't understand, Csongor. I have done something so terrible that it pains me to even think of it." Rainwater dripped off her trembling lip.

Csongor led Gordania through the entry doors and across the foyer to the elevator.* He pushed the wall button. When the elevator arrived, they entered the car. Csongor pushed the fifth floor button. The steam-powered elevator jerked momentarily and then accelerated upward until it reached an astonishing velocity of 40 feet per minute. Gordania squeezed Csongor's arm more tightly when the elevator convulsed. The car soon arrived at the fifth floor. Without speaking, Csongor ushered Gordania across the hall to his office leaving a trail of puddles behind, unlocked the door, and directed her to the chair in front of his desk. He locked the door, and a distant flash of lighting illuminated the room in synchrony with the sharp click of the key. He walked across the office, lowered himself into the chair behind his desk, and folded his hands. "Now, Miss Sinclair, please tell me what is troubling you, and we shall see if there is some way I can assist you."

---

* The first elevator was installed in New York City in 1857.

Gordania clenched the torn fabric around her neck even more tightly. "I have murdered Mr. Brewster."

Csongor drummed his fingers together. "My goodness. And how did you do it?"

"I hit him in the head with a bronze songbird. I did not mean to kill him, but he had ripped my favorite dress and was attempting to have his way with me and I panicked and grabbed the nearest thing of weight I could find and since he had pushed me against the bookshelves and I couldn't breathe and then I remembered the bronze songbird so I took it and swung it at him and I only meant to drive him away but it made such an awful sound when it hit his head and he screamed and fell to the floor and didn't move and there was so much blood and I dropped the songbird and Miss Johnson came running into the room because she heard the commotion from her room down the hall and she looked at Mr. Brewster and touched him and told me to run from the house as fast as I could and I ran from the house without taking any of my things and when I—"

Csongor arose and Gordania closed her mouth. He appeared even more relaxed after hearing the appalling story. He spoke in smooth, professional tones. "First of all, my dear, you did not murder Mr. Brewster. Murder implies an unlawful killing, particularly with premeditated malice. Did you kill Mr. Brewster with premeditated malice?" Gordania shook her head side-to-side. "I didn't think so. Would it be fair to say that you killed Mr. Brewster in self-defense?" Gordania nodded. "This is clear to me as well. Secondly, Miss Johnson—who I only met briefly in passing—gave you excellent advice. Although I shouldn't share this with you, the circumstances indicate otherwise. The death of Mr. Brewster leaves his son in full control of the family estate and its vast fortune. I have heard from Mr. Brewster himself that the son is a malignantly vindictive individual. I can therefore presume with reasonable assurance that he will use some measure of his newfound wealth to track you down and convict you to a life in prison...or worse. The family is very powerful in Boston, both socially and politically; I cannot imagine how you will escape this result, even if I were to represent you in court."

A tear spilled down Gordania's cheek. "Then what am I to do? I have nowhere to stay. I have no money. I have no clothes. Should I turn myself into the police?"

Csongor sneered sarcastically. "It would only help the family to spend less money tracking you down. No, absolutely not."

Gordania's lip quivered. "What then? What am I to do?"

Csongor bounded to Gordania's side. "Come with me, my woebegone girl. First we must dry you off and buy a new dress and shoes. A warm coat and sturdy travelling chapeau are also advised." He briefly touched Gordania's shoulder. "A few other modest changes might be in order too, if you are to have any chance of escape."

"But I have no money. What little I have saved is in my room back at the Brewster home with all of my other things. I am now completely penniless."

Csongor placed his hand beneath Gordania's elbow and encouraged her to stand. "Do not worry of money, Miss Sinclair. The charming vision of you dripping wet and splattered with mud has rendered your pastoral beauty even more alluring, and is worth far more than the price of a few articles of clothing."

"But—"

"Do not speak any more, Miss Sinclair. We have work to do, and likely very little time to do it before the police arrive. I know of a store down the street where we can find the requisite clothing. When we have completed this task, I shall tell you what I have in mind."

"But—"

Csongor touched Gordania's lips to silence her. "No more words, my lovely Gordania. It is time to make haste if we hope to succeed with my plan."

Gordania waited some distance from the busy ticket windows of the Boston, Hartford & Erie Railroad Passenger Station while Csongor dickered with the clerk. She toted a new canvas handbag with some essential toiletries and a change of undergarments and fidgeted uncomfortably in her new clothing: a simple black travel dress with black-fabric-covered-buttons and only a dash of gray trimming the high collar and the cuffs of the long sleeves; sensible ladies lace-up leather boots with flat heals (also black and suitable for running from the police according to Csongor); a practical wide-brimmed straw hat with black fabric trim and black streamers that Csongor insisted would provide some protection from the oppressive sun she would likely encounter in the Utah Territory (Csongor had found an all-black bonnet, but did not purchase it because he said it diminished Gordania's rustic beauty); a rather masculine dark-gray wool jacket with large pockets to provide warmth and to shed the rain; and Csongor's final masterpiece of disguise, a new hairstyle with braided ponytail completely snipped off, remaining locks parted in the middle and trimmed smoothly just below the jaw line, and any remnant of auburn hair dyed black as coal. She fidgeted even more when Csongor approached. Not only had she murdered, or rather killed a man—an act she would never have dreamed possible before her departure from Scotland—but she was also a fugitive from the law.

Csongor appeared oddly jubilant. "I have purchased your ticket." He opened the ticket and confirmed the departure time. "I consulted the map and have decided to send you to the most isolated place I could find. I had to make a difficult choice between Seattle and Silver City, but in the end I chose Silver City because very few have heard of it. This ticket will take you to Ogden by way of Chicago, where you will change trains.* You should have a few hours to walk around the city, if you care to, but please avoid any police or overly-inquisitive men you may encounter. When you arrive in Ogden you will have to arrange passage to Silver City via stage-coach. I don't imagine it should be too difficult."

"But Csongor, I have no money. I left what little—"

"Not to fret, Miss Sinclair. I have deposited ten fifty-dollar bills in the inside pocket of your new jacket and another three thousand dollars in your bag. This should be sufficient to buy passage to Silver City and to pay for room and board until you can find a new occupation."

"But Csongor, I could never accept such a—"

"It is but a pittance of my great fortune, Miss Sinclair. I must insist that you accept the money graciously and consider it my gift to your new life in the wilderness of Idaho."

---

* Allowed more time to research and plan, Csongor would have purchased a ticket to Kelton, six stops and 84 miles west of Ogden. Although a stagecoach line operated between Salt Lake City and Boise, Kelton was the primary transportation and shipping center for routes to Boise and then to Silver City and the mineral-rich Owyhee mountains.

"But—"

"Not another word. I will consider it a personal affront if you do not accept the money. And three more things before you board the train—"

"Three more things? But you have already done more than you should."

"One never does enough, my dear. First, the final touch to your disguise." Csongor reached inside his jacket and pulled out a pair of spectacles with dull-silver wireframes. He used both hands to guide the frames over Gordania's ears and to wedge the bridge on her nose. "There. The color blends very nicely with the jacket."

"But Csongor, my eyesight is excellent."

"No matter. The lenses are clear glass, but you will still have to clean them occasionally or they will obscure your excellent vision. And you must leave them on at all times to conceal your identity. Do not forget this."

"And the second thing?"

"An easy one, unless you choose to forget. For the time being, you must avoid using your real name. I have therefore chosen a new moniker for you. From this day on you are Alexandra Smythe from Liverpool, England. I have prepared a few notes concerning your family background, as well as a personal letter I wrote to Miss Smythe while she was changing into her new clothes. Present this letter as evidence if you must prove your identity. You cannot afford to hesitate should you find yourself in the unavoidable position of responding to questions from the authorities. You must therefore memorize the notes. And practice a new signature until you can execute it flawlessly."

Gordania skimmed the page of handwritten notes and the counterfeit letter. "Why the name Alexandra?"

"It is the name your parents should have given you in the first place."

"How long must I use this new name? I am not sure I'm very fond of it."

"It matters not whether you are fond of it or not. You must not use your real name for at least three years. Maybe longer. You will have to decide when it is safe to emerge from the charade. It is possible that you may never use your real name again."

"Then why Liverpool? Will people not recognize I come from Scotland?"

"Because you have some knowledge of Liverpool. And people will not recognize where you come from at all. They will probably think you come from Hungary."

Gordania licked her lips and swallowed. "And the third thing?"

Employing unusual sleight-of-hand (and a curious bit of misdirection), Csongor produced a small pistol from thin air. "I have acquired a derringer* for your personal protection, as well as a box of ammunition should you need to reload. Keep it nearby at all times. Sleep with it under your pillow. Should someone attempt to arrest you, dispatch them quickly with the derringer and walk away. The pistol will allow you a second shot should you miss the first time, and is much easier to conceal than a bronze songbird. I recommend some target practice when you find the opportunity." Csongor hid the derringer in Gordania's coat pocket and dropped the box of ammunition into the canvas bag.

"But Csongor, I could never kill anyone again. The experience has been too horrific for words."

Csongor snorted, "Nonsense. The second time is always easier. The third time even better."

"The third time? I do not believe you."

"Believe what you want, my dear, but what I say is true. Now, you must board the train. It leaves in less than five minutes, and I don't like you loitering on this platform out in the open."

"What will you do then?"

"I will carry on with my life, just as you will. Now board the train, and remember to wear the spectacles at all times and to keep the derringer within easy reach." Csongor lifted Gordania's elbow and guided her to the passenger car.

"Will I ever see you again?"

"I doubt it, my fair Alexandra. Now off with you."

Gordania ascended the iron steps to the car platform and turned to wave goodbye, but Csongor had already dashed through a crowd of travelers. She caught a last glimpse of his back, then walked into the passenger car. When she had settled into her seat, she was instantly overcome by exhaustion and fell into a deep, troubled sleep, but not before removing the uncomfortable spectacles in contradiction to Csongor's instructions. She did not awaken until the train stopped unexpectedly at Brookline

---

* Csongor has supplied Gordania with a new Remington derringer manufactured in 1869 with rifled over-and-under barrels, .41 rimfire caliber, silver finish, and dark walnut grips.

Station. She sat up and searched through the dusty window, and there on the platform stood two policemen with Jonathan Brewster. Gordania remembered the glasses but could not recall where she had placed them. Her trembling hands groped through pockets and around her legs. She found the errant spectacles in the canvas handbag and put them on before Jonathan and the two policemen entered the passenger car. The three men strolled down the narrow aisle, glancing from side to side at each of the seated passengers. When they reached only a few paces away from Gordania, Jonathan paused and said: "If Miss Sinclair is aboard this train, it should not be difficult to find her. She has the most beautiful auburn hair braided to a ponytail, and it hangs well below the waist. It is quite marvelous, really. And she always wears white. I have never seen her in anything else. But make no mistake, constables: Gordania Sinclair is a wicked temptress who will stop at nothing to achieve her evil goals, and I intend to see that she hangs for this outrage against my family."

Gordania squeezed the derringer in her pocket and shivered when she heard the accusation. *Only two bullets for three men. Don't know how long it will take to reload. And where did Csongor put the box of ammunition? Can't look for it now. Too suspicious. Don't know how to reload anyway. Just sit still and try to look relaxed. Heart pounding in my head. Can they hear the pounding? Heart pounding. Can they hear it? Pounding.*

One of the policemen stared directly at Gordania, hesitated, and then simply tipped his hat. Gordania readied the derringer, but he continued down the aisle. Jonathan and the two policemen stepped off the train and walked into the station. The train jerked and began rolling forward; within minutes the steam locomotive and its tail of cars raced westward. Still exhausted, Gordania tried to resume her nap, but this time the rhythmic din of wheel against rail and the troubling vision of the policeman tipping his hat—and the remembrance of nearly shooting him—haunted her and prevented sleep.

Chapter Seventeen

Chicago, Illinois
July 1870

Winging beneath a luminous blue sky horizon-rimmed with billowy cumulus clouds, and returning from a less than triumphant exploration of an offshore barge, an intrepid Rock Pigeon soared to nearly two hundred feet above Lake Michigan some distance east of the city. Straight ahead, a long timber breakwater with neatly-spaced rows of sea-blackened timber piles and random dock structures ran from left to right to hold back the swelling waters of the lake from a slender gray strip of reclaimed land bristling with closely-spaced train tracks. A single locomotive puffing black smoke and hissing white steam hauled seventeen freight cars north over the rails nearest the breakwater. Beyond the reclaimed land and tracks, a dusty promenade and rigidly-spaced grid pattern of city blocks and streets and walks and trees and commercial buildings and homes and spewing factories and undeveloped parcels flowed miles to the west before dissolving into the hazy distance. To the right, the breakwater thrust northeast into the lake and formed a geometrically-slant-sided peninsula south of a broad viaduct where various tracks fanned out into a railroad yard to connect with other docks and warehouses and two grain elevators and dreary service buildings and the massive barrel-vaulted Illinois Central Depot. The viaduct skirted the northern foundations of the grain elevators and plunged more than a mile into the city before splitting into two separate branches—one heading northerly and one southeast. Sailing ships and ships under power and barges and small boats and other vessels navigated along the waterway in both directions and spilled out into the gray, choppy waters of Lake Michigan. A passenger train, waiting patiently for departure, projected out of the nearest of three great arched openings puncturing the southern wall of the depot below the gable end of the barrel-vaulted roof. The Rock Pigeon glanced briefly at the depot, but spotting a promising flurry of companions on the other side of the promenade—beyond the slender strip of reclaimed land and tracks—glided to the left and began a rapid descent. The pigeon soon confirmed his target and then maneuvered artfully into a steep dive.

Embroiled in the fluttering chaos of dozens of swooshing pigeons, two birds in particular caught the attention of Manfred Herrmann when they viciously pecked at each other in an apparent fight to the death over the relatively large chunk of bread tumbling untouched between them. Manfred tore off another piece from the remnant of his stale loaf and tossed it directly at the sparring birds to prevent an escalation of the confrontation, but only a moment after the bread hit the ground a new pigeon plunged unexpectedly out of the eastern sky and snatched the morsel away. Pleasantly warmed by the afternoon sun and cheered by the sound of children playing somewhere down the promenade, Manfred chuckled at the comical aggressiveness of pigeons. Because his train was not scheduled to leave for several hours, he threw chunks of bread into the swarm of pigeons until he had shared what remained of the loaf, then positioned his suitcase on its end and sat on the clumsy chair before commencing a thoughtful observation of the countless people occupying the sun-warmed promenade.

A father, mother, and three daughters (each separated by roughly two years)—the entire family dressed in white except for the man's dark gray pantaloons—strolled by at a leisurely pace and chattered and laughed as they passed. *Gray pantaloons. If only he had worn white the whole family would match. A beautiful afternoon. Better than I expected when I got up this morning. I shouldn't eat so much for breakfast. Enjoyed my time here, although I silently grumbled about the trip when Professor Strathmore suggested it. Nice to see a big city like Chicago. Don't know if I would ever come back. Sort of smells like livestock and smoke all the time. Probably won't ever come back. No reason to, really. They must be happy... at least for the moment. They probably argue all the time at home.*

A short man with luxuriant handlebar moustaches and wearing a dented felt bowler and rumpled pinstripe suit scurried along the promenade in the direction of the train depot lugging two overly-large suitcases that frequently bounced on the uneven ground. *The suitcases are larger than he is. Probably heading for the same train I'm on. Doesn't leave for over two hours. What's his hurry? He could slow down and enjoy the day. Lots of Lutherans here. More than I expected. Probably never find this many Lutherans in one place ever again. Nice to meet some of them, even if our religious ideas don't match perfectly. Makes you think. I suppose that's worth something. He should get his suit pressed. And it wouldn't take much effort to remove that silly dent from the—*

A muscled workman, with flannel sleeves rolled up tightly above the elbows and toting a heavy oil-stained tool box with the handle of a hammer and the toothy end of a saw sticking out, hustled south with lengthy strides. *He looks very strong. Wouldn't want to get into a fight with him. Wonder what he's working on. A new house, maybe? A boat? Is he finished for the day or walking to another job? No way to tell by looking at him. Well-used tools. Must be a carpenter. Noble profession, carpentry... same profession as—*

A brown-roofed carriage pulled by a slavering white-and-gray-speckled mare raced across Manfred's view, but he did not look quickly enough to distinguish the occupants. *Expensive looking carriage but the horse is a bit old. Suffering in the heat of the afternoon. Like to give it some water, but nothing I can do about it. Silver City. Still don't know where it is. Hope I like it. Have to make it to Kelton first, and then Boise City, and then figure out how to—*

A young boy wearing a smudgy white shirt, tweed knickers, and a Chicago White Stockings baseball cap jogged by playing a game of hoop rolling, the hoop stick ringing pleasantly against the rolling hoop every two strides and the diameter of the hoop extending to his waist. The metal hoop bounced on a small rock and the boy skillfully tapped it back to the ground. *I used to love the same game when I was a boy on the farm in Iowa. Whacking an old wagon wheel rim along with a hickory stick. Haven't played it for years. He's very good at it. Must play a lot. Nice catch on the bounce. No, I probably won't come back here again. Rather see somewhere else. Never been to New York or Philadelphia. Boston neither. Never been to a lot of places.*

Powered by four husky oxen straining against leather harnesses, a flatbed wagon overloaded with an odd assortment of lumber rumbled south at the pace of a well-dressed gentleman engaged in a Sunday constitutional. Two men sat stiffly on the wagon seat and yelled various profanity-strewn encouragements at the oxen. Manfred sniffed the pleasant fragrance of the freshly-cut wood then focused on a spot directly forward of his makeshift seat. His vision blurred on the spot, and when the wagon had passed he quickly regained focus on a solitary figure standing beyond the path of the wagon and facing away from him toward the chilly waters of Lake Michigan. The figure rotated a quarter turn to regard the wagon. The figure rotated once more until it stared directly at Manfred sitting on his suitcase. *A pretty woman. Very pretty. But why dressed all in black on such a warm day? Black hair cut very short. Not my cup of tea, but strangely sensual. Black dress. Black shoes. Dark gray jacket slung over her arm but otherwise black. Black ribbons in the hat. Short black hair. Short. Black. Glasses. Must read a lot. An intelligent face. Mysterious face. Anxious face. Wouldn't mind meeting her, but I've other plans to attend to. Should I wave to her? She's looking right at me. Should I wave? No. Better not to wave. Wouldn't be right to wave to a strange woman dressed in black who I've never met. Prefer white. Prefer. But black is fascinating. Warm feeling in my stomach. Not right. Not right at all to feel this way. Black hair cut short. Growing warmer. Must be the sun. Must be.*

The woman touched her glasses, tugged at the brim of her black-ribboned hat, glanced at Manfred one last time, then pivoted south and hurried away. *There she goes. Missed your chance. Very mysterious. Wish I had waved, but then again, might have come to no good. Have to catch the train, anyway. Should get going. Don't want to rush. Pretty. Very pretty. Very fascinating. Very mysterious. Maybe a little too mysterious. Probably not right for you, anyway. Not right. Keep telling yourself this. What a fool. And a damn coward too. You shouldn't swear, even in the seclusion of your mind. Not right to swear. Not right. Even though you haven't spoken the words, God knows. He knows. Should have waved. Should have. Missed your chance. Never see her again. Never. Damn coward. And a fool.*

Comfortably seated facing the back of the train after stowing his suitcase, Manfred gazed dreamily through a polished window of the Pullman car that would transport him from Chicago to Kelton. He continued his observation of people walking along the train platform beneath the impressively-vaulted roof of the depot, but soon grew impatient to begin his journey. A second train, steam billowing across two sets of shiny tracks, clattered into the station on the opposite side of the next platform. Travelers poured from the train and filled the platform with chaos. A uniformed conductor appeared below Manfred's window. The conductor briefly displayed a large gold watch hanging from a gold chain before yelling something and waving his arm. The conductor backed away and the train moved. And then Manfred observed a most astonishing sight: the mysterious woman in black running along the platform with long athletic strides, skillfully dodging left and right around people and suitcases and carts and iron columns, the gray coat and a canvas bag held in graceful arms and providing a measure of balance as she swerved around each new obstacle. Manfred pressed his cheek against the window to improve his view, but when his nose had nearly touched the glass the running woman vanished from his sight. The train gained speed and sunlight instantly filled the car when it burst from the great arched opening at the end of the depot. The conductor and the running woman appeared at the end of the aisle and began walking toward Manfred. Manfred's eyes instantly fell on the rise and fall of her lovely bodice and then discovered the glistening moisture above her lip, but he sheepishly fumbled with his ticket when she unexpectedly glanced at him.

The conductor escorted the running woman to a seat across the aisle from Manfred and one row back: an unfortunate location because it allowed clear views in both directions. The conductor pointed at the seat with the flattened palm of his hand. "You can sit here, Miss. You'll have a good view of where the train is going and maybe a little privacy too. Would you like me to stow your coat and bag?"

The running woman dropped the coat and bag on the seat and deftly removed the black-ribboned hat. She fiddled with her spectacles and brushed both sides of the short-cropped black hair with her hand. "Thank you sir, but I prefer to keep my personal things close at hand. I'm sure you understand." The lilting cadence and pleasant brogue of Dunnet Head washed over Manfred. A rush of warmth tumbled down his spine before igniting a shiver across his back, a sensation he had never before experienced. The woman groped an outside pocket of the jacket and carefully folded the jacket before sitting. She braced her head against the juncture of the seat and wall, the coat spread over her legs and her hand concealed in a pocket. She seemed fast asleep in a short while.

After spending too much time observing the running woman, Manfred took a book from his suitcase (*The Innocents Abroad*, by Mark Twain) and began reading to keep his head down. Unfortunately, his eyes still wandered to the running woman every few paragraphs. After several pages of "reading," he marked his place, closed the book, and just gawked at her continuously for minutes at a time. An hour later, he paced up and down the aisle to stretch his legs, always glancing furtively at the sleeping woman when he passed by. On his fourth pass, she stirred quite violently and the jacket covering her legs fell to the floor, revealing a small pistol in her hand. Manfred looked around the car. None of the other passengers had noticed. Manfred wiggled into the seat facing the sleeping woman. He retrieved the coat, brushed it off, and spread it over the sleeping woman's hand and legs to conceal the pistol. When he released the coat, the sleeping woman flinched awake and glared directly at Manfred.

Manfred spoke first, his voice less than composed. "My deepest apology Miss. I did not intend to wake you. I merely—"

The pleasant brogue now hardened with agitation, the running woman interrupted, "What are you doing?"

"I was merely—"

She sat up and inadvertently pulled the derringer into view. "Do you have business with me?" Her hands shaking, she fumbled the pistol into a pocket.

"No ma'am, I was merely—"

"Do you not understand the danger you were in? I might have shot you. You must leave me alone... this instant."

"But Miss, please let me explain. I meant no harm. I was merely—"

The running woman's voice began to tremble. "Please go back to your seat and do not talk to me ever again. Please."

Manfred did not try to utter another word. He retreated to his seat. During the remainder of the long trip, he avoided the running woman whenever practical. He passed her awkwardly several times in the aisle to and from meals (his chest brushing her bosom once), but they never spoke. When they both sat in the passenger car at the same time, he faced away from her and read *The Innocents Abroad* or stared out the window at the endless prairie or slept. When the train arrived in Ogden, Manfred focused on the approaching depot—a crudely-built two-story gable-roofed wood structure freshly painted an astonishingly bright red—and the handful of passengers waiting to board. His mind momentarily distracted, he nearly gagged on a swallow of spit when he turned his head and looked straight into the mysterious emerald eyes of the running woman. She slid toward the window until she faced him directly and their knees nearly touched. "I want to apologize before I leave the train."

Manfred coughed to clear his throat. "Apologize? No need. You had every right to behave the way you did."

The running woman persisted. "I must disagree. I'm sorry to have responded with such anger at the beginning of our trip. I know you meant no harm."

Still flustered by his unexpected proximity to the running woman, and captivated by the hue of her eyes and the lilt of her voice, Manfred could not think of a witty rejoinder. "My… name is Manfred Herrmann… from Iowa." He clumsily held his hand out.

Without smiling or nodding or taking Manfred's hand, the running woman retorted dryly, "I suppose it would only be proper to share the same information with you. My name is Alexandra Smythe, from Liverpool."

"Liverpool? You mean in England?"

Alexandra rose and slid gracefully into the aisle. "I cannot speak more. I only wished to apologize for my beastly behavior. Goodbye, Mister Herrmann." The running woman skipped briskly to the back of the passenger car and hurriedly disembarked. Manfred rushed to the opposite side of the car and pressed his face against the window, but could not find her anywhere on the platform. He scanned the front of the station, but she had disappeared. Saddened, he returned to his seat. As he waited for the train to speed away, he thought to himself: *A lovely name. Alexandra. Alexandra Smythe. Lovely voice. Missed your chance a second time. Now you will certainly never see her again. Never. Never. Never. Just as I suspected, you are truly a damn coward. Shouldn't swear. Not right to swear. And a damn fool too.*

Although much smaller than Ogden, Kelton offered a surprising array of useful facilities including a train station, blacksmith, livery stables, two hotels (one with a second story), two saloons, a mercantile for agricultural implements, a mercantile for general merchandise, a mercantile for drugs and notions and books and stationary, a post office, and a stagecoach company. After leaving the relative comfort of the train and stepping into the dusty heat of a Utah afternoon, Manfred's first impressions of the small town did not inspire him to stay longer and he decided to immediately seek out the stagecoach company to buy a ticket. He did take some time to peruse the narrow passenger and freight depot: a one-story, wood-framed building with steep gable roofs, double-hung windows painted white, dark-stained vertical wood siding, and a raised wood platform that reduced the step off the train to only a few inches. He moved along when four men began noisily unloading wood crates and coils of rope and iron-rimmed wagon wheels from the first of two boxcars. A wizened little man directed him down the dirt street in front of the depot to the Northwestern Stage Company to make arrangements for travel to Boise. Once inside the weathered building (and horse stables), Manfred conferred with the stagecoach agent—a young and impertinent fellow who apparently thought he deserved better than Kelton—who said he had missed the stagecoach by a full day and would have to wait until morning for the next departure. Manfred purchased a ticket, and the impertinent agent admonished him to return no later than 6:00 a.m. to avoid missing the stagecoach again.

Ticket in hand, and disappointed to stay the night, Manfred asked the impertinent agent, "Can you recommend a good hotel?"

The impertinent agent scolded, "How should I know which hotel you should stay in? Never had the need to stay at any of them."

Manfred postulated (respectfully), "Well then, if you were forced to stay at one of them for reasons out of your control, which one would *you* choose?"

Realizing that the man standing in front of him had no intention of going away without an answer of some sort, the impertinent agent sneered, "The big hotel down the street, I reckon. The one to the east. It's the only hotel with two floors. I don't see how you could miss it, unless you're some sort of fool. Do you know which way is east?"

Manfred muttered something inaudibly before answering, "Yes, east is the direction I just came from. Thank you for the advice. I shall return at six in the morning."

Manfred stayed the night on the second floor of the hotel in a small room with a double bed (clean sheets and feather pillows), a chair, and a small table equipped with porcelain wash basin and pitcher (filled with clean water). He enjoyed an elevated view (through a single double-hung window) of the sun-yellowed grass, scrubby bushes, scattered rocks, and low mountains to the north. He ate dinner and breakfast in the small dining room on the ground floor. He arrived at the Northwestern Stage Company office at 5:53 a.m. the next morning and presented his ticket to the very same impertinent agent, who, surprisingly, was a bit less impatient, if not less churlish. At exactly six o'clock, Manfred heard the commotion of the stagecoach and its four rambunctious horses out front. He carried his battered suitcase outside and waited by the coach next to an elderly gentleman and his wife who he had not seen before. Weather and trail dust had scoured the once bright vermillion paint on the sides of the coach to a lackluster pinkish-red and the once lively yellow of the wheels and running gear to a muddied gray. A driver and a second man—a double-barreled shotgun slung over his shoulder—appeared. Both men wore identical mud-stained boots with tan-colored pants tucked in, yellow bandanas tied loosely around their necks, leather vests decorated with tarnished silver buttons and frayed strips of leather, and sun-faded-wide-brimmed felt hats tilted to block the sun. The two men worked efficiently together to load the passenger luggage, two canvas bags of mail, and a small padlocked strongbox with "U.S. Army" printed in white letters, into the rear boot.*

Manfred initiated a conversation with the elderly gentlemen while he waited to board the stagecoach. "On your way to Boise?"

The elderly gentleman, dressed in tweed jacket with wide lapels and a black string bow tie, supported himself comfortably on a black cane. "Yes, my wife and I are heading to Boise where we hope to find our son.

---

* The rear boot is the leather-flapped baggage compartment at the back of the stagecoach. There was also a smaller boot forward of and below the driver's seat.

We haven't heard from him in over a year." The man's wife looked away when he said this.

Manfred sensed anxiety in the man's voice. "Did he write a letter to you?"

"Yes. He was sending a letter every month, but then the letters stopped completely, and we haven't heard from him since."

Manfred suggested a plausible explanation, even though he did not believe it himself. "He probably just got busy with something and hasn't found the time to write."

The leather-vested-silver-buttoned stagecoach driver yanked the passenger door open. "Time for everyone to load up. We've got a long trip ahead of us and we're already late."

The shotgun man climbed up to the driver's seat and braced his foot jauntily against the top of the front boot. Manfred allowed the elderly gentleman and his wife to enter the coach first, and then insisted that they occupy the seat facing forward. Before Manfred could sit, the driver released the break lever and snapped the reins and the four muscular horses jerked the stagecoach forward. Plunging face-first toward the elderly wife's lap, Manfred grabbed a handful of the roll-up curtain at the top of the window to avert an embarrassing disaster. After he had regained his footing and settled into the cushioned seat, he prepared for the long trip to Boise—a dusty, sweaty, rollicking, butt-slamming, teeth-jarring, nerve-grating forty-hour journey across desolate lands through places with strange names Manfred had never heard of before: Crystal Springs, Clear Creek, Raft River, City of Rocks, the summit of Goose Creek Mountains, Oakley Meadows, Mountain Meadows, Rock Creek, Desert, Clark's Ferry on the Snake River, Sand Springs, Malad, Clover Creek, King Hill, Cold Spring, Rattlesnake, Canyon Creek, Baylock's, Black's Creek, and finally, the intended destination of Boise City. Mercifully for Manfred and the elderly couple, the stagecoach stopped at intervals of 50 to 60 miles for rest and meals at small wood-framed home stations built just for this purpose at City of Rocks, Clear Creek, Oakley Meadows, Clark's Ferry, Cold Springs, and Baylock's. In particular, the home station at City of Rocks—a rustic log building with low ceilings 13 hours beyond Kelton—offered the surprisingly comfortable amenities of sitting room, barroom, dining room, kitchen, three bedrooms with clean sheets (primarily for snowbound passengers), and a large fireplace. It was here that Manfred learned the names and home state of his traveling companions: Arthur and Sarah Pence of Pennsylvania. And it was here that he experienced the strongest (and blackest) cup of coffee he had ever tasted (or seen). Unfortunately for Manfred and his fellow passengers, City of Rocks was the first stop on the long trip to Boise, and the accommodations at the remaining home stations proved less accommodating and the vileness of the coffee intensified. But when not enjoying rest and food and coffee at one of the home stations, Manfred and Arthur and Sarah endured the stagecoach as it rushed ahead in a relentless onslaught of chaotic motion, constantly maneuvering along the tortuous trail, wheels pounding incessantly against the pulverized soil of the uneven ground, choking dust spreading in ragged plumes around the advancing coach, sweat-lathered horses straining hard against the creaking wood and leather harnesses. Some distance north of the final meal stop at Baylock's, and less than a mile from Black's Creek, the inexorable progress of the stagecoach abruptly ended.

After twenty seconds of inactivity, Sarah Pence shifted to her right and peered through the window. "It's hard to see through the dust, but it looks like there's a tall man wearing a brown duster* and a brown bandana over his mouth standing there with a shotgun. He doesn't look too friendly, if you ask me."

Arthur Pence looked through the window on his side of the coach. "The same man is standing over here, but he's wearing a yellow duster and he's not tall, and he's pointing a rifle at us instead of a shotgun. He doesn't look at all friendly either."

Manfred heard a muddled voice to the front of the stagecoach, and a muddled reply directly above. Then he heard what sounded like the shotgun hitting the ground. Annoyed and impatient, he swung the door open next to Sarah Pence and plunged into the stifling air of the late afternoon. Startled, the man in the brown duster—also wearing a brown hat pulled down to the top of his bushy eyebrows—pointed the shotgun at Manfred's chest. Manfred took one more stride before showing the man

* A duster is a long trail coat commonly worn by cowboys to provide protection from dust and rain.

his empty hands. "No reason to shoot, my friend. I am a man of God, a Lutheran Minister from the state of Iowa. I mean you no harm."

Overhearing the conversation, the man to the front of the stagecoach—obviously the leader of the robbery because of his black duster, black hat, and black bandana over his mouth—trotted to the side until he could see what problem had distracted his business associate. He chided brown duster in derisive tones. "It's just a harmless preacher man. Can't you see? Now get the damn shotgun back on the stagecoach men. They's the one's you ought to worry about, not a harmless preacher who doesn't even know which end of a gun to hold." Brown duster pivoted instantly and aimed at the seat at the top of the stagecoach. The leader waved yellow duster to the front of the horses, then scowled at the stagecoach driver and shotgun man and demanded, "Now both of you get down here where I can see what you're doing. And keep your hands up in the air so you don't get accidently shot."

The two stagecoach men complied. After the driver hit the ground, he said to the leader, "We've got the army payroll on board. You'd be making a big mistake if you took it. Don't think the U.S. Army would take kindly to it if you steal their payroll."

Brown duster fidgeted. "Can I shoot him boss? I never get to shoot anybody. Bill's got to shoot somebody. But I never get to shoot anybody."

The leader sucked in a deep breath and glared into the cloudless sky above. "Dammit Charlie, just shut the hell up! Next you'll be telling 'em *my* name. We're here to rob this stagecoach, not to shoot anyone... unless we have to because they won't give us what we come for." He resumed his discussion with the stagecoach driver and shotgun man. "That's why we're here—to take the army's money. We know all about it. You are going to just give it to us, right? I don't want to have to shoot the both of you, 'cause if I did I'd take the money anyway and you'd both be shot, which makes no sense to me. Does it make any sense to you?"

Manfred offered the driver his advice. "I'd give them the box. No reason to get killed over a little bit of money. Worldly possessions are not worth dying for."

The leader gleefully agreed. "That's right, Mr. stagecoach driver. Listen to the preacher man's sermon. Best I ever heard, if you ask me. Short and to the point. No reason to get shot over a wordy position. Now hand over the box afore I makes a mistake and tells Charlie here to blow your heads off."

Followed closely by the leader and brown duster, the stagecoach driver and shotgun man shambled to the rear of the coach, unfastened the leather flap of the boot, and pulled the U.S. Army strongbox to the ground. "I still don't think you ought to take it. Army's going to be awful mad if you take their payroll. *Awful* mad. They might just hunt you down and hang you. Then you'll be sorry you took the dang thing in the first place."

Overhearing the talk of the army payroll, the third man, the one wearing the yellow duster, deserted his post at the front of the horses and jogged to the back of the coach and kneeled down next to the strongbox. He caressed it with leather-gloved fingers. "This looks like what we're after boss. You was right again. That fellow who works for the Northwestern sure knows what he's talking about."

The leader sneered. "Damn it Bill, of course it's what we're looking for, you stupid fool. Don't you think I knows what I'm doing? Now both of you get that dang box tied to one the horses and let's get the hell out of here."

Just as yellow duster and brown duster lifted the heavy box off the ground and began to carry it to the waiting horses, a lone rider came into view a few hundred feet to the south at the top of a small rise in the trail. The two men paused and yellow duster gaped through the heat waves swirling up from the dry ground. The rider kicked his horse and advanced on the coach. The leader held his hand above his eyes and squinted as the lone rider approached within a hundred feet. The leader finally recognized the blue uniform of a U.S. Cavalry officer. The lone rider trotted right up to the three bandits and the stagecoach driver and shotgun man and Manfred.

The cavalry officer dismounted and saluted crisply to the stagecoach driver. "Major Ethan Plantagenet at your service, sir. Might I assume that you and your passengers are in need of assistance?" Yellow and brown duster dropped the strongbox. The shotgun man jumped when it clunked on a rock and rolled to its side.

Surprised, but unconvinced of any meaningful threat, the leader taunted the cavalry officer. "What the hell is this? You ride up here all by your lonesome, and then stand there like a stuffed turkey expecting us to hand over this strongbox? Charlie, go ahead and shoot him. Now's your chance."

Major Plantagenet held up his hand. "First, I did not specifically ask you to hand over the strongbox, although I will at some point in this conversation. Second, before you shoot it would be only proper to inform the three of you that I am accompanied by a dozen buffalo soldiers of the 10th Cavalry Regiment: they are escorting me to my new command at Fort Boise. It is your misfortune that we happened along by chance and are about to thwart your attempted robbery. At this moment, each of you has two Spencer Carbines* trained on your hearts. Should any one of you make the unfortunate decision to shoot me, you will die before even raising your weapon."

The leader glanced around again and snorted, "I don't see nobody nowhere, and what the hell is a buffalo soldier? Never heard of such a thing."

Major Plantagenet lowered his hand and Charlie, the one in the brown duster, froze. "I suppose—before I give the command to kill all of you in a single coordinated volley—you deserve an explanation. I'd never heard of them either until recently. They are Negro troopers. Congress formed the regiments after the war."

The leader chuckled. "Darkies? You 'spect me to shake in my boots? They probably can't hit the broadside of a barn."

Major Ethan Plantagenet confessed, "I might have thought the same a few months ago, but I have learned otherwise during my travels from Kansas to my current location. I can assure you that any one of these men can shoot a sitting crow from a hundred yards. They are only half this distance from where you stand, and I believe you are larger than a crow." Ethan spoke directly to the leader. "Are you a gambling man? Care to take a chance?"

Manfred joined the conversation. "I'd put your guns down and surrender, like the good Major says. If these men are anything like the 54th Massachusetts Infantry,† you *will* all die before lifting a finger."

---

* The .56-50 caliber Spencer Repeating Carbine was originally issued to Union Army cavalry units in late 1863. The carbine was relatively light, highly accurate, and with a seven-round magazine offered a high rate of fire.

† The 54th Massachusetts Volunteer Infantry Regiment was one of the first official all-black regiments in the U.S. Army during the Civil War. The unit saw

The leader scoffed at Manfred. "I'm not sure I believe anything this here cavalry officer says. I'm still thinking he's alone and just feeding us a bunch of bull."

Manfred assessed the demeanor of Major Ethan Plantagenet and suggested, "He looks like a man of his word to me. I'd do as he says."

Without waiting for a signal from the leader, yellow duster and brown duster dropped their weapons and held up their hands. This infuriated the leader. "Oh what the hell? Pick those guns up right now. We're not surrendering to one man just 'cause he's wearing a pretty uniform and talks pretty too. Look around! Do you see anybody? Hell, I don't even see the damn crow he's talking about."

Yellow duster responded, "I ain't going to get shot just 'cause you say so. You go ahead and get shot if it suits you. I'm listening to the preacher man."

The leader stomped his foot on the ground and snatched his hat off and threw it down and kicked it. "Dammit. I should have knowed better than to hook up with a couple of cowards like you." He drew his revolver and dropped it to the ground and held his hands in the air. Arthur and Sarah stepped from the stagecoach, and six buffalo soldiers appeared in a ragged arc to the south and began walking. Major Ethan Plantagenet strode over to the woman, grasped her hand, and raised it to his lips. "My deepest apologies, ma'am, for the regrettable events of this day. May I invite you and your travelling companions to dinner tomorrow at Fort Boise to allow me the opportunity to demonstrate the genuineness of my regret?"

Sarah Pence twittered, "Why Major, it would be our honor to join you for dinner. We would be delighted."

Manfred pondered another delay before reaching his intended destination. "I'd have to stay an extra day in Boise City, but it would not speak well of my manners to turn down such a gracious invitation. Yes, I will join you for dinner tomorrow night."

Major Plantagenet nodded. "Then I shall work out the details in the morning since this is my first visit to Fort Boise and I am not familiar with the accommodations. But let us agree to eight o'clock tomorrow night as we may not have the opportunity to communicate before dinner." He

---

extensive action, including the heroic assault on Fort Wagner near Charleston, South Carolina.

turned to the tall, brawny sergeant now standing to his right and aiming a pistol at yellow duster. "Sergeant Johnson, round up these pathetic scoundrels and load the strongbox. We shall escort the stagecoach safely to Boise City."

Sergeant Johnson snapped off a crisp salute and barked, "Yes sir," then growled at a corporal and a trio of privates lingering nearby. "You heard the Major. Round up these scoundrels and get this stagecoach loaded up. I don't want to be waiting here for any Indians who might show up to spoil our day."

The leader, the one in the black duster, spat on the ground and swore as a black corporal tied his hands behind his back and led him away. "Damn. Negro troopers. Who ever heard of such a thing? Damn."

Constructed by the U.S. Army in 1863—the same year as the founding of Fort Boise—the one-story-gable-roofed Commanding Officer's Quarters provided a pleasant venue for the promised dinner. Refreshed from a good night's rest and a bath, Manfred Herrmann swallowed scalding-hot coffee from a porcelain cup and listened to Sarah and Arthur Pence tell the story of their lost son. He noted the superior flavor and aroma of the coffee when compared to his recollection of the vile brew served at the various stagecoach home stations during his forty-hour trip from Kelton to Boise. Major Ethan Plantagenet had changed into a dress uniform for the event, and frequently expressed ardent interest in the conversation.

Arthur Pence concluded, "And this is why we've traveled all this way to Boise City. When we did not receive another letter from our son for over a year, we packed our bags and boarded the train west. Tomorrow we will begin our search."

Major Ethan Plantagenet consoled, "I understand. I would have done the same. Because I have only just arrived, I do not know the quality of local law enforcement, but I sympathize with your plight and will do what I can to help."

Sarah's lip quivered and she blinked back a tear. "Thank you Major Plantagenet. My husband and I feel very alone in this strange land. We both would appreciate your help."

"It would be my honor to assist you and your husband." Major Plantagenet adjusted the position of his chair to appraise the temperament of Manfred Herrmann, who had spoken little during the meal. "And what is the nature of your story, Mr. Herrmann? Have you also travelled to the Idaho Territory looking for someone?"

A surprisingly vivid image of Alexandra Smythe flashed in Manfred's mind. "Not at all. I'm on my way to Silver City. I hope to take the stagecoach there tomorrow."

Major Plantagenet persisted. "Silver City. Yes, I've heard of it. A wild mining town in the mountains south of here. And where do you come from originally?"

Manfred relaxed momentarily before stiffening again. "Iowa. I was born on a farm in eastern Iowa and grew up there. Worked on the farm most of my life."

"I see. And what specifically brings you to Silver City?"

"I've been sent there to establish a Lutheran mission church."

"Of course: a man of God. We could use a few more of you in this part of the world. And have you travelled the country much before now?"

Manfred hesitated. "I travelled extensively during the war."

This statement intrigued Ethan. "Really? And what places did you see during the war?"

Manfred briefly considered a canard, but then spoke honestly. "Many places I will never forget. Belmont, Missouri. Shiloh, Tennessee. Corinth, Mississippi. Many places."

Ethan appeared unruffled, but his gut had convulsed. "Shiloh? And what year did you travel to Shiloh?"

"The year? 1862. I was there April sixth and seventh."

Ethan's hand twitched beneath the table. "Would it be proper to assume that you served with the Union Army at the Battle of Shiloh, or do I assume too much?"

Manfred settled back in his chair. "Yes, but it is not something I care to talk about." After a brief silence, he disclosed, "Although I cannot escape nearly daily thoughts of that terrible day."

"Yes, it was a terrible day. May I inquire which unit?"

"The 7th Iowa Infantry Volunteers."

Ethan sipped brandy from a crystal glass and then slowly set the glass on the white table cloth. "Before we talk further of these events, I must tell you something. I served with the 8th Texas Cavalry Regiment at Shiloh. I killed many of your brethren."

Manfred's countenance did not signal any particular reaction. He sat quietly for several seconds before speaking quietly. "And I must tell you that I also killed many of yours. I believe we are equal in sin."

After an unpleasant respite, Ethan stood and reached his hand across the table. "The war is over and I have put it behind me. However, I do believe we have been made brothers by our shared experience on the battlefield of Shiloh. May I offer my hand in friendship?"

Another unpleasant pause, but then Manfred also stood and slowly grasped Ethan's hand. "I would like nothing better."

Sarah Pence, no longer willing to hold back the writhing passions of both her lost son and the astonishing forgiveness unfolding at the dinner table, wept.

Chapter Eighteen

Fort Boise, Idaho Territory
August 1870

Reflecting ragged streaks of washed-out blue sweeping across a dome of partly-cloudy skies, the smoothly-flowing waters of the Snake River swelled against the vertical sides of a flat-bottomed ferry. An overhead line guided the wood-hulled ferry across the wide river, groaning frenzied rhythms through squealing iron rollers in protest of the strong lateral forces of the rushing waters. Warm prairie breezes whistled confused tunes on the vibrating overhead line and flickered graceful songs on the surface of the waters and hummed jagged melodies along steep-sided-green-topped cliffs rising vertically from the river westerly of the ferry crossing. A long, narrow grove of black cottonwoods spreading beyond the river near the ferry landing swayed defiantly against the insistent prairie winds and added fluttering broadleaf accompaniments to the rhythmic iron rollers and whistling overhead line and singing waters and humming cliffs. Roshan Kuznetsov listened to the multifarious sounds blend with the balmy air. He lowered his flannel-sheathed belly over the weathered wood railing, iron-spiked along the side of the ferry, and watched his sun-rimmed shadow dance along the surface of the swirling waters below. He raised an arm up and down three times to verify the shadow belonged to him, then waved both arms to confirm the discovery.

Gus Glenn, founder and owner of the ferry, stood next to a young assistant ferryman on a cantilevered wood platform attached to the deck of the vessel near the back and yelled at Roshan through cupped hands, "Don't you be leaning too far over the side. If ya fall in we won't look for you until the return trip, and by then you might be pretty hard to find."

Roshan straightened up and waved politely at Gus Glenn. He moved near Tseng Longwei, who patiently held the reins of Roshan's horse. "I tell you this Longwei, even if you don't believe it is of the truth my newest of friends: if we did not the waited for a long time of your working to the finish on the railroad because of... because of... what is it you call the thing of my speaking again?"

Tseng Longwei improved his grip on the leather reins and twirled the long, braided ponytail of his black hair between the fingers of his free hand. "Do you mean to say... my sense of honor?"

"Yes, is the same thing. Because of this *sense of honor*, which you have told of me before until I am tired of the hearing of the sense, we are much to the late of riches of the land of Silver City and we are still not walking on our horses to the left when we find the day. A year has fallen from my life and, as I explained in a minute when you were not to listen, we are still never close enough from the wealth to pick the gold maggots up by our hands."

The horse twitched when the ferry rose on a gentle swell in the current. Longwei tightened his grip on the reins and sidestepped closer to the horse. "It is not because of my sense of honor and my desire to fulfill my promised commitment to the Central Pacific Railroad that it has taken more than a year to reach this point in our journey to Silver City. It is because you did not know which way to go."

Roshan offered a vigorous counterargument. "What you speak is of a truth in the way I can see when I look to it, but I must argue to the other when I tell you are full of the real horseshit, and the real bullshit too, because we do not still have the wealth it is clear to the lips we could not buy the cheap whore with the money a man of any place would give to Roshan or to Longwei for this *sense of honor* of who you speak."

Tseng Longwei spoke patiently. "And I will offer you a counterargument as well, my illogical and rambling partner of business who speaks in endless riddles. It is not because I have not enjoyed our many adventures together while we have travelled far to the east on the Oregon Trail looking for the place to *turn to the left side when I find the right day*, as you explained to me when we forged our partnership. It is because we had already travelled east of the place to turn when we first met. In truth, we only needed to travel on the tracks a very short distance to the west and turn to the right to find Silver City."

Roshan snorted and gestured with his hands. "It is not of my fault we did not forge the meeting before our time in the mountains of the golden spike. You should have found Roshan to the other side before the spike of gold and the turn to the left on the right day would have found the land of Silver City in a time of the past." Roshan stoked his beard. "But I must share of you: I too think the adventure of the things before this time of day in the happy way. It is not the bad thing to learn the blacksmith and the horse shoes in the months of our time in the land of Laramie City. And of my remember of it, we could not find more of the turn to the left when the wealth of the each has for it nothing more to spend."

"Yes, I agree. Our many months in Laramie City learning the trade of the blacksmith may be useful in the future, but I am not the one who found you, you are the one who found me, and because I do not know this strange land where Chinese and Irish build railroads for the Americans who seem to possess endless wealth, I have no way of knowing where to find Silver City. I assumed you knew the direction. I also have fond memories of our time in North Platte learning to cut and sew canvas for the many wagons and prairie schooners heading in the direction we should have headed in the first place. This skill may also be of some use in future days, although I cannot say how or when."

Roshan snorted even louder and gestured with more determined agitation. "I am not the one of this land the same as you. The land of Mother Russia is my land of home. The land of Sitka is my home of land. The land of Seattle is my home of life. The land of San Francisco is my life of home. I do not know the remains of the land of America in the same way you do not know the remains. I only know of the turn to the left on the right day, and the day did not arrive in the soon time." Roshan softened his voice and concluded: "If you will listen to the lips of my words you will see truth in the lips."

The ferry landed at the northern shore of the Snake River and scraped noisily over the gravelly sands. Gus Glenn's associate ferryman skipped down the side of the ferry and pulled the gates open. Longwei, followed by Roshan, resumed the conversation as he guided the horse over the muddy ground to the continuation of the trail. "I think it is no longer of importance if we each thought the other person knew the way to Silver City because we have learned several new trades and we are still together after travelling a long time in the wrong direction and other unfortunate events of which I will not speak at this time because they likely will be of no use in the years to come other than to cause arguments. The thing of most importance now is this: I no longer doubt our business partnership was truly meant to be."

Roshan slapped Longwei on the back. "What you say is of the truth, my tiny black hair friend, and my lips see of it and my nose hear of it. I also have not the doubt God has blessed our look for the turn to the left on the right day. It is only my wish He did not wait for the such long time to turn us on direction of the west before we found much time from the spike of gold on the day we know."

Longwei led the horse up a gentle hill. "Do not underestimate the time we have spent together travelling in the wrong direction and learning new trades and sharing many unfortunate events. It has forged the friendship necessary to survive the many hardships likely to come in Silver City. Only God knows what is right for us, but I believe He has chosen our path for a purpose."

Roshan grinned. "Yes, of this we speak on the same pages to the book. Only God knows what to do to us, and I find happiness in the words you speak on this day. But I must speak the different words to you on one thing: the land of Silver City will be of a time the greatest of wealth for the each of you and Roshan. Do not believe the other word of this."

Longwei and the horse stepped over a jagged drainage, cut through the trail by a thunderstorm two days earlier. A flock of crows squawked overhead before diving though the branches of a young cottonwood. "No, my friend. I will not believe the other word of this. But I must point something out to you: at this point I have little choice. We have sufficient food and money to reach Silver City, but then I must hope any more adventures will not turn out to be of the unfortunate kind we have experienced more than one time on our journey. Although our friendship has survived to this point, I do not believe it wise to invite another test, especially the regrettable incident with the spittoons at the general store in Ogden of the Utah Territory. I truly hope I will never again in my lifetime repeat the events of that unfortunate afternoon."

Roshan did not see the cut in the trail and nearly launched himself headfirst into a bristly pile of sharp rocks after catching the heel of his boot. He tugged at his beard after regaining his balance. "Of the spittoons and the store of generals—and I must tell of you I did not see men of generals ... why the store is called of this name it does not make the truth to me—but where the trouble fell on both together I do not speak the otherwise of you. But I must again tell to you, Roshan did not have the knowledge of anything of too many spittoons lived in the store and when the many spittoons could fly above the head of Longwei and Roshan in the same minute of time when the men who found anger with Roshan for no reason I care to remember and picked them up with many hands and—"

Longwei grimaced and a mild gag crawled along the back of his tongue. "Please do not remind me of the details of the incident with the spittoons in the general store. I too did not know such a thing was possible, or that it would cause so much trouble with so many people at the same time. The event still brings me astonishment, and I do not wish to spoil my appetite for the evening meal. The remembrance of the incident already offers the possibility of spoiling my appetite for several weeks."

"Yes, the astonishment is much of me too, but today it is enough to have the money and the food until the land of Silver City is under our feet if you ask of Roshan this question. But because the River of Snakes find us, we must walk on the back of the horse to the land of Fort Boise to ask of the way to turn to the land of Silver City to follow the lips of the man who said of this in the land of Kelton at the building of trains. I am feeling the good of our walk on today and do not find worry to think about, if you should ask me to speak of things to be sure."

Longwei plowed his heel into the ground and pulled the horse's reins. "We are both walking at the moment. One of us should ride. Would you like to take a turn on the horse?"

Roshan backed away from the horse. "I took of the last time walking on the horse. It is good for you to walk on the back of the horse in the now. I will walk not on the back of the horse when the later time is here for all to see."

Longwei bowed graciously at the waist. He pulled himself onto the saddle without using the stirrup. "Such acts of kindness keep us together when we are cursing our misfortune and burning our arms on hot iron bars fresh from the blacksmith's furnace before the barn catches fire and jabbing our fingers on dull needles when repairing canvas on many prairie schooners and wagons heading in the direction we should have been heading in the first place. Thank you, my true but unruly friend."

"It is Roshan who is of the thanks. The travel of misfortune cannot argue we are now friends of truth. And if the luck does not find a way to the days before, Roshan and Longwei will find the land of Fort Boise by the day after the time of the missing sun, if you can hear to it."

The same flock of crows returned from the east, and intentionally darted just above Roshan and Longwei and taunted them with ominous bird calls before vanishing to the west behind a lumpy outcrop of mossy boulders.

To the surprise of Tseng Longwei, he learned at Fort Boise that the Irish not only worked on the railroads of America but also provided the primary source of recruitment for the U.S. Army. Longwei and Roshan were stopped and questioned by two blue-coated Irish privates at the main entry gate to the fort. They were stopped and questioned again by an Irish corporal when they wandered randomly across the hoof-pulverized-manure-saturated soil of the broad parade grounds. And an Irish sergeant asked Longwei to wait outside while Roshan went into the commanding officer's headquarters to ask for directions to Silver City. When Roshan entered the office, he quietly inspected the floor for any spittoons. Roshan marched to the front of the fort commander's desk and introduced himself. "Do you have any spittoons of brass in the place of this room? One time ago in the land of Ogden the spittoons of the store of generals did what who would not think of such a one? I must say to you if you are to hear of my lips before you believe: you are the lucky one who did not see of the many things of the spittoons in the store of generals. Like of my friend Longwei—who stands in the outside at this very moment of the today—said when we walked on the horse to the land of Boise on the day of the other time: *what man did not know such a thing was of a possible, or it would cause of the much trouble with so many people*

at time in the same. If you were of the luck to see such a thing with the many spittoons flying in the same minute of the clock, I have the certain idea you would not wish to see of such a thing in the time of your life or you—"

The commandant stood and reached his hand across the desk. "Major Ethan Plantagenet, at your service, sir. And what is this about a store of generals? I'm not sure I've ever heard of that particular commodity sold in a store."

Roshan crushed Ethan's hand before shaking it with prolonged vigor. "Roshan Kuznetsov from the land of Sitka and Seattle and San Francisco and also the land of North Platte, if you will believe it. I come to find a way to turn to the land of the Silver City. Can you tell me of this way?"

Ethan extricated his hand and uncurled his fingers. "You possess quite a grip, Mister Kuznetsov. Yes, I believe I can help you with this question. You are actually very close to your intended destination, although I feel obliged to warn you that Silver City is a wild and lawless town. I would advise you to think twice before travelling there."

Roshan blinked twice and opened his eyes widely. "You can tell of me of the turn to the left on the right day?"

Ethan sat in the dark-stained wood chair behind his desk. "If you turn left, you might end up heading east on the Oregon Trail, then who knows where you'll end up or what adventures you might encounter. I suggest you head south on the Boise and Ruby City Road. You'll know you're heading the right direction when you cross the Snake River."

Roshan nodded. "Ah, the River of the Many Snakes. I have seen this river of the day before, when Longwei and Roshan stood on the ferry of the man who is Glenn."

Ethan intertwined his fingers below his chin. "When you reach a crossroads near Booneville, you turn to the left. Continue down the road past Ruby City. The road is treacherous with many turns and hills and numerous opportunities to fall to your death if you are not careful, but will eventually lead you to Silver City. You can't miss it."

Roshan guffawed. "I am sorry to say if you would be of great surprise to see what Roshan and Longwei can miss on the road when we cannot find the turn to the left on the right day."

Ethan stood. "I believe you. And is there anything else I can assist you with today?"

"Can you walk to the outside and point of the way to the Ruby Boise Road? My good friend Longwei stands in the outside when we speak of these things and it would be of the good to point when he can see the hand of your finger."

"It's the Boise and Ruby City Road. And yes, I can point you in the right direction." Ethan guided Roshan to the recently-painted covered porch at the front of the building. During the meeting, Longwei had waited patiently next to a soldier on guard duty who did not speak much English.

Roshan waved at Longwei. "This is my good friend of many days, who may hear of our many adventures, Tseng Longwei."

Ethan thrust out his hand. "I'm Major Ethan Plantagenet. Pleased to meet you, Mr. Longwei. Mr. Kuznetsov has spoken kindly of you."

Longwei bowed without taking Ethan's hand. "Tseng is my family name. My first name is Longwei. In China we do it in this way."

Ethan bowed in return. "Of course Mister Tseng. But let us move to the front of the porch, and I can point you and Mr. Kuznetsov in the right direction. I wouldn't want the two of you to head east by mistake." Ethan strode to the front of the weathered wood porch and pointed a little west of south with his palm held vertical and the fingers joined. "Head generally south. You'll reach the Snake River in about 25 miles. Cross the river on the ferry, and in another 20 miles you'll reach Booneville, where there is only one road to Ruby and Silver City and it heads east. You can't miss it. The road is exceedingly dangerous. Please take care."

A buzzing mud wasp drew Longwei's attention up to the shingled underside of the porch roof. He watched the wasp disappear into a bulbous gray nest at the juncture of a wood joist and beam. "You would be surprised, Major Plantagenet, at what things Roshan and I are capable of missing."

Roshan slapped his leg and howled, "This is of the truth my business of partner Longwei. But think of our many adventures on the road to the left if we could have missed the most of! Think of the horse shoes. Think of the burning barn of hot iron. Think of the canvas wagons and pricking fingers. Think of the store of generals and flying spittoons!"

Chapter Nineteen

Boston, Massachusetts
September 1870

Coldly blue, Csongor Toth's enigmatic eyes probed the young man sitting in front of him. White linen sack suit* with matching vest and not a stain or loose thread to be found: *a little baggy around the shoulders and elbows, and a bit rumpled at the knees, but otherwise a good choice for the excessive warmth and humidity of the afternoon.* Heavily-starched white shirt with stiff collar accurately closed by a stud: *would prefer a symmetrically-knotted tie with a few dashes of color, perhaps dark blue with narrow gold stripes, or even the ubiquitous silk ribbon string bow tie Americans seem to prefer, but the stud has become quite common these days and is hard to resist.* Straw boater, head band crisp and clean, obviously purchased within the last few weeks: *he removed it immediately upon entering my office, which speaks well of his upbringing and good manners.* Cream-colored shoes carefully tied: *a commendable, if not triumphant, effort to blend fashionably with the color of the linen pants.* Clean-shaven face with strong nose, slender lips, impressive cheek bones, oiled and smartly-cropped brown hair parted in the middle: *I do not personally object to a bit of facial hair, particularly when the countenance presents such an uncompromising visage and the simple addi-*

---

* The sack suit, also called a walking or business suit, first came into fashion in America in the 1850s. It was typically fabricated of linen or wool. Although less formal than the frock coat, the sack suit was often a man's "best" clothing. The sack suit of the late 1800s and early 1900s ultimately evolved into the modern three-piece suit.

tion of a neatly-trimmed moustache does much to soften the effect. Maybe his youth does not allow the possibility of a robust moustache? Smooth hands with slender fingers and clean, manicured nails: *obviously a coddled existence with few, if any, expectations of real work. The ears. I missed the ears the first time. A bit large, but why do the ears intrigue me? What is it that suggests the likelihood of....*

"Mr. Toth? Have you considered my request?" Jonathan Brewster, a line a sweat forming above his lip, spoke in stoically impassive phrases.

Csongor Toth pressed his fingers down on the well-used blotter covering the working area of his desk and escaped momentarily from his reverie. "Yes, Mr. Brewster. I expended considerable effort and time in the consideration of your request." He relapsed into deep thought without offering any continuation. *I see it now. The ears. The ears offer the possibility of....*

Jonathan Brewster waited tolerantly for an answer, and when Csongor offered none he pressed, "Then what have you decided? Will you accept the job I have offered to you?" Still no response. "You will be well compensated, Mr. Toth. Of this you should have no doubt." Silence. "Mr. Toth?"

Csongor fell back in his banker's chair and rested his hands on the smoothly-curved armrests. "I have no doubt, Mr. Brewster, that I shall be well compensated. No doubt at all."

Jonathan Brewster spoke more rapidly this time, his voice now colored with subtle but rising impatience. "Then you have accepted the job?" Csongor still did not answer. "Mr. Toth, can I assume you have accepted the job of tracking down the temptress Gordania Sinclair and bringing her back to Boston to be convicted of the brutal and unprovoked murder of my father?" Still nothing. "Mr. Toth, what do you say? Will you accept the—"

Csongor Toth lifted his chin. "Yes, Mr. Brewster, I will accept the assignment you have offered. However, it could prove expensive and difficult to find her, and once found it could prove even more difficult and expensive to bring about her return to Boston."

Although increasingly agitated, Jonathan Brewster acted undaunted. "Mr. Toth, returning Gordania Sinclair to Boston for trial is the official purpose of this assignment. But, confidentially—and I know from conversations with my father that I can trust you in this—if it is not practical to bring her back to Boston to be legally convicted in a court of law and then hanged from the neck until dead, I expect you to arrange for her demise wherever she is found…discreetly. Although regrettable, it would not sadden me if some unwashed scoundrel bludgeoned her to within an inch of her life after, say, a failed robbery. Do I make myself clear on this?"

Csongor's lip curled upward, slightly. "Quite." He briefly succumbed to the earlier reverie before announcing decisively, "I shall begin immediately. And Mr. Brewster…I shall not fail you."

Jonathan Brewster pushed himself up from the chair and carefully adjusted the straw boater to a slight downward angle. "My father always said he trusted you, Mr. Toth. I would expect nothing less."

Csongor Toth rubbed his vested stomach against the polished stone edge of the semi-circular oyster bar and gleefully tossed back the last occupant of his plate of Narragansett oysters on the half shell. After the slippery mollusk had slithered deliciously down his gullet, he lifted a tall tumbler to his lips and finished off the last of his brandy and water. He clinked the glass down on the stone bar and posed contentedly on the wood stool. He waited two minutes before ordering a second plate of six oysters and a second tumbler of brandy and water. He had consumed three of the oysters and drained half the glass before a sturdy man—an inch under six-foot tall wearing black frock coat, charcoal gray trousers with black pinstripes, and black bowler—loomed behind him. Csongor slurped another oyster before pivoting on the stool to acknowledge the man. "Mr. Connelly. As always, you have arrived exactly on time. I was hoping you would arrive after I had consumed a second plate of oysters, but I should have known better. Shall we retire to one of the booths to allow more intimate conversation?"

Dougal Connelly shrugged his muscular shoulders. "We can go wherever you please, Mr. Toth. But I do not know why we can't meet in your office like usual, if it's privacy you want. The Atwood & Bacon Oyster House* is quite crowded today, and noisy to boot."

---

* Established in 1826 at 41 Union Street by Hawes Atwood under the name *Atwood's Oyster House*, the restaurant became *Atwood & Hawes* from 1842 to 1860 and *Atwood & Bacon* from the late 1800s into the early 1900s. At

Csongor picked up his plate and tumbler, slid off the stool, and walked toward an empty booth on the opposite side of the room. Dougal Connelly followed Csongor, who rotated his head only slightly to speak. "I too prefer the privacy and convenience of my office, but I am in the habit of eating oysters on Friday afternoon, and because today is Friday I had no choice but to arrange the meeting here. Would you care for some oysters, Mr. Connelly? They are particularly succulent today."

Csongor and Dougal Connelly wedged into the empty booth on opposite sides of the narrow table. Dougal did not remove his bowler, and then planted his elbows on the table. "Can't stand the slimy things. If you ask me, feels like a gob of snot squirming down your throat."

Csongor tossed another oyster into his mouth. "Very descriptive, Mr. Connelly, but I fear you are missing one of the many delights Boston has to offer the common man. Your loss saddens me."

Dougal Connelly shrugged again. "If you like 'em so much Mr. Toth, you can have my share. But I'll certainly have a whisky, if you're paying."

Csongor waved his hand at a nearby waiter. "Garçon! A whisky for the gentleman who despises oysters to his own detriment." He finished his last oyster just as the whisky arrived, then sipped brandy and water from the tumbler. "Since we have run out of things to say of the oyster, shall we get down to business? What information do you have for me on this fine Friday afternoon?"

Dougal Connelly finished half the whisky in a single gulp then wiped his mouth with a black sleeve. "I've spoken to dozens of train men. I found a conductor who remembered a pretty woman of about the right age and height reboarding the train to Chicago—in Albany, two days after the murder."

Csongor feigned surprise. "Really. How interesting. But many pretty women must ride the train to Chicago. How does this bit of circumstantial evidence prove you have found Gordania Sinclair?"

Dougal Connelly lowered his hands until both forearms rested on the booth table. "This is the interesting thing, Mr. Toth. The woman had short black hair instead of long brown. And she wore black instead of white. But

---

some point, likely around 1915, the restaurant was given its current name of *Union Oyster House*.

this conductor fellow remembers the woman in black because she kept taking off her glasses and putting them on again, over and over, like they didn't belong to her. He also said she acted really nervous about something. I think it was Gordania Sinclair in disguise."

Csongor melodramatically amplified his surprise. "Gordania Sinclair in disguise? In disguise!?" He took a quick sip of brandy and water, set the tumbler down a little too hard to emphasize his amazement, then took another sip. "Surely you can't be suggesting you believe this woman was Gordania Sinclair simply because she appeared nervous and fiddled with her glasses. Such behaviors might lead to a preliminary suspicion of guilt, but they are not sufficient to allow any specific conclusion."

Dougal Connelly smirked, "There's more." He finally took off the bowler and fanned himself with it.

"More?"

"When I spoke to young Mr. Brewster about his recollection of Miss Sinclair, he noted the color of her hair and her height and said she was pretty, but then he mentioned something else, something quite unusual."

"Unusual?"

"Quite. He claimed Gordania Sinclair could run like a man. He also claimed she was fast, even in the white dress she always wore."

"Run like a man? Fast in a dress? Forgive my doubts, but I do not see how these observations support your hypothesis, which I must say is rather shaky at the moment."

"I'll explain. This same conductor fellow, the one I just told you about, said when the train was pulling away from the platform the woman in black had to run to catch it."

Csongor ran his finger around the rim of the tumbler. "And this is supposed to convince me of something in particular?"

Dougal Connelly stopped fanning himself and leaned across the table. He lowered his voice. "The conductor said the woman in black ran like a man. Those were his very words. *Like a man*. And then he said—"

"There's more?"

"He said she ran like the wind, fast as you please."

Csongor did not speak for several ticks of the second hand. "I see, Mr. Connelly. Well, I must admit…you may have convinced me that you have found Gordania Sinclair. In disguise, of course. Who would have imagined it? But this conclusion suggests another question. From what we know, she was very poor. How could she have managed a train ticket when she had no money?"

Dougal Connelly pulled away and resumed fanning himself with the bowler. "Simple. The young Mr. Brewster informed me of this just the other day: all the money was missing from his father's pocket when they found him dead on the sitting room floor. Not only did she murder his father, she robbed him as well. She's a cold one, Mr. Toth. Make no mistake about it. A cold one."

Csongor finished the last of the brandy and water then waved at the same waiter who had brought the whisky. "Garçon! Another brandy and water for me, and another whisky for my business associate who has still not learned to appreciate the beauty of the exquisite Narragansett oyster." He restored his attention to Dougal Connelly. "I must say, Mr. Connelly: I hired you because I was told you are the best bounty hunter in Boston."

Dougal Connelly objected to this characterization. "I prefer to be called a detective, Mr. Toth. I'm not a bounty hunter."

Csongor waved his hand. "Of course. Detective. What do you suggest now?"

Dougal Connelly squashed the bowler on top of his head when the drinks arrived. "This conductor fellow had more to say. The woman in black had a ticket to Ogden in the Utah Territory. Assuming you're willing to foot the bill, I'd like to take the train to Ogden. I should have no trouble finding the young lady in short order, and when I do..."

"Yes. I believe your instructions are clear."

Dougal Connelly inhaled the whisky. He slammed the glass on the table to signal the end of the meeting. "Couldn't be clearer, Mr. Toth. Couldn't be clearer. I'd like to leave tomorrow. I'll be sure to pack my blackjack,* just in case I might be needing it."

Csongor scooted out of the booth and stood. "I agree wholeheartedly, Mr. Connelly. The sooner Miss Sinclair is brought to justice, the better for all of us."

* A blackjack is a small leather-covered bludgeon with a short flexible shaft.

Steam-piston-chugging southerly the next morning (Saturday) on the *Boston, Hartford & Erie Railroad* line after a 6:15 a.m. departure from the downtown depot, the passenger train followed the rails along a sweeping curve a quarter-mile from the station until it had swung a little north of west, crossed Harrison Avenue and Washington street, and then drifted to the left before crossing Tremont Street and settling into a long section of tracks heading a few degrees north of west. The blustery rains of a September storm drooled across the window next to Dougal Connelly's first class seat in the luxurious Pullman Sleeping Car Csongor Toth had reserved for him. Dougal smeared away a patch of condensation with his sleeve and watched the rain-smudged buildings and streets of southern Boston blur across his vision. The steam locomotive and trailing passenger cars rattled across the tracks of the *Boston & Providence Railroad,* continued on to the three-way intersection of Brighton Avenue, Beacon Street, and Western Avenue near the Charles River, then swerved southwesterly toward Brookline. The train curved south beyond the Boylston Street crossing, and after completing another half-mile of track turned westerly before arriving at Brookline Station. Dougal Connelly dozed while passengers scurried to and from the train. He sat up when the steam engine jolted each of the passenger cars into successive forward motion. The train continued southwest a short distance, then followed a smooth succession of curves west, northwest, and then southwest before crossing several country roads and passing to the left of the Chestnut Hill Reservoir. The tracks skirted the southern foot of Chestnut Hill (south of the reservoir), then traversed a mile of serenely pastoral country before reaching the small village of Newton Center (about seven miles west of central Boston). Before the train pulled away from the station, Dougal Connelly removed his frock coat and bowler and fell into a deep sleep, the steady din of the spinning wheels and vibrating undercarriage concealing his occasional snoring. He did not wake again until the train had completed stops in Framingham and Worcester. Dougal spruced himself up several miles after Worcester, then proceeded to the dining saloon car where he enjoyed a breakfast of two poached eggs, a thick slice of fatty ham, and strong coffee laced with whisky (supplied from his personal flask) while the train completed stops at Palmer and Four Corners. After breakfast Dougal returned to his seat and chatted with a young woman on her way to visit a great aunt in Buffalo. He thought of seducing her, but realized after several minutes of conversation that such an effort would likely prove fruitless. The train passed through Springfield before crossing the Massachusetts state line.

Dougal consulted his pocket watch upon arrival at Chatham, the first stop in New York: *9:37 a.m.—right on time, give or take a minute.* Only one small brown man with a small brown suitcase waited on the platform in Chatham, and the train soon pulled away from the town after he had boarded. The train next rolled across the Hudson River and Van Rensselaer Island into Albany: one of the oldest surviving European settlements of the original thirteen colonies—road, waterway, and rail transportation center of the northeast—eastern terminus of the Eerie Canal—home of the Albany Lumber District, the largest lumber market in the nation—and capital of the state of New York. Dougal drifted into another nap after departure from the station near the Hudson River, and did not awaken until several miles west of the city. The train advanced across New York, passing through Schenectady, Fonda, Palatine Bridge, Utica, Rome, Verona, and Oneida. Then on to Canastota, Chittenango, Syracuse, Port Byron, Clyde, Lyons, Newark, Palmyra, and Rochester. Although the more efficient course would have been to stay on the train to Buffalo and skirt the southern shore of Lake Eerie through Cleveland and Toledo, Csongor had insisted that Dougal Connelly change trains in Rochester and journey along the southern strand of Lake Ontario to the suspension bridge at Niagara Falls.* Csongor had never visited Niagara Falls, but had once received an impressive post card of the bridge and falls from a former client and had argued that Dougal should not pass up the opportunity. Because of this alternate route, Dougal stayed the night in Rochester and boarded the train on Sunday morning. After travelling through Brockport, Albion, Medina, Lockport, and the town of Niagara Falls—the final New York stop before entering Canada—the train com-

* The first suspension bridge, constructed in 1848, consisted of an 8-foot wide oak-wood plank deck suspended from iron cables and wood towers. The second suspension bridge, the one described here, was completed in 1855 at a cost of $450,000 and incorporated limestone towers at each end. Because of the increasing frequency and loads of train traffic, it was replaced by a third suspension bridge of steel towers, cables, beams, and trusses in 1886.

menced its approach of the suspension bridge romantically illustrated on Csongor's post card.

Around 9:23 a.m. the train slowed to 15 miles per hour and clattered along the raised track between a pair of tall, gently-tapered limestone piers at the eastern end of the suspension bridge. The sun, ascending in a crescendo of blissful warmth slanting low above the horizon from the east, glinted on four massive iron cables (stretched in pairs over each of the elegantly-detailed architectural caps at the tops of the piers) and sparkled on smaller cables arrayed from the hanging catenaries of the primary cables down to the stacked bridge decks below—an upper deck for trains and a lower deck for horse-drawn carriages and pedestrians. Directly to the south, a few miles away but clearly visible through a wide opening in the vertical cliffs containing the Niagara River,* the broadly-sheeting waters of the falls and billowing plumes of mist refracted the early morning sun into luminescent clouds of shimmering radiance. Dougal Connelly, sitting alone at his table in the dining saloon car, finished the last of his poached eggs and prepared to lace his coffee with whisky. After crossing the suspension bridge, the locomotive accelerated to 50 miles per hour and pulled the trailing cars across the southern tip of Ontario to Paris, London, and Sarnia. In Sarnia the steam locomotive and all of the cars rolled onto a ferry to cross the swiftly flowing St. Clair River. Upon docking in Port Huron, the train rolled off the ferry onto new tracks and began a gentle southwesterly sweep through the state of Michigan: Flint, Lansing, Charlotte, Battle Creek, and Niles. The train crossed the state line and skirted the southern tip of Lake Michigan until it turned westerly then northwesterly. After an abbreviated tour of the northwest corner of Indiana, the train crossed another state line into Illinois. Within an hour the train rumbled into the Illinois Central Depot in Chicago. Following a full-day stopover (purposely arranged by Csongor Toth to allow his bounty hunter, or detective, or whatever one cared to call him, the opportunity to sightsee in Chicago), Dougal Connelly boarded the *Chicago, Burlington, and Quincy Railroad* and begin the final leg of his long journey to Ogden.

---

* The Niagara River flows north from Lake Erie to Lake Ontario.

The new engine and cars travelled south along the shoreline of Lake Michigan a short distance then curved sharply west and rolled unhurriedly through the city center and suburban rim of Chicago and then on to the town of Riverside and over the Des Plaines River and then to Naperville, Aurora, Leland, Earl, and Mendota. Then across undulating prairies and ocean-like grain fields and densely wooded hills to Arlington, Princeton, Neponset, Kewaunee, Galva, Altona, Oneida, and Galesburg (a city of 14,000 residents and home to Knox College, where Abraham Lincoln first denounced slavery on moral grounds during a debate with Stephen Douglas). After taking on water and fuel in Galesburg, the train progressed to Cameron, Monmouth, Kirkwood, Sagetown, and the iron bridge over the Mississippi River into Burlington, Iowa.

Dougal Connelly disembarked the passenger train in Burlington—a bustling steamship port of 20,000 inhabitants and home to the *Chicago, Quincy, and Burlington Railroad*—and enjoyed a leg-stretching 15-minute walk in the humid shirt-soaking heat. After loading a handful of new passengers, seven wood-slatted crates of unknown contents, two rolls of barbed wire, and three canvas bags of mail, the train hurried away from the station and travelled among the rich farmlands and expansive cornfields and sprawling stockyards and flowing wheat fields and modest hills of Iowa through the pastoral towns of Mt. Pleasant, Fairfield, Agency, Ottumwa, Albia, Chariton, and Osceola (named after a Seminole Indian leader). Then quickly speeding onward to Afton, Creston, Villisca, Red Oak, Hastings, Glenwood, and Council Bluffs (the eastern starting point of the First Transcontinental Railroad and the last stop in Iowa before the Missouri River). The train navigated the Missouri River on a wide-beamed-flat-bottomed train ferry operated by the Council Bluffs and Nebraska Ferry Company. While he surveyed the distant shore of the river, Dougal Connelly thought to himself: *too many river crossings on ferries—someone should build a bridge, here and few other places.*

The ferry arrived in Omaha, Nebraska (a thriving town of 25,000 a little over 900 feet above sea level) soon enough, and, after a brief sojourn at the busy depot, continued west. On and on the train clattered, across level grasslands and then climbing higher and higher up the westward-ascending slopes of the Nebraska plains to Fremont, Columbus, Lone Tree (1,086 feet above sea level), Kearney (2,046 feet), Willow Island

(2,511 feet), the thriving metropolis of North Platte (600 residents), Alkali (3,308 feet), Julesburg (3,500 feet), Sidney (4,073 feet), Antelope, and finally across the Nebraska state line into Wyoming at the breathless elevation of 5,000 feet above sea level (more or less).

The train completed four quick stops at Pine Bluffs, Egbert, Hillsdale, and Archer before delivering a bag of mail in Cheyenne, a community of 6,000 residents and home to Fort D.A. Russell (established in 1867 to protect workers of the Union Pacific Railroad). Then up and up again into the Black Hills to Granite Canon and Buford and Sherman and through snow sheds and along wind-battered snow fences to the rocky summit at 8,242 feet above the sea then down and down into Laramie City and Coopers Lake and the beginning of the Laramie Plains. Then on again to Black Creek, Medicine Bowl, Carbon, and northward around the jagged slopes of Elk Mountain and across the North Platte River to Fort Steele, Creston, Red Desert, and Table Rock. Then into the Rocky Mountains to Bitter Creek, Rock Springs, Green River, Church Buttes, Bridger, and Piedmont.

Dougal Connelly reposed comfortably in his first class seat and watched the kerosene lanterns flickering in the windows of the Piedmont station. A gibbous moon washed the platform—empty save the conductor—with pale blue light and brightened the trees behind the building. He clicked open the cover of his watch: a few minutes after eleven and only ten miles from Utah. Dougal unfolded the traveler's map Csongor had provided when he boarded the train in Boston and ran his finger along the route and read the accompanying text in the dim light. Next up the summit at the line between Wyoming and Utah, an elevation of 7,540 feet above sea level, before plunging down to Evanston, Wahsatch, Castle Rock, Echo, Weber, Devils Gate (a small town he could not read because of a tear in the paper), and finally Ogden. *Not long now, then begin the search for Gordania Sinclair in earnest.* He reached inside his coat pocket and fondled the blackjack. *I doubt she will elude me much longer. No one ever does.* Dougal released the blackjack, pulled a rumpled envelope from the opposite pocket, and read the bold writing on the front:

OPEN UPON ARRIVAL AT PIEDMONT

He tore open the envelope and found a single sheet of white paper. He unfolded it and began reading.

Good evening Mr. Connelly,

If you have followed my instructions to the letter, you are reading this in Piedmont. I truly hope you have enjoyed the trip thus far, and that you successfully apprehend the fugitive Gordania Sinclair and bring her to justice. However, before you retire for the night, there is one more thing I would like you to see prior to your arrival in Ogden. If you will indulge me one last time, please step outside to the platform between cars when you reach the summit, which is also, as it turns out, very near the border between Wyoming and Utah, and look to the south. I've heard the experience is unforgettable. if the sky is clear and the moon is out, you should have no trouble appreciating this assertion.

Best Regards,
Csongor Toth

The passenger car lunged, rolled a few feet, and lunged again when the steam locomotive squealed away from the station. Dougal Connelly shoved Csongor's note into his pocket and dropped the envelope on the seat. A little perturbed of playing a silly children's game, he waited ten minutes before walking to the front of the passenger car. He opened the door and stepped to the platform as instructed in the letter. *A bit cool, but the moon is out and the sky is clear.* He looked to the south at the moment the train reached the summit. *Just a bunch of trees; can't see a thing, even if the moon is out.* The door opened behind him. Dougal recognized the distinctive military-style cap, black suit, and bushy sideburns of the conductor. The conductor shut the door.

"Now what? Do you need to see my ticket again?"

"No, I do not. I have a message for you from a Mr. Csongor Toth."

"Not more children's games? What's this message? It must be terribly important by the look of things."

"Come closer and I will deliver it to you."

Growing impatient, Dougal Connelly shifted close enough to smell the sweetness of the conductor's breath. "I'm listening."

The conductor winked nonchalantly. "Your services…are no longer required." The conductor pressed the tip of a stiletto against Dougal Connelly's chest just below his rib cage and then stabbed the entire length of the blade through vest and shirt into the left lung. Dougal exhaled a wheezy breath and clutched his hands around the sharp blade, slashing both thumbs. The conductor waited until Dougal inhaled, then twisted the blade clockwise with practiced expertise. Dougal tried to speak, but only a sputtering croak passed his lips. Without releasing the blade's pressure, the conductor reached inside Dougal's jacket and pilfered his wallet, pocket watch, and Csongor's note of instructions. "You won't need these anymore." The conductor maneuvered Dougal to the side of the platform. "Goodbye, Mr. Connelly." The conductor yanked the blade downward to remove it. Dougal Connelly—blood spurting through his fingers from the mortal wound—wavered but did not fall. The conductor admired this unanticipated strength, wiped the blade clean on the lapel of Dougal's jacket, and pushed him backwards off the platform. Dougal spiraled into the darkness and vanished down a steep ravine. After admiring the cold beauty of the night sky, the conductor tossed the stiletto off the platform before returning to the passenger car to purge the contents of Dougal Connelly's first class accommodations.

Clean-shaven with smartly-cropped brown hair oiled and parted in the middle, Csongor Toth bounded from the train in Ogden dressed in a dapper white linen sack suit with matching vest, heavily-starched white shirt with stiff collar accurately closed by a stud, recently-purchased straw boater, and neatly-tied cream-colored shoes. He carried a single leather valise under his arm. He walked briskly across the wood-planked platform and entered the two-story passenger depot. Once inside the sooty building, he walked directly to the window of the telegraph office. The agent sitting behind the counter shuffled some papers before looking up. Csongor spoke with crisp, aloof words. "I wish to send an urgent telegram to Brookline, Massachusetts. Can you accomplish this task?"

The agent grunted, "Course I can. That's what I'm here for." The agent slipped a sheet of paper and a nubby pencil across the counter. "Write the message down and I'll get it off today."

Csongor picked up the pencil and began scribbling on the paper. He spoke the message while he wrote: "To Jonathan... Brewster... Linden Place... Brookline... Massachusetts... Have reliable... information... Miss Sinclair... has fled... to Brazil... South America... Will pursue... immediately... Expect departure... within... the week... Kindly arrange... transfer of... 5000 dollars... to Western Union... Ogden... for expenses... I will not... fail... to bring her... to justice... Dougal... Connelly." Csongor slid the paper and pencil across the counter. "How much do I owe you?"

The agent counted the words in the message and grunted again. "That'll be eight cents."

Csongor pulled a dime from his pocket. "Here you are my good fellow. A bargain for a message as important as this one. Please keep the entire amount as a token of my appreciation for services well done." He nodded, pivoted smoothly, and swaggered out of the passenger depot into the purifying warmth of the street. When he had progressed beyond the shadow formed by the ridge of the depot roof, he said to himself, "Maybe I should explore the potential business opportunities of Silver City." He looked both directions before speaking again. "Yes, this is exactly what I shall do—but not before I have received the money transfer from Jonathan Brewster."

Excerpt from

A Concise History of the West

by Muireall Anne Ravenscroft

The Telegraph

Although many important discoveries and inventions preceded the invention of the telegraph -- the voltaic pile by Italian physicist Alessandro Volta in 1800;

an electrochemical telegraph by German inventor Samuel Thomas von Sommerring in 1809; the electromagnet by English physicist William Sturgeon in 1825 -- the history of the telegraph truly begins in 1832 with the invention of the first functioning device by Baron Pavel Schilling in St. Petersburg, Russia. Schilling set up his primitive telegraphs in two different rooms of his apartment and successfully demonstrated the "long distance" transmission of electromagnetic signals. A year later, in 1833, German mathematician and scientist Johann Carl Friedrich Gauss and physicist Wilhelm Eduard Weber collaborated to construct the first electromechanical telegraph and then successfully communicated between two of the devices over a distance of more than 1,200 yards in Gottingen, Germany. The discovery of the electromagnetic phenomenon of self-inductance by Joseph Henry -- an American scientist born in Albany, New York of Scottish immigrants (and first Secretary of the Smithsonian Institution) -- and his subsequent work on the electromagnetic relay provided the critical component of the telegraph that allowed a weak current to operate an electromagnet over long distances. David Alter, a prominent inventor living in Elderton, Pennsylvania, invented the first known American telegraph in 1836, one year before Samuel Morse produced his first practical equipment. During the same period, English inventors William Cooke and Charles Wheatstone developed the first commercial telegraph in Great Britain in May 1837. Although originally patented as an alarm system, it began commercial use on a 13-mile segment of the Great Western Railway between Paddington Station (London) and West Drayton Station in April of 1839.

Samuel Morse, an accomplished painter as well as inventor, did not work on the telegraph in isolation: he associated with American inventor and machinist Alfred Vail to develop and commercialize the telegraph between the years 1837 and 1844. In 1837 Morse and Vail also designed a system of dots and dashes to represent numerals and letters. This system worked well with the Morse telegraph because the device used pulses of electric current to move an electromagnet which in turn caused a pen to mark dots and dashes on a running strip of paper. The telegraph was later modified to emboss the paper. Morse gave the first public demonstration of his telegraph in 1838 at the Franklin Institute in Philadelphia, but significant development did not occur until 1843 when Congress appropriated $30,000 to finance the construction of an experimental telegraph line from Washington, D.C. to Baltimore, Maryland. After completion of the line in May 1844, Morse transmitted the first successful message from the Supreme Court Chambers to a B & O Railroad depot in Baltimore: an excerpt from the Book of Numbers, Chapter 23: WHAT HATH GOD WROUGHT.

Commercial telegraph lines spread rapidly in the following years, and by 1850 nearly all of the eastern states were connected. A separate telegraph system was soon constructed to support the burgeoning economy of California. Legislative proposals to fund a telegraph line to California were submitted throughout the 1850s, but it was not until the end of the decade that Congress approved the Pacific Telegraph Act of 1860 and a contract for construction of the line was awarded to the Western Union Telegraph Company. Originally founded in 1851 as the New York and Mississippi Valley Printing Telegraph Company, the company changed its name to Western Union in 1856 to commemorate the consolidation of several telegraph lines in what were then the far western reaches of the system. Edward Creighton, a Western Union general agent, was tasked to manage the project. He subsequently hired two separate subcontractors: the Pacific Telegraph Company for construction of the eastern section; the Overland Telegraph

Company for construction of the western section. Work commenced from both directions on July 4, 1861. The Pacific Telegraph Company began in St. Joseph, Missouri, reached Fort Laramie on August 5th, and completed the eastern portion to Salt Lake City on October 18th. The Overland Telegraph Company began in Sacramento, California, traversed the more difficult terrain of the Sierra Nevada Mountains and the Rocky Mountains, and reached Salt Lake City on October 24, 1861. That evening a message was sent by Horace W. Carpenter (president of the Overland Telegraph Company) to President Abraham Lincoln. The message read: I ANNOUNCE TO YOU THAT THE TELEGRAPH TO CALIFORNIA HAS THIS DAY BEEN COMPLETED. MAY IT BE A BOND OF PERPETUITY BETWEEN THE STATES OF THE ATLANTIC AND THOSE OF THE PACIFIC. The line operated successfully until 1869 when it was relocated to follow the route of the new Transcontinental Railroad.

Although not directly related to the American West, consideration of the first Transatlantic Cable offers the possibility of historical perspective. The first attempt occurred in 1857. The American ship Niagara and the British Ship Agamemnon began the task on August 5th at Valentia Harbor in Ireland (then connected by telegraph to the rest of the British Isles). Unfortunately, the cable snapped after 380 miles. Following the manufacture of an additional 700 miles of cable, a second attempt commenced on June 25, 1858. In a revised strategy, the Niagara and Agamemnon met in the middle of the Atlantic and joined each ship’s portion of cable together. The cable broke immediately. The two ships re-spliced the cable and laid 40 miles before the cable broke again. Again the ships re-spliced the cable, and again it snapped, but this time after 146 miles. The two ships sailed back to Ireland, and despite the disheartening failures, it was determined that sufficient cable remained to make one more attempt. On July 29th the Niagara and

Agamemnon again met in the mid-Atlantic for a fifth and final attempt. This time the cable held, and on August 5, 1858 the two ships successfully completed the installation of the Transatlantic Cable from Valentia Harbor, Ireland to Trinity Bay in Newfoundland. Edward Wildman Whitehouse, originally an English surgeon but now chief electrician for the Atlantic Telegraph Company, transmitted this first message on August 16th: GLORY TO GOD IN THE HIGHEST, AND ON EARTH, PEACE, GOOD WILL TO MEN. Unfortunately, Whitehouse subsequently applied massive 2,000-volt shocks to the line in an ill-fated attempt to rectify initial performance problems, and within two weeks had damaged the cable beyond repair. ~~In response to an official inquiry, Whitehouse claimed~~ Work on a second Transatlantic Cable did not resume until 1865, and although this time only a single ship was deployed to attempt....

John Ravenscroft removed his finger-smudged reading glasses and rubbed the sweaty flesh above his nose. He nudged the brim of his wide-brimmed felt hat upward and searched down the slender length of the wharf until he located the silhouetted figure of Muireall sitting on a wood-and-canvas folding chair in front of her easel. John stood, set the manuscript down on his matching chair, placed a stone on top to prevent the gentle sea breezes of the waning afternoon from scattering the valuable pages, and advanced with leisurely strides toward his intensely-focused wife. When he arrived directly behind Muireall, he simultaneously breathed in her fragrance and studied the nearly-completed watercolor of Morro Rock. A fishing reel whirred to his right; he tilted his head in time to see a chunk of bait and trailing line zinging far off into the sparkling waters of the Pacific Ocean. After nodding at the grizzled fisherman who had executed the cast with accomplished expertise, he said to Muireall, "You're almost finished. Not bad."

Muireall swirled an oval wash brush in a cup of bluish water. "Not bad, but I need more lessons. Are you eager to leave?"

John set his hands on his hips and stretched back. “Not really. I just finished the part about the telegraph, and noted with some amusement that you have probably condemned this poor fellow Whitehouse to eternal infamy from this point forward. Did he really damage the cable right after all the effort it took to string the thing across the Atlantic?”

Muireall brushed along the bottom of one of the clouds. “Afraid so... at least such was the conclusion of the official inquiry.” She dipped the brush in the cup of water then jabbed the bristles into a smear of blue paint. “Whitehouse always claimed the equipment worked properly and it was not his fault.”

A seagull alighted on the guano-stained wharf railing and hopped comically toward the grizzled fisherman looking for a chunk of discarded bait for supper. “I suppose he would, but to damage the first transatlantic cable in less than two weeks after all the trouble it took to install it? How can one excuse this? It wouldn’t surprise me at all if the sailors on those two ships had tried to track the poor fellow down to hang him from the highest yardarm.”

Muireall yawned. “He’s probably dead by now and doesn’t care anymore.”

“Yes, but his descendants may care a great deal about the besmirched reputation of their ancestor when they read your book.”

“Unlikely.”

“Unlikely they will care?”

Muireall raised the brush to the dampened canvas and resumed painting. “Unlikely they will read the book.”

Chapter Twenty

Boise City, Idaho Territory
August 1871

Sensing an unpleasant drool of remorse at the portal to an unpleasant dream, Priscilla Kimball twitched uncomfortably on the makeshift bed of wool and straw. She rolled off the lumpy bedding against the angled sideboard of the prairie schooner before waking, her sweat-soaked dress clinging to the shivering skin of her slender legs. She jerked up to a sitting position. Without permission, her psyche absorbed the momentarily unfamiliar perceptions surrounding her. The floor shook when one of the iron-rimmed wheels jittered along the face of a shallow rock buried in the trail and a chair fell against her arm. She nearly screamed, but a clear recollection of her present circumstances arrived in time to avoid the need.

The troubling images remained surprisingly lucid before commencing a slow dissolve into subconscious oblivion. When she closed her eyes and reviewed the fading images, she recalled that the dream had emerged twice before—maybe three times—following the day she rode away from the wedding reception on Ezekiel. She also remembered that awareness of the dream's recurrence only presented itself during the precious minutes after she had awakened before vanishing into the same nothingness from which the dream itself had apparently emerged. She thought of writing the unsettling events of the dream down on a piece of paper, but had no paper or pen to accomplish the task. She considered if the dream might have some purpose or meaning (although she could not think of any at the moment); she carefully reviewed the sequence of the dream until the moment it faded from her thoughts.

Priscilla, her wedding dress restored from filthy-blood-splattered tatters to immaculate white and the jagged cuts on her thorn-slashed legs healed to youthful softness and her flowers resurrected from brown-shriveled decay to vibrantly-colorful life, rides through a glorious field of sun-yellowed prairie grasses into the light of a new morning. Milky cumulus clouds billow up into powder-blue skies above the faraway hills. She feels the warmth of the sun on her sweet face and feels the clean air swirl across her arms and shoulders and smells the musty freshness of the grasses in her delicate nostrils. It must have rained during the night; only a reminiscence of the scent floats on the breeze today. Ezekiel gallops with unusual velocity and ease over the gentle slopes of the prairie. Priscilla rides effortlessly without holding the reins or saddle or pressing her feet into stirrups. Priscilla looks down into the speed-blurred meadow rushing beneath her feet, and Ezekiel appears to float above the invisible ground without touching it with his silently-churning hooves. She lifts her head to see what lies onward, and a low hillock unexpectedly rises into her vision, suddenly bulged up by some unseen force pulsing organically beneath the swelling ground. Ezekiel charges fearlessly up the expanding slope of the hillock, his silent hooves driving faster and faster as the ridge of the hillock pushes up higher and higher. Priscilla worries of tumbling backwards off the horse when the angle of ascension increases too much, but continues to ride effortlessly in the saddle. At last, Ezekiel reaches the zenith of the hillock and plunges aggressively over the top. Priscilla expects a frightening dash down the steep slope on the other side, but the prairie beyond is again level and smooth. Ezekiel accelerates until he appears to fly several feet over the top of the prairie grasses. Priscilla raises her arms to catch the wind, but in spite of her speed the air becomes serene and motionless. She rides for many hours, enjoying the sensation of flight in her stomach. A clearing appears ahead, directly on the path Ezekiel has chosen. At first Priscilla cannot distinguish anything in particular about the clearing, but as Ezekiel approaches she sees the silhouetted form of a standing man. Ezekiel continues to rush headlong, and when he reaches within a hundred feet of the clearing Priscilla recognizes the face of her husband, Thaddeus Haglund. Terrified, she fumbles to turn Ezekiel away from the clearing, but when she touches the leather reins the halter dissolves into a swirl of translucent ash. She screams at Ezekiel to stop, but instead he convulses to a frightful swiftness. Foolishly, because of the speed Ezekiel has now achieved, she tries to swing her leg over the horse's head and dismount, but her legs are paralyzed. Within three blinks of the eye Ezekiel thunders into the clearing. Thaddeus Haglund waves and says: *I have been waiting a long time for you, my dear. Thankfully you have finally arrived.* As Priscilla listens to the words, she is now standing on the moist earth of the clearing and Ezekiel has vanished. She stutters: *Why... why have you been waiting... for me? I ran away. Do you not remember?* Calmly, Thaddeus explains: *Because my darling, it is our wedding night, and the time has come to consummate our marriage. Do you not remember?* A shiver of panic squirms up her back and she feels cold. She takes a deep breath and exhales; a plume of frost emanates from her open mouth. The cumulus clouds darken and ooze along the horizon. She notices, for the first time, the large bed with brass headboard next to Thaddeus, and the metamorphosis of her wedding dress into a nightgown. She covers her youthful bosom with her hands. *But I ran away. How did you find me?* Thaddeus motions Priscilla to the bed. She tries to resist, but a diaphanous phantom glides her along the ground and raises her into the air and pivots her horizontally and places her neatly in the center of the bed. Thaddeus sits at her side. She tries to cover her chest again but the phantom restrains her arms. *I did not find you, my dear. You rode here on Ezekiel of your own free will, just as I predicted after our wedding. Do you not remember me telling you this?* Priscilla attempts to protest, but her tongue and lips are numb and she can only mouth noiseless words. Then, in the gloomy boundary of her vision, the clearing is suddenly filled with people: her entire family, the wedding entourage, members of her congregation, everyone who attended the wedding and reception. Her voice returns momentarily, and she asks: *Why are these people here?* Thaddeus caresses her leg near the hem of her nightgown. *You are delightfully naïve, my precious little darling. I have invited these people to witness our blessed event. Do you not remember? I explained this to you before the wedding.*" The hem moves above her knees; the phantom pries her legs apart with gossamer talons. Priscilla tries to scream, but her voice has vanished again. The hem moves up her thighs. She tries to push Thaddeus away but the phantom holds her more tightly. She struggles to breath. The people gathered in the clearing encircle the bed and begin to applaud. Thaddeus smiles and waves, then returns his hand to the hem of her nightgown and lifts it above her... her... and then... and then... somehow... Priscilla realizes... she... has the authority... to stop the dream. She can stop the dream... by simply... by simply... by waking up.

Drenched in more sweat because of the remembrance of the dream, Priscilla instinctively covered her stomach and—although the late afternoon had not cooled below 87 degrees—shivered. The prairie schooner rumbled to a creaky stop, and knowledge of the terrible dream tumbled away into nothingness. A minute passed, and then another, and the lurid details of the dream faded into the gloomy shadows of her deepest thoughts. Although a hint of panic remained, Priscilla no longer appreciated the source of it. But unlike the dream, she knew a vaporous fear would linger for hours. The tattered canvas flap at the front of the schooner slapped open. Ferd Tucker poked his head through the opening and grinned. Priscilla thought he must have seen the dream to grin so knowingly. He spoke to her without admitting his knowledge of the dream. "Time to get out and give your legs a good stretch, Miss Mary Smith from Brigham City."

Priscilla attempted to conceal her distress by stretching her arms and yawning in a contrived show of serenity. "Where are we? Have we made it to Fort Boise yet?"

Ferd tied off the reins. "Right next to it. We're in Boise City. I think we'll stay here the night, seeing how it's gotten sort of late in the day and I don't much like travelling in the dark in these parts. All manner of evil things can happen when you travel in the dark. We can take you to Fort Boise in the morning."

Priscilla faked a second yawn before crawling inelegantly out of the back of the schooner because the dress kept sticking to her damp legs. She walked around the side until she found Ferd on his hands and knees inspecting the left front wheel. She had forgotten her earlier claim of wanting to go to Fort Boise. "When's dinner. Would you like me to make a nice cooking fire or cook up some beans?"

Ferd bent down a little more and cocked his head to inspect the axel. "Might need a little more grease here. Didn't sound right the last couple of miles." He sat up on his knees and clapped his hands together to shed some of the dirt. "Not yet. We're going to visit the mercantile first. Maybe buy some supplies. Maybe not. Depends on the price of things. Might get a little information on what's up ahead on the trail. Want to come with us?"

"Where's Ezekiel? I didn't see him tied to the back of the wagon."

"Dropped him off at the blacksmith while you were sleeping. Thought it might be good to have the blacksmith look at that limp."

"Where are Joniah and Seth and Clarinda?"

Ferd's back stiffened when he stood up and tried to unbend. "Joniah already headed over to the store. Last time I checked, Seth and Clarinda were tagging along. Want to head over and take a look with me?"

Priscilla scratched a persistent itch on her forearm through the sweaty sleeve of her dress. "I think I'll just stay by the wagon. I don't have any money to buy anything anyway."

Ferd wiped his hands along the sides of his pantaloons. "Suit yourself, Miss Mary. We should get back before too long. You stay close to the wagon. I did not like the look of some of the men standing in the street when we arrived. Seemed like dangerous gunslingers to me. You keep away from 'em."

Priscilla sagged against the wagon and crossed her ankles. "I will. I'll stay close to the wagon, like you said. I won't go anywhere near any gunslingers."

Ferd nodded, coughed into his dirty hand, and tromped down the street in search of the mercantile and his family. Priscilla waited until he was out of sight, then skipped away from the prairie schooner. When she reached the middle of Main Street, she slowly rotated to survey the numerous amenities of Boise City. A light rain a few hours earlier had dampened the hoof-pulverized-manure-and-urine-laced ground just enough to keep the dust down to a tolerable level. The prairie schooner, a fresh rip drooping from the flank of the canvas bonnet, had stopped just before the post office: a small building with a horizontal-clapboard-sheathed storefront and a raised wood porch with wood-shingled roof and four evenly-spaced whitewashed wood posts. A narrow alley separated the post office from the next building to the right, a much grander structure with a similar but larger storefront and porch. Three men loitered under the roof of the porch, each wearing a vest and boots and wide-brimmed hat, but not a one of them with a holster and gun. Priscilla decided they were not gunslingers. When her view had swung around far enough to align with the length of the street, she observed more storefronts and porches and alleys lining the sides as far as she could see, but except for the numerous signs and banners Priscilla could not determine any notable purpose from the look of the buildings. As she continued a slow pirouette, her eyes paused on silly things. Two scrawny trees with leafy branches scratched against a porch eave. A lace curtain fluttered through an open window above a balcony on a long building with a white horse tied up in front. A wagon pulled by two brawny mules and loaded with barrels and rusty shovels and a coil of rope creaked when it sunk into a hole. A swirl of black smoke puffed from a brick chimney on top of a brick building—one of two Priscilla had spotted—then drifted artistically in the afternoon breeze. A cloud shaped like a pig digging in a trough full of corn cobs floated indifferently. A large cat with a splash of white fur on its nose licked its butt then curled up on a broken wood step in a fading remnant of sunlight. A short woman with brown hair tied into a ball at the back of her head and a white apron swept dirt along a crooked porch into billowing clouds. Three men on horses trotted from a side street and headed directly toward Priscilla, each with flat-brimmed hat and black pants and black jacket and—Priscilla dug her heel into the hoof-pulverized-manure-and-urine-laced ground and froze. She flattened her hand and set it against her forehead and squinted. The men rode closer. Is it possible? She leaned forward a little and squinted again. The men rode closer. She rubbed the dust from her eyes, blinked twice, and squinted one more time. Her father. Her older brother James. And Thaddeus Haglund.

Priscilla sprinted back to the prairie schooner, dove to the ground, and rolled underneath. She pressed her nose against the rusted iron rim and peeked out from behind the rear wheel. The men rode closer. *What now? Hide. But where? Hide. Hide.* She sat back cross-legged and noticed a smudge of black grease oozing out between the axle and the wheel. Without thinking too much, she smeared some of the grease on the palms of both hands then rubbed the gooey slime on her forehead and cheeks and across her nose then down her chin. *Now what? Still have to hide.* The men rode closer. Priscilla crept beneath the prairie schooner until she reached the other side, but did not find the courage to run across open ground to the alley next to the Post Office. Her father,

James, and Thaddeus Haglund, now less than 50 feet from the prairie schooner, rode closer. *Hide. Must hide.* Priscilla sneaked to the front of the wagon to look for another escape route. The men rode closer. She bumped her hand against the wood tongue extending forward between the oxen (and connecting the yokes to the front of the wagon). She spotted the narrow space between the rearward pair of oxen. The men were nearly upon her now. Instinctively, she crawled underneath the front axle of the wagon, slithered up the side and along the top of the splintered wood tongue, and wedged her slender body between the colossal beasts. The ox to the right swiveled its head a little and snorted but quickly turned away, apparently uninterested. The ox on the left shifted its hooves and squeezed Priscilla. She thumped her tiny hands against the smelly brute but could not convince it to move away. The men rode next to the prairie schooner and the oxen. Priscilla sucked in a deep breath and covered her face with greasy hands. The three men rode by, but not one of them thought to look down into the narrow space between the oxen. The men rode by without speaking. Priscilla did not know it, but they had decided to visit the mercantile to ask if anyone had seen a young woman of fifteen wearing a wedding dress and riding an Arabian horse. The ox to the left moved again, prompting Priscilla to slowly exhale, but this time she did not utter a sound.

Ferd and Joniah and Clarinda and Seth returned from the mercantile with a slightly-more-than-half-full 98-pound sack of flour (which Ferd had dickered down in price), a metal spoon for ladling beans and gravy, a small jar of honey to sweeten up the morning biscuits, and three pieces of hard candy. Clarinda was eager to tell Mary Smith about the candy, but did not see her when the family approached the wagon. She ran around the prairie schooner and climbed into the back, stumbled over the wagon's precious contents to the front, and crawled over the seat. She waved her hands at Joniah and wailed: "Mother, I can't find Mary Smith anywhere. She's not around the wagon, and she's not in it neither. I wanted to tell her about the candy, but now I can't find her anywhere."

This announcement alarmed Joniah. She barked a command at her husband as he lifted the sack of flour into the prairie schooner. "Ferd, don't you worry about the sack of flour right now. You go look for Mary Smith down that alley by the post office." Ferd dropped the sack of flour and ran into the alley. Joniah cupped her hands around her mouth and began walking in circles and yelling. "Mary Smith. Where are you? Mary Smith of Brigham City, get back to the wagon right now!"

A pinched voice wafted up from the oxen standing in front of the prairie schooner. "I'm over here."

Joniah twirled around and stared at the four oxen. "Mary Smith, is that you? I can't see where you are."

"I'm over here, betwixt the oxen. I can't move because I'm stuck."

Joniah yelled out to her errant husband. "Ferd, come back here right now. We found her." She ran to the closest ox and leaned over the top. She found Mary between the two beasts pressed face-down into the top of the wood tongue. "Goodness gracious child. What are you doing down there?"

Priscilla concocted a new lie. "Three gunslingers rode into town on big black horses and I was scared of them. This is the only place I could think to hide. Are they gone yet?"

Joniah pretended to look around, because she already knew there were no gunslingers on big black horses. "Whatever you saw isn't around here anymore. I think you can come out now."

"I can't come out. I'm stuck."

Ferd hurried back from his failed expedition down the alley and stood by Joniah. "What have we here?" He suppressed an urge to chuckle. "This has got to be the strangest thing I ever saw in my entire life."

Joniah glared. "Don't just stand there and talk about it. Do something to get the poor girl out of there before the oxen squash her like a ripe June bug."

Ferd strolled casually to the back of the wagon, snatched a hickory ax handle from a small barrel filled with tools, and returned to Joniah's side with a big grin on his face. He jabbed the ax handle between the oxen and used it alternately as a lever and a club to encourage them to move apart. When the narrow space had increased about five inches, Priscilla scooted backwards and stood up on the wood tongue. She hopped to the ground and started brushing dirt off her dress with greasy hands.

Joniah seized Priscilla's hands to minimize the mess. "Why, just look at you child. Not only were you stuck between the oxen, your face and hands are black as night. What did you get into?"

Priscilla improved her lie. "When the gunslingers showed up on the black horses I hid under the wagon and got into the grease on the wheel and it made quite a mess and when I tried to clean it up it got all over."

Joniah sighed. "I can see that for myself, child."

Clarinda, who had gleefully watched the whole miserable scene from her perch on the wagon seat, yelled, "We each get a piece of candy after dinner. What do you think about that, Mary Smith?"

Ferd chuckled and spoke to Joniah. "Let's find a place to camp the wagon before you get the girl cleaned up. Then we can prepare supper and talk about going to Silver City instead of Oregon like the owner of the mercantile said. We also need to figure out a place to leave Mary, since she wanted to go to Fort Boise in the—"

Priscilla interrupted, "Can I go to Silver City with you?"

This request surprised Joniah. "But my dear, you said you were trying to get to Fort Boise. We just need to figure out a place for you to stay."

Priscilla persisted. "I don't want to stay in Boise any more. I want to go to Sliver City with you. I'm scared of the gunslingers in Boise."

Ferd corrected, "Silver City."

Priscilla continued, "Silver City is where I want to go. I won't be any trouble. I can help with the chores like always, and I won't make a lot of noise. I promise."

Joniah implored, "Ferd?"

Ferd kicked at the ground. "I don't know. . . ."

Joniah beseeched, "Ferd!"

Ferd's resolve collapsed. "Well, I suppose, if you help with the chores… and don't make too much noise."

Priscilla rushed at Ferd and hugged him around the neck, rubbing a smear of grease on his collar. "Thank you. I promise I won't be any trouble for you. I promise. I'll help with the chores whenever you ask. I promise."

Seth finally joined the family after searching for a wasp nest under the porch roof in front of the Post Office. "When's dinner? I'm hungry."

Chapter Twenty-One

Oregon City, Oregon
September 1871

Joshua Hotah and his beloved appaloosa, which he had still not named because it was not in his nature to give a name to a horse (his Sioux mother would not have approved anyway, although his English father would have found it amusing), halted within sight of the end of the Oregon Trail. Joshua shifted in his saddle to ease off a sore muscle and sensed the early-morning sun on the back of his ears. He removed a tarnished brass compass (a gift from Ethan Plantagenet) from the breast pocket of his long-sleeved flannel shirt and watched the needle settle into a steady bearing. He surveyed Oregon City from his hillside vantage. The compass indicated a perfect north-south alignment of the main street, but the position of the sun suggested northeast by southwest. He wiggled the compass and checked again, but the slender needle alighted on the same bearing. He shook his head and deposited the compass in the flannel shirt pocket. Dozens of mostly gable-roofed wood buildings and long boardwalks lined both sides of the dirt street. A woman wearing a gray dress and gray bonnet scurried along the far boardwalk in front of a small building with a sharply-pitched roof and a white balcony above the main entry door. Two young children, a boy with a fishing pole on his shoulder and a girl swinging a basket from side to side, walked haphazardly along the centerline of the street, oblivious to the purpose of the boardwalk. A square tower attached to the front of a four-story building perforated with rows of windows extended high above the ridgeline and terminated in a white cube with square openings and a flat roof that did not look like anything else in the town. Three men unloaded wood crates from a wagon near the base of the tower. A flat-bottomed riverboat with one black smoke stack and whitewashed superstructure and churning paddle wheel maneuvered in the swiftly-flowing Willamette River near the northern end of the four-story building. A moist breeze drifted up from the river and fluttered the trees to Joshua's left. The river bent around the south end of the settlement and separated it from two small islands, which appeared—from Joshua's perspective—dangerously close to the roiling waters below a horseshoe-shaped waterfall. The ceaseless roar of the falls skimmed along the river and over the town and up the hillside to Joshua's sun-warmed ears and comforted him. Saw mills and grist mills dotted the island to the left, and another riverboat waited at a dock sticking out from a heavy-timber-open-sided building on the eastern shore of the island. More saw mills and grist mills and buildings Joshua could not identify spread along the opposite banks of the river. The hum of a whirring saw shrilled from one of the mills. Behind the buildings the flat ground along the river rose up steeply into thick woods and smoothly undulating ridge lines. And to the north, just beyond where the town ended, the Willamette flowed sharply west (according to the compass) and widened before continuing on to the Columbia River.

Joshua clicked his tongue and the appaloosa trotted ahead. As they descended the last of the Oregon Trail, he reminisced of his journey from Fort Laramie to Oregon City with the appaloosa, who occasionally fluttered her ears. "We have travelled over much ground my friend. I do not know if we will find my father and mother who we have searched for these many months together, but we have seen many interesting things and have talked to many interesting people." The appaloosa stepped over a narrow drainage channel and flicked her ears. A squirrel, crouched on a rotting stump with dark green moss growing on the side, chattered a warning at Joshua and the appaloosa. Joshua acknowledged the squirrel. "See, even the squirrel agrees with me." The appaloosa did not disagree. "We have crossed many rivers and many mountains and even suffered the heat of an endless desert to find our way to the green hills of Oregon City. I do not believe either one of us has complained, at least not much I can remember." The appaloosa advanced through a saddle in the hills running along the eastern boundary of the town, and angled sharply right on a switchback that led down toward the northern end of the main street. "I did complain about the dry bones and broken wagons and dead animals we saw in the desert." The appaloosa's lips fluttered when she exhaled. "Yes, I know you did not like the dead animals either, especially when you foolishly sniffed one of your dead brothers who was ready to explode. I do not think you will do it again." When the ground leveled out, Joshua Hotah and the appaloosa turned left into a side street defined only by a few scattered buildings. After passing an abandoned hovel, the young children they had observed from the hill east of the town—the boy with the fishing pole and the girl with the swinging basket—appeared at the other end of the alley. The little girl and boy slowed their pace. When they had arrived within a few yards of the appaloosa's nose, everyone stopped. Joshua judged the little girl around ten and the little boy around seven, and decided the children were likely brother and sister and blessed by good parents.

The little girl spoke after her brother hopped behind her back. "What's your name?"

Joshua bent down a little to better hear the girl's tiny voice. "My name is Joshua Hotah, and this is my appaloosa."

The little boy peeked at Joshua around the little girl's arm, but did not say anything. His older sister was beguiled by Joshua's long black hair and dark complexion. "Are you an Indian?" She thought of pointing, but remembered her manners.

Joshua answered calmly, "My mother was Sioux and my father was an Englishman who hunted the buffalo. I am not an Indian or a white man. I am both at the same time."

The little boy tiptoed into the open to see Joshua more clearly. His older sister asked, "What's your horse's name? Can I give him an apple?"

Joshua did not know what the appaloosa would do if the little girl tried to give her an apple, but he could not think of a polite way to say *no*. "She does not have a name. I just call her *appaloosa*. Sometimes I call her *horse* if she does not do what I ask."

The little girl dropped the basket to the ground, opened the lid, and pulled out an apple. She rubbed one side clean on the sleeve of her cotton dress then stepped forward and held the apple a few inches from the appaloosa's mouth. Joshua, who still could not think of a way to say *no*, prepared to yank the reins back, but the appaloosa nibbled the apple in the tiny hand with a gentleness he had not witnessed before. He relaxed while the appaloosa finished the apple. The little girl reached into the basket and pulled out a second apple. "Would you like an apple too, Mr. Joshua? We've got one more."

At first Joshua did not think it right to take the little girl's last apple, but he reached down anyway and accepted the gift. He bit off a ragged chunk, chewed it, and swallowed the sweet fruit. "Thank you. I have not tasted an apple this good for a long time."

The little girl picked the basket up. "Do your parents live around here? I don't think I've ever seen anyone who looks like you, Mr. Joshua."

"I do not know. A woman I met at Fort Laramie told me they might live here, but I do not know." Joshua tore off another chunk of apple and chewed the pulp.

The little boy, his courage growing, finally spoke. "What's her name?"

Joshua hesitated because of the circumstances of his meeting with Martha Canary. "You would not know her."

The little girl changed the subject. "How do you 'spect to find your parents in Oregon City? It's a pretty big place and a lot of people live here."

Joshua patted the appaloosa on the neck. Another giant saw blade hummed somewhere across the Willamette River. "I do not know how I will find them. I suppose I will ride into town and ask people if they have seen them."

The little girl frowned. "I don't see how that's going to work, Mr. Joshua. What if no one wants to talk to you? *Then* what are you going to do?"

A riverboat whistle shrilled near the south end of town. "A good question. What do you think I should do?"

The little girl placed a hand under her chin to impersonate her mother in deep thought. After scrunching her face a few times, she lowered the hand and her precious eyes gleamed. "I know! You can talk to our father. He owns the newspaper. He knows just about everything there is to know about Oregon City."

Joshua's heart beat a little faster, although his countenance did not reveal it. "What is your father's name?"

The little boy seized the opportunity to rejoin the conversation. "That's easy. His name is father."

Joshua asked, "And where can I find this newspaper man who knows just about everything about Oregon City?"

The little girl answered, "At the newspaper, silly. You can find it on the main street. Just ride into town and look for a sign with *Oregon City Enterprise* on it. Shouldn't be too much trouble for you, Mr. Joshua."

Joshua tipped his Indian scout hat (now decorated with three feathers and missing the golden crossed-arrows insignia and red and white acorn-tipped braid), a gesture he had learned in the U.S. Cavalry. "Thank you, my small friends. I will go there now to speak to your father."

The little girl and boy waved at Joshua and the appaloosa as they rode to the end of the alley and disappeared around the corner of a dilapidated shack with clapboard siding in need of a good scraping and a fresh coat of paint.

After riding straight down the middle of Main Street and provoking anxious glances from more than a few of the locals, Joshua dismounted and tied the appaloosa to a weathered post in front of a narrow two-story building with the words *Oregon City Enterprise* painted above the entry. He caressed and soothed the appaloosa, then climbed up to the wood porch that extended from side-to-side across the building's storefront. He slapped the dust off his dark-blue army jacket (now sleeveless and bead-adorned to match the moccasins) and stomped across the porch. He squinted quizzically through the glass panel door before reaching down to the brass knob. When he opened the door and stepped inside, a trio of multi-pitched bells jingled a whimsical tune above his head. The sound of the bells startled him, because he had not heard anything like it before when entering a building, and he ducked around and looked up.

Slapping ink-stained hands on an ink-stained apron, Grady Hathcock strode from an open door at the back of the front office after hearing the bells. He paused behind a narrow service counter stacked with freshly-inked newspapers to observe the strange individual who now stood before him staring up at the three bells above the entry door. He waited long enough to conclude that the man had probably not come to buy a newspaper. "May I help you?"

Joshua Hotah reached up and touched one of the bells. "I have never seen such bells above a door before. It is very clever."

Grady rubbed an ink-stained hand across the front of the ink-stained apron one last time. "Comes in mighty handy to let me know if a customer's entered the front office, except sometimes I can't hear the bells above the noise of the printing press. Did you come here to buy a newspaper? They're right off the press."

Joshua could not think of any reason why he should buy a newspaper. "Are you the father of two small children who like to walk around this town?"

Alarmed by the question, Grady Hathcock shoved his ink-stained thumbs behind the apron. "You mean a little girl carrying a basket and a little boy tagging along behind with a fishing pole?"

"Those are the same children."

"Yes, those are my children. Is there something wrong?"

"Nothing is wrong."

Grady relaxed, but only a little. "Then why do you ask?"

Joshua leaned to his right and looked through the doorway. He could see another man wearing an ink-stained apron turning a wheel on some sort of machine. "These children told me you might know my parents."

Even with the feathers and missing insignia, Grady recognized the cavalry hat. "I see. And why did they imagine I might know your parents?"

"A woman in Fort Laramie told me she thought she saw them in Oregon City...less than two years ago. The children told me you know everything about Oregon City. This is why I have come here to ask if you know of my parents."

Grady chuckled. "Well, I do know most of the news of Oregon City, but I can't say I know everything that goes on in this town. What did your parents look like?"

Joshua tried to remember, but his mother's visage eluded him. "I cannot say, but I know my father was an Englishman who hunted buffalo and my mother was Lakota Sioux."

Grady briefly considered this information—then his nostrils flared. "Come over here to the desk. I want to show you something you might find pretty interesting." Joshua followed Grady to the desk. "Have a seat while I take a look. The chairs aren't very comfortable, but I don't suppose you'll mind." Joshua lowered himself to the hardwood chair and crossed his arms. Grady walked behind the desk and hunched over a dark-stained-three-drawer wood file cabinet with tarnished brass pulls curving out from the bottoms of tarnished brass frames holding slips of ink-stained paper. Grady rested his hand on the top drawer before opening the middle drawer. His ink-stained fingers fumbled through the contents of the drawer. When the fingers reached the back of the drawer, they pulled out a crinkled page of folded newsprint. Grady carefully unfolded the paper on the desk and smoothed the creases with his thumb. He pointed at a picture in the middle of the page. "Take a look at this."

Joshua used his feet to slide the chair forward. He leaned over the desk and studied the grainy newspaper picture of a seated man holding a buffalo rifle with a woman wearing a blanket standing by his side. "Who are they?"

Grady Hathcock hooked the ink-stained thumbs behind the ink-stained apron. "I think there's a good chance they're your parents. Look at the date at the top of the paper."

Joshua blinked. "August 20, 1869."

Grady pointed at the picture again. "Read the caption under the photo."

Joshua blinked again. "*A buffalo hunter and his squaw.* It does not say he is English or she is Sioux. My father was an Englishman and my mother was Lakota Sioux."

Grady noted the odd use of past tense. "No it does not, but I'm the one who took the photograph and I remember them now. I don't remember where they came from or why they came to Oregon City, but I do remember he was a buffalo hunter from England and she was a Sioux squaw. I think they almost certainly must be your parents."

"How long did they stay in Oregon City?"

Grady rubbed his chin. "Not long. When I took the picture, the man said something about Silver City. Yes, I remember now. They were planning to travel to Silver City because of the big strike there. I think they might have left a few days later, but I don't remember for certain."

Joshua stood and his legs pushed the chair back. "Where is this Silver City?"

"Idaho Territory. Head east on the Oregon Trail. When you get to Boise, ask for directions."

Joshua nodded respectfully. "Thank you, but I must ride to this Silver City."

"But you just got here."

"I know, but it is time to leave."

Grady picked up the paper with the grainy photograph and folded it twice. "Take this. It might help you find your parents."

"You do not need it?"

"Not as much as you do."

Joshua folded the paper a third time and stuffed it into his shirt. "Thank you. I will take good care of the paper." He turned without shaking hands and walked to the entry. The three bells jingled again when he opened the door.

Grady Hathcock followed Joshua across the front office. "By the way, what's your name?"

His hand still on the brass knob, Joshua answered without looking at Grady. "My name is Joshua Hotah."

"Do you mind if I take your photograph before you leave?"

Joshua swiveled his head a little, but not sufficiently to see Grady's expression. "Thank you, but I do not have time to take a picture." He hurried through the opening, closed the door, and walked briskly across the porch. He untied the appaloosa from the post, mounted easily, and cantered to the center of Main Street. He rode north (according to the compass), and after passing the dilapidated shack in need of scraping and fresh paint he turned east. Before Joshua and the appaloosa had arrived at the other end of the alley, they met the little girl with the basket and the little boy with the fishing pole returning to town. "I spoke with your father. You are right. He does have much knowledge of Oregon City. I ride to Silver City to find my parents."

The little girl swung the basket from side to side. The little boy peeked out from behind her dress when she asked, "Have you given your horse a name yet?"

Joshua Hotah lowered his hands to the saddle horn. "No, I have not. I will think about it." He tugged a beaded-leather bracelet from his wrist. "This was my mother's. I would like to give it to you…to repay you for the apples."

The little girl held her hand up and Joshua guided the bracelet over her slender wrist. "Thank you, Mr. Joshua. It is beautiful."

The little boy peeked. Joshua removed his wide-brimmed-black-felt Indian scout hat decorated with three feathers. "This is for your brother. I have worn it in many battles, but I do not need it anymore." The little girl took the hat and dropped it on her brother's head. "It don't fit him now, but I'm sure he'll grow into it." She squeezed her brother's shoulder blade. "What do you say to Mr. Joshua when he gives you such a nice gift?"

The little boy peeked under the brim of the hat. "Thank you, Mr. Joshua."

Joshua Hotah nodded but did not say another word. He clicked his tongue and the appaloosa trotted away toward the Oregon Trail and Silver City. Joshua thought of the grainy newspaper photograph as they clambered the hill out of town. He would show his parents to the appaloosa after finding a good place to camp for the night.

A Preview of *Book 2: Gathering of the Clans*

by Muireall Anne Ravenscroft,
award-winning author of *A Concise History of the West*
and other acclaimed works of nonfiction.

When Rich Ritter inquired if I had any interest in editing his most recent work, *Nor Things to Come: A Trilogy of the American West*, I vacillated because my primary focus has been nonfiction. But with gentle prodding from my husband, because John knows I hope to write a novel someday (although the storyline has not yet presented itself), I eventually agreed to the opportunity. After a year of hard work and intense collaboration (at times Mr. Ritter is overly passionate about his writing, particularly dialogue and descriptions of the weather), I completed the task to our mutual satisfaction. It was therefore not an unpleasant surprise when, six months later, he asked if I would be willing to write a preview of *Book 2: Gathering of the Clans*. Given this second chance, I did not hesitate.

As with all great stories, *Book 1* has ended with many unanswered questions. Will Joshua Hotah find his parents? How will Priscilla Kimball, a penniless fugitive from an arranged marriage, survive her desperate circumstances? What are Csongor Toth's true intentions? After helping Gordania Sinclair to escape disaster, he hires a bounty hunter to track her down (likely to bring about her demise) and then dispatches the man in close quarters with a chilling absence of compassion. Will Longwei and Roshan ever find their way to Silver City? Thus far these "partners of business" have demonstrated an astonishing capacity for misadventure. Manfred Herrmann has survived the Civil War and a stagecoach robbery, but will he survive his own dark nature? And consider the calamitous adventures of Gordania Sinclair, the singular heroine of this tale. Her father surely never imagined that he was sending his beloved daughter into a world of murder, deception, and peril when he gave her a final hug at Golspie Station. I will not answer these questions here, because I have no intention of diminishing your enjoyment of story. I will, however, offer a few clues to the delicious events awaiting you in the second book of this magnificent trilogy.

Let me begin by offering this assurance: Gordania, Manfred, Longwei, Joshua, Roshan, Csongor, and Priscilla will all arrive safely in Silver City, Idaho. And let me assure you as well that, although Mr. Ritter has already presented many fascinating supporting characters in *Book 1*, there are many more yet to come. Because of the importance of these new characters to the storyline, I will offer you a preview of *Book 2* by way of my favorites: the prostitute Nadia (her last name is never given), the mute cowboy Conrad Airingsail, the country doctor Guinevere Dupree, the entrepreneur (and owner of a worthless mining claim) Gustus De Angeles, and the black gunslinger Elijah Brown (who, to everyone's surprise, does not drink or smoke).

Nadia—a former school teacher who has been forced into her current profession by unfortunate events beyond her control—will make her appearance immediately in Chapter 1, where she will befriend a naïve Priscilla Kimball who has entered the saloon on the corner of Washington Street and Avalanche Avenue in search of a livelihood. Unbeknownst to Priscilla, a significant portion of the saloon's annual revenue is derived from the insalubrious activities upstairs. The owner of the saloon, a shrewd and unscrupulous businesswoman named Margaret, will initially hire Priscilla as a cleaning lady. But later in the story, because of pressure from one of the locals, Margaret will entice Priscilla to provide certain unspecified services in return for $1.50 per satisfied customer and every other Sunday off. Nadia will intervene to protect Priscilla, but at the cost of a ruinous deal with Margaret. To help pay her debt to Margaret, Nadia will eventually give English lessons to Roshan.

Conrad Airingsail is, on his best days, an odd duck. A secretive man who is also heavily armed in the most unusual fashion, his verbal muteness and furtive behaviors engender much suspicion amongst the citizens of Silver City. And he always smells of fresh manure, which renders him even less approachable. When he rides into town on his buckboard to purchase supplies at the general store, he unexpectedly meets Manfred Herrmann on the boardwalk outside. Manfred invites him to church services in the back room of the saloon on the corner of Washington and Avalanche, and offers a written notice with the time and place. Conrad grabs the notice, but quickly walks away and rides out of town. Conrad will return to help Manfred face down an angry mob in a later chapter.

Guinevere Dupree does not make her entrance until Chapter 7, when an agitated Joshua Hotah knocks on her clinic door in the middle of the night with a deathly-ill Nez Perce boy slung over his shoulder like a sack of writhing potatoes. Although she served the Union Army as a nurse in the Civil War, Guinevere later graduated from the New York Women's Medical College before venturing west. Her once auburn hair silvered by too much care in the waning months of the war and the slender figure of her youth now plump with age, she horrifies Joshua by announcing that she will attempt her very first appendectomy on the boy. A spirited discussion ensues in which Joshua compares what she is about to do to the gutting of a buffalo. After convincing Joshua that the boy will surely die if she does nothing, she sedates the suffering child with ether and begins.

Gustus De Angeles, a grizzled old miner with a disposition to match, discovers Roshan and Longwei burning a "piece-of-shit gold rocker" (please forgive my use of profanity: I am merely quoting Roshan Kuznetsov's own appraisal of the mining implement) on the banks of a stream when he rides into their camp on a burro. Because they appear physically fit and in desperate need of supervision, and because they graciously agree to share their meager dinner of beans, he offers them both a job working his worthless claim near Mahogany Gulch on War Eagle Mountain. Events both comic and tragic will ensue.

Elijah Brown will arrive in Chapter 13 for a nocturnal business meeting with Csongor Toth and his despicable associates: Seth, Jackson, and Miguel. Csongor will offer a job that can only be described as unspeakably depraved. When Elijah refuses on moral grounds—quite an achievement for a man who kills for a living—Csongor will pay him for his trouble and bid him farewell. Tseng Longwei will later discover Elijah, unconscious and soaked in blood, in the back of his wagon. Longwei will haul the massive man to Guinevere Dupree's clinic for treatment and then to Mahogany Gulch to recuperate, where Elijah Brown will realize that he cannot remember his name or occupation. Longwei will name him John Smith as a temporary measure.

I will conclude this delectable taste of the events to come with Gordania Sinclair, now Alexandra Smythe, as she was not mentioned in any of my previous discussions. After a sensuous bath at the War Eagle Hotel (where we learn that she conceals the derringer in a cotton holster sewn into her bloomers), Alexandra will make a surprise entrance at a masked ball. Because she is still on the run from the law—or more accurately, the malignantly vindictive son of the man she killed with the bronze songbird—the masked ball is the perfect venue to both conceal her identity and to see Manfred Herrmann again. She has asked Csongor to arrange a "chance encounter," which he accomplishes with aplomb and unclear intentions. After "discovering" Alexandra at the ball, and with encouragement from Csongor, Manfred kisses her hand and dances the night away, aggressively dissuading several would-be suitors in the process. Is this the beginning of true love? And if so, will love's sweet flower wither and perish in the flames of relentless vengeance? And what of Csongor Toth? Does his penchant for pitiless murder make him incapable of empathy, or does he conceal a warm place in his otherwise cold heart only for Gordania? Alas, you must read the remaining books of this wonderful trilogy to discover the answers. I look forward to offering you a preview of *Book 3* when you have arrived.

Chapter Notes

Prologue

1. Muireall used an Underwood No. 5 typewriter to write the manuscript. John Ravenscroft purchased the typewriter for her as a gift during a trip to New York City in 1902.
2. The City of San Luis Obispo began in 1772 with the founding of Mission San Luis Obispo de Tolosa by Father Junipero Serra. It was the fifth mission in the California chain of 21 missions. San Luis Obispo became a Charter City in 1876. (www.ci.san-luis-obispo.ca.us/briefhistory.asp)
3. Originally named the "Westport Chair" when designed by Thomas Lee in 1903 (while on vacation at his summer cottage in Westport, New York in the Adirondack Mountains), this predecessor to the modern Adirondack Chair was first patented by carpenter Harry Bunnell in 1905 as the "Westport Plank Chair." The chair featured wide armrests, and a straight back and seat fabricated in a severe rearward slant to accommodate the steep slopes of the Adirondack Mountains. (www.classicadirondackchairs.com/adk-chair-history-and-care/)

Chapter One

1. A lighthouse was built atop the 300-foot cliffs at the northern tip of Dunnet Head, Scotland in 1831 by Robert Stevenson, grandfather of Robert Louis Stevenson. Construction of a magneto-electric generator by one Professor Holmes allowed the use of an electric arc to provide illumination in lighthouses beginning in 1853. I regret that I could not confirm the date of first use of electric illumina-

tion at Dunnet Head Lighthouse, but it likely occurred between 1862 and 1879, several years later than the date of this chapter. (www.lighthousemuseum.org.uk)

2. Born in the late 1700s and apprenticed as a gun maker in 1806, John Dickson established his own company, *John Dickson & Son*, in Edinburgh in 1820. The company did in fact manufacture a side-by-side percussion shotgun in the 1850s. The company filed a patent for its famous round action shotgun in 1882. (www.john-dickson.com)
3. I used modern photographs to describe the Dunnet Head Lighthouse because I could not find any drawings or photographs from earlier periods. However, with the exception of certain structures built during World War II, the existing lighthouse, support facilities, and stone walls have the look of the early 1800s to me.

Chapter Two

1. Manfred Herrmann enlisted in the 7th Iowa Infantry Volunteers at Burlington, Iowa in 1861. Before Shiloh, the unit suffered heavy casualties at the Battle of Belmont in Missouri (November 7, 1861). During the battle of Shiloh, the 7th Iowa was attached to the Second Division under the command of Brigadier General W. H. L. Wallace, First Brigade under the command of Colonel James M. Tuttle. Other regiments in the First Brigade included the 2nd Iowa, 12th Iowa, and 14th Iowa, all infantry units. General Wallace was killed in the afternoon of the first day at the Battle of Shiloh. The 12th and 14th Infantry Regiments were cut off and surrounded when they attempted to retreat from the Hornet's Nest and then forced to surrender.
2. Brigadier General T. C. Hinden's First Brigade was attached to the Third Corps commanded by Major General W. J. Hardee, and consisted of the 2nd Arkansas, 5th Arkansas, 6th Arkansas, 7th Arkansas, and 3rd Confederate Infantry Regiments, and the artillery batteries of Miller and Swett. In reviewing maps of the battle prepared by the Civil War Preservation Trust and others, it appears that the 5th Arkansas did not participate in the advance on the Hornet's Nest in the early afternoon of April 6th.
3. The 8th Texas Cavalry Regiment, originally called "Terry's Texas Rangers," was organized and led by Benjamin Franklin Terry in

Houston in September 1861. Colonel Terry was killed during the regiment's first combat action near Woodsonville, Kentucky in December 1861. The regiment elected Lieutenant Colonel Thomas Lubbock as its new leader after Terry's death, but he died of illness before assuming command. John Austin Wharton was then elected to fulfill the role, and led the regiment in the Battle of Shiloh. Engaged throughout the battle, the 8th Texas Cavalry Regiment protected the retreat of the Army of the Mississippi at the end of the second day. (www.terrystexasrangers.org)

4. Originally developed by Captain Claude Etienne Minié of France in 1849, and later improved by manufacturers in the United States prior to the Civil War, the minie ball was a cylindrical-shaped, soft-lead bullet (manufactured slightly smaller than the intended firearm bore) with three grease-filled grooves and a conical hollow in its base designed to allow rapid muzzle-loading of rifles. The minie ball and powder were supplied together in a paper cartridge. A soldier simply tore open the cartridge, removed the minie ball, dumped the powder into the rifle barrel, rammed the minie ball into place, and fired. Expanding gasses deformed the cylindrical sides of the minie ball against the barrel rifling providing spin for improved accuracy, a good seal for longer range, and at the same time cleaning the barrel of debris. By allowing the possibility of several accurate shots per minute, the minie ball dramatically increased the lethality of military weapons and rendered previous battlefield tactics ineffective. Capable of causing terrible wounds and shattering bones, widespread use of the minie ball by infantrymen during the American Civil War produced inconceivable casualties. (www.civilwar.si.edu/weapons_minieball.html)
5. Avila Beach, a tiny stretch of pristine sand located on the north shore of San Luis Obispo Bay a little over 10 miles from the inland community of San Luis Obispo, was originally occupied by the Chumash Indians who exploited the area's rich fishing, hunting, and gathering opportunities. The Portuguese explorer Juan Rodriguez Cabrillo first encountered the Chumash in 1542, and five Catholic missions were established within the Chumash Nation by 1772. The population of the area increased in the late 1800s with the growth of agriculture

and quarrying, both facilitated by the construction of the Southern Pacific Railroad. John Harford built a wharf in 1873 to facilitate trade, but the area's history as a tourist and recreation destination began in 1876 with the construction of the Marre Hotel at Port San Luis. (www.nwfsc.noaa.gov/research/divisions/sd/communityprofiles/California/Avila_Beach_CA.pdf)

6. John and Muireall Ravenscroft drove to Avila Beach in a 1907 Ford Model K Roadster. They purchased the vehicle in San Francisco.
7. I used the following primary Internet and other resources to write Muireall Anne Ravenscroft's excerpt in Chapter 2 titled *Shiloh: Prelude to the Decline of the Confederacy:*
   Understanding Shiloh: The Death Knell of the Confederacy, an essay by W. Keith Beason, www.civilwarhome.com/shiloh.htm, http://militarypower.wikidot.com/battle-of-shiloh, www.nps.gov/shil/historyculture/shiloh-history.htm.

Chapter Three

1. The Taiping Rebellion in China, one of the bloodiest civil wars in human history, spanned fifteen years from 1850 to 1864 and resulted in the deaths of over 20 million civilians and soldiers. Some historians place the death toll even higher. (As Western points of reference, the Crimean War occurred from 1853 to 1856, and the American Civil War began in 1861 and concluded with General Lee's surrender in 1865) At one battle alone, the fall of Nanjing in July 1864, up to 100,000 people were slaughtered in three days. The rebellion found its roots in the Chinese population's dissatisfaction with the ruling Manchu Dynasty (also called the Qing Dynasty), which was generally viewed as corrupt and ineffective. Contributing factors to this view included the humiliating British defeat of Imperial Chinese forces in the first Opium War (1839-1842) and the inability of the Manchu Dynasty to control growing lawlessness and the growth of secret societies in the countryside. The founder and eventual leader of the Taiping Rebellion, Hong Xiuquan was born of a farming family in Guangdong Province in 1813. In 1836, after numerous failed attempts to pass the imperial civil service exams, Hong suffered a prolonged illness (some suggest that it may have been a nervous

breakdown) in which he experienced visions that convinced him that he was the brother of Jesus Christ and that he had been sent to spread his particular version of Christianity throughout China and to purge the country of the corrupt Manchu Dynasty. Hong Xiuquan established the *Taiping Heavenly Kingdom,* also called the *Heavenly Kingdom of Peace,* in 1851 on his 38th birthday. A 60,000 man Taiping army took the city of Nanjing by force in 1853 and eventually converted it to the capital of the *Heavenly Kingdom of Peace.* (www.taipingrebellion.com)

2. The ancient city of Nanjing is nestled between the Yangtze River to the west and Zhongshan Mountain (448 meters above sea level) to the east, each providing a natural defensive barrier. Construction of the city's perimeter wall began over 600 years ago and required 200,000 laborers and 21 years to complete. The layout deviated from previous Chinese walls in that it responded freely to the complex topography of the area, creating a serpentine defensive structure, rather than adhering to the traditional style of a square or rectangle. Originally constructed with 13 gates, the number had grown to 18 by the conclusion of the Manchu Dynasty (1644-1912), the last ruling dynasty of China.
3. The Ever Victorious Army, active only during the years 1860 to 1864, in fact consisted of Chinese soldiers trained and led by foreign officers. However, I liked the impressive sound of *The Ever Victorious Army,* and have fictionalized the idea of a Chinese major. The size of the unit reached around 5,000 men at its zenith, but because it was equipped with modern weapons and trained in European military tactics, the Ever Victorious Army often defeated much larger Taiping forces. After experiencing several setbacks, the unit was disbanded in June 1864, approximately one month before the fall of Nanjing. The Ever Victorious Army was led from 1863 to the end of its service by Charles George Gordon (1833-1885) of Khartoum fame.

Chapter Four

1. Legislation founded the California Polytechnic School in San Luis Obispo as a vocational high school on March 8, 1901. The first day of class occurred October 1, 1903, and the first bachelor's degree

was awarded May 28, 1942. The name of the school was changed to California State Polytechnic College in 1947 and then to California Polytechnic State University in 1972.

2. The San Luis Obispo Carnegie Library was built in 1905 from a grant of $10,000 provided by steel tycoon Andrew Carnegie. Architect W. H. Weeks of Watsonville, California designed the Romanesque-style building and the Stephens and Maino construction company of San Luis Obispo built it. After the construction of a new city library, the building was converted to a museum in 1955.
3. Fort Sedgwick, originally called Camp Rankin and renamed after General John Sedgwick (killed in the Civil War), was located near Lodgepole Creek (a tributary of the South Platte River) about one mile upstream from present-day Julesburg, very close to the northeast corner of Colorado. The fort was established in 1864 to protect settlers and the overland stage and freight route to Denver—the town of Julesburg functioning mainly as a stage and freight station—and later the construction of the Union Pacific Railroad. Primarily in response to the Sand Creek Massacre (November 1864), over 1,000 Cheyenne, Arapaho, and Sioux warriors attacked the fort in January 1865, but failing to take it turned their attention to the town of Julesburg. The Indians attacked Julesburg again two weeks later and, after the few remaining citizens had fled to Fort Sedgwick, burned the town to the ground. The U.S. Army abandoned the fort in 1871. (www.legendsofamerica.com/co-forts3.html)
4. Fort Hays, originally named Fort Fletcher after the governor of Missouri and then renamed in 1866 after Brigadier General Alexander Hays (killed in the Civil War), was located a little northwest of the center of Kansas. The fort began operations in October 1865 and closed in 1899. This western outpost originally protected the stage and freight wagons of the Butterfield Overland Dispatch traveling to Denver. The fort closed in May 1866 after the stage line went bankrupt, but then reopened a quarter mile away near Big Creek in October 1866 to protect the approaching railroad workers of the Union Pacific Railroad. When it became apparent that the railroad would actually pass five miles to the north of the fort, it was relocated again next to the railroad right-of-way in June 1867, but not before a flood nearly

destroyed the old fort and killed nine soldiers and civilians—two weeks prior to the move. (www.kshs.org/places/forthays/history)

5. I used the following primary Internet and other resources to write Muireall Anne Ravenscroft's excerpt in Chapter 4 titled *The Horse and the Indian: A New Way of Life: The West*: A film by Stephen Ives, www.newadvent.org/cathen/12554b.htm, *Spanish Colonial Horse and the Plains Indian Culture*, an essay by O. Ned Eddins, www.amappaloosa.com/history/story.htm.

Chapter Five

1. The U.S.S. Ossipee, a 207-foot wooden sloop-of-war with three masts (foremast, mainmast, and mizzenmast) and steam engine propulsion (top speed 10 knots), was built in 1861 at the Portsmouth Navy Yard for service in the Civil War. The vessel served with the North Atlantic Blockading Squadron and the West Gulf Blockading Squadron (off Mobile, Alabama), participated in the invasion of Mobile Bay, and was one of the ships that pursued the Confederate steamer CSS Web during its daring attempt to escape down the Mississippi River to the sea. Decommissioned at Philadelphia, Pennsylvania at the end of the war, the U.S.S. Ossipee was recomissioned in October 1866 under the command of Captain George F. Emmons to protect American interests in the Pacific. The ship weighed anchor in San Francisco Bay on September 27, 1867 to transport a group of Russian officials and other dignitaries to Sitka for the transfer of Alaska to the United States at a ceremony on October 18, 1867. The vessel served in the North Atlantic from 1873 to 1878 and with the Asiatic Squadron, Atlantic, from 1884 to 1887. The U.S.S. Ossipee was decommissioned at Norfolk, Virginia in November 1889. (www.history.navy.mil/danfs/o4/ossipee.htm)
2. The Russian Orthodox Church built the original Saint Michael the Archangel Cathedral in Sitka between the years 1844 and 1848. The Russian Orthodox Diocese governed all of North America from Sitka during the years 1840 to 1872, and thereafter Sitka functioned as the seat for Alaska. The current structure was actually rebuilt after a devastating fire in 1966 burned the church to the ground. According to the National Park Service, Saint Michael's Cathedral is the "...prin-

cipal representative of Russian cultural influence in the 19th century in North America." (www.nps.gov/akso/CR/AKRCultural/CulturalMain/2ndLevel/NHL/NHLStMichael.htm)

Chapter Six

1. What is today called Eötvös Loránd University began in 1635 as a Catholic University for teaching theology and philosophy in the rural town of Nagyszombat. During the years 1770 to 1780 the university was moved to Buda and later to Pest and, with the support of Maria-Theresa (Empress of Austria and Queen of Hungary), became the Royal Hungarian University. The university was reorganized in 1950 and renamed after one of its professors, the renowned physicist Loránd Eötvös (1848-1919). The Faculty of Law and Political Sciences was established in 1667 and is one of the oldest faculties at the university. The Eötvös Loránd University was the only institution in Hungary to offer curriculums in law and political sciences at the university level until 1872.
   (www.elte.hu/en/elte_brief_history, www.elte.hu/en/law_and_political_sciences)
2. I found a high-resolution photograph on the Internet of a Bösendorfer baby grand piano manufactured in the 1860s, and it had 85 keys (7 octaves) beginning and ending with A. A modern piano, like the one sitting in your grandmother's living room, has 88 keys (7 octaves plus a minor third) beginning with A and ending with C.

Chapter Seven

1. Brigham Young—accompanied by a group of Mormon pioneers comprising 143 men, three women, and two children—founded Salt Lake City in the Salt Lake Valley in what is now northern Utah on July 24, 1847. The Mormons originally travelled to the Salt Lake Valley to escape religious persecution. Interestingly, the area was part of Mexico until an 1848 treaty ceded it to the United States, and in 1850 the area became the Utah Territory. Construction of the Mormon temple began in 1853. U.S. Soldiers were stationed in Salt Lake City during the Civil War. Men drove the "Golden Spike" into the last tie of the

Transcontinental Railroad at Promontory Point (66 miles northwest of Salt Lake City) in 1869. The Mormon Church officially ended the practice of polygamy in the 1890s, and Utah became the 45th state, and the third to extend the vote to women, in 1896. (www.utah.com/cities/slc_history.htm)

2. Muireall Anne Ravenscroft will write more extensively of the Transcontinental Railroad in a later chapter, but I did want to provide some basic information here. The First Transcontinental Railroad was built by the Central Pacific Railroad of California and the Union Pacific Railroad between 1863 and 1869. The Union Pacific route began at Council Bluffs, Iowa, and travelled through Nebraska, Colorado, the Wyoming Territory, and the Utah Territory where it connected to the Central Pacific route at Promontory Summit approximately 66 miles northwest of Salt Lake City. The Central Pacific route began in Sacramento, California and travelled over the Sierra Nevada Mountains into Nevada and then on to Promontory Summit, Utah Territory. The western route was extended from Sacramento to Alameda, California and then to Oakland at a later date. The east and west were not directly connected until construction of the Missouri River Bridge in 1873. Between 1869 and 1873 trains were ferried across the Missouri River. (www.cprr.org/Museum/Maps/_traveler%27s_rr_guide_1882.html)
3. Originally bred by the Bedouins for war and long treks across the scorching deserts of the Middle East, the Arabian horse is an ancient breed and likely the oldest known breed of riding horse. The Arabian is renowned for its endurance, speed, intelligence, and gentle disposition. Famous riders of the Arabian have included Genghis Khan, Napoleon, Alexander the Great, and George Washington. Because the Bedouin tribes zealously maintained the purity of the breed, the modern purebred Arabian is practically the same horse that thrived in ancient Arabia thousands of years ago. (www.arabianhorses.org/education/education_history_intro.asp)

Chapter Eight

1. The Pacific Mail Steamship Company (PMSSC) was originally established in 1848 to service the profitable U.S. mail contracts. In

a quirk of history, the PMSSC Steamer "California" departed New York in 1849 on route to the company's first trip to San Francisco. The steamer stopped in Panama to pick up a few passengers, but instead was boarded by hundreds of adventurers seeking transportation to the gold fields of California. When the California arrived in San Francisco on February 28, 1849, most of the crew disembarked the ship with the passengers to seek fortune at Sutter's Mill. Although the sudden loss of his crew angered the captain, the California Gold Rush ensured the long range financial success of the company. The Pacific Mail Steamship Company launched the first trans-Pacific steamship service in 1867 with an initial route between San Francisco and Yokohama, with stops in Hong Kong and Shanghai. The Pacific Mail Steamship Company became the principal method of transportation for the Chinese immigrants who built the First Transcontinental Railroad. The wooden side-wheeler steamer "China" was launched in December 1866 specifically for the trans-Pacific route, and provided services between Asia and America, including Shanghai and San Francisco, from September 1867 through 1883. (www.sfhistoryencyclopedia.com/articles/p/pacificMail.html)

2. The sou'wester of 1867 included jacket and hat and would have been fabricated from oilskin. Oilskin was typically a heavy cotton fabric waterproofed with linseed oil. Another type of oilskin was sailcloth waterproofed with a thin layer of tar. I use the word "waterproofed" only because it is part of the definition. It is far more accurate to describe the garments of this age as "water resistant." Although I could not determine the justification, the jacket and hat are both called a sou'wester.
3. The history of Shanghai begins in the 10th century and spans eight Chinese Dynasties into the modern era. The city grew rapidly during the Qing Dynasty (the last Chinese Dynasty, 1644-1912) because of its strategic location at the mouth of the Yangtze River and potential for trade with the West. British forces temporarily controlled Shanghai during the First Opium War (1839-1842). During the Taiping Rebellion, an offshoot of the rebellion called the Small Swords Society occupied the city in 1853. In 1854 the Shanghai Municipal Council was created to manage the foreign settlements

including the British, American, and French concessions in Shanghai. British and French troops used modern artillery to inflict heavy casualties on Taiping forces at the Battle of Shanghai (1861-1862). The French concession dropped out of the Shanghai Municipal Council in 1862, and in the following year the British and American concessions formally joined to create the Shanghai International Settlement. As more foreign powers (including Germany and Denmark) negotiated treaties with China they became part of the administration of the settlement, but it continued as a primarily British affair until the late 1930s. Although the Shanghai International Settlement was administered and controlled by foreign nationals, unlike Hong Kong it always remained sovereign Chinese territory. (Wikipedia)

4. The earliest archeological evidence of human inhabitation of the San Francisco area dates from approximately 4,000 B.C. Although some historians have promoted the hypothesis that Sir Francis Drake landed at Point Reyes just north of the Golden Gate in 1579, this is only one of several theories. It is more likely that Europeans did not arrive in the area until 1769, when a Spanish expedition led by Gaspar de Portola ventured north from Southern California. At that time the Ohlone people, a complex hunter-gatherer culture that maintained as many as 50 distinct tribes and villages, thrived in Northern California from the northern tip of the San Francisco Peninsula south to Big Sur and east to the Diablo Mountain Range. Seven years later, in 1776, the Spanish established the Presidio Real de San Francisco. The Catholic Church established the Mission San Francisco de Asis shortly thereafter. Englishman William Richardson built the first independent homestead in 1835, and then with Mayor Francisco de Haro laid out the first street plan for expanding the settlement of Yerba Buena (the original name of the town). After the Mexican War of Independence concluded in 1821, San Francisco became a part of Mexico. On July 9, 1846, during the Mexican-American War, Captain John Montgomery landed with 70 sailors and marines and took possession of the Yerba Buena settlement in the name of the United States of America. At that time the population of Yerba Buena amounted to 462 people living in tents, shanties, and adobe huts. The town was renamed San Francisco in January 1847. Mexico ceded

California to the United States in 1848 after the end of the Mexican-American War. The California Gold Rush, which began in 1848 after the discovery of gold at Sutter's Mill, prompted thousands to flood into the area and by December 1849 the population of San Francisco had increased to 25,000. California was granted statehood in 1850, and Sacramento became the state capital in 1854. It is interesting to note that the state legislature met in San Francisco in 1861 due to flooding in Sacramento. The immense wealth generated by the gold rush prompted rapid entrepreneurial development in San Francisco including Wells Fargo Bank in 1852, the Bank of California in 1864, and expansion of the Port of San Francisco to establish the city as a major center of trade. Levi Strauss founded the first company to manufacture blue jeans in San Francisco in 1853, and Domingo Ghirardelli established the Ghirardelli Chocolate Company at Ghirardelli Square in 1852. The Army Corps of Engineers fortified Alcatraz Island into a military outpost between 1853 and 1858 and Civil War prisoners were housed there as early as 1861. By 1870, three years after Tseng Longwei's arrival, the population of San Francisco had expanded to over 149,000 people. (www.yerbabuenagardens.com/history.html, www.sfgenealogy.com/sf/1867g/sfgr67.htm)

Chapter Nine

1. The Seattle of 1907, the year Muireall Anne Ravenscroft completed her history of the American West, was a much different place than the Seattle of 1868, the year Roshan Kuznetsov worked in the Yesler Sawmill on the waterfront of Elliot Bay. According to a poster prepared by the Seattle Mayor's Office of Arts & Cultural Affairs and the 1907-2007 Seattle Centennial Project, 1907 is "The Year Seattle Became a Real City." The poster further states: "... Seattle was a city in name only prior to 1907. Then, in the span of one remarkable year, it shed the mud and rude manners of a rough-and-tumble frontier port for the genteel sophistication of a major Pacific Rim metropolis." As proof of this transformation, the following evidence is provided: 1) the population of Seattle increased from 80,671 in 1900 to 237,194 in 1907; 2) a number of major institutions including Children's Orthopedic Hospital, United Parcel Service, the Moore Theater,

St. James Cathedral, the Episcopal Church of the Epiphany, and Pike Place Public Market were founded in 1907; and 3) the towns of Ravenna, Ballard, West Seattle, Southeast Seattle, Columbia City, and South Park were either annexed or voted for annexation in 1907, mainly, it appears, to gain access to improved utility systems (water, sewer, and electrical), because of difficulty in keeping up with road improvements necessitated by the "birth of the auto age," and because of mounting municipal debt.

2. I used the following primary Internet resources to write Muireall Anne Ravenscroft's excerpt in Chapter 9 titled *The Birth of Seattle:* www.lonelyplanet.com/usa/seattle/history, www.native-languages.org/puget-sound.htm, www.historylink.org.

Chapter Ten

1. The S.S. Tarifa—an iron-hull, 292.5 foot, single-screw steamship with two auxiliary masts and capable of a top speed of 11 knots—was built for the British & North American Royal Mail Steam Packet Company (later the Cunard Steamship Company) by J & G Thomson of Glasgow and launched in December 1865. The Tarifa offered accommodations for 50 first class and 650 third class (steerage) passengers. And—this is the exciting part—actually completed a voyage from Liverpool, England to Queensland, Ireland to Boston, Massachusetts in July 1869. The voyage likely required 15 days and began on July 10, 1869. It is interesting to note that the passenger manifest for this voyage included several women in their twenties from Scotland. (www.olivetreegenealogy.com/ships/tarifa1869.shtml)
2. Gordania's complete train route from Scotland to England in 1869 was as follows: Beginning in Golspie then to Inverness, Aberdeen, Dundee, Perth, and Glasgow; then across the English border to Carlisle, Preston, Wigan, and finally Liverpool, where she disembarked at the Liverpool Exchange Railway Station near the docks. The Golspie to Inverness route was constructed in 1868. Additional rail routes from Thurso, very close to Dunnet Head, to Golspie were not constructed until 1871 and 1874. Thurso, Scotland is currently the United Kingdom's most northerly railroad station. (www.brassett.org.uk/rail/rindex.html)

3. I made an assumption that Gordania would have traveled to the Liverpool Exchange Railway Station to complete her journey near the Princess Dock, although I did not mention this in the chapter. The website www.liverpoolmuseums.org.uk/nof/docks presents an excellent and detailed history of the Liverpool Docks along the Mersey River, but I could not determine with certainty that a passenger bound for Boston would have boarded a steamer at the Princess Docks during the year 1869. The website did note that the Cunard, White Star, and Canadian Pacific Lines visited the "Princess Landing Stage" to pick up passengers in 1876. And, as noted above, the S.S. Tarifa was originally built for the company that became the Cunard Steamship Company. In the 1840s two northern train routes were constructed into Liverpool: one from Bury via Bolton and Wigan by the Lancashire and Yorkshire Railway (LYR), and one from Preston by the East Lancashire Railway (ELR). A joint terminus for the two lines was opened in 1848 at Great Howard Street. Heavy traffic soon rendered this station inadequate, and an extension was opened in 1850 at Tithebarn Street on the outskirts of the Liverpool business district. The website www.disused-stations.org.uk/l/liverpool_exchange notes the following: "The station was a grand affair that had required the demolition of 540 houses in an area that had become a notorious slum. The station was 25 feet above street level being supported on brick arches. The Station frontage was a two story affair in the 'Italianate' style. It was connected to Tithebarn Street by a set of steps. The station had five platforms which were provided with an overall roof for the comfort of passengers." You will note that Gordania describes the station to Csongor Toth quite well. The station had two names early on because of its joint use. The LYR called it the "Exchange Station" and the ELR called it the "Tithebarn Street Station." The station did not receive its final name of "Liverpool Exchange" until the LYR and ELR merged into a single company, the Lancashire and Yorkshire Railway, in 1859. (www.disused-stations.org.uk/l/liverpool_exchange, www.liverpoolmuseums.org.uk/nof/docks)

Chapter Eleven

1. According to the Wartburg Theological Seminary website, the roots of the seminary originate with the missionary vision of Johann Konrad

Wilhelm Loehe (Löhe in German), a Lutheran pastor who served in Neuendettelsau, Bavaria. The New Schaff-Herzog Encyclopedia of Religious Knowledge (a document I found nearly unreadable at times) notes that he ended up in this "...inconsiderable and unattractive place..." in 1837 after numerous run-ins with the civil and ecclesiastical authorities in Kirchenlamitz and then Nuremburg, primarily due to his penchant for denouncing sin without fear like the prophets of old. He served as the village pastor of Neuendettelsau from 1837 until the end of his life. His relationship with the Bavarian Church was further strained during the years 1848 to 1852 because of his frequent thoughts of separating from the church. Loehe's discontent derived from his tendency to measure the condition of the church against his own ideal standards. This conflict between reality and the ideal created incessant turmoil in his mind, and ultimately led him to present a petition to the General Synod in which he demanded "...the withdrawal of secular supremacy over the Protestant Church, complete purification of confession, and the strictest adherence to the symbols of the church." At one point the Bavarian Church proposed the suspension of Loehe, but many voted against the measure because its enactment would have led to an actual split of the church due to his strong following. But his relevance to this story derives from his missionary work, and in 1852 pastors from Neuendettelsau (the "inconsiderable and unattractive place" noted above) founded an educational institution in Saginaw, Michigan. The following year the school moved to Dubuque, Iowa and the seminary began in 1853. Unfortunately, the seminary experienced financial problems three years later and was forced to move to Clayton County, Iowa where the St. Sebald Church was later constructed. The St. Sebald Lutheran Church website provides the following information: "The church was named for Saint Sebaldus, a legendary missionary to Germany. A church in Nuremberg bears the same name... In 1867, the present frame building was erected for a cost of $3,400. It had no steeple, bell, or basement. The windows were of clear glass, pews handmade, and the walls were left as plastered. The alter was constructed from a large dry-goods box." It was during this time that the name *Wartburg Theological Seminary* was chosen. If you are a Lutheran, you will almost certainly remember that Martin Luther stayed at Wartburg Castle from 1521 to 1522 after his excommunication by Pope Leo X where he further irritated the Pope by translating the New Testament into vernacular German. In 1875 Wartburg Theological Seminary moved to Mendota, Illinois due to the need to expand. The seminary did not return to Dubuque, its current location near the Mississippi River and the confluence of the state borders of Wisconsin, Illinois, and Iowa, until 1889. (www.wartburgseminary.edu, *New Schaff-Herzog Encyclopedia of Religious Knowledge*, www.sebaldlutheran.com)

2. I've added this note for readers who wish to learn more about the five dimensions of Loehe's Ecclesial Theology. This information is briefly summarized from an article by Craig Nessan on the Evangelical Lutheran Church in America website, which you can find at the following address: www.elca.org/What-We-Believe/Social-Issues/Journal-of-Lutheran-Ethics/Issues/February-2010/What-Does-Wilhelm-Loehe-Have-to-Say-to-Us-about-the-Christian-Life.aspx. First, his ecclesial theology was *pietistic*. Loehe's pietism strongly influenced his interest in mission, which ultimately led to "...his involvement in preparing pastors and teachers to serve the German immigrants in the American Midwest." Second, Loehe's ecclesial theology was *confessional*. He persistently defended the Lutheran confessional identity and strongly opposed 19th century pressures to unify Lutherans and the Reformed Church. Third, his ecclesial theology was *liturgical*. Loehe's scholarly study of the liturgical traditions of the early church became the basis for the liturgical order published and used throughout the Lutheran Church in Germany and America. Fourth, his ecclesial theology was *diaconal*. "He took initiative in the founding of a deaconess order and the charitable institutions that continue to minister in Germany to this day." And fifth, his ecclesial theology was *missional*. To quote Loehe himself from his *Three Books about the Church*: "For mission is nothing but the one church of God in its movement, the actualization of the one universal, catholic church.... Mission is the life of the catholic church. Where it stops, blood and breath stop; where it dies, the love which unites heaven and earth also dies. The catholic church and mission—these two no one can separate without killing both, and that is impossible." I do

not know if these five dimensions of Loehe's Ecclesial Theology are a modern invention or were understood as such in the 19th century, but for the purposes of this fictional story it does not really matter. (www.elca.org/What-We-Believe/Social-Issues/Journal-of-Lutheran-Ethics/Issues/February-2010/What-Does-Wilhelm-Loehe-Have-to-Say-to-Us-about-the-Christian-Life.aspx)

Chapter Twelve

1. I applaud you, dear reader, if you have actually read every chapter note up to this point. If you have skipped any, then you are only deserving of faint praise. But assuming you have read them, the chapter notes are either very compelling or you have exceptional discipline to read anything placed in front of you. But this particular note is about Boston, not about your skill as a reader or my prowess as a writer. I have some fondness for Boston, even though I have only visited this great city once, in 1985. I attended an American Institute of Architects national convention with my business partner, Paul Voelckers. My other business partner, Robert Minch, did not see fit to attend because he was, and still is, quite cynical about the cost/benefit of such events.* We arrived at Logan International Airport very late the night before the first day of the conference. Due to a misunderstanding with our office manager, we stayed at the Holiday Inn in Roxbury that first night (instead of the Holiday Inn near the convention center). I must say that the room was very comfortable, the service excellent, and the buffet breakfast exceptional (including a few dishes I had never before experienced). We attended a spectacular performance of the Boston Pops, and the orchestra blew back what little hair I had at the time when performing *March of the Charioteers* from the movie *Ben Hur* (composed by Miklós Rózsa). We walked the campus of Harvard University (the oldest institution of higher education in the United States) and I noted that the graduates of the School of Business had more money and made larger postgraduate donations than the graduates of the School of Architecture. I learned to avoid eye contact with Boston drivers when using the crosswalks. I met a police officer with

* I retired from the firm in 2005 after 28 years.

a thick Irish accent. I slurped raw oysters with horseradish sauce at the stone bar of the Union Oyster House (established in 1826, the oldest restaurant in Boston—and we sat very near the "Kennedy Booth"). I counted "smoots" on the Harvard Bridge between Boston and Cambridge. I bought a pair of penny loafers at a shoe store near Harvard Square. I experienced my first roundabout in an unfamiliar rental car during rush-hour traffic (fortunately, I was not the driver). After the conference we drove to Newburyport and stayed the night in a delightful, quirky, picturesque, stone and shingle, two-story hotel, the name of which I cannot remember. After dinner at a tony converted fire station, we walked the quaint streets of Newburyport until after eleven without getting arrested. The next day we ate lunch at a very old restaurant with splendid views to one of the oldest bridges in America, the name of which also eludes me. All-in-all a memorable trip.

2. After researching the Lindens area of Brookline for this chapter, I wish I had taken a side trip there during my visit to Boston in 1985 (see above). On its website, the Brookline Historical Society provides this information taken from a pamphlet published by the Brookline Preservation Commission: "The Lindens area is the earliest planned development in Brookline and was laid out as a 'garden suburb' for those wishing to escape the growing congestion of Boston. As originally conceived in 1843, it reflected the latest ideals of planned residential development for a semi-rural setting. One commentator remembered in 1900 that, 'The houses built at this place were considered at the time of their erection, beautiful structures and the colony was rather aristocratic. It was a beautiful section of town and the land to the north and west, now covered with houses, was then a beautiful woods, with a brook running through it.'" You will note that this succinct description inspired much of the creative imagery woven into the second part of the chapter. I also used many of the photographs, drawings, and maps provided by the website to propel my writer's imagination. I should note that the characters in the chapter are completely fictional, and, to the very best of my knowledge, bear no resemblance to any person—living, dead, or otherwise. (www.brooklinehistoricalsociety.org/history/presComm/linden.asp)

3. The Mourning Dove (scientific name Zenaida macroura for those of you who care about such things) is one of the most widely distributed and abundant birds in North America. Mourning Doves are highly adaptable and thrive in nearly all ecologies (within their range) except marshes and heavily-forested areas. The Mourning Dove's year-round range extends across most of the United States, Mexico, and Central America, with migrations into southern Canada during breeding and southern Central America during the winter. Mourning Doves are generally grayish-brown and buff in color with black spotting on the wing coverts and near the ears; 11 to 13 inches in length, with a wingspan of 17 to 19 inches; weigh 4.4 ounces, on average; and have delicate bills, long pointed tails, and reddish legs and feet. Mourning Doves form strong monogamous relationships that persist through at least one nesting season, and may raise up to six broods per season in warmer climates. Clutches usually consist of two white eggs, and both parents participate in nest building, incubation of the eggs, and feeding the young. And—in a poignant example of one of the Mourning Dove's more human qualities—the male carries small twigs to the nesting site, but the female gets to decide how to arrange them in the nesting platform. (Natural Resources Conservation Service, *Mourning Dove (Zenaida macroura)*, Fish and Wildlife Habitat Management Leaflet Number 31, February 2006)

Chapter Thirteen

1. Fort Laramie—first established in 1834 at the confluence of the Laramie and North Platte Rivers in southeastern Wyoming; strategically located on the Oregon Trail; the only sign of civilization for Brigham Young and his Mormons during their 1,000 mile western trek to New Zion in 1847; witness to the migration of more than 30,000 Forty-Niners during the California Gold Rush; defended by skeleton crews of Kansas, Ohio, and Iowa infantry and cavalry volunteers during the Civil War; guardian of prospectors after the unfortunate 1874 discovery of gold in the Black Hills; staging area for thousands of U.S. Army Troopers during the 1876 campaign against the Sioux and Cheyenne; abandoned and then rudely stripped of its doors, windows, and fixtures in 1889 when it no longer served any

useful purpose—played an undeniably essential and colorful role in the expansion of the American West. At the time of its closure in 1889, this wilderness outpost offered a wide range of facilities to the western traveler including a hospital, administration building, the "Old Bedlam" (a two-story commanding officer headquarters and bachelor officers quarters complete with verandas, and the oldest structure in Wyoming today), five separate double-occupancy buildings for officers and their families, cavalry and infantry barracks, several mess halls, Sutler's Store complete with separate barrooms for officers and enlisted men, a sawmill, a magazine, a parade ground, a commissary storehouse, a bakery, an iron and concrete bridge across the Platte River, and various guardhouses and other supporting structures. Although a photograph taken of Fort Laramie in 1870 (the year before Joshua Hotah's arrival) indicates fewer structures, the encampment still sprawls impressively along the bending shores of the Laramie River. The photograph also shows numerous white canvas tents and a few more permanent structures across the Laramie River southeast of the main camp, but I could not determine if they were military or civilian. A map of the Fort Laramie National Historic Site indicates several civilian facilities north of the main camp including the Rustic Hotel and stagecoach stables. As a point of interest, Fort Laramie was garrisoned by Companies A, B, H, and I of the 14th Infantry and Company A of the 5th Cavalry during March and April of 1871. (Mattes, Merrill J. *Fort Laramie Park History, 1834-1977*. Washington, D.C.: U.S. Dept. of the Interior, National Park Service, 1980. Print; and www.nps.gov/archive/fola/units.htm)

2. I used the following primary Internet resources to write Muireall Anne Ravenscroft's excerpt in Chapter 13 titled *The Buffalo Hunters*: www.buffalofieldcampaign.org/aboutbuffalo/bisonnativeamericans.html, www.legendsofamerica.com/we-buffalohunters.html, www.texasbeyondhistory.net/kids/forts/13.html, www.tshaonline.org/handbook/online/articles/lns02.
3. Martha Jane Canary, born circa 1850 and better known as Calamity Jane, worked from time to time as a prostitute at the Three-Mile Hog Ranch near Fort Laramie around the year 1874. Since I have fictionalized the establishment of the ranch prior to 1871, Martha's period

of employment has shifted earlier as well. A photo taken of Martha at a young age presents a surprisingly-attractive woman—a drastic contrast to the gun-toting tomboy in men's clothing seen in later photographs—and accounts from her early life describe her as a "pretty, dark-eyed girl." It is obvious that a harsh life on the Great Plains and addiction to alcohol aged her far beyond her years. She displayed a gentler and more compassionate side of her otherwise rugged personality when she helped nurse victims of a smallpox epidemic in the Deadwood area around 1876. She died at the age of 53 in South Dakota in 1903. (www.enotes.com/topic/Calamity_Jane, www.eskie.net/superior/west/calamity.htm)

Chapter Fourteen

1. The prairie schooner was a descendent of the Conestoga wagon, a much heavier freight carrying vehicle that originated in the Conestoga region of Pennsylvania, circa 1725. The early pioneers traversing the Oregon Trail quickly learned that the massive Conestoga wagon was unsuitable for the demands of the trail: the heavy wagons often killed even the most vigorous oxen with a third of the journey still remaining. The full length of the prairie schooner, including the tongue and neck yoke, measured around 23 feet. The height from the ground to the top of the canvas cover (bonnet) measured approximately 10 feet. The wheelbase of the wagon extended a little over 5 feet. The prairie schooner weighed about 1,300 pounds empty. Because of its lighter weight, as few as 4 oxen or 6 mules could successfully pull a fully-loaded wagon. Other interesting features include the following: 1) The sides of the wagon bed measured 2 to 3 feet high and were usually sealed with tar to allow the wagons to "float" across slow moving rivers; 2) The front wheels were fabricated slightly smaller than the rear wheels (typically 44 inches compared to 50 inches) to allow the wagon to negotiate tighter turns; 3) The only springs in the prairie schooner were located beneath the driver's seat. Passengers riding in the back of the wagon suffered directly the inevitable roughness of the trail. (www.coggonharvesthome.com/prairie_schooners.htm, www.encyclopedia.com/topic/Conestoga_wagon.aspx#1-1E1:Conestog-full)

2. Abraham Lincoln signed the Homestead Act on May 2, 1862. By this time, 11 states had seceded from the Union. The act provided a three-step process for the acquisition of a homestead. First, a U.S. citizen (or one who had intentions of becoming a citizen) who had never borne arms against the government could file an application for 160 acres of surveyed government land. Second, the homesteader had to improve the land within five years by building a minimum 12-foot by 14-foot dwelling and planting crops. And third, the homesteader had to file a deed of title at the local land office after proving residency and completing the noted minimum improvements. The local land office would then forward the submitted paperwork to the General Land Office in Washington, DC, where each case was reviewed and valid claims were granted a patent to the land free and clear—except for a small registration fee. Daniel Freeman, a Union Army Scout, filed the first land claim on January 1, 1863. (www.archives.gov/education/lessons/homestead-act/)
3. Muireall Anne Ravenscroft devoted an entire chapter in her history of the American West to the Oregon Trail. It is impossible to reproduce it all here, so I have instead inserted the following excerpt from her original book outline:
    a. President Thomas Jefferson organizes the first American expedition to find an easy overland route west to the Pacific Ocean. Meriwether Lewis, William Clark, and a small group of a few dozen men reach the Pacific Ocean on December 5, 1805, but the route is far from easy and completely unsuitable for travel by wagons.
    b. Inspired by the Lewis and Clark expedition, and seeing an opportunity for profit through fur trading, the world's richest man, John Jacob Astor, funds two different groups to find a suitable route to the mouth of the Columbia River in 1810. The first group voyages by ship around Cape Horn and arrives safely. The second group travels overland but experiences death and loss of sup-

plies attempting to cross the Snake River and therefore judges the river unnavigable.

c. Lieutenant Zebulon Pike leads a military expedition west in 1806 to explore the Great Plains and Rocky Mountains. He calls the plains, "The Great American Desert." This designation discourages western migration.

d. Major Steven Long leads a military expedition west in 1819. After passing through what are now Nebraska, Colorado, Kansas and Oklahoma he confirms Lieutenant Pike's earlier assessment and declares the entire region unfit for human habitation. This also discourages western migration.

e. In spite of this unfavorable publicity, adventurous men continued to drift west during the early decades of the 19th century. These intrepid individuals lived thousands of miles from civilization, survived off the natural bounty of the land (elk, buffalo, etc.), carried all of their possessions on their backs, and roamed hundreds of miles each year in search of beaver pelts. In 1808 mountain man John Colter discovered the steaming geysers of today's Yellowstone National Park. In 1825 mountain man Jedediah Smith discovered a pathway through the Rocky Mountains. In 1832 mountain man Joe Walker blazed a trail to California. In 1840 mountain man Jim Bridger established a fort in what is now Wyoming to sell supplies to emigrants traveling overland to Oregon.

f. Marcus and Narcissa (note to self: do not use this name for a daughter) Whitman complete the first successful trip to Oregon in a covered wagon in 1836.

g. An 1843 wagon train of a thousand pioneers (later called "The Great Migration") initiated a mass migration west on the Oregon Trail. Over the next 25 years more than a half-million people move west.

h. The vast majority of emigrants used steamships to travel on the Missouri River from St. Louis to Independence, Westport, St. Joseph, Omaha, or Council Bluffs.
i. The first emigrants travelled to Oregon by ship, and some still travelled this way after the great western migration on the Oregon Trail had begun. However, few pioneers could afford the fare of a sea journey, most pioneers originated in the central states far from any seaport, and travelling overland in a wagon required four to six months while the sea voyage consumed a full year.
j. Many hardships awaited the pioneer families travelling on the Oregon Trail. River crossings claimed hundreds of lives. Many, including children, were crushed to death after falling beneath wagon wheels. Pioneers were killed or injured by lightning strikes and hail storms. And many died from cholera, a deadly and incurable disease. Some wagon trains lost two-thirds of their pioneers to cholera.
k. The initial segment of the Oregon Trail passed between the Cheyenne to the north and the Pawnee to the south. Early encounters with Indians involved the trading of clothing, tobacco, and rifles for food and horses. Later, as the migrating pioneers depleted prairie grasses through overgrazing and consumed all available firewood, many tribes along the Platte River experienced great suffering. The pioneers worried endlessly of Indian attacks, but, in fact, very few emigrants were actually killed by Indians. However, attacks did occur, and notable examples include the Grattan Massacre of 1854 and the Massacre Rocks Incident of 1862.
l. The "glory years" of the Oregon Trail end in 1869 with the construction of the First Transcontinental

```
Railroad. Nonetheless, pioneers continue to use
the trail into the 1890s.
```

(www.isu.edu/~trinmich/Oregontrail.html)

Chapter Fifteen

1. I used a Southern Pacific Bulletin published in May 1928 by Associate Editor Erle [sic] Heath titled: *A Railroad Record that Defies Defeat—How Central Pacific laid ten miles of track back in 1869* as my primary historic resource to write the opening scenes of this chapter. Before the effort to lay 10-miles of track commenced on April 28, 1869, men and two-horse teams had already hauled and distributed over 25,000 wood ties along the previously-graded rail bed, and had actually placed and spaced the ties for some distance. The material trains therefore carried only iron rails, bundles of fish plates, and kegs of bolts and spikes. The article notes that the one-day effort required 4,000 men and hundreds of horses, and that only a few hundred of the men were white (Irish). The remaining 3,800 (plus or minus) men were therefore Chinese. The article also offers the following speculation and then summarizes the quantity of materials: "If the roadway had been perfectly level and straight, these men could have laid fifteen miles of track. The task had involved bringing up and putting into position 25,800 ties, 3,520 rails averaging 560 pounds each, 55,000 spikes, 14,080 bolts, and other material making a total of 4,462,000 pounds." After lunch the men encountered ascending slopes and many more curves, and could not maintain the frenetic pace of the morning.
2. I used the following primary Internet resources to write Muireall Anne Ravenscroft's excerpt in Chapter 15 titled *The First Transcontinental Railroad: Technological Marvel of the 19th Century:* www.bushong.net/dawn/about/college/ids100/history.shtml, www.pbs.org/weta/thewest/resources/archives/five/railact.htm, www.civilwarhome.com/jdavisbio.htm, cprr.org/Museum/index.html, www.academickids.com/encyclopedia/index.php/First_Transcontinental_Railroad_%28North_America%29#History, *When Railroads Were New* (Chapter 7) by Charles Frederic Carter (see http://cprr.org/Museum/When_RRs_Were_New.html).

Chapter Sixteen

1. A group of Boston printers, collaborating under the name John A. French & Company, established the Boston Herald in 1846. At the time, the newspaper consisted of a double-sided single-sheet publication and sold for one penny a copy. The Sunday Herald was added in 1861 in response to increased demand for news about the Civil War. I have assumed that the paper in 1870 consisted of more than one sheet. (www.heraldmedia.com/heraldMedia/history.html)
2. Alfred Dubucand, born in Paris in 1828 and died in 1894, was a proficient sculptor of horses, dogs, birds, and other animals, and had a particular interest in the nomadic people and animals of Northern Africa. His bronze casts are notable for exceptional detail and finish without portraying excessive romanticism. Dubucand's approach to modeling, particularly his ability to capture motion, imbued his subjects with a lifelike appearance that set his work apart from many other animal artists of the time. (http://bronze-gallery.com/sculptors/artist.cfm?sculptorID=19)
3. I could not find any evidence that the Revere Bank Building in Boston provided elevator service in 1870. However, the Otis Elevator Company had installed elevators in New York City, London, Newfoundland, and Nashville, Tennessee by the same year. Because the Revere Bank incorporated and then leased space in the building at the corner of Franklin and Devonshire Streets in 1859, the building likely did not include an elevator. I have therefore fictionalized the possibility of a renovation prior to 1870. It is interesting to note that the Revere Bank did install a vault on the second floor. (www.otisworldwide.com/d31-timeline.html)
4. I must confess, dear reader, that I spent far too much time one Monday evening attempting to determine which railway station Gordania would have used to travel from Boston to Ogden, Utah. After studying numerous maps available through the Norman B. Leventhal Map Center at the Boston Public Library (particularly an 1870 map titled *Boston and Its Vicinity* by George Coolidge), I realized that the *Boston, Hartford & Erie Railroad* passed through Brookline. Because this fit very well with the storyline, I chose the B. H. & E. R. R. Passenger Station at the corner of Federal and Broad Streets as the

point of departure and merely assumed it would eventually connect to the First Transcontinental Railroad. I also assumed the train would stop at Brookline Station, but this is likely a reasonable conjecture. (http://maps.bpl.org/)

5. The Remington Company manufactured its version of the "derringer" from 1866 to 1935. Designed by William H. Elliot and sometimes called the "Double Ace," this pistol was in production longer than any other Remington handgun; it is estimated that the company manufactured roughly 150,000 units. The Remington Double Derringer is the compact pistol you are likely familiar with from TV and movie westerns. The generic term "derringer" is actually a misspelling of the last name of Henry Deringer (1786-1868), an American gunsmith who designed and manufactured small pocket pistols beginning in 1825. The Remington design added a second barrel and incorporated an upward-pivoting reloading system. Because the .41 caliber rimfire bullet poked along at a relatively slow 425 feet per second, the Remington Derringer was a deadly close-range weapon. (www.nramuseum.com)

Chapter Seventeen

1. I used the following sources (all but the last from the Chicago Historical Society) to extrapolate the Rock Pigeon's view of the Chicago waterfront near the Illinois Central Depot in 1870: 1) A photograph taken from the southwest of the depot titled *Illinois Central Railroad Depot, 1858*; 2) A "birds-eye view" (how appropriate) drawing of the waterfront and depot as it appeared in 1857; 3) A photograph titled *Illinois Central Railroad north from Harrison Street toward Van Buren Street Station and Viaduct, 1896*; and 4) An undated but clearly antique sepia map of Chicago with the footnote *Rand, McNally & Co., Engr's, Chicago* printed at the bottom. This map provided especially good detail of rail lines and depots.
2. Chicago developed into a major hub of railroad transportation between 1830 and the late 1850s, and became the primary termination point for all main lines arriving from the east and the starting point for all main lines heading west. By 1860 Chicago had established

itself as the nation's primary shipping center with the construction of warehouses, factories, and similar industrial facilities for the handling and processing of timber, wheat, hogs, cattle, and other commodities. Study of a railroad map for travelers (copyrighted by Alfred A. Hart in 1870) indicates that Manfred Herrmann and Gordania Sinclair would have traveled from the Illinois Central Depot in Chicago to Ogden, Utah on the Burlington Route via the Chicago Burlington & Quincy Railroad, the Union Pacific Railroad, and finally the Central Pacific Railroad. The Burlington Route ultimately terminated in San Francisco after passing through such cities as Burlington, Council Bluffs, Omaha, North Platte, Cheyenne, Laramie, Ogden, Elko, Winnemucca, Reno, Sacramento, and San Jose (to name but a few of the many stops). (http://cprr.org/Museum/Maps/_Hart_Burlington.html#enlarged)

3. The facilities available in Kelton, Utah at the time of Manfred's arrival were determined from a National Park Service publication titled: *Rails East to Promontory – The Utah Stations*. The list is derived from a directory dated 1880: it is therefore possible that one or more of the amenities mentioned in the story were not existent in 1870. With the exception of the cemetery, very little remains of the town today. The article notes the following: "Kelton served as a section station and major shipping and travel connection to the mineral rich mountains and open rangeland of the Northwest. Kelton was the southern terminus of the Utah, Idaho, and Oregon Stage Company and a station on the Overland Mail route. In a typical year during the 1870s, six million pounds of supplies were loaded from trains on to wagons in exchange for wool and furs from the intermountain north." (www.nps.gov/history/history/online_books/blm/ut/8/sec2d.htm)
4. The Northwestern Stage Company (Fuller, Parker & Company, Proprietors) was awarded a U.S. mail contract for routes from Kelton to Virginia City, Boise, Winnemucca, and other destinations on July 1, 1870. The company enjoyed a stagecoach monopoly in southern Idaho until July 1, 1878 when it lost the mail contract and sold major interests to the Utah, Idaho, and Oregon Stage Company. According to a reference article published by the Idaho State Historical Society (#146, 1971), at its height of operations, "...the Company owned

85 stations, employed 50 drivers, owned 800 horses, utilized 50 wagons or stages and maintained their own repair shops. They also had 12 local agents and four division agents." The Northwestern Stage Company also operated a route from Boise to Winnemucca via Silver City during the same eight-year period.

5. The Abbot-Downing Company of Concord, New Hampshire (incorporated under this name in 1873) manufactured the familiar stagecoach of the American West. The history of the company began in 1813 when Lewis Downing, a wheelwright from Lexington who had learned his trade in his father's blacksmith shop, produced the first "Concord Coach" in November of that year and immediately sold the vehicle to a local merchant. He purchased land in Concord and built a small factory three years later, and hired a dozen men to assist in the manufacture of wagons and chaises.* Lewis Downing engaged the services of J. Stephens Abbot, an expert carriage maker and a native of Maine, in 1826 and the two men formed a partnership a year later. The partnership was dissolved in 1847 by mutual consent, and Abbot and Downing built coaches separately until 1865. In the same year, the sons and families of the two men reunited and ultimately incorporated the business as the Abbot-Downing Company in 1873. The company continued to thrive and build coaches into the early years of the twentieth century. The website http://theconcordcoach.tripod.com/abbotdowning/ offers this description of the stagecoach: "Their sturdy bodies were glowing carmine or bright vermilion and their running-gear a jaunty yellow. Their interiors were lined with sleek leather and flowered damask,† and they had the pictures of famous beauties painted on their footboards. There was color and dash in every line of them, and they carried men on colorful adventures all over the world. They were the Concord Coaches, the last and finest triumph of the stagecoach era, and for fifty years they made their quiet little Merrimack Valley town a famous by-word in the world of transportation." In the end, the advent of the automobile signaled the end of the American stagecoach.

---

* A chaise is a two-wheeled, horse-drawn carriage with a collapsible roof.

† Damask is a heavy linen or woolen fabric with woven patterns.

6. I relied on a National Park Service website article titled *The Kelton Road – "The Stage Era"* to accurately describe the City of Rocks Home Station, the distances between stations, and the quality of the coffee. The website offers the following assessment from an early traveler: "The greatest annoyance one meets on this route is the station-houses where meals are served, as it is almost impossible to get a decent repast at any of them. The usual meal is fat ham and eggs, or boild [sic] pork, potatoes, and bread that looks as if it were baked in black ashes, while the coffee is the very vilest stuff. One place at which I stopped did not furnish any fresh meat, although hundreds of cattle were grouped around the house; and no milk although several cows with calves were within 20 yards... After a ride of 13 hours [from City of Rocks] I reached Kelton...and was pleased to find myself on a line of railway once more." (www.nps.gov/history/history/online_books/ciro/hrs2j.htm)
7. The appearance of members of the 10th Cavalry Regiment—one of the original "Buffalo Soldier" units—near Fort Boise is not historically perfect, but does serve to provide the reader with a broader perspective of the American West during the years following the Civil War. Established by Congress in 1866, the all-black units included the 9th and 10th Cavalry Regiments and the 38th, 39th, 40th, and 41st Infantry Regiments. The 38th and 41st were later reorganized into the 25th Infantry Regiment and headquartered at Jackson Barracks in New Orleans, and the 39th and 40th were later reorganized into the 24th Infantry Regiment and headquartered at Fort Clark, Texas. The 10th Cavalry Regiment (originally formed at Fort Leavenworth, Kansas but soon transferred to Fort Riley, Kansas in 1867), saw extensive service during the Indian Wars from 1866 through 1874. During the years 1867 and 1868 the regiment served under General William Tecumseh Sherman in winter campaigns against the Cheyenne, Arapaho, and Comanche. In 1868 Companies H and I participated in two noteworthy combat actions: the Battle of Beecher Island on the North Fork of the Republican River, and a combined action with the 5th Cavalry near Beaver Creek in Colorado. Medal of Honor recipient Captain Louis H. Carpenter commanded Company H in the first action and both companies in the second. The 10th Cavalry

Regiment was stationed at several forts in Kansas and the Indian Territories (present day Oklahoma) from 1868 into the early 1870s, and in 1873 companies of the 10th Cavalry Regiment were transferred to Forts Richardson, Griffin, and Concho in Texas. Buffalo Soldiers of the 10th Cavalry Regiment charged up San Juan Hill on foot with Teddy Roosevelt in 1898 during the Spanish-American War. (http://buffalosoldiersmuseum.com, www.globalsecurity.org/military/agency/army/7-10cav.htm, http://civilwarcavalry.com/?p=606, www.texasalmanac.com/topics/history/buffalo-soldiers-texas)

8. The .56-50 caliber Spencer Repeating Carbine was originally issued to cavalry units of the Union Army in late 1863. This lever-action repeater proved itself an effective cavalry weapon during the Civil War, especially when fired on horseback. Because it provided "accurate and withering fire" against the often overwhelming attacks of the Plains Indians, the Spencer Carbine became a mainstay of the U. S. Cavalry in the late 1860s and into the 1870s. The carbine had a capacity of seven rounds (loaded into a tube that was then inserted through the back of the stock), weighed 9 pounds 6 ounces, had a length of slightly over 39 inches, and included an adjustable ladder-type rear sight. The Spencer Repeating Firearms Company was sold to the Winchester Repeating Firearms Company in 1867. (www.romanorifle.com/html/spencer.html)
9. As explained in the booklet *Shaping Boise – A Selection of Boise's Landmark Buildings* (published by the City of Boise Department of Planning & Development Services in 2010), the Hudson's Bay Company originally established Fort Boise as a fur trading post in 1834 at the mouth of the Boise River, approximately forty miles west of the current location of modern Boise. The Hudson's Bay Company provided supplies and other services to travelers of the Oregon Trail from 1841 to 1854, but then abandoned the fort because of the declining fur trade. The discovery of gold on the Clearwater River in 1860 prompted a flood of miners into Northern Idaho, and two years later the discovery of gold in the Boise Basin led to another rush to the Boise Valley. The U. S. Army established a new Fort Boise at the intersection of the Oregon Trail and the roads leading south to the mines of the Owyhee (Silver City) and the Boise Basin (Idaho

City) on July 4, 1863 (one day after the conclusion of the Battle of Gettysburg) to protect the local mining industry from Indian attacks. The city of Boise was quickly platted between the new Fort Boise and the Boise River, and the fort subsequently became a natural community center for religious services, theater productions, Christmas activities, and other events. The booklet includes photographs of two substantial buildings constructed at the fort in 1863, prior to the date of this story: the commanding officer's quarters and the quartermaster building. The founding of Boise City itself took place on July 5, 1863, a day after the founding of Fort Boise. The booklet also includes photographs of two significant public buildings constructed in Boise City with local sandstone in 1872, two years after the timeframe of this chapter: the two-story United States Assay Office, and the Old Idaho Penitentiary. The first building of the penitentiary, "…a seventy-by-forty-foot building…designed to hold thirty-nine prisoners in three tiers of cells and [including] bathing rooms and another section for eating and administration." was built in 1870, the same year as this story.

Chapter Eighteen

1. As I neared the end of the first draft of Chapter 18, I realized that I had failed to write even a single chapter note in support the historical authenticity of Roshan's and Longwei's travels from the Promontory Mountains to Fort Boise via North Platte, Nebraska. I therefore offer the following for your enlightenment. The spittoon (also known as a cuspidor in more sophisticated circles) is a bowl-shaped vessel used for spitting. Although brass is the material most commonly associated with the fabrication of spittoons, other common materials included iron, porcelain, and cut glass. The spittoon is intrinsically linked with the tobacco chewers of the American West in the middle to late 1800s because of frequent appearances in movie and TV westerns, but widespread use of spittoons in public places began in America around 1880 and continued through the years of World War I when public health concerns about the spread of tuberculosis initiated a precipitous decline in popularity. As proof of the ubiquity of spittoons in the early twentieth century, the 13th annual Public Health Service Conference

(May 1915 in Washington, DC) promulgated a recommendation that when an entire car of a train was used for smoking and chewing, spittoons should be cleaned frequently and spaced one for every three seats. The recommendation allowed the option of additional spittoons if so desired by the train company. *The Social History of Missouri*, a famous mural by Thomas Hart Benton located at the Missouri State Capitol in Jefferson City, depicts the poor aim often encountered around public spittoons: the courtroom scene incorporates a brass spittoon with several brown saliva stains on the floor. Spittoons are still performing both useful and symbolic functions into the 21st Century. Professional wine tasters use spittoons to avoid intoxication. The white porcelain vessel next to a dentist's chair is technically a spittoon. One can find spittoons on the floor of the U.S. Senate as a symbol of a bygone era. And, according to Wikipedia, a spittoon resides next to the seat of each justice of the U.S. Supreme Court. I did not bother to corroborate this latter claim because it sounds quite plausible to me. (*American Heritage Dictionary*, www.suite101.com/content/the-rise-and-fall-of-spittoons-in-the-united-states-a232444)

Chapter Nineteen

1. In 1870 America, the two primary choices for more formal menswear were the sack suit and the frock coat. The sack suit typically consisted of matching wool or linen coat, pants, and vest, and was usually accompanied by a straw hat or bowler. Typically large and baggy when first introduced in the 1850s, the sack suit became more fitted during the 1860s. One of the primary reasons for the sack suit's popularity was that working men could purchase the garments ready-made at affordable prices. Although a banker might wear a sack suit to a company picnic, a cowboy or farmer would wear it to church. Significantly more formal than the sack suit, the frock coat was usually black, single or double-breasted, and incorporated a square-shaped bottom hem that hung down to the knee. In the 1850s and 1860s men commonly wore matching black trousers with black frock coats. After the 1860s fashion dictated a preference for charcoal gray or pinstriped trousers. An excerpt from an 1879 publication titled *Our Deportment* states the following: "The morning dress for

gentlemen is a black frock coat, or a black cut-away, white or black vest, according to the season, gray or colored pants, plaid or stripes according to the fashion, a high silk stove pipe hat, and a black scarf or necktie. A black frock coat with black pants is not considered a good combination. The morning dress is suitable for garden parties, Sundays, social teas, informal calls, morning calls and receptions." Note that Dougal Connelly may have committed a social blunder by wearing a bowler with his frock coat. At least he got the pants right. (walternelson.com/dr/attire)

2. Since I have had some experience with the Union Oyster House (see chapter 12 note #1), I decided to feature the restaurant in this chapter and weave it into the storyline. Founded in 1826, the Union Oyster House is the oldest restaurant in Boston. According to the National Park Service (NPS), the first known serving of oysters to the public occurred much earlier in a New York cellar that opened for business in 1763. However, the Union Oyster House retains the distinction of the oldest American restaurant still in continuous operation. The only well-known oyster house to approach this achievement is Antoine's Restaurant in New Orleans, which opened in 1868. The NPS also notes that the famed oyster bar at New York's Grand Central Terminal dates from 1913. Famous patrons of the Union Oyster House have included Daniel Webster (1840s and 1850s); and Presidents Calvin Coolidge, Franklin Roosevelt, John F. Kennedy, and William J. Clinton. The Union Oyster House website notes the following, which I attributed to Csongor Toth to add authentic color to the story: "It was at the Oyster Bar that Daniel Webster, a constant customer, daily drank his tall tumbler of brandy and water with each half-dozen oysters, seldom having less than six plates." Although I like oysters, I could not imagine consuming six plates each with a tall tumbler of brandy and water, and therefore deemed it sufficient for Csongor to order only two plates and two tumblers. (www.nps.gov/nr/travel/maritime/oys.htm, www.unionoysterhouse.com/)

3. I used three different maps to create a description of Dougal Connelly's route from Boston to his ultimate demise on the boundary between the Wyoming and Utah Territories. I revisited the 1870 map titled *Boston and Its Vicinity* by George Coolidge for information on

the route between Boston and Newton Center (see chapter 16 note #4). From there I relied heavily on an elaborately-rendered map titled *Map of the New York Central and Hudson River Railroad and its Principal Connections* produced by Rand, McNally & Company in 1876. To determine the route from Chicago to the Wyoming boarder, I once again studied the railroad map for travelers copyrighted by Alfred A. Hart in 1870 (see chapter 17 note #2). The 1876 map incorporates a graphic of a hand pointing a finger at the route between Albany and Rochester with the following text: "The Only 4 Track Railroad in the World All Laid With Steel Rails." I used the Amtrak website to extrapolate the time of travel from Boston to Chicago because I could not find a train schedule from 1870. Consequently, the arrival and departure times presented in this chapter are estimates.

4. Because Western Union did not introduce the telegraphic money transfer until 1871, Csongor Toth could not have transferred money to the Western Union office in Ogden in September 1870. I have therefore fictionalized the event to a slightly earlier time (possibly less than a year) to work with the chronology of the storyline.
5. I relied on the following primary Internet resources to write Muireall Anne Ravenscroft's excerpt in Chapter 19 titled *The Telegraph*: http://inventors.about.com/od/tstartinventions/a/telegraph.htm, www.ieeeghn.org/wiki/index.php/Milestones:Transcontinental_Telegraph%2C_1861, http://corporate.westernunion.com/history.html, www.history-magazine.com/cable.html.
6. To confirm the train crossing from Sarnia to Port Huron via ferry, I found a drawing titled "Rail Car Ferry International approaching Port Huron, MI" credited to John C. McArthur in the *Canadian Illustrated News* dated April 8, 1876. I also found the following quotation from a research paper by Suzette Bromley (University of Michigan – Flint, 2005) to confirm that a train ferry was in operation in 1870, the year of Dougal Connelly's trip west: "The year of 1859 was an important year for Port Huron and its environs. East of the St. Clair River, the Grand Trunk Railroad completed its 800-mile route from Portland, Maine to Sarnia, Ontario. Under the name of the Chicago, Detroit, and Canada Grand Trunk Junction Railway, a fifty-seven-mile track

was completed that connected Port Huron to Detroit. A car ferry was introduced that eliminated the need to unload and reload cargo as the new ferry could transport the railway cars themselves across the river. This ferry, known as the 'Swing Ferry,' extended from a cable anchored at Fort Gratiot and used the strong water current to propel it across the river. The vessel, the first of its kind, and the only one in the world for twenty years, was used constantly until 1867 when its cable was severed in a collision with an up-bound steamer. Subsequent train ferries could transport up to twenty-two loaded cars at one time (1872), and in 1888, there were 332,000 cars carried across the St. Clair River." (www.rootsweb.ancestry.com/~miporthu/PH_Railroad.htm)

7. The Union Pacific Missouri River Bridge between Council Bluffs and Omaha first opened on March 25, 1873. Prior to this date, trains on the First Transcontinental Railroad crossed the Missouri River using the Council Bluffs and Nebraska Ferry Company.

Chapter Twenty

1. By 1870 there were 22,573 flour mills in the United States. Millers originally packed flour in barrels weighing 196 pounds: a carry-over of the British system of weights (196 pounds equals 14 English stone). By the late 1800s the advent of the sewing machine allowed the less expensive packaging of flour in sacks. The common sack size was half of a barrel, or 98 pounds. Smaller sacks for home use did not appear until after 1900. (from an essay by Norman Reed published in *Columbia* magazine, Vol. 22 No. 4, Winter 2008-2009)

Chapter Twenty-One

1. The magnetic declination at Oregon City in 1871 was 20 degrees 54 minutes east, which approximately matches the alignment of the town's main street. Ethan Plantagenet evidently neglected to mention declination when he gave Joshua the compass. (www.ngdc.noaa.gov/geomagmodels/struts/historicPoint)
2. Oregon City, the first Euro-American settlement in the Willamette Valley and the first incorporated city west of the Rocky Mountains, was originally founded in 1829 on the Willamette River just below

the Willamette Falls. Surprisingly, the 1,500-feet wide by 40-feet high horseshoe-shaped falls are the largest in the Pacific Northwest and the second largest, after Niagara Falls, in the United States. The Clowwewalla, Cashhooks, Molalla, and Clackamas Indians inhabited the area prior to 1829, but by the year of the founding of Oregon City smallpox, cholera, and other diseases introduced by early explorers had decimated the tribes. Dr. John McLoughlin first established a two-square mile claim near the Willamette Falls on behalf of the Hudson's Bay Company, and soon developed a small fir trading center and a millrace.* By 1839 the settlement consisted of the millrace and a small group of houses inhabited primarily by employees of the Hudson's Bay Company. In 1833 the Methodist Episcopal Church approved the Reverend Jason Lee and his nephew, Reverend Daniel Lee, to establish a mission in the west. The Lees travelled to Fort Vancouver to reconnoiter the possibilities and there met Dr. John McLoughlin, who encouraged them to explore the Willamette Valley. The Lees subsequently established the Willamette Mission in present-day Marion County. Later, the Reverend Jason Lee presented a series of lectures in Peoria, Illinois during the winter of 1839-1840 to promote settlement in the Oregon Territory. His lectures inspired the "Peoria Party" to make the first overland trip to the Willamette Falls settlement in 1840. Others arrived by ship to reinforce the Methodist Mission, including George Abernathy and the Reverend Alvin F. Waller in June 1840. George Abernathy was appointed manager of the first community store. The Reverend Waller established the Island Milling Company in 1841, and by 1842 was also operating a small sawmill and developing plans for a flour mill on a portion of Dr. John McLoughlin's original claim. In response to this intrusion, and in an effort to solidify his claim, McLoughlin platted the growing village and named it Oregon City in 1842. Construction of a Methodist Church, the first protestant church west of the Rocky Mountains, was completed in 1843 (the materials and land were donated by Dr. John McLoughlin). That same year, a provisional government under the jurisdiction of the United States was established,

* A millrace is a fast channel of water that drives a mill wheel.

and a year later Oregon City, which had expanded to 75 buildings, was incorporated. By 1846 the population had grown to 500 people and by 1849 to over 900. The Oregon Territory was officially created in 1848 (statehood was granted in 1859) and Oregon City became the first territorial capital. With the construction of lumber and flour mills the town expanded its industrial infrastructure, and in 1850 the first steamboat on the Willamette River was built to provide improved shipping between Oregon City and the upper Willamette Valley. Oregon City's prominence declined in the 1850s when the territorial capital was moved to Salem and Portland emerged as the territory's primary transportation and population center. Oregon City responded by transitioning from a service and shipping economy to one based primarily on manufacturing. Construction of the Imperial Flour Mills was completed in 1864. The Oregon Manufacturing Company (Oregon Woolen Mills) was founded in 1864. The Pioneer Paper Manufacturing Company was established in 1866. And in 1869, two years before Joshua Hotah's arrival, the Oregon and California Railroad Company completed the first railroad line in the state between Portland and Oregon City. (www.orcity.org/planning/brief-history-oregon-city)

3. The *Oregon City Enterprise* began as a four-page, seven-column, weekly (Saturday morning) newspaper on October 27, 1866. The paper was enlarged to eight columns in July 1867 to accommodate an increasing demand for advertising. At the time, a one-year subscription cost $3.00, and advertising cost $2.50 for the first square of 12 lines and $1.00 for each subsequent insertion. The newspaper survived into the late 1900s. (www.heritagetrailpress.com/Newspapers/Newspaper_OREnter_Hist.cfm)

www.ingramcontent.com/pod-product-compliance
Lightning Source LLC
LaVergne TN
LVHW020531100826
845148LV00010B/1415

* 9 7 8 1 5 9 4 3 3 5 5 2 5 *